RF IP

FAST ATTACK

D1388160

WALLACE

Severn River Publishing
www.SevernRiverPublishing.com

This is a work of fiction. Names, characters, businesses, places, events and incidents are either the products of the author's imagination or used in a fictitious manner. Any resemblance to actual persons, living or dead, or actual events is purely coincidental.

ISBN: 978-1-951249-07-6 (Paperback)
ISBN: 978-1-951249-01-4 (Hardback)

ALSO BY WALLACE AND KEITH

The Hunter Killer Series

Final Bearing

Dangerous Grounds

Cuban Deep

Fast Attack

Arabian Storm

Hunter Killer

By George Wallace

Operation Golden Dawn

By Don Keith

In the Course of Duty

Final Patrol

War Beneath the Waves

Undersea Warrior

The Ship that Wouldn't Die

Never miss a new release! Sign up to receive exclusive updates from authors Wallace and Keith.

Wallace-Keith.com/Newsletter

The Navy must be at sea, underway. We must be present in key areas of the world protecting American interests, enabling access to international markets and trade, responding to crises, and providing security. The muscle and bones of the Navy are our ships, submarines and aircraft, highly capable, exercised daily, well equipped, and ready to operate at sea and far from home.

-Admiral John Richardson, Chief of Naval Operations, US Navy

PROLOGUE

Alistair Peabody was quite proud of himself. He had just successfully completed making love to his wife, an accomplishment that nowadays occurred with a frequency best measured in years, not days. Damned pesky circulation issues! It was his age—seventy-four—and decades of cigarettes, bottom-shelf Scotch, and greasy fish-and-chips lunches that had caused such an affliction, of course. That and sitting day after day for forty years behind a desk at Royal Navy Command Headquarters in Portsmouth, attired in a proper suit and tie, studying dim photos and fuzzy video of submarine periscopes to identify which one belonged to which of the world's navies.

At the moment, though, he stood quite naked on the after deck of his cruising sailboat, gazing out at the broad Atlantic. Conception Island, lying somewhere a couple of miles to the west, was a thin glimmer on the horizon. His battered copy of *Bahamas Cruiser Guide* said that the tiny island was uninhabited except by a bird sanctuary. Unlike Nassau, a day's sail to the north, Conception Island had none of the cruise ship folderol. Had the Peabodys been sailing there, he would not have dared to throw out the sea anchor and climb down into the cabin for the opportune romp in the sack. One of those hundred-thou-sand-ton sea-going condominiums could steam right over the top of his tiny Irwin 54 without noticing or causing even a ripple in one of the behemoth's topside swimming pools.

Another day or two here on the sunrise side of the Bahamas, and then it would be time to venture out again. He and the wife would start the last leg of their dream cruise, sailing along for the south coast of England and Plymouth. It certainly did not seem as if two years had passed since they picked up their Irwin, fresh from a major refit in Singapore, and headed out across the tropical Pacific. Where had all the time gone?

Now that he and his wife had partaken of the consecrations that modern medical science had once again made possible for them, he was no longer in need of such a blessing. He hoped a brisk wind off the ocean would counter what the little blue pill had unleashed. Otherwise it would certainly be a run up to emergency care at Princess Margaret Hospital in Nassau to medically reverse Alistair Peabody's personal-best erection. That would be an embarrassing discussion with some amused young triage nurse.

There was no wind. The sea anchor was holding well. He glanced at the GPS and compared their current position to where they'd been when he first got the glimmer in his eye. They had drifted barely a nautical mile.

Something was working, he thought, happily noting the beginning of a drop in pressure in the general area just below his sizable gut. Maybe it was the lovely, relaxing view that was lowering his heart rate, backing down his rushing blood pressure.

Be careful what you wish for, old bean. Alistair smiled. *An over-abundant blessing is no blessing a'tall.*

Then something far out in the water caught his eye. A quick movement. A splash.

A petrel diving for shrimp? No, it was something vertical, solid, and it left a decided rooster-tail in its wake as it moved quickly north to south. Alistair always kept his binoculars ready next to his deck chair. Sometimes girls on yachts removed their tops to sunbathe. On a good day, their bottoms, too.

He quickly found and focused on what he had spotted. He caught his breath.

He knew instantly what he was seeing. Alistair Peabody was one of maybe a few hundred people on the face of the planet who could identify it, one of maybe two dozen who would know the precise details of it. Even so, he had never seen this particular one in real life. But he had certainly seen enough images of it—the distinctive shape, the detail, the markings—to recognize what was boldly poking up from beneath the sea surface.

And it was absolutely not supposed to be there.

"There is no bloody way," he whispered. "No bloody way."

Alistair knew what he must do. He turned and dashed inside, past his gently snoring wife, to the closet. There he procured his digital camera, praying there was space left on the card. Grace often carried it with the strap around her neck, her ample bosom constantly poking the shutter button, inadvertently taking high-resolution photos of feet, decks, and water.

In all the excitement, he hardly noticed that his engorgement problem was quickly becoming a non-issue. The mysterious object was still out there but would soon be beyond his vision. He snapped photo after photo until he could no longer locate the staff in the viewfinder, then raced to the satellite phone in the main saloon, remembering to first spread a towel on the divan. Grace fussed mightily when he sat bare-arsed on the furniture.

He concentrated hard on remembering the Portsmouth telephone number. He hadn't had occasion to dial it since retiring four years ago and heading out on their grand water adventure.

Then, as the ringtone pulsed, he thought long and hard about who exactly he should request to speak with. Who might he know that was still there by now? Who would believe the ramblings of an old, retired analyst phoning in with such an outlandish report?

A report that he had just seen a submarine periscope off a bird sanctuary on a lonely stretch of water east of the Bahamas. A periscope of a Russian submarine model that was still undergoing sea trials half a decade ago when the old analyst had first seen photos of it.

Alistair could not determine if the youngster who now worked in his old section believed his report or not. He certainly would when the images showed up in the cheeky booger's email inbox. Even now, years removed from it all, Peabody knew what a stir this would cause. A Russian submarine in Bahamian waters. So close to shore. So close to that ultra-secret US Navy underwater test facility out there just beyond the horizon, on the other side of those reefs.

Peabody was so caught up in making his breathless report to Royal Navy HQ and downloading and sending off the images that he had lost track of time.

He also had failed to notice that his old soldier had rallied mightily, even though the blue pill's magic should have long since waned. He once again stood ready for service.

Alistair Peabody stepped inside to wake his wife. Later, he might even tell her about the Russian submarine periscope.

But now, otherwise occupied, he was not aware that the submarine in question had slowed before executing a long arc of a turn.

It was now headed directly toward the Irwin, steadily gaining speed.

1

The bluish light from the overhead halogen lamps painted the labyrinth of pipes, hoses, and thick cables in stark brightness and shadow. The brisk breeze blowing down the Western Branch of the Elizabeth River carried little hint that it would soon be another torrid August day, nor did the slight salt smell it bore offer much in the way of confirmation that the vast Atlantic Ocean was so close. But the summer heat was brutally inevitable once the sun came up, and the ocean lay northeastward, just beyond Willoughby Spit and the Hampton Roads Bridge Tunnel.

The usually busy shipyard was about as quiet as it ever got in these very early morning hours. Normally only a few yard birds—shipyard workers—would be out and about, but tonight, this particular corner of Norfolk Naval Shipyard was bustling with activity. A shipyard crane, resembling some giant prehistoric robin's-egg-blue insect, ponderously made its way down the tracks that ran along the wing wall of the massive dry dock. Bells clanged and colossal iron wheels screeched on steel rails, marking its passage.

Joe Glass carefully picked his way through the clutter, deftly dodging a forklift that was lugging a heavy crate down the pier. Somewhere to his left, deep in Dry Dock 2, buried under a complex of scaffolding and Herculite tenting, his beloved *Toledo* rested on blocks, suffering the ministrations of the shipyard's best workmen. One of them, using an angle grinder, unleashed a torrent of white-hot sparks into the pre-dawn shadows and into the basin below the submarine. Lights flashed, welding torches flamed, and hammering and banging echoed all around the vessel.

Glass hurried along the dry dock wall, gritting his teeth as he stared down into the ugly industrial confusion. Already a year of this without the wind in his hair, an eternity without going back to sea. It was too much to ask of a submariner.

On a whim, he took a quick shortcut across the huge steel caisson that kept the muddy Elizabeth River out of the dry dock basin. Glass ducked between the nucleonics shack and the shift supervisor's trailer and double-timed across the pier. The gray two-deck living barge—the crew's temporary home while their submarine was undergoing refitting—was tied up there, partially blocking waterside access to Dry Dock 1.

Sam Wilson, the Naval Reactors Regional Office representative—commonly called the "NRRO Rep" for short—was waiting for him on the barge's cramped quarterdeck. Glass was struck once again at how much Wilson resembled an egg by the way the man's bald head flowed smoothly into remarkably narrow shoulders, along with his rotund physique. This egg had a bite, though. Wilson was well known for both his irascible personality and his close connections with the all-powerful Naval Reactors. One quick phone call and he could immediately sink any submariner's career.

"Morning, Mr. Wilson." Glass nodded affably and offered his hand. "To what do I owe this early morning visit?"

"Captain, I've been doing a monitor watch on your ship,"

Wilson growled, ignoring Glass's outstretched hand. Instead he flipped open his spiral steno pad, pointedly avoiding pleasantries and eye contact. "The Work Authorization File in Maneuvering is a disgrace. The Work Authorizations are not being filed in chronological order as clearly required in NAVSEA Instruction 4790.2C. I found at least three cases where they were transposed. The required weekly audit is almost twelve hours overdue. I will expect a written critique and course of corrective action on my desk by the end of the day."

Before he could respond, Glass's smartphone buzzed in his pocket. He held up one finger and took a look at the phone's screen. He recognized Jon Ward's number.

"Pardon me, Mr. Wilson," Glass said. "This is Commodore Ward. I need to take this call. If you will excuse me, we can discuss this later."

Without waiting for the demanding bureaucrat's permission, he touched the phone's screen.

"Morning, Commodore. To what do I owe this very early morning call?"

"Hi, Joe. I figured you might be on the boat early," Ward replied, then dispensed with any more chitchat. "Are you somewhere where we can go secure?"

"Just a second, Commodore. I'm on the quarterdeck. I'll get up to my office." Joe Glass bounded up the ladder to the second deck, leaving the NRRO Rep standing there with steno pad in hand. The ladder dumped him off in the passageway right outside his office/stateroom. Two steps and he was inside the tiny cubicle.

"Okay, Jon, ready to go secure." Glass swiped up an app on the phone and keyed in the password. The screen flickered as a red banner momentarily flashed across the top of the screen before it switched to a solid green.

"I hold you secure," Glass reported.

"I hold you the same," Ward responded. "How is shipyard life treating you these days?"

Glass let out a long sigh as he settled into his desk chair.

"Jon, I need to get back to sea. The bullshit is driving me nuts. This shipyard stuff is no place for a sailor. And to top it all off, that little gnome Wilson was waiting for me on the quarterdeck, howling about a crisis with the WAF log, of all things."

"Wilson is a real work of art," Ward replied. "His ranting is famous. Just try to stay off his bad side. According to reports, he doesn't have a good side, so don't even ask." Ward quickly changed the subject. "How are our science experiments?"

"Well, you and those eggheads up at NUWC have sure cut up my boat," Glass answered, rubbing his chin. "The new pump propulsion system has the whole ass end cut up. I'm still trying to wrap my head around how it's even supposed to work. I've certainly never seen anything like it. No shaft. No screw. Just some pumps out in the mud tank that are supposed to provide enough oomph to push around something as big and heavy as *Toledo*. You really think it's going to work?"

Ward chuckled. The digital artifacting on the secure line made his laugh sound brittle and alien.

"The lab rats' numbers show that you will be a couple of knots slower at Flank, but you will be ten to twenty dB quieter. Once we test it out on you and your boat, we can make any necessary changes and then start planning it for new-construction boats. What about the active cancelation system?"

Glass reached over and grabbed a notebook out of his safe. He flipped to a schedule page.

"The ACS is on schedule, according to the engineers." He turned to a system description page. "This thing reads like a Romulan cloaking device. Never thought the US Navy would go all *Star Trek* on me."

"Pretty much," Ward answered. "It sucks up any audible

signature and pulses out a perfect copy of the signal, only one-eighty out of phase. It should not only mask any active sonar, but you will literally look like a black hole in the ocean."

"If only it would work on Wilson." Glass chuckled. "A shipyard cloaking device would be worth its weight in dilithium crystals."

"Well, be ready. We've got a couple more new toys that we're sending your way," Ward went on. "A team up here has come up with a new hull treatment we want to try. It's a combination of something they are calling a bubble meta-screen and a shark skin. The bubbles are embedded in a new silicon rubber and are purported to absorb any sound energy. The shark skin is supposed to work like the dimples on a golf ball, giving you a couple of knots more speed."

"I hear a little too much 'supposed to' in that pitch, Jon," Glass shot back. "Just between a couple of old shipmates, what's the real story?"

"Well, we're not sure how those bubbles will behave with depth changes," Ward answered slowly, deliberately. "The computer modeling shows that they work fine, and then they worked great in the hydrostatic test chamber. But those were little test patches. A whole boat is a different deal altogether. And on top of that, there's always the problem of the adhesive. The polymer-epoxy stuff that they plan to use is real ticklish."

"Okay," Glass snorted. "I guess that's what we get for being the fleet's designated guinea pig. Any other little unexpected gifts coming my way?"

"Matter of fact, there is," Ward answered. "NUWC has a pod we are strapping on the deck just aft of the sail. Think dry deck shelter with some added twists and a couple of pods below the waterline. I'm not at liberty to tell you exactly what they are for yet, but you will be seeing the work documents to install them soon. When we can get together in a SCIF, I'll brief you on them. Okay, I have to go now. Even commodores have bosses who like to call early-morning meetings. Try not to piss off Wilson too much. I may not be able to save your ass if you make him too mad."

The line went dead.

Ψ

The submarine *Igor Borsovitch* hovered at one hundred meters depth as if treading water. The *Igor Borsovitch* was the Russian Navy's newest modified Severodvinsk-class nuclear attack submarine. Captain First Rank Konstantin Kursalin took great pride in commanding what he considered to be the finest, most powerful submarine in the world. Nothing else could match the power, speed, or stealth of his ship, not even the Americans and their much-vaunted *Virginia*-class submarines.

Conception Island, Bahamas, lay only ten kilometers to the north-northeast. The shallow reefs leading to the secret American base at Tongue of the Ocean were straight ahead. It was time for Kursalin and his crew to complete this part of their mission.

"Launch the *podvodnaya robot,* the undersea robot," the captain ordered.

The vessel swam out of the *Igor Borsovitch*'s sixty-five-centimeter torpedo tube and headed due west, climbing up to a depth of five meters. As the vessel moved quickly away from the Russian mother sub, a hair-thin fiber optic line trailed behind it. The unmanned submarine, a little over ten meters long and weighing almost two thousand kilos, swam silently up and over the broad, shallow reef that had always protected the American facility from submerged prying eyes. A small, skinny antenna barely protruded above the water for a few seconds while the mini-sub used GPS to instantly calculate its position.

After a minor course change, the vessel completed its passage over the reefs, then immediately dove deep into the darkness and set out on its mission. The unmanned robot sub navigated to a precise location in the test range and hovered there quietly for a few minutes. A small sensor pod dropped from its bottom and sank to the sea floor. Then the sub continued on to the next waypoint and again dropped a sensor pod.

After dropping off four more pods, the robot turned and headed back up and over the reef. The sun was just making its appearance on the horizon when the little vessel returned to rendezvous with the *Igor Borsovitch*. Once there, the robot sank to the bottom and sent a pulse out over the fiber line activating each of the sensor pods.

"Captain, we have communications with the robot submarine," a technician reported. "All the sensor probes are working properly."

Captain Kursalin rubbed his chin. An uncharacteristic smile played at the corners of his mouth.

This was truly a delicious moment, a turnaround from all the embarrassment that the Americans had caused when they had illegally tapped into those Russian undersea cables in the Sea of Okhotsk. Now, the shoe was on the other foot. He only had to go off and hide in deep water for a few days while this little undersea sensor system did the dirty work for them.

Then, they would enjoy a front row seat while the braggart Americans tested each of their newest and most secret weapons.

Ψ

The Coast Guard HC-144A Ocean Sentry twin-engine turbo-prop aircraft circled the area one more time. The Emergency Positioning Indicator Radio Beacon blared away at 406 megahertz, informing the plane's crew that down below them an Irwin 54 yacht registered to one Alistair Peabody, a vessel out of Portsmouth, England, had met some disaster requiring rescue. The HC-144A dropped to a thousand feet and made another pass. Even with the most modern radars, forward-looking infrared, and electronic sensors, nothing was showing up on the surface of the sea. Nothing except the beacon.

The co-pilot pointed to their fuel indicator and grunted. They were almost bingo for fuel, so it was time to RTB. Maybe they could vector a Seahawk down this way come morning to see if they could have better luck finding something.

The thirsty Ocean Sentry climbed back to cruising altitude and pointed northwest.

2

The president of the Russian Federation watched the bright, sharp images on the large-screen display with great interest. The video feed emanated from an orbiting drone as it zoomed in on a line of his country's newest T-14 Armata main battle tanks roaring across the Belarusian peat bogs. The ugly, squat tanks, looking for all the world like monstrous green bugs on steroids, threw up great sprays of brown mud behind them as their 1,200-horsepower diesel engines propelled the low-slung war machines at high speed.

President Grigory Iosifovich Salkov ignored the bustle in the room around him as he stood and watched the monitor. He allowed the faintest of smiles to play at the corners of his thin, taut lips. Had anyone dared look at him, they might even have seen a twinkle in the president's dark, moody eyes.

The command center, buried deep in the bedrock below the Kremlin, was a mixture of high-tech communications technology and Soviet-era gaudiness, leftovers from a time long since passed. The yards-thick cement walls were covered with the latest gargantuan motion-activated displays, interspersed with heavy, dusty crimson draperies. The large, heavily carved oak conference table was almost hidden beneath the mass of keyboards and thin-screen monitors.

President Salkov surveyed the room. Most of his ministers were present, as were each of their deputies—at least those who were not currently out of favor with Salkov for one reason or the other. Only one was unexpectedly missing. Dmitry Sharapov, the Minister of Sports. No matter. He held his position only because his father was a billionaire and a staunch supporter of the Federation. Sharapov was probably out riding one of his prize horses. Or one of his half-dozen mistresses.

The president's attention was drawn back to the scene playing out on the center display. The Armata tanks maneuvered in perfect unison, making a wide, sweeping turn to the right. These twenty tanks had rolled off the Uralvagonzavod Research and Production Corporation assembly line only the month before. They were the very first of the next generation of Russian armor, equipped with the very latest technology, but they had not yet been battle-tested. Even so, already they were in action, supporting the rightful Belarus government in its fight against Western-backed-and-armed separatist rebels.

Grigory Iosifovich stepped closer to the screen, remembering the frantic plea for help from Minsk. He was only too glad to test these new toys against real, live targets.

With the Russian economy having dreadful issues—which the Americans and their blabbering media liked to term as "in the tank" without acknowledging that a primary cause was their country's inexplicable sanctions—and as oil prices flirted with new lows, the Russian people were beginning to grumble. There had very nearly been riots when Salkov raised the price of vodka the previous week. With these problems, the new threat on his borders was the very diversion he required.

When there was a menace from outsiders, when someone tried to violate the sovereignty of their country, no one rallied around the flag like the Russian people. A thousand years of history had implanted that blind loyalty in their genes. Napoleon learned that bitter lesson in the Patriotic War of 1812. Then Hitler in the Great Patriotic War in 1945. Now, Salkov would do precisely as so many other Russian leaders had done before him—he would employ that patriotism to his advantage. And, of course, for the ultimate survival of his people and country.

There was a sudden flash of bright orange-red in the upper corner of the screen. When the pixels recovered, a yellow trail bisected the display, aiming directly for the row of tanks and proceeding at lightning speed.

"Anti-tank rocket!" Ignot Smirnov, the Minister of Defense, shouted.

At the same instant, the turret on the nearest tank spun around amazingly fast, facing the incoming weapon. The 12.5 mm heavy machine gun, hung on a pod on the outboard of the turret, lurched upward, spewing out a stream of lead that met the menacing rocket head-on. The thing exploded harmlessly, still more than a kilometer from the line of tanks.

Then, as the men in the room watched wide-eyed, as if they were viewing one of those American military thriller movies, the same tank's 125 mm 2A82-1M smoothbore cannon spat once. A laser-guided high-explosive round made a long, flat arc as it rose out toward its target. The drone video panned to a gray pickup truck with a rocket launcher bolted to its bed hidden behind a copse of trees five kilometers away. The scene had just come into focus on the monitors when the truck suddenly ceased to exist amid a billow of smoke and flames.

Salkov smiled broadly, actually showing teeth. Even those in the room who had known the president since his time with the KGB had never before witnessed such a display of gleeful satisfaction.

His Armata tanks had just passed their first live fire test. All the technologies had worked without a glitch. Even more important politically, the insurgents had dared to fire on the Russian tanks. It was a clear assault on their sovereignty. The president now had this vicious affront recorded right there on video for all the world to see, including the Western-backed media and the Westerners who sought his demise by continuing to support the rebels.

The Russian television news would pounce on it, of course. So would others around the world, in countries already struggling to maintain their levels of military spending or who questioned their governments' involvement in such a distant scuffle. And the United Nations would find it very difficult to deny this clear assault on the peaceful Russian army, which was simply out testing their new defensive weapons when they were so viciously attacked without provocation.

Turning to the Minister of Defense, the president smiled and politely said, "Please call our friends in Minsk. Our intelligence has confirmed that the West is sending arms to the rebels across the Polish border. We are offering five divisions of armored infantry to help them protect that border."

"And if they refuse our kind offer, Grigory Iosifovich?"

The Russian president smiled again. Twice in three minutes. The ministers were impressed.

"In the words of the corrupt American gangster movie, 'Make them an offer they cannot refuse.'"

On the monitors behind him, the tanks dashed, spun, and careened through the muddy bog. Clouds briefly obscured the drone's lens. Lightning streaked on the far horizon. Just as quickly as the lightning bolt had unzipped the sky, the smile left the president's lips.

"It is time to further test the Americans," he announced, now facing his Chief of the General Staff, General Boris

Lapidus. "Send two *Blackjack* bombers over the Arctic toward North America. You will approach within the American Air Defense Identification Zone, but you will not enter sovereign airspace. Do you understand what must happen, General?"

"Yes, Mister President!" the tall, lean commander answered in a crisp, clipped tone, snapping to attention. Then he had a second thought. "Should the bombers have their transponders energized?"

"Of course not! How would that test the Americans?" the president snapped back. "Now, is there any word from the *Igor Borsovitch*?"

General Lapidus hesitated, bending to search for a particular sheet of paper on the desk in front of him. He finally found it.

"Yes, I received their latest traffic just as I was leaving my office. The submarine reports that they have successfully implanted the sensor net as well as the communications node, precisely as planned. The data from the first monitoring period is already being analyzed."

"And?" Salkov asked pointedly. The president was aware that his Chief of the General Staff was stalling. He also noticed a bead of sweat forming on the general's high forehead and trickling down his cheek and neck to his tight, starched collar.

Lapidus was not relating the entire story. The man swallowed hard and went on.

"Captain First Rank Konstantin Kursalin reported that a small sailboat may have detected their presence as they were taking station to launch the unmanned submarine. Though they are convinced the sailboat's occupants would have no idea of the nature or identity of anything they may have seen, Captain Kursalin did the prudent thing and disposed of the threat before they could possibly raise any alarm. The Bermuda Triangle has simply claimed yet another 'victim.' Another inexperienced sailor has gotten in over his head and provided fodder for the reality television shows."

The president of the Russian Federation turned and stared, presumably at the tanks on the display still zooming about the Belarusian countryside. A hard rain had begun to fall there.

For the moment, he decided to pretend not to notice the telling discomfort of his Chief of the General Staff. But the submarine's captain, Kursalin, would pay for his carelessness. He had invested billions of rubles, years of research, and the best efforts of the Federal Intelligence Service, the infamous SVR, into making the *Igor Borsovitch* totally invisible to American sensors.

And all for what? So that stumbling incompetent could get his vessel detected by some drunken playboy on a sailboat.

Just as Lapidus knew it would, the slight bit of bad news about the submarine had severely dented the president's sudden good mood. In his world, even the tiniest of errors— even one that had been effectively corrected by quick, decisive action—would not be offset by anything, not even the wonderful performance by the new tanks in the peat bog.

There would be hell to pay.

Ψ

Jim Ward sat back in the netting, struggling to find a comfortable position. Even in the big airplane's inky-black cargo bay, the SEAL team leader found sleep impossible. He would never get accustomed to what passed for a seat on one of these big albatrosses. The MC-130W Combat Wombat droned on, boring through the night sky to the designated drop zone. Twenty thousand feet below them, the Caribbean Sea's wave tops passed by at slightly better than three hundred knots.

Bill Beaman plopped down in the seat next to the young SEAL. He tapped Ward on the knee.

"Your team ready for this jump?"

"Yes, sir," Ward answered. "At least it gets us out of Little Creek for a little fun in the tropical sun. But you still haven't told me why you're jumping with us, sir?"

"What you really want to ask, but don't have the balls to, is, 'Why is an old codger like you out doing a night jump with us young'uns?' Well, we old codgers can still show you world beaters a thing or two. Just try to keep up when we get on the ground."

"Just making sure you are not babysitting me," Ward said, only half-kiddingly.

Ward's father was Commodore Jon Ward, former submarine captain and Bill Beaman's longtime friend. When Jim Ward was born, Beaman was one of the first to visit the Navy hospital to see the lad, bringing him a baby-sized snorkeling set.

"You know better than that, kid," the older SEAL told him. "You're more likely babysitting this old, worn-out..."

Just then, the jumpmaster yelled above the engine noise, "Costa Rican coast in five minutes. Ten minutes to the drop zone." Master Chief Rex Johnson rousted out the rest of the SEAL team.

"All right, babies! Let go of your wieners and get your hands out of your pants! Nap time is over. Saddle up and check your gear, then double-check your buddies' gear. Everybody on oxygen right damn now."

"Ah, come on, Master Chief," one of the team members grumbled. "How many hundreds of times have we done this?" Even so, Tony Martinelli slipped on his oxygen breathing apparatus.

"Martinelli, I didn't stay alive in this business for as long as I have by being careless. I ain't about to get careless now. Oh, and by the way, you just volunteered for 'Tail-end Charlie' on this jump. Make sure we don't leave anything behind up here. The Air Force ain't inclined to put your lost luggage on the next flight."

Despite the grousing, the SEAL team eagerly checked and double-checked their gear as their ride climbed steeply to attain jump altitude. They were about to do a HAHO: a High Altitude-High Opening jump. From 28,000 feet, the team would use their aerodynamic chutes to literally fly for more than a hundred miles before finally touching down in the landing zone in the middle of the Costa Rican jungle. HAHO jumps were a perfect way to slip into an area without creating unwanted attention. Tonight's jump was yet another practice one, just to sharpen their skills. Down on the deck, a "hostile" team was out to spot and catch them. Or at least try. Exercise or not, this was still no walk in the park.

"Five minutes to drop zone. Ramp coming down," the jump-master yelled.

The large cargo ramp at the rear of the aircraft slowly tilted downward. From inside, the men could see a starry, moonless tropical night sky above them. Below was a thick cloud layer.

On a pillar beside the jumpmaster, a light suddenly glowed bright red. The SEALs, with Beaman and Ward leading the way, lumbered toward the ramp in all their heavy jump gear and stood in line, waiting.

The jumpmaster held up one finger. One minute until they were over the drop zone.

The red light blinked out, replaced by a green one. The jumpmaster waved vigorously, urging them out onto the ramp. Beaman, Ward, and the rest of the team strolled down the ramp. Then, as if stepping off a curb, they walked into the emptiness.

As usual, it took Jim Ward a few seconds to get oriented. He pulled the cord to open his parachute five seconds after he cleared the aircraft and its hurricane-like prop wash. After quickly referencing his GPS jump computer, he gave a few tugs on the steering cords to set up on course to the landing zone, then glanced over his shoulder to make sure that everyone was stacking up behind and above him.

A crackle of static on his headset preceded Martinelli's voice. "Everyone clear and on course, Skipper."

At fifteen thousand feet altitude, the team was swallowed up by the dense clouds they had seen from the airplane. Ward strained to even make out the digits on his jump computer. If he could not see his own boots, he certainly could not see the rest of his team. From here on out—or at least until they dropped through the bottom of the clouds, assuming they had a bottom—every man was on his own to follow the planned course.

At ten thousand feet, Ward felt the first tinges of worry. With these HAHO jumps, a couple of degrees inaccuracy would leave his men scattered over miles of real estate. Nothing to do but follow the jump computer as best he could. A jump computer manufactured by the lowest bidder, as Ward's dad so often reminded him.

At five thousand feet, Ward was aware that they were in serious trouble. The team could be anywhere when they landed. The jump computer said he was still on course, but what about everyone else?

At a thousand feet—less than the height of the TV towers preferred by so-called "free jumpers"—Jim Ward's senses were screaming. His heart was pounding. The drop zone should be right in front of him, but there was no way in hell he could confirm it. Even with his night vision goggles, he could see nothing but soupy, swirling fog.

Suddenly tree branches lashed his face. Before he could react, the ground rushed up to meet him, the impact slamming him to his knees. Instinctively, the young SEAL tucked and rolled, trying to deflect as much of the shock force as he could. Even so, the impact drove the breath from his lungs and he felt tooth grit in his mouth.

Still, he seemed to have landed okay. No damage. He hoped the rest of the guys were as fortunate. And nearby.

Just then he heard a heavy thud and a sharp, ominous snap somewhere from behind and above him. Hitting the quick release, Ward ditched his chute and ran toward the sounds. Above him, in the swirling mist, he could see Bill Beaman slowly rappelling down from a tall, thick-leafed espavel tree. The older SEAL grunted in pain as he landed on the ground. He collapsed into a heap, his right foot dangling at an unnatural angle.

Ward knelt next to Beaman.

"I think you'd better call the MEDEVAC chopper," Beaman said, gritting his teeth from the pain. "Something tells me"—he glanced at the leg—"that I've finally broken the damn thing this time."

3

A contented shiver ran through Sarah Wilder's perfectly toned body. The light from the candle on the table in front of her accented the highlights in her auburn hair as she toyed with the final sip of her third glass of merlot. The Connecticut country-side was arrayed below her window-side vantage point high up in Foxwood Resort's Paragon Restaurant. She watched as lights began to wink on in the distant houses, cued by the sun's inevitable dip below the western horizon, dropping toward California, her home for most of her growing-up years.

This life of hers was infinitely better than what Dr. Marsha Jacobson, her advisor at Berkeley, had foretold. At least she was now following the feel-good, politically correct pursuits Marsha had urged. "Socially conscious engineering" was the way Dr. Jacobson phrased it. "If you don't believe that a project is for the good of all mankind, you should work to bring it down," the advisor evangelized, the words a perfect echo of her father's philosophy, too. But only since her graduation from college had she learned just how committed her dad had been to such a viewpoint.

That place and time at Berkeley returned to her now as she

watched that same sun signal the end of another day, five years after that prophetic conversation. The picture of the two of them sitting on Marsha's deck high up in the Oakland Hills, watching the sun set beyond the bay, past the silhouette of the Golden Gate Bridge. Even now, sitting in a packed restaurant a continent away, Sarah could almost feel the cool breeze ushering in the fog from the Pacific and smell the sweet marijuana smoke drifting up into the night sky.

It was also at Cal-Berkeley that she had met Alexi, in her senior year in Dr. Jacobson's Ethics/Social Implications of Technology class.

Alexi, with the deep blue eyes and shock of golden hair. Alexi of the muscled, Adonis body; infinite, contagious lust; and thought-provoking ideas. Unafraid to challenge Marsha Jacobson in class or Sarah Wilder in bed, his place or hers. Or in Golden Gate Park or in his car parked on a side street in the Embarcadero or any other place where their desire boiled too high and spilled over.

It was Alexi who soon convinced Sarah that everything she thought she knew was wrong. That she actually did not prefer women to men. That her feelings for Dr. Jacobson were more out of misguided respect than love and desire. Ultimately, Alexi had helped sway Sarah into seeing that she should take her Cal engineering-degree-with-honors and her wonderful mind and go to work for the government. That Sarah should go to work specifically for the highly classified Naval Undersea Warfare Center, twenty-five hundred miles and light years away from academia and socially-conscious engineering. But that she should actually take seriously Dr. Jacobson's admonition, the one about using her knowledge and abilities to bring down those forces working against the common good.

It was Alexi who had Sarah Wilder on the verge of

becoming a spy for his native country, with him not only her lover but her handler as well.

But it was someone else who ultimately pushed her over the edge: her father, Rex Wilder. Their father-daughter chat the night after commencement was a revelation for her, and apparently a proud, long-awaited moment for him. Over sprouts and sushi at a dimly lit restaurant in Sausalito, he shared with his only child that not everything she knew about her dad was true. For example, he had not been born in Sacramento at all. His diploma and yearbook from Foothill High School were both fake, as were the photos of him with the math team and chess club. So impressive were his bogus transcript and legit SATs, the admissions department at Cal Tech had never questioned any of it. His birthplace was actually a small village a hundred miles east of Leningrad, in Russia. It was true that his extraordinary skills in math and physics marked him early as a potential engineer or scientist. However, others in high places in Moscow tabbed him as someone who could be of considerable value if strategically placed in a particular role in another country, such as the United States.

Sarah listened wide-eyed as her father told her he was what was termed a "sleeper spy," embedded in the aerospace industry in Southern California, and had been so engaged since the Cold War. The information he gathered for Mother Russia was not earth-shattering or spy-novel fodder. None of the secrets he passed on caused anyone to be hurt or killed, but it was all useful, valuable, when completing the espionage puzzle. He was well compensated, both by his unsuspecting employer and by the KGB.

But it was not just the money. He believed completely in his mission, he assured Sarah. It had been his firm conviction from the very beginning that his native country truly was the world's best bet to untrack mankind's mad race toward nuclear annihilation.

He carefully watched his daughter's face as he shared his secret life with her, gauging her reaction. It was a secret not even his late wife—Sarah's mother—had known. When it was obvious she was not going to run screaming into the night, that she was taking the news very well, he took the next step.

Rex Wilder informed her that he was aware that Alexi was recruiting her for a commitment very similar to his. The Russian and his superiors—some of the same handlers with whom Rex had worked so well—first came to him when Sarah, still in high school, showed her inherited strengths in math and computer science. They asked directly if he would be interested in helping groom his daughter for service similar to his.

"The risks are remarkably low, legally or physically," her father assured her. "I would never suggest you follow my lead otherwise. Nor would I do so if I did not truly believe that your efforts would put no one else at risk of injury. On the contrary, you will help save lives, possibly millions of them, by helping prevent atomic Armageddon, an unwinnable war driven by those who want to dominate the world and those who want to make their fortune by creating weapons for such tyrants."

Sarah's head was spinning by then. Even so, she told her father how proud she was of him, of the risks he had taken for something in which he so strongly believed.

Then Rex Wilder closed the deal. He explained that he could call on his own contacts within the Navy to assure she was offered the position at NUWC—the job Alexi wanted her to take—and that the beginning salary would be exceptional. Sarah told him she would seriously think about all this. But with the two most important men in her life aligned, her decision was a foregone conclusion.

Sarah and Alexi drove cross-country together in her Prius,

stopping far more often than necessary along I-80 for a quick roll in the hay, sometimes with the benefit of a motel room, sometimes not. Alexi moved into a nice little apartment on the Upper East Side in Manhattan, just blocks away from his job at the Russian Consulate. Sarah took a tiny little place in Warwick, Rhode Island, far enough from Newport and the NUWC labs that she could easily conceal her white-hot relationship with Alexi from her strait-laced employers.

She quickly began feeding secrets to Alexi. At first her jobs were mundane and her access was limited. He was uncharacteristically patient with her. Then, gradually, her talent for deciphering the complexities of submarine electronics became more known and appreciated around NUWC. Soon both colleagues and supervisors were bringing her the knottiest problems to solve. Of course, as soon as she and Alexi interrupted their coupling long enough to come up for a breath, she shared everything she knew with him.

The Russians paid well but not extravagantly. With that money and her government salary she would soon have put enough away to pay cash for the Tesla that she dreamed of. Enough to spring for an occasional Caribbean vacation for her and Alexi during the horridly cold New England winters and not feel even a tinge of the guilt her tight-wad dad had instilled in her.

But money was not the reason she risked prison. Sarah had almost convinced herself it was not even love. She was merely applying socially conscious engineering, just as her dad had done. Soon, with Alexi's guidance, she came to understand that she would have done it all for free. This was her way to help bring down the greedy rich crowd, the ones who put profits and power over the elimination of human suffering. The ones who stoked the furnace of war not for patriotism or freedom for the masses but just so they could join the ranks of the mega-rich.

Not caring that the products of their commerce were maiming and killing oppressed human beings in distant lands.

She checked her lipstick in her reflection in the soup spoon from her table. Alexi was driving up to be with her tonight! She felt the warm tingle in her loins, and it was not from the three glasses of merlot. Weeknight trysts were unusual anymore. They both had jobs that filled their days and often stretched well into the evenings. His trip, beginning with the choke of rush-hour traffic northeast of New York City, then continuing through the rich-folk suburbs of Connecticut and up I-95, took so much time. And there was always the real risk of someone affiliated with work seeing her with a young man with a Russian name, accent, and passport.

This hastily arranged visit would surely be for something very special. But now he was running quite late. That was also very unusual. The after-work slot players in the casino below had already laid claim to their favorite-themed machines, and the first show of the evening in the lounge was screeching and booming hollowly.

Sarah heard a stir over by the restaurant's entrance. She turned from the dark night outside the window. It was him. Tall and straight, striding across the room to her in that familiar authoritative gait. Women all along the way looked up from their prime rib, past their dining mates, to stare unabashedly as he passed.

Finally, he was here. A quick dinner, another glass of wine, then down to the suite she had booked and the night she had anticipated since their last meeting two weekends before.

Alexi smiled only slightly as he kissed her on the cheek, a brotherly buss, and plopped down across from her. Without even glancing at the menu, he waved the impatient waiter away.

"I do not have much time," he said abruptly. "I have to get back quickly. There is much going on. Two things, my sweet.

Our friends send their deepest appreciation for the last gift you sent them. It is most interesting and will have great value to our cause."

He paused to quickly pour himself a bit of the wine and take a swallow, then stared for a moment at a spot where he had spilled a drop of the liquid on the white tablecloth. Sarah could sense the drink was part of a purposeful pause. Something was not quite right. Even at his most distracted, Alexi was always able to be attentive, direct with her. Now he seemed hesitant.

"And?" she finally questioned.

Alexi looked out the window, avoiding her eyes. He began slowly, quietly. She had to strain to hear his words above the tinkle of cutlery and the murmur of conversation in the dining room.

"There has been a change. We need for you to have yourself transferred to NUWC's secret facility down in the Bahamas. You doubtless know of it. They will soon be testing new submarine technologies down there and we need to know what those technologies are and how they work." He reached across the table and took her hands in his before staring into her eyes. She could see something new in his face—sadness. "There is one other thing. We cannot meet again for a while. There is a possibility that we could be found out. You are now too important an asset... an asset for the cause of peace... for us to risk any more face-to-face meetings. Or any contact at all for the time being. We are simply at too important a point in time, and you are too valuable, to take risks just to fulfill my own selfish desire to be with you. You will soon be contacted about how to pass information once the transfer is completed and you are established at your new employment location. And do not worry. We will know when you are in place and ready to serve the cause of peace."

He dropped her hands as if they had suddenly become

painfully hot. Alexi swallowed the last of the merlot and set down the glass too near the edge of the table, then rose and walked briskly out the door. His wine glass tipped over, rolled off the table, and shattered on the floor.

Sarah Wilder stared blankly at the door where her beloved Alexi had just disappeared. Then the first tear traced a slow path down her soft, flushed cheek.

Ψ

The light was slowly fading to the west, out beyond where the heroes at Arlington National Cemetery slept eternally. No one behind the thick, bullet-proof glass protecting Admiral Tom Donnegan's office in the Pentagon's E-ring—one of the building's most coveted locations—bothered to notice the nightly show. Instead, all eyes were on him. Even in shirt-sleeves and devoid of the expected accoutrements of the US Navy's top spy, Donnegan dominated the room and held the full attention of the two men there with him.

Seated opposite each other at the large, battered oak conference table were Captain Jon Ward, Commodore of Submarine Squadron Six, and Rear Admiral Stanley "Steam" Elsworth, the Navy's topmost submarine engineer as well as the Commanding Officer of the Naval Undersea Warfare Center, usually referred to by its acronym, NUWC.

First things first, when his visitors walked in the door, Donnegan had immediately asked Ward about his wife, Ellen, and their son, Jim, the Navy SEAL. Donnegan was not just Jon Ward's boss. He was also an old family friend, since long before Ward commanded submarines. The younger Ward was Donnegan's godson. The admiral was informed that Jim was off in Central America practicing jumping out of perfectly good airplanes with his SEAL team, accompanied on the training exercise by no less than another old friend, SEAL Captain Bill Beaman. And Ellen was doing well, still teaching college-level botany to bored frat boys and sorority girls.

"Okay, good to hear my god-kid is doing something more productive than his old man. And he's hanging around with a much better element than you do, Jon." Donnegan took a moment to spit out bits of the cigar stub that he habitually chewed, then swallowed one more gulp of thick, black coffee from his huge mug, the one that his aide made certain was never empty. "Now, Jon, Steam, kindly explain to me why the two of you have come charging up here to intrude on my evening reverie with your damn hair on fire?"

Elsworth was the first to speak. "Admiral, we need to talk about all that stuff we are putting on *Toledo*. We have been trying to cram every off-the-wall, game-changing gizmo that we can on her. Make her the test platform for every single system, tool, and whiz-bang apparatus we can fit between bow and stern before we commit the taxpayer mega-bucks to stick some of the stuff on the new *Virginia*-class boats. So far we've been real lucky that no one has questioned why that boat has been sitting there in Norfolk Shipyard for so long and what we are doing to her. We're worried that she might be drawing unwanted attention from some folks who have no business knowing ours."

"You talking about the damn Russians or the damn Government Accountability Office?" Donnegan grunted through the stogie.

Ward suppressed a dry laugh and picked up the line of conversation. "Probably a little of both. The Russians will only shoot at us. Congress will take away all our money and dole it out to some senator who kisses the correct posteriors." The men nodded in sober agreement. Ward continued, "Our money is way deep in the black budget. So deep that GAO will have to dig through a whole pile of spook funding to find us. We're more worried right now about Russian interest. The way they are building boats these days, they have to be watching what we do really, really close. And we have reason to believe they are watching us even closer than we thought."

"Look here, I'm supposed to be the spy-guy in this scenario," Donnegan replied, rubbing his jaw and looking at Ward and Elsworth from beneath his bushy gray eyebrows. "Now here you yahoos are, in my office, telling me you are suddenly getting your sphincters all puckered up about spies. So tell me exactly what it is that has you two birds so bothered that you are up here telling me how to do my job."

Elsworth reached beneath the table and pulled up a leather satchel with two large, sophisticated-looking locks. He carefully placed an index finger on one of the lock pads while Jon Ward did the same with the other. The satchel popped open, and Elsworth extracted a thick sheaf of papers. The folder cover was crosshatched with broad red lines and prominently marked, "TOP SECRET: SPECIAL ACCESS REQUIRED – PROJECT RED STEALTH."

Elsworth flipped to the first chart in the stack of paper.

"Everything that we have done to *Toledo* so far has been primarily evolutionary. Even the cloaking device is only a new application of a very well-known technology. Known to us, certainly known by now to the Russian military. We merely leveraged a lot of computing power and some rather innovative algorithms. Technologically speaking, it will keep us ahead for a few years, maybe." Elsworth flipped to a new chart, using just a bit of flourish. "This, now, is something totally revolutionary. It is based on a lot of work that our friends over at DARPA have been playing around with."

Donnegan leaned in to read the caption beneath the image on the graphic.

"RADAR? What the hell are you talking about, Steam?

RADAR is hardly a stealth technology for a sub. Everyone knows that RADAR works in air, not water. You telling me that you plan on surfacing and using RADAR to somehow find submarines?"

Ward held up his hand.

"Just hear us out, Admiral. I think you'll see where we're going. Think active sonar, only using electromagnetic waves instead of sound. This is entirely an underwater operation. You remember those ELF transmitters we used to have up in Northern Michigan?"

Donnegan nodded. "Yeah, we used them to call up the boomers when they were deep. The tree-huggers thought the RF caused cancer in gopher gonads or some such silliness. Got the place shut down years ago. So?"

"The important thing is that ELF penetrates water for very long distances," Elsworth said, jumping back in. "The VLF transmitters we use today penetrate water as well, but the distance is measured in meters rather than thousands of kilometers."

Ward leaned in to point to charts on the page in front of Donnegan. "Looking at the hydrogen bonding vibrational spectrum and the Nyquist sampling frequency we need, three kilohertz in the myriameter band is about the perfect transmit frequency and bandwidth for maximum data transmission. To detect a submerged object at any distance means that we will be processing petabytes of data per ping. Calculations show that we should expect ranges on the order of ten nautical miles for a submerged target the size of a submarine."

"We put the transmitters in a row of pods on *Toledo*'s hull and use the thin-line towed array as a receive antenna," Elsworth explained, tag-teaming with Ward. "Since *Toledo* isn't anywhere near the size of the Upper Peninsula of Michigan, we'll have to do some fancy synthetic aperture processing to get a usable wave form. We'll use some big data processing to put this all back together. The key is a very narrow transmit frequency, a long receive antenna, and a lot of computing power to put it all together."

Donnegan smiled for the first time since Ward and Elsworth interrupted his evening meditation.

"And I suppose that you are going to tell me next that the best part is, no matter how quiet a boat is acoustically, this radar will find it."

"That is exactly what we believe will be the case," Ward said. "And unless they are looking for RF at this very particular frequency underwater, it is completely undetectable. We just need *Toledo* to verify out there in the ocean what we are seeing in the lab. Obviously, the key is to keep the whole technology under wraps so that our stealthy friends who are so enamored of the color red aren't looking for RF energy in that precise frequency range and wave form."

"That's why we prefer not to be installing the system in the Norfolk shipyard as has been planned all along," Elsworth piped in, closing the sale. "Tongue in the Ocean in the Bahamas is the perfect place to install this system and test it without the fear of any prying eyes. Or electronic surveillance."

Both men stood up straight and looked at Donnegan. The old admiral studied the charts for a long moment.

"And you are telling me this because...?"

Ward did not hesitate.

"There are those here in this building who, for reasons of their own, think taking anything new to the Bahamas, or anywhere else besides Norfolk or Newport, for that matter, is a big risk. A powerful congressman or two—you can probably guess which ones, and already know that they have a pipeline to your bosses over here—maintain that we cost their states high-paying jobs if we go off-shore with any of our test programs.

They also think Salkov is ready to negotiate to get out from beneath the sanctions and is no longer a real threat to us. So why spend the money on science fiction stuff? Or risk antagonizing the bastards if they learn about any of the new things we are doing? Those congressmen know just enough to be dangerous, but they head the two committees that could put a halt to the entire *Toledo* experimental program if they get their underwear in a bunch."

Tom Donnegan took a long drink of coffee.

"I think I see the method in your madness," he rumbled. "You're asking me to put my ass on the line so you guys can go down to the Bahamas and play disk jockey on the microwaves."

"That about sums it up," Ward confirmed, while Elsworth shrugged and nodded.

"I don't know precisely how I'll cover this up, or how I'll deflect the shit-storm if anybody hears about it," Donnegan told them. "But I'm buying what you two are selling. I have reasons to suspect that Newport has a leak as well, but we haven't been able to figure out just where yet. We will, but it may take some time. Meantime, get *Toledo* down there where it's secure, get that RADAR installed, and see if it can even find a clam in a bucket of bilge water." He looked for a moment at the well-chewed end of his cigar. "It better work, boys. And the damn Russians better not ever find out about what it can do. Ever!"

4

Captain First Rank Konstantin Kursalin put the periscope crosshair precisely on the bridge of the unsuspecting ship. The huge vessel's brilliant lights were almost blinding. Even at ten thousand meters, the cruise liner was so large that it filled the periscope's field of view. Such a large and inviting target, filled with probably two or three thousand tourists sipping fancy, sweet rum concoctions, floating blissfully from one tropical port to another. Not one of those tourists could possibly dream that Kursalin and his submarine were out here, fully capable of putting their massive seagoing hotel on the bottom.

"Shoot number one tube on periscope bearing," Kursalin calmly ordered.

Behind him, he could hear muttered orders as the weapons officer worked to launch the torpedo. Then he heard the satisfying swish of a high-speed water turbine and the rush of a thousand liters of seawater as the deluge flushed out the torpedo tube.

"Number one tube fired," the weapons officer reported. Then he added, "Simulated torpedo running normally."

Kursalin nodded and stepped back from the periscope. The device slid smoothly down into the scope well.

"Very well," he responded. "Secure from torpedo drill. Make your depth fifty meters."

The Russian submarine slid silently back down, plowing deeper into the darkness of the Atlantic Ocean.

Kursalin looked around the control room of the *Igor Borsovitch*. The crew hummed with the efficiency of a well-trained group that had worked together for many months, but he could now sense the teamwork beginning to fray at the edges. Even with a new toy—the finest submarine and most advanced underwater technology in the world—to play with, they were growing complacent.

Too many days lolling around here in the warm waters south of Bermuda. Just "boring holes in the ocean," as the Americans put it. He had tried to keep them busy while they waited for the underwater spy sensors to dutifully collect their data. The sensors remained where Kursalin's crew had strung them along in the deep waters on the far side of the coral reefs, over in the American test range at Tongue of the Ocean. Now they could only wait for them to deliver the data to the spy node on this side of the reef.

How did the missile boats do it? How did they tolerate the boredom when their entire mission was to sit and wait and twiddle their thumbs for months at a time? Konstantin was certain he would go stark raving mad on such a mission. His Cossack genetics did not allow him the patience to remain idle. He was a predator, one that needed to be on the prowl.

He knew, too, that every time he rendezvoused with the communications node, he was giving the Americans one more opportunity to detect the presence of *Igor Borsovitch* and uncover his secret.

The Russian shook his head slightly, as if to dispel the anxiety, and stepped over to where his first officer, Captain Second Rank Kaarle Garlerkin, was studiously analyzing the sonar display.

"Captain, we..."

"First Officer," Kursalin interrupted with a growl and an impatient wave of his hand. "Bring the submarine back to periscope depth. You will make the next approach on the cruise liner. It is time to copy the broadcast and see what instructions Moscow has for us. Then you may once again interrupt their shuffleboard game and 'sink' the decadent Americans."

"Yes, Captain," the first officer replied with only a hint of hesitation. Then he nodded.

The tall, lanky Garlerkin stepped up to the periscope and ordered, "*Sdelat' skorost' desyat' kilometrov v chas.*" ("Make your speed ten kilometers per hour.") "*Sdelat' svoy glubina dvadtsat' metrov.*" ("Make your depth twenty meters.")

The submarine ascended smoothly back toward the surface, slowing to a pace roughly equivalent to a fast walking speed so her tall periscope would not send up a watery, white feather on the sea, something even a drunken tourist at the rail of the ocean liner could spot against a coal-black ocean. It was best his scope's rooster tail did not end up as a post on Facebook.

Garlerkin raised the periscope and stared through its eyepiece, making a quick 360-degree sweep of the horizon. He needed to be sure that only the *Igor Borsovitch* and the cruise liner shared this particular part of the Atlantic.

There it was, exactly where he expected to see it. The cruise liner was plodding on, making big circles to convince its passengers that they had been on a real boat ride, before heading to Nassau. At this speed and with the intentional detours, they would arrive in port early the next morning. Perfect for disgorging the tourist crowd onto the waiting economy, ready for their shore excursions designed to separate them from their dollars in exchange for a few "authentic" trinkets freshly imported from China and some barely drinkable duty-free rum.

"Bearing on the cruise ship," First Officer Garlerkin called out as he depressed the periscope's bearing button.

"Three-two-zero degrees," a *michman* called out, reading from the numerical display above his head.

Another *michman*, seated in front of the torpedo fire control display, called out, "Matches the solution."

Just then, a tinny voice over the boat's announcing system interrupted the sea wolf's quiet approach on her prey.

"Captain, come to Radio. Message from Moscow onboard."

Kursalin moved from his perch behind Garlerkin and headed toward the submarine's tiny radio room aft of the control room. As he entered the cramped space, the radioman handed him a printout of the message. He read quickly.

"To Commanding Officer, Eyes Only.

1. The *Igor Borsovitch* will proceed immediately to a position of 36 degrees 33 minutes North Latitude and 74 degrees 36 minutes West Longitude. You must arrive in the mission area within forty-eight hours of the date-time group of this message. You will remain in the mission area for fifteen days, unless orders are modified later.

2. After arriving on station, you will observe the sea trials of new American *Virginia*-class submarine expected to occur in the next five days. You will record all possible telemetry and acoustic data. Collect any photo intelligence that may be available.

3. The *Igor Borsovitch* will remain undetected at all times. If detected, *Igor Borsovitch* will make all efforts to break contact and evade. Under no circumstances will *Igor Borsovitch* be identified as a VMF Rossii submarine. Use of all weapons is authorized for self-protection and concealment.

4. Commanding Officer to open sealed document labeled

'*Spetsial'naya Instruktsiya Odin*' and comply with instructions. *Stels ustroystvo* (stealth device) will be employed for duration of this mission.

5. *Udachi* (good luck). Igno Ivanovich Smirnov sends."

Kursalin scratched his chin thoughtfully. He vaguely remembered a bunch of engineers crawling all over the *Igor Borsovitch* shortly before they departed Polyarny. That happened periodically. But this time, after the inspection, the senior engineer had handed him a thick, securely taped envelope. With a serious face, the man had instructed him to lock the envelope in his safe and only open it if told to do so.

That, too, had happened a time or two on previous runs with his various commands. No instructions to open the envelopes had ever been issued, so he had no reason to anticipate that happening this time.

But it just had. And once he opened the envelope and read the contents, perhaps he would finally learn what this *stels ustroystvo* was and what it was supposed to accomplish.

The commanding officer turned and strode back through the control room, still clutching the message. He barely noticed the crew restoring the room from its battle stations condition back to normal cruising.

"Captain," First Officer Garlerkin called after him. "Your instructions?"

Kursalin hesitated for a second and then ordered, "Come to course north, depth one-five-zero meters. Come to normal cruising speed." He waited for Garlerkin to confirm his orders before adding, "When you have *Igor Borsovitch* on course and speed, join me in my stateroom. We have some matters to discuss."

Kursalin entered his cramped little stateroom and spun the dial on the heavy safe built into the bulkhead above his desk. When the safe's door swung open, he reached in and grabbed the red *Spetsial'naya Instruktsiya Odin* envelope. Slitting it open with his pen knife, he removed a thin binder labeled "*Stels Ustroystvo*" in large red letters. Below that in smaller red letters was "*Instruktsiya po Ekspluatatsii* (Operating Instructions)." And stamped in several places were the ominous words "*Sovershenno Sekretno* (Most Secret)."

Only the most closely held information bore such an ominous classification. It had been drilled into Kursalin's head many times over his career that any information classified "Most Secret" must be guarded with his life.

His hands shaking, the captain slowly opened the thin document, then slumped down into his chair and began to study it. The instructions were actually very simple. He only needed to take a magnetic key taped to the back of the document and place it into the system's controller module. Then he should type in the correct code. From there, the system was entirely automatic.

Kursalin shook his head in disbelief as he digested the words on the pages in front of him. Evidently the *stels ustroystvo* device was designed to make his submarine disappear from all sonar sensors. Not merely make it quieter, but actually make it disappear. The equations and electronics were gibberish, but he slowly deduced that the system copied any noise it detected and then transmitted a second noise that was exactly 180 degrees out of phase and at precisely the same amplitude as the incoming noise. That would totally cancel it out.

The captain was still contemplating the implications of this new device when First Officer Garlerkin knocked quietly on the door. Only after his commander's grunted, "*Vvodit'* (enter)" did he open it. Quickly stepping inside, he shut the door and plopped down on the bed, the only other available seat in the tiny room.

Without a word, Kursalin handed the first officer the flimsy single-sheet message. As Garlerkin began to read, he stopped at the first line and gave the captain a questioning look.

Kursalin answered him before he asked.

"Those shore-bound idiots in Moscow do not understand that there is no way to run this ship without my first officer knowing everything I know."

Garlerkin nodded, looking pleased. It was truly rare when his captain shared anything with his second-in-command. He read the short message in its entirety before again looking up at Kursalin.

"Captain, I will plot a course to our new mission area." He paused for a few seconds as calculations coursed through his head. "We are about 1,500 kilometers south of the mission area." Glancing back at the message and reading the day-time group, he added, "We will need to transit at fifty kilometers per hour to arrive in the mission area with enough time to sanitize it before we start the mission."

Garlerkin knew that transiting that fast would make them detectable to the ever-present American ASW ships. Why was his captain not worried about such a risk?

Kursalin nodded, again anticipating the first officer's question. He had already been doing the same planning in his head and reached the same conclusion. He handed the red-bound binder to his second-in-command.

"Just read this."

Twice in less than two minutes, the captain had shown unusual confidence in Garlerkin. And this document was clearly of the highest level of importance.

The XO began to study the information. His eyes grew wider with each sentence.

5

Admiral Tom Donnegan carefully closed the thin report and placed it on top of one of the many stacks that covered his cluttered desk. Stroking his chin, he reached for the red phone and punched in a well-remembered number. The call was answered on the second ring.

"Fleet Forces Command, Admiral Bradburn's office, Chief Jones."

Donnegan cut the practiced litany short. "Chief, this is Donnegan. Put me through to the admiral."

Seconds later Admiral Joshua "Brad" Bradburn came on line. "Tom, we haven't caught up in a while. How're things up there in the Puzzle Palace?"

"Brad, we may have a problem." Donnegan, the Navy's top spy, usually dispensed with all pleasantries, even if the nature of the call was not quite so urgent as this one. "I've been reading all the reports on Russia's recent activities and I don't like the way it's adding up. Too many pieces moving around. Salkov is one sneaky son of a bitch, but he always has a plan. And it is never good."

"What has that notoriously vivid imagination been cooking

up now?" Bradford questioned. As the commander of all the Navy ships and aircraft in the Atlantic, he was more than aware that his team would be on the front line, no matter what.

"You've seen the reports on him sending armor and troops into Belarus. NATO has their pantyhose all in a knot with a couple of hundred thousand Russian troops on their border. And the Russian Air Force has been testing our Air Defense zones pretty regularly for a while now. If you've seen today's intel brief, you know that we can't find several of their newest subs: a couple of their new boomers, several diesel boats, and a half dozen or so attack boats. It doesn't take any damn imagination to smell this pot of shit!"

"You think he is hell-bent on starting World War III?" Bradburn asked, his tone clearly one of disbelief.

There was a short pause on the line. When Donnegan replied, his words were unusually measured.

"Brad, we don't have any really good insight on Salkov's motivations. He never plays by the normal rule. He zigs just when you think he will zag. Don't really think he wants to start a war, but he has some real internal problems that aren't easily solved and a history of throwing his weight around to gin up some good old Russian pride and deflect any brave critic. Bottom line, I don't like the way this is going down. We need to keep our eyes open on everything we do."

Admiral Bradburn clicked his tongue in frustration.

"Tom, we're spread real thin right now. You know that as well as anybody. With all the budget cuts, sequestrations, and every other gimmick Congress can come up with, we don't have enough of the right assets. The last Congress hurt us real bad when they laid up the *George Washington* and the *Carl Vinson*. That has us down to eight carrier battle groups max, and those we do have can barely get under way, what with all the deferred maintenance. Now you tell me I need to get everything ready for some big crisis just because the Reds are rattling some swords. What am I supposed to do?"

"Life ain't fair," Donnegan answered. "We do what we can with what we have."

"My God!" Bradburn suddenly shouted. "We've got the *George Mason* heading out on alpha trials. She's the most advanced sub we've ever built. All the bells and whistles, and we are testing them all. *Toledo*'s going out with her, too, and you know what kind of new technology she's carrying. You don't think Salkov would try anything with them, do you?" Without allowing Donnegan to answer the question, he continued, "I'll make sure we have a full-court press on the security for her. I'll have all the ASW I can muster to protect her... what few assets I have available."

Tom Donnegan's voice was low, deep, barely audible.

"I hope I'm wrong for once, Admiral. I really do. But I don't think so. I hope you can muster enough of something to call whatever bluff that son of a bitch is about to play."

Ψ

Joe Glass re-read the message. Finally, a release from the shipyard! It was time to go to sea and be a sailor again.

TO:USS TOLEDO
FROM:COMSUBLANT
SUBJ:OPERATIONS ORDERS

1. ON OR ABOUT 0800Z 15 OCT, WHEN CERTIFIED READY FOR SEA, USS TOLEDO WILL GET UNDERWAY FROM NNSY AND PROCEED TO VACAPES OPAREAS BRAVO TWO THREE AND BRAVO TWO FOUR.
2. TOLEDO WILL CONDUCT SEATRIALS TESTING

IAW SEATRIALS PLAN TO BE COMPLETED NLT
1600Z 17 OCT. REPORT RESULTS TESTING PUMP
JET PROPULSION, ACS SYSTEM SOONEST.

3. AT COMPLETION OF SEATRIALS TESTING
   TOLEDO WILL ESTABLISH AN ASW BARRIER
   SEARCH ALONG WESTERN BOUNDARY OF
   ASSIGNED OPAREAS. TOLEDO IS TO DETECT
   AND REPORT ANY SUBMERGED INTRUDERS
   ATTEMPTING TO MONITOR GEORGE MASON
   SEATRIALS IN VACAPES OPAREAS THREE
   THREE AND THREE FOUR.

4. WHEN RELEASED, TOLEDO WILL PROCEED
   VIA ASSIGNED TRANSIT ROUTES GOLF,
   SIERRA, BLUE TO ARRIVE AUTEC NLT 1200Z
   24 OCT.

5. FURTHER INSTRUCTIONS TO FOLLOW

BT

Glass well knew how much he needed to accomplish and
how little time he had to get it all done. Charts to be plotted,
stores and weapons to load, maintenance to wrap up. A thousand details. And in addition to checking all the new systems on
Toledo, he was assigned to nursemaid Brian Edwards, his former
XO, and the *George Mason*, Edwards's spanking new *Virginia*-
class submarine. But one thing about his orders bugged Glass.
Why was SUBLANT so concerned about someone snooping
around the new boat that they had put the rush on and sent
Toledo out to guard the barn door? Especially when the effec-
tiveness of his own boat's new propulsion system and the other
gear she now carried had not yet been adequately tested?

Happy as he was to be underway, he still felt a bit of appre-
hension. Glass stood and yelled through the head that sepa-
rated his stateroom from the executive officer's.

"XO, grab the COB, Nav, and Engineer. Meet me in the wardroom in ten minutes."

Glass sipped his cup of coffee without tasting it as he rifled through the rest of the message traffic, killing time while the XO rounded up the troops. All pretty routine, the comings and goings of the submarine fleet. He quickly browsed the latest update on the Red Stealth project. It appeared NUWC was gathering their best engineers for what amounted to a Caribbean vacation. The security access message contained twenty-two names.

Ten minutes passed quickly as Glass finished reading and headed down to the submarine's wardroom, located in the middle-level operations compartment. Lieutenant Commander Billy Ray Jones, the new XO, sat to the right of Glass's seat at the head of the small table. LCDR Doug O'Malley, the Engineer, slouched in the chair to his left. Master Chief Sam Wallich, the Chief of the Boat, sat across the table from the Engineer. LCDR Jerry Perez, the Navigator, was fiddling with a keyboard. He was attempting to get the chart up on the wardroom's wide-screen television so he could display a projected track.

Jones glanced up as Glass entered the wardroom through the tiny pantry at the aft end.

"We're all here," he said, his South Alabama drawl thick as ribbon-cane syrup. Jones came from a long line of submariners, tough guys who rode the *S*-boats before World War II, the *Gato*s and *Balao*s in the Pacific during the war, and helped put the first of the nukes into service in the 1950s. "Nav is puttin' up the projected tracks now."

"And the keyboard is kicking his butt, as usual," O'Malley chimed in.

Glass chuckled. "Play nice, boys. We have work to do. COB, I need you to honcho a stores load tomorrow, and just to make things interesting, we'll be doing a weapons load at the same time."

Wallich winced and shook his head. Trying to accomplish both evolutions simultaneously would be hard, slow work for the crew. It would also make access through the forward part of the boat next to impossible. Loading weapons would block the weapons shipping hatch as well as remove the deck in upper- and middle-level operations. The stores load would block the forward escape trunk, the only other access to the boat's front end.

"We'll get it done," the COB said. Glass next turned to O'Malley.

"Eng, I need you to have the reactor up on line by sixteen-hundred tomorrow. Shore power off by twenty-hundred at the latest. Make sure that you test the mains, or whatever the hell we are calling them now. We're going to get out ahead of the *George Mason*."

"Aye, sir. We'll be ready," O'Malley responded, smiling. "Oh, and the main turbines are still the mains. They just power those pumps back in the mud tank rather than a screw. I have to admit it's a neat arrangement. Inlets flush to the hull just forward of the rudder, then a multi-stage pump jet shoots high-pressure water out the back like some jet fighter."

"Damn sight different from those old diesel boats Grandpa used to drive," Jones added.

Glass grunted, still not completely convinced this new technology would work like his reliable old screw, regardless of what made it turn. He understood perfectly how that big bronze propeller moved a ship through the sea. But how well would these newfangled pumps perform? He could not help but imagine them working like a flushing toilet.

Perez finally found the right combination of keystrokes to

get the image up on the screen. The team settled in to plan out the multitude of details for their next few hectic days.

Ψ

1500Z 15 OCT

"Station the maneuvering watch!" came the blaring command from the 1MC announcing system.

Commander Brian Edwards tried to massage the aching knot from the back of his neck. Preparing a brand-new submarine for her first taste of seawater had consumed his existence for months. Every detail, from critical reactor safety records to the sea trials menu, had crossed his desk for approval. He was exhausted, but all the work and worry were about to pay off. The USS *George Mason* was finally as ready for sea as she would ever be.

Edwards grabbed his jacket and ball cap before heading out of his stateroom and up the short ladder to the upper-level operations compartment. Master Chief Dennis Oshley met him at the bottom of the long ladder leading up to the bridge.

"Big day, Skipper," Oshley said with a broad grin. He handed Edwards his favorite binoculars. "It's going to be damn good to get back to sea."

Edwards slapped his COB on the shoulder.

"Sure will be, and even better to get away from these yard birds and bureaucrats. With so much brass onboard, we'd better check the pre-dive trim very, very carefully."

"Let's see, you only have a four-star, two three-stars, and a two-star up there," Oshley noted, nodding upward toward the vessel's bridge. "Way I figure it, if you keep the four-star and two-star on one side of the playpen and the two three-stars on the other side, we won't have to worry too much about the weight of the egos causing us to list one way or the other."

"Right," Edwards agreed with a grin. "Tell you what, COB. You try to tell Naval Reactors, SUBLANT, NAVSEA, and PEO SUBS where they are supposed to stand." He shook his head, pulled his ball cap farther down over his face, and zipped up his jacket. "What's the weather report?"

"Sunny and mild. Temps in the seventies with light winds out of the southeast. You won't be able to chase them off the bridge with any bad weather."

"Thanks for nothing, Chief. Well, we'd better get this show on the road." Edwards started the long climb to the bridge of America's newest submarine. "The guests will be getting restless."

The *George Mason* glided smoothly down the James River, past the I-664 and Hampton Roads Bridge tunnels, and on out into the Chesapeake Bay. As the Thimble Shoals Light passed off their port beam, Edwards said goodbye to his harbor pilot and tug escorts. He brought the sub around to line up on the narrow space between the north and south islands of the Chesapeake Bay Bridge Tunnel. An inbound container ship heading for the Norfolk Port Authority Terminal, her decks stacked high with China's best exports, passed down the *George Mason*'s port side. Dozens of motor boats jetted across the bright blue waters, making the most of the fine autumn weather and catching a look at the new warship. A squadron of sailboats raced around a closed course at the mouth of Lynnhaven Inlet to the south.

With the Chesapeake Bay Bridge Tunnel astern, Edwards brought the boat around to a course of due east, out into the Atlantic Ocean. As expected, his escort vessel, the USS *Bulkeley* (DDG-84), was waiting there and took station a mile off the *Mason*'s starboard beam. The *Bulkeley*, a guided-missile destroyer, would be their constant companion and link to the outside world until Alpha Trials were completed, as well as the command center for all the ASW efforts to cordon off the sea trials area.

Now safely in open water, Edwards finally turned to the assembled high-ranking dignitaries gathered behind him.

"Admirals, please join me in the wardroom for lunch. We have four hours until we reach the dive point. We'll be doing routine surface testing until then."

Ψ

Eighty miles to the east, the *Toledo* sped silently along as she slipped beneath the waves. Joe Glass sat on the fold-down stool aft of the number two periscope and watched his crew perform. So far everything was normal. The maneuvering watch was uneventful, but the crew was shaking off the rust from too much time in the shipyard. The new propulsion system had worked fine on the surface. Now it was time to see how this fancy new technology performed in a submerged submarine.

"Officer of the Deck, coordinate with the Engineer and increase speed to Flank," Glass ordered.

Lieutenant Pat Durand, the on-watch officer of the deck, answered, "Captain, Eng reports all temperatures and pressures are normal at Standard. Recommends increasing speed to Ahead Full. Shifting pumps to fast speed."

"Very well," Glass acknowledged as *Toledo* surged ahead. The boat settled out at an indicated speed of twenty-four knots.

"Sonar, Captain. What do you hear on the towed array?"

Just forward of the control room, Master Chief Randy Zillich watched his sonar operators as they leafed through the displays. He keyed the 27MC microphone.

"Skipper, that system is really quiet. It almost sounds like there is no sub in front of the array."

"Captain, Engineer reports everything normal at a Full

Bell," Durand interjected. "Proceeding to Flank."

Glass watched as the pit log crept up—twenty-six, twenty-seven, twenty-eight knots before it finally peaked at just shy of thirty-one knots. Not quite what she once did with a screw shoving her along, Glass acknowledged. But boy, she sure as hell was quiet!

The captain stood and stretched, trying to work the kinks out of his back. It was time to "walk the store," move around and see what was happening throughout his boat.

"Officer of the Deck, slow to Ahead Two-thirds," he told Durand, and walked back to the navigation plot. "When you are in Op-area Three-three, stream the thin line towed array, energize the ACS cloaking device, and establish an ASW barrier search on a north-south line."

It was time to see if all these new gizmos were worth what the taxpayers spent on them. And if they would help them keep an eye on their brand-new sister.

Ψ

As the *George Mason* pulled away from Norfolk and *Toledo* played with her new toys a hundred miles to the north, the Russian submarine *Igor Borsovitch* was finally slowing to search speed after the quick transit from near the Bahamas. Captain First Rank Konstantin Kursalin stared intently at his sonar display. The only contact was a container ship a hundred miles to their southeast, trudging its way up the East Coast, likely headed toward New York with a load of cheap Korean cars.

Kursalin felt his heartbeat quicken. It was time to go to work.

"First Officer, rig the ship for quiet. Commence sonar search for the American submarine." He hesitated for only a second. "Energize the *stels ustroystvo* device."

6

Captain First Rank Konstantin Kursalin peered intently at the electronic chart displayed on the large screen on the control room's aft bulkhead. The *Igor Borsovitch* had arrived at the designated spot in the Atlantic a full six hours ahead of schedule. Now his crew needed to make sure that they were the only submarine lurking off the Virginia coast of the USA.

"First Officer," Kursalin said as he turned to Kaarle Garlerkin. "Deploy the acoustic towed array. It is time for us to go shark hunting."

Back in the free-flood area above the *Igor Borsovitch*'s engine room, the sonar towed array reeled out behind the submarine as she slowly steamed forward. Soon it stretched more than a thousand meters astern. With a sonar array this long and sensitive, Kursalin knew that any American submarine within twenty kilometers would be easily detected and tracked, long before the cocky Americans even suspected that the Mother Land's finest submarine was hunting them down, right there in their own home waters.

Kursalin sat back and tried to make himself somewhat comfortable for what he knew would likely be a long, boring search. Of course, if and when they detected anything of interest, it could get very exciting—and very dangerous—very quickly. Far too quickly for him to prevent a disaster if he did not already have all of the available information needed to make the proper moves. The only way to make sure that he had all the necessary information to make the best move if the time came was to sit out here in the control room and absorb it as it came in.

"Captain, we have completed a search with the array," Garlerkin reported. "We are now ready to turn."

Kursalin nodded as he acknowledged the update.

"Very well, come to course three-zero-zero. Let us sneak in a little closer to the coast while we search. Do we have any contacts on the hull arrays?"

"Nothing except the merchant traffic that we have held all day."

The Russian submarine moved slowly toward the Virginia coastline even as she continued to conduct a sonar search for any American submarines in the area. Kursalin knew that he should have few worries about being discovered there, swimming boldly in the very heart of the American submarine home waters. Russia's finest engineers had assured him that the *stels ustroystvo* device made him totally invisible to the Americans' much vaunted sonar.

Still, the experienced submariner knew it was best to be certain. And prepared to act if necessary.

Ψ

At that very moment, two thousand yards to the north—just over a mile away—the *Toledo* slowly steamed to the southeast of the Russian vessel, conducting a sonar search, specifically looking for any submarine that might try to sneak into the

George Mason's private party. Joe Glass sat on his familiar stool at the back of the periscope stand, watching the sonar displays for any contacts that might show up beyond the merchant traffic that they had already been tracking. The new ACS system seemed to be doing its work, making the *Toledo* acoustically invisible.

Still, Glass sipped his coffee as the screens continued to show him nothing new out there. Nothing at all.

The hours stretched on as the two submarines blindly danced around each other. The *Igor Borsovitch* slowly worked her way in closer to the coast while the *Toledo* gradually "mowed the grass" in her operating area, guarding the outer door.

Ψ

"Captain, sonar is picking up detections to the west, between us and the shore."

The Russian skipper cocked his head. "Tell me."

"I believe we have two contacts," First Officer Garlerkin responded. "One of them sounds like an American destroyer, probably one of their *Arleigh Burke*-class. Looks to be doing about thirty-two kilometers per hour. Best bearing is two-six-five."

"And the other?" Kursalin queried.

"Best guess is a US submarine on the surface," Garlerkin reported, unable to hide a wolfish grin. "Sonar says that it is close, inside five kilometers."

"Well, I believe we should go take a look." Kursalin rose from his seat. "First Officer, maneuver to take a position three thousand meters off the submarine's starboard bow. That will put the submarine between us and the destroyer and will allow us to watch as the Americans steam happily past us."

Kursalin stepped back to watch the maneuvering unfold on

the large-screen chart display. The line of blue dots representing the *Igor Borsovitch* curved around the two rows of red dots portraying the American warships. He patiently waited until everyone was in almost a perfect position to observe the passing ships.

"Launch the ESM buoy. We need to know what their periscope detection radars are doing."

The *michman* manning the weapons control console reached up and flipped a switch on the panel above his head. Up in the sail, a small launch door flipped open and a canister about ten centimeters in diameter and two meters long floated up to the surface, trailing a skinny fiber line behind it. When the buoy popped to the surface, a small antenna slid out of its housing and immediately went to work, searching for high frequency radar signals.

"Captain, the buoy is detecting many radars." Garlerkin gave the results from the device even as he continued to read the information that had popped up on his computer screen. "The destroyer's Aegis SPY-1D is very strong, but poses us no threat. We are detecting many commercial navigation radars, two with very high signal strength, probably close. There is an APY-10 radar from an American *Poseidon* aircraft and an APS-147 from an American MH-60R helicopter. Both have periscope detection modes. Both appear to be weak. Those, of course, could be a problem for us."

Kursalin walked quickly back toward the periscope, his mind racing. Here was the perfect opportunity to watch an American *Virginia*-class submarine up close and gather invaluable photographic intelligence. It was a priceless chance. But the risk of detection was high. If the Americans found him in the middle of their sea trials, they might very well attack. Without a doubt, the Russian Navy would attack had the situation been reversed.

There was a possibility he might be sunk. Or worse, go home in disgrace.

By the time he reached the periscope, the captain knew what he had to do.

"First Officer, bring the ship to periscope depth."

Ψ

Slowly circling 20,000 feet overhead, the P-8 *Poseidon* ASW aircraft, Tail Number 441, integrated the line of SSQ-101 ADAR passive sono-buoys working in conjunction with data from the three SSQ-125 Multi-Static sono-buoys that it had seeded to detect any submarines in the area.

The Tactical Radar Operator watched his spanking new APY-10 multi-function radar as he leafed through the displays. Boredom set in early on these training missions. The squadron commodore, sitting up in the command pilot's seat, had briefed them before the flight. This was a real-world tactical mission, just as surely as if they had been over the Barents Sea instead of in the Atlantic off the East Coast of the USA. Even so, Tony "Spanks" Smith knew very well that the coast of Virginia, not the Kola Peninsula, was a hundred miles to his west.

The APY-10 was almost as much fun to play with as *Call of Duty*, except the graphics were not quite as good. Spanks flipped through the synthetic ISAR mode and took a radar "picture" of the USS *Bulkeley* running fifty miles to the west and then one of the *George Mason* steaming along on the surface. He could make out figures standing up on the submarine's sail, but it sure would be great if the graphics were good enough to really see who they were.

Then Smith flipped over to the high-resolution automatic periscope detection mode, APDM. Nothing out there to look at, but it might still be fun just to see what the system would do.

Almost immediately an alarm window flipped down and the display auto-slewed away from the *George Mason*, instantly zeroing in on a spot a couple of thousand yards to the north. Smith thought he saw a flicker of black for a millisecond before he was looking at sea-return again.

Naw, it couldn't be! Had to be some equipment anomaly. You could count on every damn new system to go on the fritz at least once.

He wanted to be a team player, though. Smith keyed the inter-cabin communications system and called out to Lt. Julie "Hoolihan" Marsh, the Tactical Control Officer.

"Hey, Hoolihan. Got a hit on the APDM. Went sinker immediately."

"Right, Spanks," she responded, adding an incredulous snort. "That's the *Red October* on alligator drive out there, sneaking in to the North Carolina coast for asylum for Sean Connery. Weren't you paying attention in the pre-flight? Besides, the sono-buoys are showing *nada*."

"Aw, come on, Lieutenant," Smith shot back. "You don't have to bust my balls just because this system picks up every beer can floating in the ocean."

"Okay, Spanks. We'll see what the Pax River eggheads come up with on post-flight data analysis. I'll put it out on Link 16, just in case anyone else has contact."

Ψ

"Hey, Tacco, Charlie Three Whiskey just reported a poss-sub on the link." The Link 16 operator on the *Bulkeley* was glad something had broken the monotony. "Two thousand yards off the port side of the *George Mason*."

Lieutenant Commander Sayegh Husiyen, the young Tactical Action Officer, stared at the large-screen display on the bulkhead. The tracks were getting pretty confused with all the traffic they were monitoring in the congested VACAPES OpAreas.

"Is Alpha Four Sierra reporting contact?" the TAO asked, inquiring about the MH-60R ASW helicopter searching out to the northwest.

"Negative," the link operator shot back. "She is blank on her buoys as well as her APS-147 periscope detection radar."

"What about the tail?" Husiyen asked the sonar monitor. They had launched the TB-37 MFTA multi-function towed array early that morning and, since then, had been carefully searching with its sensitive hydrophones, listening hard for any unwanted guests.

"Nothing on that bearing," was the answer. "We hold the *George Mason* weakly on the surface at bearing three-four-one, best range ten thousand yards. That's the only submarine contact held."

"Okay, classify the contact a false alarm, and report out on the Link," the TAO ordered.

Nobody was down there. Nobody at all.

7

"Captain, picking up transients to the southwest," the 27MC speaker blared. "Best bearing two-three-one. Correlates to Sierra Two-Four, the *George Mason*. Sounds like she is opening her vents."

The *Toledo*'s crew was still keeping a close eye on the big rectangle of Atlantic Ocean in which their brand-new sister and her destroyer escort swam. Not only was making certain nobody crashed their coming-out party important, but this excursion was also an excellent opportunity for real-world training on all the experimental systems that had recently been installed aboard the boat.

Joe Glass grabbed the microphone from its holder and confirmed receipt of his sonarman's report. "Captain, aye. She's going to get real quiet now. Be ready. Don't lose her in the grass."

"Sonar, Captain. We ain't gonna lose her." Master Chief Randy Zillich's voice was as confident as always. "I got her tonal map programmed into the BQQ-10, and the TB-29 towed array is acting like a champ for once. Holding her on three-hertz and twenty-hertz tonals. Weak but trackable. Tracker assigned and holding."

Glass sat back, took a sip of lukewarm coffee, and relaxed for a few seconds. Master Chief Zillich had reason to be confident. He was the best sonarman in the fleet, bar none. He had been on *Toledo* for almost his entire career, refusing to transfer to any other boat and even turning down much deserved shore duty several times. The chance to test and learn all the new Buck Rogers gear on his boat had led to yet another transfer rejection by Zillich only the week before. If there was an erg of acoustic energy anywhere in the ocean, Randy Zillich would find it and track it all the way back to its source. If any of this new stuff strung up all over *Toledo* helped do that, he wanted to get first crack at it.

"Captain, aye," Glass answered. He set his mug down, stood, and stepped over to the navigation plot at the back of the control room. Colored dots, lines, and smudges on the screen looked like some primitive video game. "We'll stay on this course for a few more minutes to make sure we have solid contact and then we will reverse course to the south. The last thing we need to do is run out of our box."

Randy Perez, the Navigator, glanced up from his own analysis of the electronic chart display.

"Skipper, we got twenty minutes at this speed and course before we get to the boundary."

The little yellow-light blip representing *Toledo* tracked across the ECDIS, the electronic chart display, toward a red line drawn perpendicular to their present northerly course. Off to the west, another red line ran up and down—north and south— denoting the western edge of their assigned operating area. A tiny blue diamond well to the west of the north/south line showed where the destroyer USS *Bulkeley* was steaming along on the surface. A small shallow "U" with a dot in it, also blue and well to the west, represented the vessel they were all keeping an eye on, the newly-launched submarine *George Mason.*

Glass shook his head in wonder as he watched the colorful palette of the ECDIS screen. Gone were all the paper charts and graphs that had historically been used to navigate and figure out where everybody else was in a patch of the sea. No guess-work involved to integrate all the information. These electronic displays did it for them. As Glass's former skipper, Jon Ward, liked to say, "It was like God was looking down from above and seeing everything at once."

But what was it that Ward, now a commodore, usually added to that simile?

"Just remember it's that snake in the grass you don't see that can coil up and bite you."

It was true, of course. Even as their ability to see and hear got better, the capabilities of other countries' submarines—friendly and not so friendly—improved as well. It was a compli-cated and expensive but crucial game of leap-frog.

Joe Glass turned away from the colorful screen. For right now, he would assume they were hearing and seeing all they needed to.

Ψ

Captain First Rank Konstantin Kursalin carefully watched the sonar displays in the *Igor Borsovitch*'s control room. The new American *Virginia*-class submarine was quiet and very difficult to track. His own vessel's acoustic towed array was barely sensi-tive enough to hold contact on the American, even though she was a mere two thousand meters away. The sensitive spherical sonar array in *Igor Borsovitch*'s bow space did not have any contacts at all, except for the American destroyer and several merchant ships off in the distance.

Kursalin was well aware that they were performing a delicate dance. He needed to stay close to the American submarine if he hoped to gain any intelligence, and she certainly appeared to be worthy of some serious monitoring. There was no doubt this was the new vessel on sea trials that he had been assigned to find and observe. The recordings he was taking were priceless. The analysts at the special intelligence section of the Severomorsk Division of the N. N. Andreyev Acoustical Institute would be able to sift out every vulnerability of this new American submarine. He just needed more recordings. But he also needed to remain undetected.

As long as the American cooperated and kept his speed down, it was relatively easy to stay close enough. However, if he went much above twenty-five kilometers per hour, the flow noise on his own acoustic towed array would become too loud to hold contact.

"Captain," Kaarle Garlerkin called out. "The American submarine is speeding up. His signal is getting weaker. Sonar reports that they are experiencing problems holding contact."

The first officer was not telling Kursalin anything he could not already see for himself on the sonar display. If he tried to speed up to catch the American, he would lose contact because of the increased noise. If he did not go faster, he would also lose contact because he would have allowed the range to grow too great. There was no good option.

The Russian captain stroked his chin, feeling the coarse stubble. A thought occurred to him.

He remembered his own experiences with the *Igor Borsovitch* during her initial sea trials. He had been forced to operate in a very small box so the escort ships could keep close track. They had to be close enough to immediately find him and conduct a rescue, if possible, in the event any disaster happened with the untested vessel. It must be the same for the Americans.

"First Officer, steer for the American destroyer," Captain Kursalin ordered, just the hint of a satisfied smile playing at his lips. "Keep us within three thousand meters of him. We will simply allow the American submarine to come back to us."

Ψ

Over on the *George Mason*, Commander Brian Edwards was more than ready to put his new submarine through a series of maneuvers. He reached up and pulled down the red handset from its clip above BYG-1 Command Console.

"Quebec Six Zulu," he said into the underwater telephone. "This is Three Golf Whiskey. Going to Flank, changing course to one-eight-zero. Conducting max power runs on north-south courses. When at grid position six-point-two, whiskey-point-four, will proceed deep for emergency blow test. Confirm you stay at least six thousand yards from grid position six-point-two, whiskey-point-four."

Edwards's words were digitally encrypted and then broadcast out on a sonar pulse that sounded very much like background noise to anyone listening on a system not equipped to decipher this particular racket. Sonarmen termed such sounds as "biologics" and routinely ignored them.

"Three Golf Whiskey, this is Quebec Six Zulu," the perfectly understandable but mechanical-sounding voice replied from the *Bulkeley*. "Copy all. Standing by six thousand yards from grid position six-point-two, whiskey-point-four. You are cleared for high-speed run and emergency blow test."

Edwards nodded and smiled. Time for a little fun after some very boring—but very necessary—component testing.

"Pilot, increase speed to Flank," the skipper called to one of the two chiefs sitting in front of a series of flat-panel monitors. Their screens displayed a remarkable array of ship's data and system status statistics. "Make your depth seven hundred feet."

"Speed to Flank, depth to seven hundred feet, Pilot, aye," the chief promptly responded as he reached up to one of the touch screen displays. He scrolled down until the readout showed "Flank," then scrolled down another column and tapped his index finger on the selection "700 ft." Every man aboard felt the submarine smoothly accelerate as she angled slightly downward. Without anyone touching any controls, the massive underwater vessel leveled out precisely at seven hundred feet as their speed went past twenty-five knots.

The pit log had just registered thirty-two knots when the pilot called out, "Captain, Maneuvering reports that we are at one hundred percent reactor power."

The submarine tore through the ocean depths along an invisible but sweeping race track while the engineers swarmed over her power plant taking readings and analyzing every nuance of her performance. At last, satisfied that they had all the data they could possibly want, the senior shipyard engineer told the boat's captain that they were done with this phase of testing.

"Slow to ahead one-third and head for grid position six-point-two, whiskey-point-four," Brian Edwards told the officer of the deck as he walked out of the control room. "Call me when we are ten minutes out."

So far, so good.

Ψ

Konstantin Kursalin paced the control room deck like a caged tiger. The *Igor Borsovitch* was slowly circling not far from the American destroyer, assuming that the elusive new submarine would soon return. They had lost all contact two hours before and, since then, had seen no sign of a submarine anywhere in the vicinity.

First Officer Kaarle Garlerkin bent over the sonar operator, intently watching his screen and ordering alignment changes. Why would the ship venture so far from their escort during such early trials? Not even the haughty Americans would be so vain as to assume there could not be some kind of failure in a brand-new vessel, one built by corrupt lowest-bidding capitalists. The first officer could only continue to study every bit of data in the hope that he could make the contact suddenly reappear. He did not want to even imagine the repercussions from Moscow should they not be able to re-acquire their quarry and complete the observation.

Suddenly Garlerkin froze. A blip—a very large and angry blip—appeared from nowhere on the screen. Whatever that tangle of pixels represented was very close and very loud. Before he could even open his mouth to report the impossibly sudden contact, the Russian submarine's hull started to reverberate from the sound.

"Captain!" he shouted. "Something very loud and close. Sounds like it is immediately below us!"

"Ahead Flank!" Kursalin barked. "The American is testing his emergency surfacing system! And he is right below us!"

The *Igor Borsovitch* jumped ahead as the throttleman whipped wide open the control wheel in front of him, pouring massive amounts of high-pressure steam into the main engines. Anyone standing had to grab something to hang onto or was thrown hard to the deck.

The Russian submarine raced at better than sixty kilometers per hour away from where she had been hovering, missing the *George Mason* by mere feet in the pitch-black deep. The crew could clearly hear the roar of the American submarine as she hurtled upward and past them. There was no need for fancy hydrophones when they were this close.

Surely the Americans must have detected them as they poured on the steam. Konstantin Kursalin quickly ran the possibilities through his mind. With an encounter that close, and with the amount of noise they had just made in evading an underwater collision, even his fancy new stealth device would not hide them.

There was no hesitation, no other option. He had to get away. Put range between his ship and the Americans. Allow things to settle down.

The *Igor Borsovitch* raced to the east to clear datum, no longer even trying to be quiet. Kursalin felt his heartbeat slow to normal.

"Captain, there is...impossible!" Garlerkin suddenly yelled, his eyes wide, disbelieving. "It is another American submarine! Unmistakable signature! Dead ahead and closing fast! We are trapped!"

Kursalin knew at once what would happen next. If two American submarines detected them, they were caught. The Americans would certainly know what Kursalin's submarine was doing there and would not allow them to escape with whatever data they had gathered so far. The American captains would also know what the Russian ship would do if caught and would attempt to act before that was possible.

"Shoot tubes one and two!" Kursalin shouted. He had no choice but to shoot his way out of this trap.

The two Russian Fizek-1 533mm electric homing torpedoes would take care of the American gate-guard submarine, giving him an escape hatch into a vast, open ocean.

Even through the sudden rush of adrenaline, Captain First Rank Konstantin Kursalin sensed a glimmer of satisfaction when he felt the slight kick as the two deadly fish were flushed from their tubes and sent on their way to search out and destroy the American sub blocking his escape.

Ψ

Joe Glass had just returned to *Toledo*'s control room after a quick run to the wardroom. His ship's baker was responsible for some of the most sinful cinnamon rolls in the Atlantic Fleet. Glass had finally succumbed to the temptation to snatch a couple of those fresh, hot, and fragrant rolls from the oven. That meant an extra fifteen minutes on the treadmill every day for the next two weeks, but those pastries were more than worth the sacrifice.

"Captain, we have a problem," Master Chief Randy Zillich called through the control room door.

"What you got, Master Chief?"

"That damn ACS system has gone on the fritz. It is broadcasting exactly in phase with our signature instead of 180 degrees out of phase. If anybody out there is listening, we sound like a party bus all of a damn sudden."

"Can we fix it?" Glass asked, still chewing the last cinnamon roll.

"Don't know for sure. Maybe it's just a simple adjustment," Zillich speculated. "Could be a component failure, and we're a long way from the closest Radio Shack. May be a design problem. Just don't know."

"Well, secure it for now. We'll have the NUWC eggheads take a look at it when we get back to Norfolk," Glass told him.

"Okay, and then I think I may try one of those cinnamon…"

"Hey, Master Chief!" the sonarman manning the passive broad band stack suddenly interrupted. "You running another drill on us? I hear what sounds like a pair of those new Russian torpedoes inbound."

Zillich stopped, grabbed a set of headphones, and listened hard for five seconds, all the while staring at the steadily building splash of information displaying on the screen.

"Shit!" he yelled. "Captain, torpedoes inbound! Fizik-1s."

"Ahead Flank!" Glass immediately roared. "Right full rudder. Launch two evasion devices." Then, a beat later, he asked of nobody in particular, "What the hell is going on?"

The *Toledo* jumped ahead obediently as the huge new water jets ejected a massive stream of high velocity water. Two acoustic evasion devices tumbled out into the swirling midst of the turbulence and began releasing a wall of acoustic energy, an auditory mess designed to blind and confuse any in-rushing torpedoes.

But the Fizik-1s were smart devices. Smart and damned diligent.

"Best bearings two-seven-three and two-seven-four! Both in active search!" Zillich called out, his voice sharp but under control.

"Counter fire!" LCDR Billy Ray Jones called out. The Executive Officer's eyes were wide. "We need to counter fire!"

"At what?" Glass queried. "We don't have any contact, and shooting back toward the torpedoes would be straight at the *George Mason*."

The *Toledo* raced ahead, already approaching top speed. Their only chance was getting out of the Russian torpedoes' acquisition cone as quickly as possible.

"Torpedoes blew past the evasion devices!" Zillich yelled. Jesus. They were smart!

"Master Chief, get that ACS working. It may be our only hope!" Glass called out.

Zillich jumped up and began punching buttons on a temporary control panel that technicians had hung overhead in the sonar room.

Only chance or not, Jones ordered two more evasion devices launched. Maybe they would miraculously decoy the on-racing death.

"Incoming weapons are range gating!" the sonarman yelled, his voice trembling. The young sailor had never been in this situation outside drills. He knew precisely what was happening, though. The torpedoes were not confused. They knew exactly where *Toledo* was and were heading her way. "Both weapons bear two-seven-one!"

"Master Chief?" Glass yelled. "How you coming?"

Sweat poured down Zillich's face.

"Doing all I know to do!" Then, under his breath, "Damn thing didn't come with an instruction manual."

"Incoming weapons still range gating! They have us for sure!" the sonarman called out, his voice now rising an octave.

Zillich scrolled frantically through the words and numbers on the anti-detection system's screen. He chewed on his lower lip as he stared hard, squinted, wiped sweat from his eyes, and quickly punched at another selection on the monitor.

"There!" he yelled. "I think ACS is back on line!"

The two experienced submariners held their breath. So did every other crewman aboard who was aware of what was happening.

Normally "think" was insufficient. They were supposed to know.

"Torpedoes stopped range gating!" the sonarman reported, the relief palpable in his words. "Sounds like...yes...they have both resumed search mode."

Toledo had once again become virtually invisible. And not a second too soon.

Master Chief Zillich slumped down into his seat, his shirt soaked with perspiration. He grabbed a headset and put it on, making no effort to disguise his trembling hands.

"Torpedoes bearing zero-nine-four and opening," he reported.

The deadly fish were swimming away from them, no longer able to detect the *Toledo*'s presence. But somewhere out there was the submarine that launched the pair of predators in the first place.

And she had plenty more just like those two.

8

Gentle waves lazily lapped at the sandy shore as an early-autumn sea breeze rustled through the salt grass. This particular three-mile arc of prime beachfront at Naval Base Dam Neck in Virginia Beach was far removed from the tourist hustle and bustle and remained restfully quiet.

On the other hand, the scene inside the concrete-and-blue-steel building just on the landward side of the dunes was anything but restful. The Naval Ocean Processing Facility Dam Neck was the Atlantic home for the Integrated Undersea Surveillance System. Housed deep within the nondescript but still foreboding building, behind multiple locked and heavily guarded doors, highly trained and very specialized analysts were busily sifting through a vast compilation of data that had been gathered from undersea surveillance arrays scattered around the world. Some of them, like the SOUSUS arrays, were left over from the Cold War. Their whereabouts and capabilities were well known by most of the world's militaries, but they still provided useful information.

Other arrays were known by only a very few people holding very special clearances.

Today the building was in an unusual uproar. Analysts and their supervisors were desperately trying to sort out what had just happened not that far from their front door. Amazingly powerful network servers whirred, coldly considering data, while humans checked what results the machines spit out, smart people and unconcerned computers working in tandem to try to make some sense of all the accumulated ones and zeroes.

Meanwhile, in a very private, guarded, and sound-proofed conference room off one of the main hallways in the center portion of the building, a loud and profane discussion raged.

"What the bloody hell is this?" Admiral Tom Donnegan thundered, waving a slim folder over his head like a battle flag. "Jon, what the hell do you make of this crap? Either of you two have any thoughts on this that I haven't already shit-canned as too damn silly to even remotely be a plausible explanation?"

The admiral tossed the offending file across the battered gray steel table toward where Captain Jon Ward sat at the far end, grim-faced but quiet. "Hell, even if it is ludicrous, I want to hear it," Donnegan continued his rant.

Ward deftly blocked the incoming folder with a forearm, like a hockey goalie. A "TOP SECRET, SPECIAL COMPART-MENTED INFORMATION" banner screamed across the top of the cover. Just below it, a similar title—the letters just as large but not in all caps— identified the folder's contents as "Report of Hostile Encounter with Unidentified Submarine."

Ward flipped it open and started to read the executive summary as quickly as he could manage. Donnegan did not wait for him to finish.

"Here's what it says. The Airedale types over at Pax River finished their analysis of the periscope detection radars. From the mission tapes, that P-8 had solid contact on a confirmed periscope for fifteen seconds. The MH-6oR had tenuous contact for a couple of seconds. And this son of a bitch was less than three thousand yards from the *George Mason* at the time!"

By the end of his recap, Donnegan was roaring again. He sat back, spent, and ran his hands through his thick, gray hair.

Ward looked across the table, shaking his head. "And the TAO on the *Bulkeley* called it a false contact because he didn't have any sonar contacts? That right?"

Donnegan pursed his lips, ready to explode again, but Rear Admiral Stan Elsworth chimed in before he had the chance. The commander of the Naval Undersea Warfare Center held up his hand and cleared his throat. "Look, Admiral, my guys went over the sonar tapes from both *Bulkeley* and *Toledo*. We looked at them every way we could. We even had the guys at Johns Hopkins Applied Physics Lab verify our results, just to be sure."

He paused for a second to let that information sink in. The rivalry between NUWC and Johns Hopkins APL was bitter and infamous. Something had to really be critical for either outfit to allow the other the opportunity to second-guess its results.

"There was nothing at all on any tape that we hadn't already accounted for. All of the ASW sensors held the *George Mason* intermittently when she was close. They didn't hold any other submarines until the *Toledo*'s ACS system went on the blink, and then there she was, big and bold on all the screens. Nothing else was in the area. Nothing. Not a damn thing. Those torpedoes appear to have been launched from absolutely nothing. Back-plotting, we can determine that they came from somewhere and suddenly showed up about halfway between the *Toledo* and the *George Mason*. And less than five thousand yards from either one. That area was absolutely empty of any acoustic signals at all. I'll say it again. There was nothing there. If there was, it was invisible."

Donnegan shook his head and threw up his hands as if in surrender. "We had our best sensors out there," he said quietly.

"Airborne, surface ship, submarine, all the first team all the way around. Even the new Advanced Fixed Distributed Array didn't catch so much as a sniff of any intruder. And yet, some bold-assed bastard waltzes right into the middle of our little bash, right here in our front yard, and leaves a big turd in the punch-bowl. Then, to add insult to injury, he politely takes a couple of pot shots at us on his way out. And here we sit, with the most technologically advanced navy in the history of the world, yet we have not one damn idea of who he is or where he came from or where he went! We can't even prove he exists!"

Even the heavy steel table shook as Donnegan slammed his fist down hard. "We damn well better find out who it was! Ain't no way in hell we can let anybody rub it in our faces like that and get away scot-free with that kind of caper."

As the admiral ranted, Jon Ward was considering the cold lines of print on the page in front of him. He idly massaged the bridge of his nose, lost in thought, ignoring Donnegan's anger. Then, after the reverberations of the admiral's blow to the table died away, he looked up.

"What if someone else has an ACS system like ours, or something very similar? Wouldn't we see just about what we saw yesterday? Nothing. Nothing until the Fizik 1s are out and making lots of noise on their own. The way I see it, there are only two possibilities for who might have developed that level of technology, and, who, by the way, would also be equipped with Fizik 1s. Norfolk is too far away for the Chinese to have a boat here. My money is on the Russians."

Stan Elsworth cocked his head and leaned forward.

"That is the only plausible explanation, Jon. And since Joe Glass got his ACS back on line to escape those torpedoes, you can bet he disappeared from that Russian's sonar screens, too." Both Ward and Donnegan were nodding in agreement. "So we have to figure that when they analyze their tapes, some smart guy over there is going to realize that we have a working stealth system, too."

"That, and that same smart guy will know that we know that they know. Damn."

Tom Donnegan looked as if he had just bitten into something bitterly vile.

"Jesus. Considering President Salkov's current tendency for ranting and raving, I'd say that we've got ourselves one big, steaming pile of horse hockey. I'd be glad to let either one of you boys make my next couple of phone calls. Starting, of course, with POTUS himself if he is not off on vacation again."

Ψ

President Grigory Iosifovich Salkov brusquely called to order the impromptu meeting of his most trusted advisors. He visually took quick attendance.

Dmitry Sharapov, the Minister of Sports.

Ignot Smirnov, the Minister of Defense.

Chief of the General Staff, General Boris Lapidus.

Salkov considered this team to be a strange mix of personalities and abilities. Even so, each man had proven to be ruthlessly effective and would do without hesitation what was required to further the goals of their president. There were many others with bigger titles and higher rank in the sprawling bureaucracy. However, this little group was the real power behind the Russian government. The president could trust them as he could no others. Their loyalty was without question.

When strings needed to be pulled or buttons pushed, this was the group that did the work. When stronger methods were required, these were the ones powerful and connected enough to know who to engage to do the dirty work and do it correctly, with no political backlash.

The group was comfortably seated in their leader's favorite venue, the great hall of Salkov's summer dacha, located a few kilometers outside of Kstovo in the Nizhny Novgorod Oblast. The ancient building rested high on a bluff overlooking the Volga River. The spot was some four hundred kilometers east of Moscow, an easy hour by private jet from the Kubinka Air Base.

As beautiful and peaceful as this retreat was, the true draw for President Salkov was *samozashchita bez oruzhiya*, or Sambo, the Russian martial art of unarmed combat. Kstovo was the home of the World Academy of Sambo. The president was ranked a "*Mastera Sporta*" or "Master of Sport" in the discipline. It was a distinction well earned, not given simply because of whom he was.

Salkov had just finished a vigorous practice combat with his private trainer. His red kurtka was still sweat-soaked from the lively session.

"Minister Smirnov," Salkov began, nodding toward his Minister of Defense. "Would you please bring us up to date on tank production?" Salkov took a deep swig of *sportivnyy napitok*. One must keep his body's electrolytes in balance after such a vigorous workout. "The figures that I am seeing are most disappointing. The numbers out of the Uralvagonzavod facility are well below what you promised."

Sweat ran in rivulets from Smirnov's brow and down his cheeks, briefly collecting in his jowls before dripping off his chin.

"The problem is Kartsev and Venediktov. Together they run the place. They are demanding more *den'gi kak predmet vzyatki* (bribe money). They are of the opinion that they have us in a corner. We must have the new tanks in service if we are to challenge NATO, and they have the only factory that can produce them."

"How much more are they asking for?" demanded General Lapidus.

"They are demanding five billion rubles each," Smirnov replied, almost choking on the number, and glanced quickly to his president to gauge his reaction to the factory managers' extortion.

President Salkov first grinned and then laughed out loud. He waved his hand dismissively.

"Have the Minister of Finance pay them both out of the Treasury. Then arrange for Kartsev to be denounced for corruption. I never could stand that weasel. He needs to spend some time in Lubyanka. Make sure our people confiscate all his bribe money and return it in total to us personally. That is a nice stipend for each of us. At that point, Venediktov will be more than willing to get assembly of the tanks up to speed. I would wager that the vehicles will be rolling off his production line at a record pace the same day."

Salkov next turned to Lapidus. "Now Boris, what do you have to tell us?"

The old general sat back in his over-stuffed chair, not even bothering to stifle a yawn as he gathered his thoughts.

"Well, Grigory Iosifovich, there is, as the Americans like to say, good news and bad news. For the bad news, as we have already discussed, I cannot really begin troop deployments toward the Polish and Lithuanian borders until I get another thousand tanks. We cannot be conducting 'exercises' if we do not have the equipment to exercise. And, of course, to flaunt in the faces of NATO."

Lapidus pushed his fingers inside his uniform jacket and shirt and scratched himself idly as he continued.

"For the good news, Captain First Rank Konstantin Kursalin, captain of the submarine *Igor Borsovitch,* has reported that he has successfully completed his mission to spy on the new American *Virginia*-class submarine's sea trials. He says that he has some very interesting sonar recordings and remarkably good tapes and pictures of activity. Our experts are already analyzing what he was able to send on the satellite link." Lapidus suddenly seemed to notice that he was scratching himself. He paused, withdrew his fingers, and sat up straighter. "Captain Kursalin also reports, though, that there may be a problem with the newly installed stealth device on the *Igor Borsovitch*. At the conclusion of the mission, as he was departing the area, he was almost trapped by a second American submarine. He claims he had no other choice but to shoot his way out, launching two torpedoes. He is presently transiting back to Polyarny and will be able to give a full report on the incident when he arrives."

Salkov frowned.

"I have not seen anything in the briefings from the American press about any submarine combat incident—or 'accident,' as they would probably term it in their media—anywhere near their coast. Or anywhere else," President Salkov added quietly. "The Americans, for all their secrecy, would have had to explain the disappearance of a submarine and its crew. I gather from this that Kursalin's torpedoes missed their mark. For that, at least, we must be grateful. That and the fact that he and his submarine were not blown out of the water by the Americans after they were attacked. We have no obligation to inform the public of such a loss, of course, but it would have been a terrible forfeiture of valuable intelligence data if he had been sunk. That hot-headed Kursalin could have caused a major upset in our timetable. You must have him and his crew punished for their poor marksmanship. But not too harshly, of course. We do not want any hesitation if he needs to launch torpedoes at the Americans again anytime soon."

President Salkov pulled the chair away from his desk and sat down. Leaning forward, staring at his team, he started to lay out the details of his strategy. "When we finally have the forces in place to move, we must have already nudged NATO into a corner where they can't react. History and *realpolitik* shine on us. Those bureaucrats are so lethargic that they will not move until the fires burn hot, and so lacking in unity that they will not be able to decide what to do. They would prefer to ignore our actions and do nothing, because any kind of move could destabilize their economy, even if they have to relinquish some of the territories they stole from Mother Russia. And the new American president, this Grayson Whitten, is still trying to find his office. He has no foreign policy experience that we know of. He will be a kitten. But there is much work to do to nudge them into the correct corner."

The trio watched with rapt attention as Salkov continued, his ice-blue eyes holding them with pure ferocity.

"I calculate that we need at least ninety days to achieve our objectives and consolidate our gains from the time we decide to initiate the plan. It will take NATO at least three weeks to react and move their initial forces into engagement."

"We will brush those meager troops aside like so many gnats," General Lapidus scoffed. "The EU has decimated their armies over the years and the US has moved nearly all the American troops home. They can muster barely a battalion of armor and a squadron or two of fighters."

Minister of Defense Smirnov nodded in agreement. "I concur with General Lapidus. The European part of NATO is a very weak and toothless tiger." He took a deep breath. "But the Americans are a different matter. If we give them the opportunity to reinforce and resupply Western Europe, this game of ours could easily spin into World War III."

Salkov gazed quietly out the large picture window toward the Volga River far below. The silence had already become uncomfortable when he finally spoke.

"My friends, when Ignot talked of a game, he was quite correct. This is a game, a massive multi-player, multi-level game of chess. And no one is better at chess than we Russians. We merely need to have our chessmen in place before the opposition can counter our gambit."

Smirnov was not so easily convinced. "We say that we need at least ninety days to consolidate our position. When Saddam Hussein misguidedly invaded Kuwait, it took the Americans less time than that to muster a crushing force in the middle of the Saudi desert. How do we prevent that from happening to us? The American Navy and their aircraft carriers control the resupply lanes to Europe."

President Salkov allowed himself just the glimmer of a smile. "Let me make some phone calls. I think we can keep the American Navy very busy elsewhere."

Dimitry Sharapov smiled and indicated with a slight wave that he had something to say. His contribution would not likely be about submarines, torpedoes, or tanks, and Salkov welcomed the diversion. The president had already made his points. He nodded to his Sports Minister.

"Grigory Iosifovich, I think I have better news than what our general reports. A young girl, Nadinka Karkhiv, has been showing great talent at our gymnastics institute. You awarded her a medal at two different meets in which she had perfect scores. Now she dreams of being on the Russian World Gymnastics team and is anxious to do whatever it takes to receive such an honor to compete for her country."

"So?"

"She now awaits you upstairs for a private interview."

The meeting was immediately adjourned.

9

Joe Glass peered through the eyepiece of the Type 18 periscope as he swung the instrument around in a slow, smooth, deliberate circle. He did not stop until he was satisfied that nothing was up there except the incredibly starry sky of a tropical night.

Lieutenant Pat Durand, the officer of the deck, stood beside the submarine's skipper and talked into the red secure voice radio-phone. The young officer was barely visible in the dark "rigged for black" control room. Every light not serving some vital function was secured. The only illumination was the faint glimmer from dozens of dials and screens.

"Captain, Range Control confirms that we are the only ship on the range," Durand quietly informed Glass. "We are cleared to surface."

"Very well, Officer of the Deck," Glass responded. "Surface the ship."

Master Chief Wallich, standing watch as diving officer, spoke up.

"Captain, Chief Johannson needs to surface as a prac fac for his dive quals."

Glass glanced down at the portly A-gang chief. Johannson was new aboard *Toledo* and already working eagerly on his qualifications.

"You ready for this, Chief?" Glass asked him. "These boats handle a little different from the boomers you're used to. And with that new drive system, *Toledo* handles a lot different from any other 688I."

"Yes, sir!" Johannson's answer was quick and confident. "COB and I have been over this a dozen times. I can do it."

"Okay," Glass answered. He liked the man's self-assuredness, though they were about to determine if it was justified. Glass turned to the officer of the deck. "Mr. Durand, surface the ship with Chief Johannson under instruction."

Pat Durand nodded. "Diving Officer, surface the ship."

"Surface the ship, aye," Johannson responded, then followed up with a rapid-fire burst of orders, each initiating a series of well-choreographed actions by the watch team.

"Helm, ahead two-thirds, full rise on the bow planes. Full dive on the stern planes. Chief of the Watch, on the 1MC 'Surface, surface, surface.'"

The big boat rose majestically out of the depths until her mass was held on the surface by her forward speed and bow planes, her heavy stern supported by the stern planes.

Pat Durand was watching through the periscope. He called out, "Decks awash," and then, only a few seconds later, "Decks clear."

"Four-zero feet and holding, five degree up angle," the chief of the watch reported.

Chief Johannson hesitated for a second, a bit unsure of what came next. Master Chief Wallich dug a not-so-subtle elbow into his ribs.

"Blower!" he grunted under his breath.

Johannson brightened. "Yeah, the blower. Chief of the Watch, start the blower on the after main ballast tanks."

The low-pressure blower—in reality nothing more than a really big and powerful fan—sucked air from the outside down through the snorkel mast. From there it sent the air out through a series of pipes into the after group of main ballast tanks. The air forced water out of the grates at the bottom of the tanks.

Slowly, as the weight of all that water was shoved out of the ballast tanks, the angle came off the ship until the chief of the watch reported, "Three-nine feet and holding, angle on the ship three degrees."

"Shift the blower to all main ballast tanks. Zero the planes, rig in the bow planes," Johannson sang out.

Finally, seconds later, the chief of the watch called out, "Three-six feet and holding."

Chief Johannson breathed an audible sigh of relief. "Officer of the Deck, the ship is surfaced."

Before heading forward to his stateroom, Joe Glass ordered, "Officer of the Deck, rig the bridge for surface, then shift control to the bridge. Call me when you are ready." As he stepped out of the control room, he paused by the diving officer's chair.

"Nicely done, Chief."

Ψ

A warm, humid breeze, carrying the aroma of seawater and warm sand, wafted down the bridge trunk as Joe Glass made the long climb up. Glass swore that he could smell the suntan lotion from tourists in the Bahamas. He emerged onto the bridge and was once again struck by the star-filled night sky. The moon was a bare glimmer on the western horizon, swimming lazily in a thick mist from the ocean's surface. To the east, the shadowy mass of Exuma Island jutted out of the black water. The darkness was only broken by a few lights scattered along the water and the warm glow of Farmer's Hill, the only real town on the small Bahamian isle.

Closer, only a couple of miles from *Toledo*, a jumble of bright working lights illuminated a strange-looking structure that appeared to be floating on the water in the middle of Exuma Sound.

Sighting through the alidade on the bridge gyrocompass repeater, Glass lined up the reticule on the center of the lights. He read the compass bearing and then ordered, "Officer of the Deck, come left, steer course zero-seven-one."

Doug O'Malley was exercising his prerogative as senior watch officer by also being the officer of the deck. It just happened that he loved night surface transits. He responded to his captain's order with, "Come left, steer course zero-seven-one, aye."

After passing the necessary orders down to the helmsman, who was sitting in the control room twenty-five feet below them, O'Malley turned to Glass. The skipper was watching *Toledo* swing obediently to the new course.

"Skipper, you know you could have just read all that off the VMS bridge repeater. Quicker, easier, and more accurate."

Glass chuckled, taking no offense to his engineer officer's suggestion.

"Yeah, Eng, I know. But I still like to do things the old way sometimes. Simple, sure, and I ain't relying on some Air Force satellite twelve thousand miles overhead to tell me what to do."

O'Malley grinned. "Here we are with the hottest technology ever to go to sea on a submarine, and I have a Luddite for a skipper."

"Just aim all this batch of hot new technology for the center of those lights over there," Glass shot back. "We need to be under cover before first light. We sure as hell don't want any prying eyes to see us down here and start putting two and two together."

Toledo pulled closer to the odd structure. By now they could see what was floating out there—two massive multi-storied barges anchored in open water, about five miles out in Exuma Sound. Between the barges, a very large tent-like structure covered a stretch of open water that looked to be about forty or fifty feet wide. As *Toledo* drew nearer, a couple of pusher boats cast off from the barges and headed out to greet the newcomers.

With a series of small rudder orders, Doug O'Malley expertly centered the big submarine between the two barges, though they were still a couple of miles off. Then they simply allowed the gentle breeze to nudge them to the southeast. The pusher boats were quickly tied off on the submarine's port and starboard sides, bound to the number three cleat, just aft of the sail. There they could fine-tune the vessel's heading as she moved closer to the tight space beneath the cover.

"Rig out the outboard and shift to remote," O'Malley ordered when they were still a mile away. "All stop. Lower all masts and antennas."

Both periscopes and the OE-538 multi-purpose communications mast slid smoothly down to their housed positions. Back in the aftermost part of the engine room, on the aft hemispherical bulkhead, the engineering watch supervisor shifted a series of hydraulic valves. Out in the ballast tank, just aft of where he stood, a small electric outboard lowered on a shaft until it extended a few feet below the hull. The little outboard, barely more than three hundred horsepower, could be trained around like an overgrown electric trolling motor to push the big submarine's stern left or right. Or, if aimed dead ahead, it could prod the sub forward.

"Outboard lowered and shifted to remote," the EWS reported.

Toledo inched forward, gliding to a stop a hundred yards from the opening between the two barges.

A Boston whaler pulled up alongside them and passed two lines to the line-handlers who were standing and waiting topside. They slipped the eyes over the two forward-most cleats, port and starboard. The other end of the lines led to massive capstans on the far end of each barge. The capstans then began to rotate.

Both lines came taut, water sizzling out of the fibers as the strain built. Almost imperceptibly, the massive submarine began to move forward, slowly, inch by inch, into the confined space between the two big barges. As *Toledo*'s rudder passed the back end of the barges, a canvas cover suddenly snapped down, concealing the submarine from any prying eyes. Anyone wanting to see what was parked there would have to pull back the drapes to get a peek.

It was not lost on anyone that such a high-tech vessel was now being protected from some equally high-tech spy satellites by such an old-fashioned means.

As *Toledo* was being secured, a brow slid across from the starboard barge. It had no more than landed on the submarine's deck when the first man charged across, obviously on a mission.

It was Commodore Jon Ward. Cupping his hands around his mouth to be heard over all the noise, he yelled up to where Joe Glass stood on the bridge of the sub.

"Joe! Welcome to your new home for the next couple of weeks. You can almost see the beach from here, but I'm afraid this is as close as you are going to get."

Joe Glass grinned and shrugged. He had expected nothing more.

Meanwhile, behind Ward, workers and technicians were

already scurrying over the brow, carrying piles of tools and parts onto the newly-arrived submarine. They were clearly ready for all the work they had to do in a short amount of time.

Ψ

Back on the barge and standing away from the crowd, a young, attractive woman in a lab coat but sensible tennis shoes watched all the hubbub with considerable interest.

Sarah Wilder had not been in a position to know why this submarine had been called in to the floating covered docks and why it would be occupying this precious space and garnering so much attention for the next two weeks. Nor could she guess why someone as high up the chain as Commodore Jon Ward was here to personally greet the *Toledo*.

Wilder casually sipped an iced coffee from a paper cup and surveyed the scene, hiding her increasing interest. This was all quite unusual. What was it?

And most importantly, how could she safely get word to Alexi and the others?

Merely the thought of her precious Alexi caused her to blush a deep red. A tear formed in each eye. She glanced around to make sure no one noticed and quickly wiped away the tears with her napkin.

She would learn more about what was going on. Then she would share what she knew with those who were serving the cause of peace, not nation-building and imperialism.

And hopefully that would include Alexi. In person. In a bed with sheets still tangled and damp from their love-making.

She blushed again. Damn! She tossed what was left of the coffee into a nearby trash barrel. The caffeine. That's what was causing her face to flush and her pulse to race.

Sarah Wilder turned and walked quickly back to the office to see what she could learn while everyone else was out there fawning over the new arrival.

10

Admiral Tom Donnegan leaned back in his chair, put his feet up on his battered old oak desk, and held the telephone loosely to his ear.

"Bill, what the hell is going on? The doctors are telling me that you have been a bad boy and not at all a model patient," he said, the light tone in his voice belying the underlying steel. He could hear Bill Beaman, at the other end of the call, breathing deeply, deciding how to respond.

"Well, Admiral, the truth is..." the SEAL began.

"Spare me the bull hockey, Bill," Donnegan shot back. "You are strapped in that wheelchair because you were too bull-headed to listen. If you don't stay there and allow that busted leg of yours to heal, that rolling chair may become a permanent part of your furniture. Who the hell knows what kind of infection you might have picked up down there? And the Navy does not have any place for a one-legged SEAL."

"Well, I think they have a pretty good..."

Donnegan snatched a folder from one of the stacks of paperwork that covered most of the desk and rudely interrupted Beaman.

"Bill, I know you well enough to realize that you will go bat-shit stir-crazy if you aren't out doing something useful for your country. How much liberty did you take after that little jaunt up to Polyarny that time with Joe Glass and *Toledo*? A long weekend after helping save the Free World? So I'm not going to let a rough landing in a tree in Central America get you all sideways. Here's the deal. I got a hell of a boondoggle job for you. We need a temporary head of security at the Bahamian Acoustics Lab for the Naval Undersea Research Facility." The gruff old admiral couldn't suppress an uncharacteristic chuckle. "I don't know who the Pentagon gets to come up with these acronyms. This one's NURF BAL. Nerf for brains is more like it. Some damn contractor charging the taxpayers a million bucks per letter while we need…"

Donnegan's rant trailed off as he took a swig of coffee. Bill Beaman was quiet, not even bothering to laugh at the admiral's joke. He was still absorbing the news of the security assignment.

"Well, Admiral, I can certainly handle…"

"Here's the deal. Get your one-legged ass down to Exuma and take over the shore-side security. Spend some time in the sun. Drink some of those rum drinks with the funny umbrellas poking out of 'em. I hear they have marvelous medicinal quali-ties. Keep an eye out for anything that doesn't look, smell, or feel right. And no matter what, you keep your ass in that wheel-chair until everything clears up. That's an order."

"But what if…?"

No what if. Tom Donnegan had already broken the connec-tion. His aide had just dropped a stack of satellite images on his desk.

Something told him he needed to take a look at them right damn now.

Ψ

Captain First Rank Konstantin Kursalin stood on the bridge of the *Igor Borsovitch*. A biting north wind bore the first insinuation of yet another long Arctic winter. Already the thermometer registered minus-2 degrees Centigrade. The sun had just edged above the horizon even though his watch confirmed that it was a few minutes past 0900 local.

Kursalin pulled up the collar on his heavy bridge coat and gazed out at the sea. It appeared to him as if the entire Russian Northern Fleet was steaming past in review, putting on a show just for him and his crew. Among the myriad frigates and destroyers, he had spied the massive *tyazholiy avianesushchiy kreyser*, the heavy aircraft cruiser *Admiral Kuznetsov*. The vessel had a squadron of bright blue SU-33 Flanker-Ds perched on her flight deck, as if they might be launched momentarily. The *Kirov*-class nuclear heavy cruiser *Pyotr Velikiy* steamed along close behind.

In all his days, the submarine captain had never seen such a display of naval might. Nor any equal show of military bluster. Not even at one of those interminable May Day spectaculars in Red Square back in the old days of serious saber-rattling. He could only guess at how many of his brother submariners might be steaming stealthily below but, like all the others, heading the opposite direction from the *Igor Borsovitch*. The submarines, of course, would not be visible to the satellites of the Americans and others that no doubt circled overhead at the moment. The rest of the armada certainly would be.

That, without a doubt, was intentional. And the rest of the world would know it, too.

The message traffic the previous day—in the same communication that ordered him to surface his submarine for all the world to see as he rounded Nordkapp, Norway—had described a new naval exercise to be conducted out in the Norwegian Sea. Every ship in the entire Northern Fleet that could sortie on short notice was steaming around the cape at Flank speed and on a course that would point them down toward Iceland and Scotland.

That is, every ship in the fleet except the *Igor Borsovitch*. She was headed home, against the grain. The Minister of Defense, Ignot Smirnov, had made a point of informing Kursalin that he would be there on the pier to personally greet them. That could not portend anything good.

The captain gritted his teeth and pulled his collar tighter against the chill wind.

Now, where was that damn pilot boat?

Ψ

Bahamasair Flight 357 had seemingly just left Nassau before the pilot was already bringing the small turbo-prop back down again, circling over a tiny airport, its single runway gouged from sand and porter weed, with water close on each side. They made the short final approach on runway twelve. The pilot skillfully kissed the macadam deck with the plane's gears. After a short run out, applying full reverse pitch the whole way, he turned onto the taxiway and pulled up to the cramped, pale yellow, single-level terminal.

Bill Beaman had no choice but to remain in his seat, even as the temperature in the cabin rapidly climbed. He wore a loud Hawaiian shirt and cut-off shorts—just like all the other passengers—but he would be the last off the plane. He required help, a condition that rankled him considerably. Still he waited patiently for the traveler assistance aide to bring him a chair and wheel him out into the tiny terminal, but he wondered how that person would ever get him out of the plane and down the portable gangway to the tarmac.

"Mon, I'm Raul, and I be takin' care of you." The aide

grinned broadly, showing off two prominent gold front teeth. His island accent was so heavy that Beaman could barely understand him. "Let's get us out of here and into some sone-shine, what do you say, mees-tuh?"

The muscular black man lifted Beaman effortlessly out of his seat, carried him down the short steps, and eased him into the wheelchair.

Exuma International Airport was really a grand overstatement. It was small, even for a regional commuter airport. Regular routes to Fort Lauderdale and Miami justified the claim of international status.

Through the airport to the rack where Beaman's bag could be claimed, Raul kept up a steady, happy chatter. There was no part of Exuma that he did not know in detail and very little that he did not talk about as they waited for the bag to show up. By the time they were headed for the exit, the SEAL felt like he had enjoyed a crash course in out-island Bahamian culture and geography.

The warm, fragrant sea breeze actually felt good as Raul wheeled him out to the waiting handicap taxi.

"This here mon, he be my brother, Elliot," Raul said, introducing the taxi driver. "He be de best driver in Exuma and he not yet killed anybody dat we know of dis year."

The cabbie, almost a twin for Raul, flashed a broad, toothy grin of his own that included similar gold teeth.

"Mon, we gone do our very, very best to get you to Hotel Peace and Plenty. You be needin' some peace. Dat and plenty of their Bahamas rum punch. Best you be wary. It don't come by de name 'punch' for nuttin'!"

Beaman found it impossible to do anything but sit back, smile, and relax. The welcome from these two was as warm as the morning sun.

"Elliot, if you don't mind, let's drive around a little first so I can get my bearings. Then let's make a quick stop at NURF BAL."

"Ah, NURF BAL." The cabbie nodded knowingly. "Sure ting, mon."

He gave Beaman a broad wink. The cabbie was clearly familiar with the clandestine nature of the occasional visitor to the Navy's facility on his island. The van sprayed gravel as it jumped away from its spot in front of the terminal.

Ψ

Six hundred miles west and south of the Cape Verde Islands, located a thousand miles west of the African coast, a small area of low pressure slowly formed in the open stretches of the Atlantic Ocean. Heated by the warm tropic sea, the air gathered moisture as it rose higher into the atmosphere. Cooler air rushed in to fill the space, only to also be heated and rise high. Slowly a huge heat engine was being formed, drawing energy from the warm waters. The Coriolis effect nudged the in-rushing air around to the left. The resulting counter-clockwise winds picked up energy as they formed a whirling cloud of moisture many miles wide and many thousands of feet tall.

Cape Verde hurricanes were the largest and most feared of the Atlantic storms. The disturbance had actually started as a tropical wave on the African savannah several days ago and gathered energy as it moved across the continent's steppe. By the time it reached the Atlantic, even though the tropical wave was still dry, it had become a full-fledged tropical disturbance.

High overhead, satellites finally took note of the storm as it came together in the classic birthplace of these big, frightening cyclones. As winds near the center officially hit thirty-four knots and transitioned from a tropical depression to a tropical storm, meteorologists at the National Hurricane Center in Miami gave the mass of moving air the next name on the list for the season's storms.

Tropical Storm Penny had just become the sixteenth named storm of the year.

Ψ

The sun was a pale-yellow orb, barely visible in the dune-colored sky. A steady wind out of the west did nothing to ease the scorching heat as it filled the air with desert sand. The master of the motor vessel *Morgan Star* kept the bridge doors firmly shut as he attempted to steer his two-hundred-thousand-ton tanker and its cargo of Iraqi crude oil through some of the heaviest shipping traffic in the world, despite visibility being down to mere yards.

The master checked his wristwatch and glanced at the electronic chart display. Only ten more minutes until he was clear of the tiny but heavily fortified Iranian island of Jazireh-ye Forur. Then he would change course to one-zero-five and fair up on the first outbound leg of the TSS Tunb-Farur traffic separation scheme.

That was when the radar alarm buzzed angrily. He glanced at the radar screen to see at least a dozen small blips approaching at high speed. Grabbing a bridge-to-bridge radio and aloud-hailer, the master rushed out to the port bridge wing in time to observe several heavily armed runabouts start to circle his ship.

The radio began to crackle with a demanding, metallic voice.

"On the *Morgan Star*, come to all-stop and lay to. Prepare to be boarded. You are the prisoners of the Iranian Revolutionary Guard Navy. Do not attempt to escape."

11

"Conn, Sonar. Multiple contacts all around us. Sounds like the whole damn Russian Fleet is up there!"

Sonar Chief Stan Alexander had not heard so many warship sonar signatures at one time in his fifteen years riding the boats. He counted at least twenty independent ships that he could hear for sure. Just as many—and probably more—were either too weak or masked by a louder ship. In his mind's eye, the experienced sonarman pictured an armada churning away in the choppy Barents Sea, all painted blue-gray, armed to the teeth, and looking for him and his submarine.

Captain Harold Swanson, commanding officer of the submarine USS *Florida* (SSGN 728), flicked through the display screens on the BQQ-6 sonar, doing all he could to tease out what the Russians were doing a mere hundred feet above his head.

He glanced across the control room to see his executive officer, Lieutenant Commander Barry Morgan, working with the tracking party, also trying to get a handle on all these contacts.

"XO," Swanson called out, "did you see anything on the intel broadcasts about anybody having a parade around here?"

"Nope, not a word, Skipper," Morgan answered. "But it has been almost twelve hours since we copied the broadcast. We're due in twenty minutes."

Swanson nodded and chewed his lower lip for a moment. Then he grabbed the 21MC mike to talk to Chief Alexander. "Sonar, Conn. Any estimate on range?"

"Closest contact is about four-five-hundred yards, bearing rate and received frequency both going down," the sonarman shot back. "Evaluated as opening. Classified as a tentative *Admiral Grigorovich*-class frigate. Definite ASW threat."

The sub captain shook his head, a frown furrowing his brow. The Russians were certainly pulling out all the stops up there, strutting their newest and best stuff. The *Admiral Grigorovich*-class frigates were so recently put into service that no one had actually seen one at sea before. Everybody had questions, though. How good was this new warship? What surprises did it hold in store for the rest of the world's navies?

"Captain," Morgan called out. "Geo solution is looking like they are steaming in two columns about ten thousand yards apart. We are pretty much right smack between them. They are on course three-one-six, plus or minus five degrees. Wouldn't surprise me one bit if Grigory Salkov himself was up there water-skiing behind one of those warships."

Swanson stepped over to where Morgan stood, staring hard at the large-screen display.

"XO, what say we come up on a course of one-three-six?" the skipper told him. "Let the boys back home know that the barn door is wide open. We'll see if we can grab some imagery on that new frigate. I know our folks would love to get a good look at her. Then we can hightail it out of here before they decide to test that new tub of theirs on us."

"Conn, Sonar, picking up hits on the TB-29," Chief Alexander interrupted. "Multiple submerged contacts. Bearings three-three-seven, three-five-two, and zero-six-one. Weak tonals, evaluated as distant. Based on the received frequencies, best guess is two Oscars and an Akula III."

Barry Morgan distractedly ran his hand through his thick hair, brushing the brown mop away from his forehead. He looked over at his captain.

"Skipper, it's getting real damn crowded around here. Let's get out from under all this traffic before we pop up to tell the boss the Macy's Parade started early this year."

Both men well knew the risks involved in coming to periscope depth and sending a radio message in the midst of a Russian task force. The risk of anyone detecting the very narrow-beam, very low-power, burst-pulse transmission was minimal. But it was not zero. The real risk was someone spotting the photonics (PMV) mast or the high data rate (HDR) comms mast, even if they would only be protruding above the waves for a few seconds. They were each the size of rather large trash cans and easily visible, even in the churning waters of the Barents.

Swanson laughed mirthlessly and looked at Morgan.

"XO, no balls, no blue chips. Let's go up, grab a few pics, and drop back down. Then we can run out from under all this heavy stuff before we call home and tell 'em that we have some nice photos for their Instagram account."

Morgan nodded but was clearly not convinced that putting anything above the surface was a good idea. Harold Swanson was the *Florida*'s skipper, though. And it was, after all, peacetime. They were in international waters, too. The worst thing that could happen would be getting themselves detected. That would be embarrassing. Especially if the Russians let the world know they caught an American boat harassing them. And that they would certainly do, loudly and clearly.

Swanson stepped across the control room and stood before

the photonics large-screen display. He called out very distinctly to assure there were no mistakes.

"This is the captain. I have the conn. Dive, make your depth seven-zero feet. Raising the photonics mast."

Up in the *Florida*'s sail, the pole slid smoothly upward in the universal mast module (UMM). Unlike the conventional optical periscopes, the photonics mast did not require the skipper to squat around a metal tube as a periscope rose out of the deck. There was no eyepiece to look through, either. The captain merely stood in front of the large-screen monitor, holding an Xbox video game controller. One of Hollywood's favorite submarine movie clichés, the skipper with his hat on backwards staring out the periscope while everyone else waited blindly, was no longer valid for the newer boats.

When the mast emerged at the surface of the sea, Swanson keyed the controller so that the view rapidly spun around, searching a 360-degree swath. The screen was filled with warships. No matter which way they pointed, there was a Russian vessel.

The captain had barely started his look around when the Early Warning Receiver began buzzing like a very angry hornet.

"Conn, ESM. Receiving numerous radar hits. Several evaluated 'threat.' Recommend lowering all masts and antennas."

The Electronic Support Measures system operator, located in the radio room just aft of the control room, was doing all he could to sort out a very complicated assemblage of radar signals to determine which, if any, were threats.

"Captain," Barry Morgan called out, noticing a helicopter's spinning rotor. "Looks like a Helix lifting off from the *Admiral Grigorovich* and another from that cruiser to the left. Skipper, it's time to get out of Dodge!"

"Conn, ESM. Picking up possible periscope detection radar. Carried on an AN-40 *Albatross*."

"Dive, make your depth five hundred feet," Swanson quickly ordered. "XO, I agree. I think we may have overstayed our welcome." Feeling the deck tilting beneath his feet already, he grabbed something solid and held on. "And can somebody tell me what the hell an AN-40 *Albatross* is?"

Ψ

The aide knocked gingerly before entering Grigory Iosifovich Salkov's private study. The Russian president sat at his imposing desk, working his way through a stack of documents. The aide waited patiently for the president to look up and acknowledge his presence. He finally did, with an impatient snort.

"Excuse me for interrupting, but the Defense Minister is on the secure phone." The man spoke just above a whisper. "He says it is most urgent that he speaks with you."

Salkov slid open a drawer and pulled out the phone stored there. He waved impatiently to the aide to leave the room.

"So what is so urgent, Ignot?" Salkov asked, as usual dispensing with any preliminary courtesies.

Ignot Smirnov, long familiar with Salkov's no-nonsense personality, was not bothered at all by his president's clipped approach.

"Grigory Iosifovich, two things. First, the Iranians have started. They report capturing several tankers in the Gulf. Satellite imagery shows the American *Nimitz* battle group steaming through the Strait of Hormuz, inbound."

Salkov allowed himself a bit of a smile. The plan was in play. Next the Iranians would start their missile exercises in the Arabian Sea.

"You said two items, Ignot. What is the other?"

"The Northern Battle Fleet reports that they have contact on an American nuclear submarine," the Defense Minister continued. "They have seen its periscope in the middle of the task force. What are your orders?"

Salkov thought for a moment, and then a slow smile transformed his typically severe countenance.

"Confirm it is not one of ours gone astray. Then sink it. We have long claimed the Barents as an historical inland sea. It is time to enforce our entitlement."

The Defense Minister gasped.

"But won't the Americans call this an act of war? Are we prepared for the consequences?"

Salkov chuckled drily, the sound like lightning static on a radio.

"The American president will bluster and posture. He will do nothing else. The man has no *yaytsa*, no balls, as the Americans like to say. He has allowed a warship to threaten our vessels in an area that we claim. It is a provocation of intense seriousness. We have no choice but to defend. Order the attack."

"I will do as you have instructed, my president," the Defense Minister answered, but doubt weighed heavily on his words.

Ψ

"Conn, Sonar. Picking up ten-kilohertz active sonar," Chief Alexander barked. "Bearing zero-seven-six, SPL ten. Fifty percent probability of detection." The sonarman was reporting that the SPL, the sound pressure level, indicated the Russians likely already had a good bead on the *Florida*.

Barry Morgan grunted. The captain had ignored his suggestion about getting out of Dodge, and now they appeared to be in a stare-down with a sea full of well-equipped Russians.

"That's one of the Helixes," he said. "If they get contact, we'll have hell to pay getting loose from this bunch."

"Conn, Sonar. Multiple three-kilohertz surface ship active sonars. SPLs all over the damn place. Second ten-kilohertz, bearing one-eight-six, SPL fifteen, seventy percent detection probability." Chief Alexander's normally calm, business-like voice cracked at the last, betraying his anxiety. Then, seconds later, he had some more bad news to deliver. "Conn, Sonar. Active sonobuoys dead ahead!"

Sweat ran from Captain Swanson's forehead and soaked his collar. This cat-and-mouse game had suddenly become far more than a game.

"Chief of the Watch, launch two of the six-inch evasion devices," he ordered, struggling to keep his own voice under control. "Wait thirty seconds and then launch two more." He glanced over at the diving officer. "Dive, as soon as the second two are launched, come to course north with a full rudder."

He looked over at Morgan and started to tell him something but was interrupted by a couple of loud bangs coming from just outside the hull.

The skipper's eyes grew wide, but then he realized what they had just heard. Two of the six-inch evasion devices, stored in tubes in the free-flood area below the sail, had blasted out of their launch tubes and begun filling the ocean around them with what the *Florida* crew hoped would be a covering shroud of noise.

"XO, tell the torpedo room to get an EMATT ready to launch on my order."

The Expendable Mobile ASW Training Target had originally been developed as an anti-submarine warfare sonar training device. Then someone figured out that it was often easily confused with a real submarine, making the EMATT a valuable evasion device as well.

Swanson looked around the control room. His entire team was riveted in place, waiting for what would happen now, for their captain's follow-up order. It was a familiar scene, but this time, it was no drill.

The next two evasion devices blasted free of the *Florida*. The massive submarine barely heeled over when the helmsman threw the rudder over. A few seconds later, they had pointed the bow northward, away from all the noise they had set loose in the water. They maintained the relatively slow pace at which they had been running, though.

"Speed?" Morgan asked when the skipper did not order a new one.

"This big hog ain't fast enough to get out of her own way," Swanson shot back. "We're going to slink out slowly and quietly. If we can."

"Conn, Sonar. Ten-kilohertz dipping sonar. Bearing three-five-five, SPL plus twenty. Probability of detection better than eighty percent."

"Shit," Swanson muttered. "They're playing leap-frog on us with those Helixes. They can do that all day and until we run out of ocean. There ain't a damn thing we can do about it but..."

"Conn, Sonar, high-speed screws close aboard," Alexander shouted. Then, two seconds later, he screamed, "Torpedo in the water! Bearing zero-seven-six. Closing fast! Closing fast!"

"Launch the EMATT," Swanson ordered. "Launch six-inch devices. Launch ADCs out of both signal ejectors!"

They needed to get as much noise in the water as they could. Maybe enough to confuse the torpedo that was homing in on their submarine, intent on killing it and every man aboard. Their best hope now was that the damn thing would go after the EMATT instead of the *Florida*.

"Second torpedo, bearing zero-six-five. First torpedo bearing zero-six-nine," Alexander reported. "Both drawing right."

"Captain!" Morgan shouted. "We got to get out of here! Recommend Flank and test depth."

Swanson shook his head and pounded the desk in front of him with a clenched fist.

"No way that'll work. They'll just track us and keep expending ordnance until they get us. All stop. Prepare to hover. Left full rudder." He took a deep breath. "We'll just sit here and try to look like a big, quiet hole in the ocean. Let them chase down the EMATT."

"Torpedoes bearing zero-six-four and zero-six-one, still drawing forward. EMATT active and bearing zero-three-one." The sonarman's voice was tight, strained.

Barry Morgan closed his eyes. For an instant, in the midst of all the tension, a thought entered his head. Of two young men, twins, soon to walk the stage at commencement at Charlottesville. Of his wife and himself, sitting there in the crowd, holding hands, proudly watching their sons graduate with honors. If he lived to see it. Many others, up and down the length of the *Florida*, had similar thoughts of home, of family, as they otherwise paid attention to what they were supposed to be doing.

Just as quickly as he had drifted away, the XO was back in the moment. But he was still not breathing, bracing himself, anticipating the ear-splitting blasts that were about to rip his submarine apart and allow the cold Barents seawater to roar in through the rents in her hull.

Harold Swanson was praying hard that his idea would work, his lips moving silently with the desperate words. If the EMATT maneuver failed, they were dead. But in the back of his mind, he was asking himself one big question.

Why in hell were the Russians shooting at them? They were clearly in international waters. Why not the usual posturing, the typical growling without the bite whenever they encountered each other? The same silly little dance both sides had done since the Cold War.

But torpedoes in the water? Armed and deadly? It simply did not make sense.

"Captain, commenced hovering at five hundred feet," the diving officer informed him. "Speed one knot and dropping. Rudder still full left, passing two-two-zero."

"Hover up to eight-zero feet. Maybe we can get lost in all the surface clutter those warships have stirred up," Captain Swanson answered. And maybe some of his men could escape at that depth if they somehow survived the detonation of those two deadly fish.

"Torpedoes bearing zero-five-four and zero-four-nine. EMATT bearing zero-two-seven."

Swanson stepped over and stood next to Barry Morgan. The men watched wide-eyed as the geo plot played out a best guess of what was happening, all from a view from directly above them.

"What you think, XO? They have us or do they have the EMATT?" Swanson asked. "Twenty bucks says the EMATT is a dead duck."

Morgan shook his head. Hell of a thing to make a wager on. If he won, he would never collect. Not in this life.

"Can't tell yet," the XO said. "We're both still in their acquisition cone. I'd bet we are about to find out, though."

Swanson nodded grimly. "Now might be a good time to pray that their torpedo designers were smart and programmed in a zero Doppler algorithm."

"New dipping sonar, bearing zero-two-zero, SPL plus ten." Chief Alexander gave the update. "The EMATT is responding to the active."

Along with having a taped replay that sounded like the *Florida*, the EMATT was also programmed to respond to an active sonar with a signal that looked to the Russian sonar operator exactly like a huge nuclear submarine. As an added twist, and to increase the realism, the EMATT was programmed to turn away and speed up, just like a real submarine would be expected to do if executing a getaway.

"Torpedoes bearing zero-two-one and zero-two-four. Down Doppler on both. Skipper, they turned away! They're heading for the EMATT."

Alexander was all but shouting by the time he got to the last words of his report. A collective exhale of long-held breath was heard throughout the conn.

"Loud splashes and explosions on the bearing to the EMATT," the chief said, affirming what they could all hear. "Sounds like that cruiser unloaded with an RBU-6000." The RBU was an older anti-submarine rocket, a more modern variant of the World War II "Hedgehog." Dumb as a box of rocks but deadly effective when fired point-blank at a detected submarine. Then, a few seconds later, Alexander reported, "More loud explosions on the bearing to the EMATT. Lost both torpedoes. They're gone, Captain. Gone!"

Harold Swanson turned to his exec. Both men's faces were white and covered with sweat.

"Well, Barry, looks like our little friend sacrificed itself for the *Florida* and the US of A."

Morgan pulled a handkerchief from his pocket and wiped his forehead.

"So what do we do now, Skipper?"

"We sit here and we continue to do our best impression of seaweed until these bastards clear out. Right now, they think they sank an American submarine. Let's let them keep thinking that. As soon as we can, we need to call home, tell them we got ambushed, and see if we can find out what the hell is happening." Then, quiet enough so only his XO could hear, he added, "Right now, though, I think I'm going to lie down for a few minutes and see if I can hang onto my breakfast."

Ψ

Six hundred and fifty miles out from the Cape Verde Islands, Tropical Storm Penny was slowly building strength, drawing energy from the warm water and bouncing off the sub-tropical ridge to the north. The storm had already gained enough energy that winds were rushing around counter-clock-wise with gusts at seventy knots near the clearly formed eye. An eyewall was building up to an altitude of nearly thirty thousand feet.

Penny started a slow trek across the Atlantic, heading gener-ally due west. The National Hurricane Center in Miami issued its first warning advisory for mariners and air crews to let them know a full-blown hurricane was brewing.

And to warn them that this was a tempest that could grow into something much, much bigger and far more dangerous before it was finished.

12

The President of the United States strode into the White House Situation Room and plopped down into a massive chair, one clearly reserved for him and him alone. A gold-rimmed porcelain cup, decorated with the presidential seal and filled with steaming café au lait, two teaspoons of organic honey and extra cinnamon sprinkled on the foam, awaited his arrival.

He seemed completely oblivious to the room full of people, each of whom had jumped to his feet when the president entered. He also seemed unaware of the posse of aides and other attendants who trailed in his wake, each wearing identical black suits and understated ties. All were male but one. She, too, wore a black pants suit and black ribbon as a necktie. They were obviously dressed so as not to upstage their boss, who sported a mauve silk shirt with a peach-hued ascot, a tight blue double-breasted jacket, and pewter chinos.

Grayson Whitten had only taken office the previous January. The freshman senator from New York had lost the general election but won easily in the Electoral College by capturing the key states with millions of dollars spent and a social media campaign that would long be analyzed and studied in marketing classes. He and his advisors crafted a platform heavy with social policy, promises of governmental economic reforms that would restore the struggling middle class by punishing through higher taxation those who dared make fortunes via selfish entrepreneurship, and with a vague pledge to bring peace to the world, not with weapons and threats but through negotiation and good intentions.

Whitten's primary claim to fame was getting through the campaign without a major scandal. His campaign manager made very sure that all his sins were politically correct and that any media type who tried to say otherwise paid a very dear price. Since the candidate had no real body of work to target for criticism, the only thing the media could—or would—discuss was his vague but hopeful "promises."

The president was still feeling his way through foreign policy, though. International strategy mostly bored him. With nothing to gain from such claptrap, he quickly grew irritated with those who wanted to take his time to discuss Arabs killing each other or some backward dictatorship that might try to develop its own nuclear weapons, regardless of how unlikely that might be.

Better to spend his time lobbying Congress to get his tax plan passed. After all, none of those people in Europe or Asia or the Middle East could vote for him or those candidates from his political party. There was a midterm election coming, and he really needed to get a majority back on one side or the other on Capitol Hill. Military readiness and commitment to NATO and all the rest simply ate up time and money that could be used to get the right people elected. And him back in the White House for a second term. Never too early to get to work on that!

He set his coffee cup down and looked across at the Chairman of the Joint Chiefs of Staff sitting impatiently way down at the far end of the mahogany table. The president had already questioned which of his staff had approved this meeting. That particular aide would, as punishment, miss out on his next jaunt to talk trade in Cancun before leaving for an international cultural exchange in Paris.

"All right, General," Whitten snapped. "Please make it quick. I have a tee time at Greenbrier in an hour and you are not going to make me late." As if the President of the United States could ever be considered late, he thought to himself.

General William Willoughby, who was also unaccustomed to waiting for anyone, was so livid he could not control his characteristic nervous tic. Under stress, the general's left eye winked uncontrollably. There were very few men with the guts to use the old "Winking Willy" nickname from his plebe days at West Point. Right now, though, the eye was working like a Gatling gun.

The president did not seem to notice. He took another sip of coffee and waved for Willoughby to get on with the brief, whatever the hell the military suits thought was so damned important that they would risk delaying his tee time. A Wall Street banker waited at the first tee box, one with considerable money that could turn the tide in a few key Congressional district races.

"Mr. President, there are two situations that I need to bring to your attention today. First, the Iranians are acting up again. Their Revolutionary Guard Navy has captured several outbound tankers and has declared the Strait of Hormuz closed to all shipping traffic. They are patrolling far more heavily than we have seen in the recent past. It looks like their land-based anti-ship missile batteries are on high alert and three of their *Kilo* submarines are unaccounted for."

Whitten set the coffee cup carefully back in the saucer before asking, "And what have we done? I trust that all the money we have poured into the Navy is being put to good use."

General Willoughby answered crisply, "The *Nimitz* battle

group along with the submarines *Hawaii* and *Topeka* have transited the Strait and are operating in the Gulf. The *Theodore Roosevelt* battle group and the *Makin Island* expeditionary group are heading to the Arabian Sea through the Suez Canal. They should be on station in four days."

Whitten nodded. "That's a lot of horsepower. I gather that you people over in the Pentagon think we should take this seriously. What does the Secretary of State say?"

The Chairman bit his tongue as he answered. "Mr. President, Secretary Samson is in transit back from the World Peace Conference in Bali. His plane reports that he is sleeping and is not to be disturbed. We will meet with him when he lands."

"And what was the second item?" President Whitten asked.

"The Russians are in the process of making a large-scale, unannounced deployment of most of their Northern Fleet," General Willoughby answered. "It is an unprecedented show of force. We are tracking over sixty ships headed around North Cape, apparently bound for the Norwegian Sea. But as you must know already, that is not the worst of it. One of our submarines, the *Florida*, stumbled across them as they were crossing the Barents. The Russians fired on the submarine, sir. By great good fortune and no little skill by our men, their attack was deflected by counter-measures, including one of our new EMATs. Thank God the *Florida* escaped and reported in."

The White House Chief of Staff, who by chance had been the president's college roommate at Princeton as well as his dearest friend, bent to whisper in his ear.

President Whitten held up a hand, telling the general that he had heard enough.

"So I am given to understand that the Russians claim the Barents Sea as something they call—let me make sure I get this right..." He looked up at his Chief of Staff. "A historical territorial sea." The man nodded. "Is that right, General?"

Willoughby's eye blinked even faster. He swatted at the question as if it were an annoying mosquito.

"What those sons of bitches claim is neither here nor there, Mr. President. The Russians can claim anything they damn well want to, but it doesn't mean jack-shit. By international law and long-set precedent, the Barents is international waters. But, sir, they attacked one of our ships. That is an act of war! We have to do something to retaliate, or the entire world…"

Willoughby's voice trailed off as he pointed a finger directly at the president.

Grayson Whitten ignored it. He pulled a handkerchief from his breast pocket, carefully dabbed his upper lip, and precisely re-folded and replaced the handkerchief in his pocket. When he finally addressed the general, his tone was that of a school-master addressing a particularly dense student.

"You say that they destroyed the EMAT, the evasion device? Only last week, you and your associate Joint Chiefs were complaining profusely that the Russians shot at one of our submarines. And that they also miraculously missed sinking the vessel because of some new stealth technology gizmo or another. General, if they were shooting—and I emphasize the 'if'—then they quite obviously had no intention of hitting either of our submarines. They were simply attempting to frighten us away so we would not learn too much about their equipment. We would have done the same, I would guess. I would also say, from all appearances, they have succeeded spectacularly well. If I may be totally honest with you, General Willoughby, you and the others are using this little dust-up as a ploy to justify that impossible increase in the defense budget you have been lobbying for in the media already. And we simply can no longer accept such wasteful spending of limited resources. Not when we so desperately require the funds for our domestic social agenda, to rebuild the infrastructure, and to jump-start the economy."

The Chairman was still sitting there, his finger pointed at the president. The general's left eye was beating a blinding tattoo.

Decision made and delivered, the president rose and strode out of the Situation Room. Then he paused in the hallway, turned, and looked pointedly at the general.

"I want you to quit trying to piss off President Salkov. He is a good friend. Remove all of our vessels from any waters that he considers to be his territorial seas. Understood, General? Now, if you will excuse me, your Commander-in-Chief has a golf game."

Ψ

"Sonar, Conn, report all contacts," Captain Harold Swanson ordered over the 21MC.

The USS *Florida* had the appearance of a ghost as she slipped through the murky waters twelve miles off the Russian Murmansk coast. The Russian fleet had beaten up the waters around the EMAT for more than six hours, expending several more ASW torpedoes and RBU-6000 salvoes, all to attempt to send the US submarine to the bottom, before finally steaming off over the horizon.

Just to be sure, Swanson had kept *Florida* hovering, hiding for several more hours before slinking off to the south. Now they had arrived in the area where they were supposed to perform their real mission, the reason for which they had left the submarine base at Kings Bay, Georgia, in the first place. Before they had been trampled by an ocean full of Russian warships.

"Conn, only contact is a fisherman, bearing zero-three-six,

distant. We have been unable to drive bearing rate on him at all," Chief Alexander replied from Sonar.

Swanson turned to the officer of the deck, a young lieutenant junior grade.

"Mr. Arello, hover at one-five-zero feet. Prepare to deploy the URLMs in both tubes twenty-three and twenty-four."

Phillip Arello brought the mammoth submarine to all-stop, hovering at precisely one hundred and fifty feet below the roiling surface. The *Florida* barely rocked at all where she sat even though things were plenty rough above them. Once the sub had coasted to a halt, hatches on missile tubes twenty-three and twenty-four quietly and smoothly opened. The tubes had once housed deadly Trident-5 submarine-launched ballistic missiles, capable of flying over five thousand miles before landing a nuclear weapon with pinpoint accuracy and deadly results. Instead of an SLBM roaring out of the tube in a cloud of steam and flames, a hydraulically operated rail slid upward from each tube. Each stopped at almost forty feet above the sub's broad, flat missile deck. A tray slowly pivoted around on the rail mechanism until its contents were horizontal. A large diameter unmanned submarine—an LDUUV—lifted from each tray and, as if each had a mind of its own, swam silently away. The tray rotated back to vertical, the rail glided back into the missile tube, and both doors closed and locked. The entire evolution took ten minutes.

"Captain, both LDUUVs deployed, both URLMs are restowed, missile hatches shut and locked," young Arello reported. "Launch control reports normal network link on launch. Both LDUUVs beyond link control now."

Swanson nodded. "Very well, Mr. Arello. Our work here is done. Let's get out of Dodge and then we can tell the boss. Come to course north, ahead one-third."

The OOD repeated his captain's order and *Florida* was once

again on her way, hopefully for safer environs, where nobody would be shooting at them. Still, Harold Swanson could not relax.

International waters apparently meant little to some folks these days. There was a reason why they had been so unexpectedly and determinedly attacked. And when the president ordered the inevitable retaliation, *Florida* would not only be the closest boat to where that strike would likely come.

She would also be the one with the most incentive to launch it.

Ψ

The two LDUUVs headed out on their mission, large fuel cells providing the energy needed to cover long distances. One LDUUV dropped off a large pod, almost three quarters of its cargo, in deep water ten miles out from the entrance to Kola Bay, southeast of Murmansk on Russia's frigid, rugged northern coast. The cargo sank to the bottom, over one hundred fathoms in the inky darkness, before gently landing. The device promptly deployed a pair of arms and a small crawler that worked its way across the mud bottom for a hundred yards, laying out a strand of tiny fiber optic cable behind it. At the end of its tether, it stopped and waited obediently.

The same LDUUV then proceeded farther down into the Kola Bay, dropping off two more packages at predetermined positions. Those also sank to the bottom before deploying acoustic, magnetic, and pressure sensors.

The second LDUUV was busy as well, dropping off its eight sensor packages even deeper into the Kola Bay, going as far as the major Russian naval base at Severomorsk to deploy the last one before prudently turning around. The two then returned for a rendezvous with the home pod, each nestling up to one of its arms to recharge and download its information. The crawler sent a small float to the surface, where it deployed an antenna used to report success to an orbiting communications satellite. The system then waited, listening for instructions to gather whatever information the sensors might detect.

The little unmanned vessels had just set up a particularly high-tech party line that was eagerly listening for gossip.

Ψ

Bill Beaman expertly wheeled his chair into Ramon's Beach Bar. The place was little more than a ramshackle bamboo-and-palm-leaf structure that leaned like a drunken sailor against the Hotel Peace and Plenty's yellow stucco walls. Ramon's had quickly become the SEAL's home away from home for the week he had been on Exuma Island. The Bahamas rum punch really was a killer drink, and Beaman firmly believed Tom Donnegan was correct when he claimed the concoction had medicinal qualities as well. He was already feeling much healthier, and the busted leg from his rough landing during the drill in Costa Rica seemed to be quickly healing.

Ramon had his drink waiting for him on the bar. Chilled beads of condensation coursed down the sides to form a pool on the highly polished teak. Beaman knew that the conch fritters and roasted plantain would be out before he was halfway through the first drink. Whatever today's catch was would be up only a couple of minutes later, just off the grill.

As he took his first sip of the punch, Beaman noticed that he was sharing the bar with a stranger sitting mostly in shadow down the way. Most nights it had only been him and Ramon, sharing tall tales and watching American football on the TV above the bar. The new patron was young. Beaman guessed late twenties. He was a handsome man, clearly muscular and very fit, not the typical pasty, rotund tourist.

The big SEAL continued his chat with Ramon. If the stranger wanted a conversation, he could start one.

When Ramon went back to check on Beaman's red snapper, the young man finally slid his way, nodded a greeting, and tipped his half-empty glass.

"Evening, friend. These drinks, they pack quite the thump, huh?"

"They give a man his money's worth of dizzy for sure," Beaman responded.

"Always this quiet around here?"

"Don't know about 'always,' but yep. The whole island is a real quiet place, and Ramon's is no exception." Beaman took another sip. The guy seemed okay. No harm in chatting him up. Besides, he had noticed something curious about the man's enunciation. "The accent—Russian, isn't it? Somewhere from around St. Petersburg, if I had to guess."

The stranger frowned, waited a telling beat, and then smiled and nodded. "Good ear, my friend. You're very good. My name is Alexi Gorbenov. I was born and raised in Ryabovo, a little town a few kilometers outside St. Petersburg. But I have lived in the States for quite a while now. Most people do not catch the accent anymore. Say, friend, Ramon tells me you are in some kind of security business. That sounds like exciting work. What kind of security?"

Beaman grinned and completely ignored the question. "Well, accents are a bit of a hobby of mine, Alexi. I figure it is always a good thing to know where people come from. That sometimes tells me where they might be going. What you doing way down here in Exuma? It's a bit off the beaten path."

To Beaman it was abundantly clear that Alexi—or whatever his real name might be—was friendly and talkative enough. But friendly and talkative in order to attempt to be subtly inquisitive.

The Russian tipped back his drink and drained his glass before responding.

"Taking a little vacation from the day job. I brought my boat down yesterday. I read somewhere that the swordfish were hitting any bait you throw their way in the deep water east of here."

"Swordfish, huh? Yes, sir, they are a pretty gullible fish. Anything that dazzles them they want to try to swallow."

Ramon was back then, carrying a large plate with a luscious snapper draped across it, grilled to smoky perfection, swimming in butter, and covered with steamed clams and fried conch fritters.

"Ramon, you are an artist!" Beaman told him. "Only thing I need now is one more of those rum punches, if you please. And one for my friend here, too. My friend Alexi, the swordfish catcher from St. Petersburg."

The Russian waved his hand.

"No thank you. I have work to do. Getting the boat ready, you know. And I need a clear head for tomorrow when I stalk the broadbill." He paused to crunch noisily on a piece of ice from his glass. "They may be gullible but they can also go deep when they want to. Very, very deep and with great stealth. And their eyes. You know the swordfish, like the shark, have special organs next to their eyes to keep them warm so they better see their prey." Alexi stood, left a twenty-dollar bill on the counter, and headed for the door. "Good night, my friend. Enjoy your snapper. At least that is one fish that did not get away."

Then the Russian disappeared into the black tropical night.

Ψ

Out in the mid-Atlantic, Hurricane Penny had gained considerable strength. She had now become a category two hurricane. One tanker, cautiously skirting her might, reported waves at forty to fifty feet and sustained winds of better than ninety knots. Air traffic control was already routing the South America-to-Europe flights well to the east.

Satellite images showed a well-defined eye surrounded by over a hundred miles of ugly, rotating, deep-gray clouds. She was moving westward, seeking warmer water to stoke her energy furnace.

She clearly did not care who or what might be in her way.

13

Admiral Rufous Clark, Commander US Pacific Command, listened as his counterparts from both Vietnam and the Philippines pleaded for his help. Admiral Thanh Ng, Commander Vietnam Navy, was particularly incensed.

"Admiral Clark, the Chinese are grasping ever further into the South China Sea. As you well know, they have military airfields on man-made islands in the Paracels and Spratleys as well as on Scarborough Shoals. These facilities are within our territorial waters."

Admiral Escario nodded in agreement. The Scarborough Shoals airfield was almost visible from Luzon, the Philippines' largest island.

"And my sources tell me that the *Liaoning*, the PLAN aircraft carrier, and a large battle group are refitting in Zhanjiang, preparing for a large-scale operation in the Spratleys," Escario added. "Admiral, we need for you to move the *Lincoln* battle group into the South China Sea for our protection."

Admiral Clark nodded. His satellites had already photographed the *Liaoning* being loaded with Shenyang J-15 fighters as a gaggle of frigates and destroyers filled the piers at

Zhanjiang's sprawling naval base. Something was clearly afoot, but the *Lincoln* battle group, homeported in Yokosuka, Japan, was already busy dealing with yet another North Korean crisis. Instead, Clark had ordered the *Eisenhower* group to the Spratleys at best possible speed over twenty-four hours ago. But, with over seven thousand miles to steam from Hawaii, they wouldn't arrive for almost two weeks.

Clark looked the other two admirals head-on.

"I am sorry, gentlemen. At the moment, and because of commitments elsewhere, this is the best we can do. I pray it is enough to keep this flickering little flame from setting this entire hemisphere afire."

Ψ

The sun had just made a grand entrance over the eastern horizon in an explosion of red and orange. Elliot, the cabbie, wrestled his battered taxi, trailed by a cloud of blue smoke, into the tiny parking lot next to the Naval Undersea Research Facility. The NURF BAL lot was normally empty at this early hour, but today a sedan was parked next to the building that served as a combination cafeteria and gym. It was clearly a rental, marked by the sticker on its windshield.

Bill Beaman knew the car belonged to the man he was supposed to meet this early tropical morning. He labored to pull himself out of the cab with his one good leg and muscled himself upright. The crutches were still difficult for him to handle, which irritated the SEAL captain far more than he was willing to admit. He could carry a wide array of bulky, heavy equipment and weapons through thick, clutching jungle or across sucking desert sand, but these damn props the Navy had issued him were a trying test of his patience.

Once upright, he paused, allowing the sea breeze to cool his face, and looked to the east. The sky behind the burning orb of the sun was streaked with brilliant red. Beaman muttered the old sailor's proverb, "Red sky in the morning, sailor take warning," just loud enough so the cabbie could hear him above the distant shrieks of the sea gulls.

"You be right, mon," Elliot said with a laugh. "Looks like dey be a big blow brewin' out there a'ways. All the boats in the marinas, they be clearin' out real soon, movin' they asses to the mainland."

"Yep. I expect so," Beaman said as he handed Elliot his fare and a good tip. He turned toward the gym door as best he could on the crutches. "How about you pick me up about 1700? I don't want to miss one minute of the action at Ramon's tonight."

Elliot grinned broadly at the shared joke. The island life on Exuma was so quiet and laid-back that Beaman normally had Ramon's Beach Bar all to himself, save for the occasional NURF BAL civilian employee who wandered in for some liquid anesthesia. Or mysterious guys with Russian surnames.

"Right, Mr. B. I will get you there early so you get your usual front-row seat. Anyt'ing else you be needin', you let me know."

He flashed his now familiar knowing wink, backed the old cab away, and, with no first gear, double-clutched it into second and jerked out of the lot, leaving a spray of gravel and oyster shells.

Beaman lurched clumsily toward the gym. He was already suspecting that Elliot the cab driver had other duties, maybe on behalf of the Bahamian government. Maybe Beaman's own. As the SEAL worked his way up one step at a time, the door suddenly swung open and a bear of a man emerged. He offered Beaman his hand and helped him ease up to the landing at the top of the steps.

"Morning, Captain. I'm Thomas Anthony. Admiral

Donnegan said I should head down this way and see how you were coming along."

"So the old goat is checking up on me?" Beaman replied with a laugh. "He surely knows that I can't get into too much trouble around these parts. So what exactly does he suggest you check up on?"

As they stepped into the empty gym, every inch covered with the latest exercise equipment, free weights, or mats, Anthony reached into his sweatpants to retrieve a cell phone, then pushed one button on the face of the device and handed it to Beaman.

"First off, the 'old goat' wants to talk with you."

Beaman grabbed the phone and put it to his ear just in time to hear Donnegan's familiar growl.

"Well, Bill, you must be getting in tune with the slower island life. It's nearly 0600 and you are just now getting to the office. All this sleeping in is going to make you fat and lazy."

"Admiral, your orders were to come down here to check out the security and get some R&R. All I am doing is following orders."

"Well, toad, the R&R is over," Donnegan shot back. "Dr. Anthony tells me that it is time for you to start rehabbing that leg before you turn into a permanent fixture on some barstool somewhere."

Beaman looked up. Anthony was leaning against a Stairmaster machine, just out of earshot.

Donnegan went on, "We checked out your friendly fellow barfly, Alexi Gorbenov. That took a surprising amount of digging for some immigrant investment banker. Turns out that his real name is Alexi Markov. He works out of the Russian Consulate in New York City. He purports to be some minor-level diplomatic functionary. I'd bet my rather broad, black ass that he is really working for the Foreign Intelligence Service, the SVR. And I'd double-down on that bet that he is part of their Directorate S, illegal intel. They are primarily responsible for recruiting and handling foreign agents. It strikes us as a bit of a coincidence that he has used his earned comp time to enjoy a nice fishing trip that just happens to take him to within spittin' distance of our facility there on Exuma, and at a time when we are testing all that new stealth gear on *Toledo*, launching a truly new boat, and dodging damn torpedoes shit out by subs owned and operated by the fellow countrymen of one Mr. Markov."

Beaman leaned on a crutch and rubbed the stubble on his chin. He had not bothered to shave since landing on Exuma.

"Interesting, Boss. Also odd that a low-level diplomat is able to afford an expensive open-ocean fishing boat and the men to crew it. I doubt he is down here in this backwater to catch swordfish."

Donnegan snorted. "So, Einstein, it looks to me like you have some work to do figuring out the solution to that particular puzzle. We sort of need to know why the Russians have posted him there. And do it without letting them know that we know. And considering that this rather interesting new character is on the scene, I'm sending your kid protégé, Jim Ward, down to help you with holding down those barstools. Hell, you know the drill, Bill." Beaman could hear Donnegan take a noisy slurp of his coffee. "Oh, and by the way, let me give you fair warning. Dr. Anthony's workouts? They can be damned brutal. We've contemplated moving him into interrogation."

The admiral abruptly hung up.

Beaman, very familiar with Admiral Donnegan's brusqueness, handed the phone back to Anthony.

"So, it's Dr. Anthony, is it?"

The big man laughed and winked.

"Yes, but my friends and victims call me Thomas the Tank.

Now, what say we get busy making that leg function the way it's designed to? You might need it again someday."

Ψ

Sarah Wilder pushed back from her computer desk, sighed, and rubbed her eyes. So far, her time onboard the barges had been incredibly boring. She filled her days solving minor—and extremely easy—electrical design problems, each of them pushed at her by her boss with the urgency of some catastrophe that could bring down the whole military-industrial complex if not solved before lunch. The guy was a moron, plain and simple. He was living, breathing proof that anyone could reach well beyond his level of competency as a bureaucrat if he just aligned himself on the politically correct side of every problem. For that, the guy had an uncanny ability.

Wilder's nights were even worse. There were no issues, easy or not, to occupy her attention. No place to get a good wine or even a decent latte. And certainly no place to shop for something new and sinfully provocative to wear when she finally had a chance to be with Alexi again.

Alexi. She missed him so much. Although a considerable number of available men were stuck on that dreadful barge with her, each more than willing and eager to help resolve her boredom and loneliness, none could even come close to filling the void left by Alexi. She was not even tempted, and their continued sophomoric efforts were beginning to annoy her, just like everything else on this godforsaken garbage scow.

She touched the keyboard to once again check her personal email account, just in case Alexi had finally sent her some hint of when they could once again be together. She was well aware that they had to be careful. And that they had much important information to discuss. But she actually hurt, physically felt pain in her stomach, at the thought of feeling him next to her, kissing her, doing all those wonderful things to her that he did so well.

Then she considered sending a note to her father. Maybe he could give her a digital pep talk without saying anything too risky. He was, after all, the expert at all this spy stuff. He could also remind her again why her job was so important. She decided not to email him either. That communication would be much too perilous as well.

Then she saw movement at her open door. She quickly brought the software system dashboard back up on her monitor. The intruder was Sam Smithski, the moronic boss. He knocked but stuck his head in without waiting for permission, just as he always did. She scowled at him but he did not seem to notice.

"Sarah, I need for you to go down on the boat and supervise the technicians working on the stealth projector processor interface."

So far, Sarah had avoided getting anywhere near the horrid black whale that had invaded the space under the canopy between the two barges. Just the sight of that evil device made her shudder. The sooner she and those of a like mind could free the world of such deadly machines and the men who used them to murder and maim, the better it would be for everyone.

The young engineer started to protest. Smithski held up his hand.

"Sarah, look, everyone else is extremely busy, and, after all, you are the subject matter expert on the stealth system. Hell, I just nominated you to be the tech warrant holder on the system when it becomes a program of record. Nobody in the world knows it better than you. And right now, I need you down there onboard *Toledo* making sure those technicians don't screw anything up. It would also be a good political move for you to introduce yourself to the submarine's captain when you get down there, too. His name is Glass. Joe Glass."

With that, Smithski turned and quickly walked down the passageway, trying to appear intent on some other pressing matter, but in actuality he was simply avoiding any conflict with his lovely but difficult employee.

Sarah shook her head, ran her hands through her long hair, and thought for a moment. Maybe the moron had just unwittingly opened a door for her. Now might be the perfect time to put her new plan into effect. She only needed a few minutes to load some computer code into the stealth processor, and this visit would give her that opportunity. Just a few simple lines of code that would toggle the projectors off if a specific coded acoustic pulse was detected by the system.

Alexi and Dad would be so proud of her!

She grabbed her laptop and ID badges before heading out the door. Going down the ladders to the main deck of the barge was fairly easy, even with that black monster ominously filling the space between her and the other barge. Crossing the brow, the gangway from the barge deck to the sub, to actually step onboard the evil vessel, was a different matter. Her hands shook as she gripped the handrail and started over, taking small, hesitant steps.

"You all right, ma'am?" A young sailor stood across from her on the rounded hull of the submarine. "You're white as a sheet and shaking like a leaf. Let me help you onboard. *Toledo* won't bite."

Sarah Wilder gave the young man a wan, forced smile. Won't bite? This vessel was made to bite. And bite hard.

"Thank you. My first time on a sub. I guess I need to meet with your captain."

"Sure. This way, ma'am."

Sarah wished the kid would quit calling her "ma'am." She

was not much older than he was. And the last thing she wanted to do was meet a submarine captain, a man trained to do all sorts of murdering and destruction in the name of democracy and nation-building.

Following the sailor, she carefully and slowly crawled through the hatch and then climbed down the steel ladder. At the bottom, she found herself in a narrow passageway enclosed by Formica-clad steel walls. She was disoriented by the tight space, but looking down the corridor—she guessed that direction was aft—the passage seemed to open into a larger space, one filled with machines and many men who appeared to be working on them.

The sailor guided her to an open door just before the larger room. He nodded a "here we are" to her and knocked.

Inside, an older man paused in the conversation he was having with another person and held up a finger, indicating they should wait a moment. He turned back to the other man and finished his thought.

"Eng, I understand that the techs are having problems with the electrical hull penetrators. See if the divers can rig cofferdams to replace them. That system won't work if the power can't get out to the pods." Then the man stood and turned to greet his visitor with a friendly-enough smile. "Welcome onboard *Toledo*. You must be Dr. Wilder. Sam Smithski promised me that you were going to fix all my headaches with the stealth system. Glad to hear that. I have enough headaches with the other gizmos that NUWC is loading me down with."

Wilder smiled back and extended her hand.

"It's Sarah. And thank you. I'll do what I can. This is my first time on a submarine and I'm afraid I don't know my way around. I know it is odd considering that I spend so much time with systems designed specifically for them, but it just never was necessary that I actually go aboard one. Can someone show me where the stealth projector processors are?"

The second man in the room rose and introduced himself.

"I'm Doug O'Malley. It's good to finally meet you. I'm the engineer here, and I've seen your name on enough paperwork that I feel like we are old buds. The processors are up in the sonar equipment space just down this passageway. I'll be happy to show you where your handiwork actually gets to live. You like a cup of coffee? A soda?"

"No, thanks."

If she drank anything, she would have to pee. She had no idea how that would work on a submarine full of men.

After a half dozen steps they were standing in front of equipment that was very familiar to Wilder. Two technicians already had their laptops out on the deck, working complicated diagnostic routines on the interface layer. She ignored their stares as she booted up her laptop, connected a cable to the system test port, and punched a few keys before tapping her computer's touchpad.

Within seconds, her special bug was safely downloaded and nestled among millions of lines of other far more complex computer code.

She only hoped the others had not noticed her throbbing pulse or the sweat beads that had appeared on her forehead.

Ψ

Alexi Markov carefully rigged the portable davit into a bracket on the transom of his yacht. The Voyager 56 was equipped with twin Volvo D-12 diesels and extended range fuel tanks, a necessity for this mission. It was big enough to comfortably do these kinds of jobs and, since it was built in 2006, old enough not to attract undue attention when tied up in any marina in this part of the world.

The full electronic navigation and communications suite would not arouse any suspicion either. Not on an open ocean vessel of this size. Not even with the few extra antennas poking up topside. And the large hold, meant to keep trophy fish fresh until they could get the catch back to port, was perfect for hiding the ROV robot vehicle they needed for the task that lay before them this day.

The only problem was the crew. To operate the boat and equipment, he needed at least three crewmen. And they had to be completely loyal and trusted. That meant Russians. Russians with family back home they wanted to keep healthy and not in prison, thus assuring their loyalty. However, a boatload of Russians in the Bahamas—and especially so near the American submarine facility—was bound to draw scrutiny. Gorbenov solved this problem by restricting his crew to the boat and explaining to the owners at the Kidd Marina, around the point from the Peace and Plenty Hotel, that there had been a snafu with their papers. Though the thirsty men craved time at the island bars before the fishing trip, they would not be able to come ashore. The marina personnel were very familiar with these "documentation" problems and were more than willing to take a few extra dollars to look the other way.

Now, with the sun climbing but mostly obscured by high clouds, the big yacht worked through the twisting channel around the rocks and islets, out into the open water east of Exuma. As they cleared Fowl Cay, the Atlantic rollers hit the vessel dead-on. The state-five seas caused the yacht to pitch and roll considerably more than was comfortable.

Alexi spun the wheel around and pointed the boat almost due north. He punched a series of coordinates into the autopilot to steer them to a spot a few miles west of roughly halfway between Cat Island and Conception Island.

The seas were broad on the starboard beam now, making for an even more uncomfortable ride. Fortunately, the Voyager was stoutly built and could take the buffeting. And this was not, after all, a pleasure cruise. If the crew was bounced around a little, Alexi really did not care. They had a vital mission to complete.

With the sea state, the Voyager could only make six knots good, and so the short trip took over four hours. Once they arrived, they quickly lowered the ROV, which swam to the sunken robot waiting on the sea bottom. The devices mated and quickly downloaded the data stored on the robot. Then, replacing the robot's batteries took another hour.

Finally, Alexi gladly spun the wheel around and headed back to Exuma. As they transited, he uploaded the data to a satellite orbiting 23,000 miles overhead. By the time he slipped his mooring lines around the bollards at Kidd Cove Marina, Russian Naval Intelligence would already be analyzing the data. That chore done, he and his crew could now concentrate on navigating the building seas on the way back.

The rogue wave caught him completely by surprise. Far larger than the rest, it appeared from nowhere and swept across from the stern quarter. The swirling wall of seawater rose high above where Alexi stood in the vessel's wheelhouse, blocking out the steel-gray sky. He knew instantly that the wave had the capability of swamping the boat and sending them all to the bottom.

The surge crashed down. The entire stern disappeared beneath its roiling green waters. Alexi grabbed something solid and held his breath, poised to swim for it, sure that they would be flipped over and swept out into the churning sea. He finally exhaled as, amazingly, the stern cleared and the last of the water flowed through the flooded scuppers.

He relaxed for a moment. Then something odd struck him. The davit. The damn thing was gone. In its place was a large, ragged hole where shattered wood had been torn from the transom.

The ROV! It was gone, too. And there was no way to retrieve it. The device was still dangling from its tether but several hundred feet down like a heavy, hooked fish. At just over two hundred kilos, there was no way the four of them could lift the ROV back aboard. Especially not in this pitching sea, or without the davit to give leverage.

Scuttling the expensive piece of hardware was, of course, not an option. His masters would not look kindly on an agent who aborted a mission and lost several million rubles' worth of equipment, all in a few seconds.

Nothing to do but swim the ROV home. Its best speed was maybe three knots. They would have to be careful not to snag something or foul the line. That and keep a better lookout for another rogue wave so they could at least brace themselves against getting washed overboard, even as the upsurge all around them threatened to shove the boat right over.

Alexi steered the ROV around so that it followed the Voyager like a reluctant puppy on a long leash. He then punched the coordinates to the Kidd Cove Marina into the autopilot and strapped himself into the captain's chair.

It was going to be a long, uncomfortable night.

14

President Grayson Whitten despised the secret people mover that ran from the White House under the Potomac to the Pentagon. His problem was primarily the symbolism it suggested, the subtle implication that the Leader of the Free World was sneaking over, hat in hand, to plead with the military honchos to please do what he was asking. Still, it was a necessary evil. At least the press would not see him. Dealing with the military was easily the most distasteful part of his job. Any interaction—or the lack thereof—thus far in his presidency had resulted in less-than-good poll numbers and still more rabid sniping from the news networks and talk shows.

Secretly installed during the Reagan Administration, the high-speed shuttle very privately connected the White House and the Pentagon with an underground rail system. Everything in Washington required an acronym. The secret transport, called PURS, short for the Presidential Underground Rail System, was one of the shortest—and probably most expensive —rail lines in the world. Only a very select few even knew of its existence. Even fewer had access to it.

Slipping through a locked and guarded steel door just

outside the White House Situation Room, the president climbed into the cramped little car. With the push of a button, he and those traveling with him were whisked under the Potomac River and directly to a similar door just outside the National Military Command Center, buried deep beneath the fortress that was the Pentagon. It was impossible for an eager reporter or vigilant foreign operative to deduce that something was happening important enough to require the presence of the Commander-in-Chief at the Pentagon. There were no charging motorcades or buzzing helicopters to tip them off.

In minutes, the car slid smoothly and silently to a halt. An immaculately uniformed Marine guard swung open the steel door, admitting President Whitten into the NMCC. The waiting Joint Chiefs snapped to attention. The Service Secretaries followed suit but with much less vigor.

Whitten merely waved rather than return the salutes. Then he strode briskly across the huge room, barely glancing at the array of geographic displays on the banks of massive monitors that filled every inch of wall space. He did not look at any of the men and women working there either, even as they tried to concentrate on their keyboards and monitors as their big boss walked past. He followed his chief of staff toward a small, private, and windowless conference room set off by itself. The president sat down in the chair at the head of a large table that filled most of the room, then motioned impatiently for the Joint Chiefs and Secretaries to find their seats. It was clear he was irritated, impatient.

Turning to his Secretary of Defense, Paulene Wilson, the president snapped, "Now, what is so important that interrupted our deliberations on the national education policy? Paulene, you know that I have the nation's top education experts cooling their heels in the White House while I traipse over here. It better be important."

Secretary Wilson, sitting on President Whitten's right hand, said, "Mr. President, we think this is very important and requires your immediate attention. General Willoughby will lead the brief."

Whitten barely nodded as Winking Willie Willoughby rose. Pointing at a large-scale chart on the video monitor, the Chairman cleared his throat and began.

"Mr. President, last week the Russian Navy began an unprecedentedly large exercise in the area of Norway's North Cape. In reality, the exercise stretched from the White Sea all the way around to the GIUK Gap, the line between Greenland, Iceland, and the United Kingdom. It is by far the largest Russian naval exercise since the fall of the Soviet Union. We have seen all their major combatants participate, including some that have never deployed outside home waters before."

Whitten nodded. He had heard all this already in his daily intel briefs. "General, don't try my patience. Tell me something I don't know."

"Well, Mr. President," Willoughby went on with barely a pause, "last week, the Iranians attacked and captured several tankers in the Persian Gulf. They have declared the Strait of Hormuz closed to all traffic, including military vessels, voiding the rights of innocent passage. We immediately deployed the *Nimitz* battle group and two submarines into the Gulf to protect our interests. Today, the Iranian government has stated that the Strait has been mined and any ship that dares to transit does so at its own risk."

The Chairman stopped to take a drink of water.

"It will take at least a month to sweep the Strait while we maintain continuous air cover to both protect the sweep operation and prevent any re-seeding. That is going to fully engage the *Nimitz* as well as the *Roosevelt* when she gets on station." Willoughby pointed at Eastern Asia and the South China Sea.

All eyes were on the dot of light from his laser pointer as it danced from one trouble spot to the other.

"Mr. President, the *Eisenhower* battle group is a few days out from taking station off the Spratleys and the *Lincoln* is being kept busy by the DPRK's latest antics."

Putting down his pointer, the general turned to face President Whitten. "Sir, my point in all this is to make very clear that we are being stretched very, very thin. I only have eight carriers right now. Four are actively engaged as we have just discussed. The *Bush* and the *Reagan* are both in the yards for maintenance. With *Gerald Ford* still fighting through her electronic arresting gear problems, the only carriers I have are the *Stennis* in the Pacific and the *Truman* in Norfolk."

Grayson sat back in his chair. A calm look crossed his face as he set his jaw and gazed at each man there. They had seen that expression many times before. The time he blasted his opponent in the first presidential debate, responding with the perfect rejoinder that flip-flopped the poll numbers the next day. The night before the election, at the end of a strategically placed hour-long campaign commercial, when he looked into the TV camera and promised the American people he would bring peace, income equality, and a booming economy in his first term. The cold day in January when he delivered the eloquent and moving inaugural speech that many pundits proclaimed the greatest in history.

"Here is what you will do," the president said, his voice now calm, his finger still stabbing the air in front of him. "You will do nothing to antagonize President Salkov. He can count just as well as you can. If we need to, we can always bring the *Roosevelt* back through the Suez to reinforce Europe or bring the *Stennis* around to help out. Besides, it's all bluster. Grigory Salkov is really a peace-loving man. He will not start any war in Europe."

President Grayson Whitten rose and walked out of the briefing room, heading back toward the hated PUR.

Ψ

Bill Beaman carefully set the night vision binoculars atop the tripod. The 10-power-magnification military binoculars were far too large and heavy to be handheld. He focused the optics on the marina about a mile across the harbor. It was easy to find what he was looking for over there. The lone boat still tied up at Kidd Marina popped into focus. The dim lights at the shore end of the pier were more than ample for the night vision binoculars to make the view—despite the blowing sea spray and pre-dawn darkness—about the same as a sunny, clear day.

It was good fortune that Beaman had seen the Voyager limp slowly into the empty marina. He and Elliot had been on the way to the Exuma International Airport to meet the nightly flight from Fort Lauderdale, to pick up fellow SEAL Jim Ward, when he spotted the Voyager limping in to Kidd Marina. He had been surprised to see the alleged fisher back in Exuma. Everything else that would float had abandoned the island ahead of the approaching hurricane, seeking the protection of the better harbors on the US mainland. He had also figured Alexi would have either completed whatever it was he and his crew were down here to do or abandoned it for now with the storm threatening.

Apparently not.

He had asked Elliot to take him to the naval facility to pick up the binoculars and tripod and then detour to a spot from which he could look across the dark, choppy waters at the pier. The cabbie gave his usual knowing wink.

"You not be the first that needed to watch the marina, Mr. B. I know the perfect spot."

It was. From there, he could immediately determine the yacht's likely reason for being back in port. A large piece of the boat's transom was missing, violently torn away based on the jagged edges of the wood and fiberglass. As he watched, two members of the Russian's crew were trying to work some kind of repair to the transom. He could also see Alexi Markov and the fourth crewman laboriously working to pull a large cable bundle up from the water.

A sudden powerful gust of wind blew salt spray all the way back to where Beaman had set up his observation post at the edge of a wall of tangled underbrush more than thirty feet from the shore line. Above, threatening dark clouds played hide-and-seek with the moon and the last of the night's stars.

The SEAL heard movement behind him in the underbrush. He spun around as best he could on one leg, his hand on the butt of his pistol. Jim Ward dropped a load of gear and plopped down next to Beaman.

"You're sure as hell milking the 'broken leg' thing for all it's worth, Captain," the young SEAL grunted. "Elliot and I have lugged all this gear over here while you have been lounging around on the beach."

Beaman could barely suppress a chuckle. It was the same type of banter and trash-talk he had so often exchanged with Ward's father. And sometimes in far more dicey situations than this one so far appeared to be.

"Best you be careful who you slip up on, kid," Beaman shot back. "I could have easily blasted your balls off before I realized you weren't worth wasting the round."

"You still able to qualify with that sidearm, Father Time? I figured at your advanced age, you'd hardly be able to hit the side of a battleship at thirty yards."

"Well, I can still manage to do about anything I want. Except walk. That's something of a challenge these days. Anyway, about time you showed up. I've just been sitting here waiting for you to bring the beer. You did remember the beer, didn't you? Ice cold with lime wedges, the way I like it?"

Then Elliot appeared, moving noisily through the sea grapes, horse bush, and love vine that covered the ground on the short walk from where he parked his hack. The tangled vegetation made for tough going but it was ideal cover.

"I hear you say you be wantin' a beer, Mr. B?" he asked. "I be happy to drive down to Exuma Market and get Kalik when they open at sun-up. Best beer in the islands."

Beaman laughed and waved away the idea.

"No, Elliot. You and I are going to sit here and watch our young friend take a nice early morning swim."

Turning to Ward, he quickly brought him up to speed on the Russian in the bar, his supposed fishing trip, the crew on his boat that was almost certainly Russian military, and how they had unexpectedly shown back up at the marina during the night towing something heavy and mysterious.

"You got all the rebreather gear with you, right?" Ward nodded. "We need you to swim across Augusta Bay and check out that boat you see over there." He motioned for Ward to take a gander through the binoculars. "You see that cable bundle they are pulling up on deck? Something on the other end is awfully heavy and valuable enough for them to tow it here in the middle of a gale to try to retrieve it. I'm betting it ain't a swordfish."

Ward looked at the stretch of water between them and the marina, at the white caps and blustery sky, at the slight glow in the east that would be full-blown sunrise in another couple of hours, hurricane feeder bands or not.

"So you want me to swim over there and see what the catch of the day is, right?" Ward murmured. "Sounds simple enough."

"Probably will be," Beaman agreed. "But be careful. The

guy in charge, Alexi Markov, is an agent for Directorate S of the Russian SVR. Odds are that the other three are his muscle. And I'd also wager that whatever it is they've hooked, they will do whatever it takes to keep you and me from finding out."

Jim Ward began pulling on his gear as Bill Beaman resumed scrutinizing the yacht. Elliot sat back in the nest of sea grapes and watched, wide-eyed.

Ψ

The first scattered birdshot of raindrops pelted Ward as he pulled on the tight-fitting black wetsuit and strapped the Mark 25 rebreather to his chest. The cumbersome device was awkward and heavy on land, more so than a standard SCUBA system, but it had the distinct advantage of not leaving a tell-tale stream of bubbles above and behind the swimmer, making it ideal for clandestine diving work.

Ward strapped his wickedly sharp diving knife to the inside of his right calf, and then another smaller one to his left forearm. Then he clipped a small underwater camera to his buoyancy vest. Grabbing his fins and mask, Ward made his way slowly down the beach and out into the dark waters of the bay. Taking a final compass bearing on his target, he adjusted his goggles and swam away from shore. Seconds later he disappeared from Beaman's view.

The churning tropical waters were pleasantly warm. Certainly warm enough that he did not necessarily need the wetsuit. On this swim, the suit was mostly to help him stay hidden. Ward had barely gone a hundred yards when he stopped to take a bearing and vent some water into the suit. There did not seem to be much current, but the increased sea state had kicked up enough silt from the bottom to make the water very cloudy. Visibility was barely twenty feet. Even the IR dive light did not help penetrate the murk.

The swim, a little over a mile, took the SEAL almost thirty minutes. Dousing the IR light, he came shallow, just close enough to the surface that he could make out the dim pier lights. He had very little chance of being seen in the choppy dark water, even if he stuck his head above the surface, but there was no reason to risk it.

Sure enough, he had come up thirty yards off the pier, to the stern of the yacht. Time to go to work. Ward dropped down and headed for the bottom.

Ψ

Elliot had been recruited to spell Beaman at watching through the binoculars while the SEAL captain prepared to give Admiral Donnegan an update by cellphone. The cabbie suddenly gasped.

"Mr. B., you need see this!"

Beaman dropped the phone and gazed through the scope. Despite the downpour, he could see the stern of the yacht, where two of the boat's crew were donning SCUBA gear. They were obviously getting ready to roll over the side, into the water. Glancing at his watch, Beaman did some quick mental calculations. Ward would almost certainly have arrived at the marina by now.

He grabbed his crutches and moved as quickly as he could through the tangled undergrowth, heading toward the taxi. He called back over his shoulder to Elliot, "Come on! We need to roll now!"

Ψ

Ward sensed more than heard the two divers drop into the water above him. He was hand-over-handing the thick umbilical back from the yacht, working his way toward whatever was on the other end of the cables. That was when he realized he was no longer by himself.

He let go of the cable, grabbed the big diving knife strapped to his calf, and swam as hard as he could for the shallow bottom. Shallow or not, he would be better off down there where there was at least one direction from which nobody could sneak up on him. Powerful kicks brought him not only to the muddy bottom but also to what was hooked to the end of the cable. He immediately recognized what was clearly a submersible robot vehicle of some kind.

So that was what they were trying to recover! Now, what were a Russian spy and his henchmen doing with an ROV tied to a yacht in the Bahamas, only a few miles from a stealth submarine facility? Ward knew that he had stumbled onto something very interesting. And probably very dangerous. Whatever was going on here, the SEAL knew that he had only a few seconds to act.

Suddenly two golden lances of light pierced the gloom above and behind Ward. Two swimmers were rapidly approaching from above, likely bound for the ROV. Their bright lights implied that they did not expect to find anyone else down there.

If they had not already, they would soon spot Ward in the dense silt below them. He quickly reached down and unpinned the steel lifting cable from the submersible device. With a couple of knife strokes, he severed the electrical umbilical as well, completely separating the ROV from the surface. That would make their problem a whole lot more difficult to solve regardless of what happened to him in the next few minutes.

The light from one of the other divers danced across Ward

as he finished. They had seen him now for sure. They swam in fast and hard, obviously skilled in this sort of thing. Both had their knives drawn, ready to fight. Ward pretended he had not yet seen his attackers, and then, just as the first swimmer arrived, he deftly ducked the man's lunge while he parried the knife with the blade of his own weapon. The man spun off, trying to reorient himself in the three-dimensional fight.

The second swimmer closed in, diving at the SEAL before he had a chance to recover from the first attack. Ward felt the knife bite hard into his left shoulder as he spun to meet the onrushing diver. Avoiding the instinct to slash wildly, ignoring the pain and billowing blood from the stab, he drew back and waited for the exact instant when he knew he could thrust the knife for best advantage, the slightest opening he instinctively knew would come. It would be his only chance.

The SEAL's knife plunged into flesh and bone, then severed the attacker's air hose as he slashed upward with all his strength. Suddenly the dingy water was filled with crimson bubbles and the attacking diver disappeared in the wall of venting air.

Ward turned to again face the first man, fully expecting to find the Russian on top of him already. But he was not there, instead swimming wildly upward and away, wanting no part of the enraged SEAL. Ward could see a pair of flippers beating a hasty retreat toward the yacht.

He struggled to control his wild breathing as he clutched his wounded shoulder, trying to stop the bleeding with direct pressure. It was a serious wound. He needed to get ashore and stop the bleeding.

Ward swam back toward Beaman and the beach. It would be a long, very painful transit. His left arm was no longer responding to his will and would soon be useless.

He steeled himself for the effort as he stayed deep, kicking away.

Ψ

The racing taxi squealed into the marina parking lot and screeched to a halt in front of the padlocked gate that blocked the roadway down to the piers. Beaman grabbed his crutches from the back seat, checked that his Glock 40 was locked and loaded, and then hobbled to the gate. He was about to shoot the lock off when he realized that the hasp was not engaged. The gate swung open freely.

He shouted over his shoulder for Elliot to stay where he was and call for backup from NURF BAL. Beaman well knew that the small detachment of rent-a-cop security guards at the lab would take a half hour or more to arrive, even if they were not asleep on the job. Any confrontation would be long over before that. But he did not want to involve the helpful taxi driver in what was sure to be a very dangerous situation. Better to leave him up here to direct the cavalry.

Beaman rounded the corner of the yacht house. The Voyager was tied up at the end of the nearest pier, and frenzied activity was occurring on its stern. A diver was being helped aboard by one of the crew while Alexi yelled and gestured wildly.

The Russian grabbed something from the deck and threw it out into the water as far as he could. Seconds later the surface of the bay humped up in a boiling cauldron. An underwater explosion ripped the night.

He had thrown a hand grenade! He was trying to stun or kill Jim Ward with the concussion!

Beaman grabbed the Glock from its holster and, with both hands around the gun and using his crutches as support, fired off two quick rounds. Just as he shot, Alexi Markov bent to grab another grenade off the deck. Both shots went zinging harmlessly over the Russian's head.

Then, as Beaman sent two more shots his way, Markov reared back to throw. One of the rounds caught Markov in his right shoulder, and the grenade fell from his hand onto the deck as the force of the bullet knocked him off his feet.

For an instant the world stood still. Even the freshening wind seemed to hold its breath in anticipation.

Then Alexi Markov leapt off the boat just as the grenade's blast ripped the stern open. When the wind blew the smoke clear, Beaman could see that two of the crewmembers were slumped over the transom of the burning vessel, which had already begun to list and sink, taking on water quickly.

Somehow, instinctively, Bill Beaman knew that Alexi Markov had cleared the vessel before it exploded. Rats had a way of surviving any catastrophe.

Then, out in the water about fifty yards or more, Beaman could just make out something in the first early light. Something bobbing in the surging waves.

Jim Ward! And he was lifeless, not moving, making no attempt to swim. The first grenade explosion must have done its job, knocking him unconscious. Or killing him.

Beaman staggered on his crutches down to the end of the pier and, without hesitating or even considering an armed Markov could be stalking him, jumped into the churning water. Using his arms and what little he could of his good leg, he beat a path directly to the stricken SEAL.

It was a tough go. As he rode up and over the incoming waves, it felt like every roller was pushing him back toward the marina. In frustration and rage he grabbed handfuls of water, using every ounce of strength to cover the distance as quickly as he could manage.

Finally he reached Ward. The young SEAL was unconscious, barely breathing. Beaman reached down and inflated Ward's buoyancy vest so his head was held clear of the waves. Turning back toward the marina, Beaman began a steady one-armed stroke, towing Ward with the other arm.

It seemed like forever before he hit the sandy bottom with the knee of his bad leg, sending pain shooting up through his hip.

Thank goodness Elliot had disobeyed his order to stay back and now stood at the water's edge, waiting for them. He waded in and helped drag both SEALs onto the sand next to the marina pier.

Gasping for breath, Beaman sat up. A thick trail of blood led from young Ward back into the water. He looked at the kid, his fellow SEAL, the son of his best friend.

If the boy was breathing at all, it was barely. Off in the distance, Beaman could just make out the wail of an approaching siren.

15

_____

Alexi Markov was flailing wildly as he swam the last few laborious, painful strokes to the narrow beach. A wave smashed him to his knees just as his feet touched the sand bottom, and he struggled to pull himself back up to the surface without swallowing too much more seawater. The pain where the bullet had ripped into his shoulder was almost more than he could stand as he struggled out of the water, crawling on his hands and knees. Finally able to stand, he gasped for breath, retching, coughing, and spitting to clear his lungs and throat.

Only then did he look back up the shoreline toward the marina, the pier, and the burning hulk of his yacht. As he watched, what was left of the vessel slid beneath the waves with a whoosh of steam and smoke. His career—and likely his life—went down with the boat. His bosses did not tolerate failure.

Beyond the pier, Alexi could just make out a shadowy form tugging what appeared to be something heavy from the water. Before the man was obscured by blowing rain, he dragged his load into the glow from the floodlight at the foot of the pier. Markov immediately recognized the man. Bill Beaman. No surprise that the SEAL was the one who had wrecked the recovery of the ROV and sent his boat and crew to the bottom of the bay. But how had he known they were at the marina? What they were up to? Had he been the one the crewmembers struggled with at the ROV?

Markov gritted his teeth, as much in anger as pain. He would take care of Beaman as soon as he was able. And, if possible, still find a way to retrieve the ROV. That might just be enough to save the spy from the ultimate wrath of his superiors even if his black ops career was now certainly unsalvageable.

He shoved aside his anger and frustration. Right now he needed to disappear into the maw of the approaching storm. It was time to hide, find medical help, mend, and then he could see what he could do to make sure that Captain Beaman would no longer be around to prevent the Russian spy—or his successors—from doing what had to be done.

Ψ

Bill Beaman caught a glimpse of Markov's shadowy figure as he stood and ran across the narrow beach and into the undergrowth. There was no hope of pursuing him. Besides, the SEAL was plenty busy, desperately trying to stop the ominous bleeding from Jim Ward's shoulder wound. Though he would have relished catching the bastard and coaxing his story from him, right now there was far more important work at hand. He would deal with the fleeing spy later. He would be unlikely to get off the island in the midst of a hurricane. And Beaman would find him, wherever he took to ground.

Although the knife gash across Ward's shoulder was nasty enough, and even though the young SEAL had bled a good bit, Beaman was far more concerned about the apparent concussion from the explosions in the water. Ward's breathing was barely detectable and his pulse was weak and erratic. Beaman knew that the kid was desperately clinging to life. He needed to get Ward to real medical help and fast.

"We need to move him now!" Beaman shouted to Elliot, who watched, wide-eyed, the wind and rain lashing his face.

"No problem, mon," the cabbie replied. He stepped over, lifted Ward, and slung him across his shoulders, employing a surprisingly good fireman's carry, then struck out toward his waiting hack. Again Beaman wondered if this guy was really nothing more than a cab driver on a sleepy island in the Atlantic.

However, he did not have time to do much speculating. Beaman turned and stumbled forward, doing his best to help Elliot get the unconscious young SEAL the help he so urgently needed. If anything, the blowing wind had grown even stronger, whipping the sand and driving rain with equal force, beating their exposed skin raw with its power. Palm fronds skittered across the parking lot, threatening to tackle them. For what was supposed to be a glancing blow, this damn hurricane was sure packing one hell of a punch already.

Elliot laid Ward in the back seat while Beaman climbed in the other side of the taxi, cradling the SEAL's head in his lap and resuming pressure on the wound.

"NURF BAL and quick!" Beaman ordered, but Elliot was already cranking up and jerking the vehicle into gear.

The taxi skewed sideways as a gust of wind hit them just as Elliot kicked the gas pedal hard. He twisted the steering wheel to regain control and sent out a spray of crushed coral from the rear tires as they shot out onto the deserted road.

Beaman awkwardly dialed Tank Anthony's number on his cell phone. The doctor answered on the second ring. After listening to the hurried report on Jim Ward's condition, he immediately re-directed them to Exuma International Airport. There was neither the time nor the facilities to treat Ward on the island. He needed heavy-duty care and he needed it immediately.

Ψ

The gray sky had given way to a sickly yellow color by the time the two cars arrived at the airport. The sun had risen above the horizon and was trying to break through the ominous wall of deep black clouds that filled the eastern sky. Neither the taxi nor Anthony's rental hesitated at the airfield gate. Both rolled directly into the big open doorway on the leeward side of one of the large gray metal hangars that lined the taxiway. This building had been leased by NURF BAL to handle logistics shipments. As part of the deal, the Navy made certain the structure was able to remain operable, if possible, even in the middle of a hurricane. Now the large steel building afforded some protection from the howling wind and driving rain.

Tank Anthony was just completing his quick examination of Jim Ward when they heard the heavy, high-pitched whine of twin turbines. Then they watched through the downpour as the MV-22 Osprey aircraft flared to descend almost vertically, make a short run across the tarmac, and stop next to the hangar. The after door was already down, and two airmen, lugging a stretcher, came running toward them before the bird had even come to a complete stop near the entrance.

"Lieutenant Ward?" asked the senior man, wearing the twin bars of a lieutenant. Beaman and Anthony both pointed to the near-lifeless man at their feet as the lieutenant stated the obvious. "Look, we need to move quickly. Conditions are marginal and getting worse. Let's get everyone aboard."

They lifted Jim Ward into the stretcher and hurriedly strapped him down. The two airmen picked him up and double-timed back toward the plane as Dr. Anthony ran alongside them.

Bill Beaman did not move.

"Captain," the lieutenant yelled over the wind and engine noise. "We need to get airborne."

Beaman waved for them to go on without him. "I still have unfinished business here," he declared.

"We have orders, Captain," the lieutenant protested. "To evacuate one injured man, Dr. Anthony, and you. To get you all out ahead of this storm." He waved back toward the open hangar doors. Right now, "ahead of the storm" seemed impossible. Most of the top of a king palm blew past the doorway, narrowly missing the plane's nose.

"Well, your orders just changed," Beaman answered with a sideways smile. "I suggest you get moving while you can still get that ugly aircraft of yours off the ground. Take care of that SEAL for me."

The lieutenant shook his head but turned and ran toward the Osprey. He and the rest disappeared into the aircraft. Beaman and Elliot stood there in the hangar, water dripping from their drenched clothes, and watched as the bird did a short take-off roll and disappeared to the west, away from the power of the storm. The plane was immediately lost in the swirling wind and deluge. Even the rumble of its engines was overpowered by the wail of the hurricane.

"Well, guess we'd better find ourselves a place to hunker down until this little blow is over with," Beaman said to the taxi driver. Hurricane resistant or not, he did not want to stay any longer than he had to in the hangar. The thing could cause one major headache if it decided to come crashing down. "Then I am going snake hunting. Got a good place in mind?"

Elliot smiled and winked.

"The Peace and Plenty. I think she be as good as any. The old place has weathered many a big wind. I hope it'll get us through this one."

Ψ

Joe Glass stared disbelievingly at the barometer. The instrument had been steadily dipping for the last couple of days, but now the bottom had fallen out of the damn thing. It now read twenty-eight-point-five inches of mercury and was dropping so quickly that Glass swore that he could see the needle twitching.

The XO, Billy Ray Jones, dashed from the passageway into the wardroom where Joe Glass was enjoying a solitary cup of coffee while he quietly worried. Jones held the aluminum message board in his hand. He was out of breath.

"Skipper, SUBLANT is ordering us to do an emergency storm deployment. They are authorizing an emergency start-up and heat-up. Orders are to get to deep water and submerged as soon as possible. Evidently this Hurricane Penny is the real deal."

"Show me that, Billy Ray," Glass said as he snatched the board from the XO. He glanced quickly at the single sheet of paper.

"I guess they've been getting their storm forecast from Channel 7 Action News! Looks like the thing didn't take the turn north they expected and now they tell us we better haul ass." He looked up at the XO. "Grab the Engineer and get a condition-two watch stationed aft ASAP. Doug knows what to do, but stay with him for some adult supervision. Make sure everyone understands the emergency start-up/heat-up procedure and get the pre-crit going. I'll have the COB to get things moving up here. I don't know what they'll do with these barges but that's not our problem at the moment."

Billy Ray Jones nodded as he ducked back out the wardroom doorway. A thousand details whirled through the XO's head as he went in search of Doug O'Malley. The next few hours would be very busy. Had they been at sea, this would have simply been a matter of going deeper, away from the raging storm. No matter the weather on the surface of the sea, there was calm water several hundred feet down. Now, with technicians leaving doors and panels open and exposed all over the boat, which was still harnessed to a couple of monstrous barges, it would be much more complicated to get ready, pull away, and dive deep.

Joe Glass was just leaving the wardroom when the outside phone rang. Since that line was only connected to the NUWC barges, only a limited number of people could be calling. Obviously they had just received the orders to scram, too.

The skipper grabbed the receiver from its cradle.

"*Toledo*, Commander Glass."

"Captain, this is Sam Smithski." The senior NUWC engineer's voice sounded as if he was on the ragged edge of panic. "I have a very big problem over here. We've been ordered to evacuate the barges but the winds are already blowing so bad and the seas are so rough that I don't think it's safe for my people to take a boat to shore right now."

"Sam, I don't think they would have told you to evacuate if..."

Smithski interrupted Glass.

"Captain, you don't have the vantage point I do. It's damn rough out there and they're telling us it will get worse. I'd need to make at least two and maybe three runs with the work boat to get everybody off these barges and to Exuma. I've got a hundred and thirty-five men and women out here. Now the Navy is telling me that Penny will be a category-five hurricane when it hits us. Category five! She's taking them all by surprise, the way she suddenly blew up and didn't go to the north. These barges were not built to survive that. What am I supposed to do?" Smithski was almost in tears.

Glass took a deep breath. There was really nothing to decide, or any other option.

"Sam, get your people down and onboard *Toledo* as quickly as you can. It might be a little cozy for the next couple of days, but I think we can handle it."

"Thank you! Thank you, Captain."

Joe Glass hung up and went searching for the Chief of the Boat. They already had a lot of work to do to prepare to get underway, and now they also had to get ready for company. Just then the 1MC announcing system crackled to life.

"Commencing an emergency reactor start-up. Dosimetry is required in the engineering spaces."

Glass grinned. Jones and O'Malley were certainly busy already.

Glass found Sam Wallich, the Chief of the Boat, topside busily inspecting the mooring lines that had been holding the submarine securely between the two barges. The wind had built up so much that it was hard to speak and be heard over its bellowing, and the seas were strong enough to strain mightily the doubled mooring lines, even with the protection of the two huge barges, which were now rocking noticeably. It was already a dangerous situation. If one of the lines snapped, it could cut a man in half.

"COB," Glass yelled, "I need you to rig lifelines and get the civilian workers over here and below-decks without feeding any of them to the sharks."

Wallich nodded and yelled back, "I kind of figured that. Got a team rigging safety lines to the forward escape trunk. We'll move 'em to the torpedo room and mess decks for now so they won't be in the way." The chief motioned toward a group of sailors straining at a heavy Kevlar line up on the submarine's bow. "Right now, I'm a lot more concerned about rigging storm mooring until we can get out of here. I've re-enforced the night riders fore and aft. Then I'm adding extra spring lines at cleats four and five on both sides. I sure as hell hope that holds."

Glass nodded grimly. Of all the *Toledo*'s seamen, Sam Wallich had more experience at this sort of thing than any three of the others put together. "Good thinking, COB. It's going to make getting underway a little slower but it will sure help to hold us reasonably steady."

A blast of salt spray stung Glass's face as the wind sent his hat off his head and skidding across the water.

Glass wiped the spray from his eyes and then dropped down the forward escape trunk hatch. From there, he quickly climbed the ladder to the upper level. In the control room, he found his navigator, Jerry Perez, poring over charts at the after plotting table.

"Nav, I need you to take charge forward and make preps to get us underway."

Perez nodded and gave Glass a thumbs-up.

"Got you covered, Skipper. I just talked to the XO. Pre-underways are in progress. We'll be ready to go when the Eng has the reactor up. Ain't going to be pretty, but we'll make it. Weps is working on buttoning up all the shipyard work to support the underway. He's down in the torpedo room making sure all the hull penetrations are good. We ain't going to have any SUBSAFE certifications for this underway."

"Well, we sure as hell don't have time for the paperwork. We'll catch up on that later. Let's concentrate on getting out of here safe, and in the process let's try to keep the water out of the people tank."

"Roger that, Skipper," Perez said with a smile.

Glass stole a glance at the barometer. It read twenty-seven-point-five inches now. My God! It had dropped an inch in just a little over an hour! This hurricane was promising to be a real screamer!

Joe Glass dropped down to the torpedo room. The first of the NUWC engineers and workers were already trooping onboard, looking scared and worried as they huddled in little groups, watching all the activity around them.

"The reactor is critical," the 1MC announced. Some of the NUWC workers now looked even more worried, but the engineers among the group assured them "reactor critical" was a good thing.

Pat Durand jumped up as Glass strode into the torpedo room.

"Skipper, we're just closing out the last work package now. Believe it or not, most of these systems are ready to test. We may actually be productive on this underway."

Glass smiled, pleased with his weapons officer's enthusiasm and flexibility.

"Okay, Weps. But let's get out of this big garage in one piece first. Then we'll worry about testing the new stuff."

The 1MC blared once more. "The reactor is at the point of adding heat. Commencing an emergency reactor heat-up."

This told Glass that it would not be long now. Time to get the last of the NUWC staff aboard and below decks. They should also be getting the maneuvering watch stationed.

As if Jerry Perez were reading his mind, the Nav's voice rang out over the 1MC, ordering, "Station the maneuvering watch. Line handlers lay topside."

Glass stopped by his tiny stateroom to grab a rain slicker and safety harness before he climbed to the bridge. It promised to be a wet, rough hour or so before they would be able to drive into open water and submerge the boat.

Sam Smithski stopped by to speak to Glass as he was pulling on his foul-weather gear.

"Commander, I am eternally in your debt," the engineer told him. "All my people are now onboard your ship. The barges have been evacuated. I don't know what we would have done if you hadn't helped us." Smithski was shaking noticeably. "You and your crew have saved us all."

Glass shook the offered hand, then told the engineer to take a seat in his stateroom since it might be a little rough going for the next little bit.

"Why don't you rest here? I'll have one of the mess specialists bring you some coffee."

As he began the long climb to the bridge, Glass heard another 1MC announcement reverberate throughout the boat.

"The electric plant is in a normal half-power line-up on the port turbine generator. Divorcing from shore power."

The skipper doubted if the shore power cables would be carefully craned back over to the barge, as was the usual procedure. In this situation and with the necessary urgency, the sailors on deck probably just dropped them over the side.

Glass poked his head out above the bridge combing and was smacked rudely in the face by a howling gale. The wind now blew the rain and sea spray horizontal.

Pat Durand was already on the bridge, huddling in a protected corner. "Evening, Skipper," he yelled above the roar of the wind. "Maneuvering reports that the reactor is in the green band. Propulsion is on the main engines. The outboard is lowered and shifted to remote. The electric plant is in a normal full-power line up."

"Very well," Glass yelled back. "Let's get out of here. Single up lines three and five. Cast off lines one, two, four, and six."

The singled spring lines would keep *Toledo* from being pushed forward while they maneuvered to back out from between the barges. Bumping into one of the barges could damage the submarine's fiberglass bow.

"Take a strain on lines three and five."

The line handlers would keep those ropes taut and use raw muscle power to prevent the seven-thousand-ton submarine from being shoved forward.

As they waited for the line handlers to complete their tasks, Glass yelled over to Durand to explain the tricky maneuver they were about to attempt.

"Weps, we're going to back out of here. As soon as the stern clears the barges, I expect the wind to catch her and push the stern over, and that could cause us to crash into the starboard barge. The rudder is not going to have much effect going astern, but put it left full to let the pump wash push us to port." Durand nodded and gestured that he understood. Glass went on, his voice cracking with the strain of yelling, "Train the outboard to port nine-zero. Let's pray that the rudder and outboard are enough to counter the wind. Otherwise, we're going to put a big old dent in the taxpayers' nice submarine."

The phone talker, crouched down in the bridge access, yelled up to Glass.

"Captain, topside reports lines one, two, four, and six are cast off. Lines three and five singled and being held taut."

"Very well. Mr. Durand, back one-third."

The big submarine started to inch backward. As the stern cleared the meager protection afforded by the barges, the seas immediately swept over the after deck. If the line handlers had not been wearing safety harnesses, they would have instantly been swept over the side and lost.

"Cast off line five!" Glass yelled to the phone talker. "After line handlers lay below." The captain looked back aft of the sail in time to see the lines drop and disappear into the churning water. "Cast off line three. Forward line handlers lay below. Shut the upper escape trunk hatch."

Glass watched as the last pair of lines fell into the maelstrom. Waves were already churning up and over the deck, pouring a cascade of seawater down the open hatch. There would be a mess to clean up below decks, but the drain pump could certainly keep up with the deluge.

Out on the deck, a soaked Sam Wallich saluted up to Glass, who returned the gesture. Then the Chief of the Boat dropped down the hatch and swung it shut after him.

As Glass predicted, the howling wind shoved the big submarine's stern toward the starboard barge. Colliding with the barge would be catastrophic for that vessel but would significantly damage the submarine as well. The worst scenario was for them to become entangled and for *Toledo* to be unable to break free. If this storm intensified much more, as it was expected to, such a thing would be a real disaster. Everyone on *Toledo* would be in mortal danger.

"Left full rudder," Durand ordered. Glass could hardly hear him though he shouted into the microphone. "Start the outboard. Back two-thirds."

In response to Glass's questioning look, Durand yelled, "Figured the quicker we get clear of here, the less time the wind has to hurt us."

Glass nodded in agreement, simultaneously shaking raindrops off his nose and forehead. Then he watched the starboard barge as it loomed ever closer. As the submarine's sail passed the barge's stern, Glass's concern shifted. Now there was considerable risk of *Toledo*'s bow slamming into the port barge as the wind pushed them sideways in the narrow space. Glass held his breath, silently praying that he had calculated correctly.

"Back full!" he yelled over to Durand. Maybe a final spurt of speed would be enough to push them clear.

Then, just when it appeared the tempest would have its way with the powerful submarine, the bow barely eased past and clear of the barge. They had made it. By a mere few inches, but they had escaped. Now they needed to skedaddle before the hurricane blew them right back from where they had just come.

"Mr. Durand, come around to a course of two-seven-zero," Glass ordered. "Ahead one-third. Rig the bridge for dive. Let's get underwater, where we damn well belong."

Pat Durand smiled and responded with an enthusiastic, "Aye, sir."

The song of the dive klaxon had never sounded so sweet.

Ψ

Meanwhile, below decks in *Toledo*'s torpedo room, Sarah Wilder scowled as she sipped the coffee someone had given her. It was not at all satisfactory, much too strong and bitter.

She kept her thoughts to herself, though. At least she was no longer confined to the barge, which had begun to rock and sway ominously earlier that morning, waking her from a deep sleep. By the time she got to her office, some of her co-workers had already turned pale and begun feeling ill. Then came word that they were evacuating to the submarine.

Now here she sat on one of the torpedo skids, surrounded by fifty or sixty other NUWC engineers, technicians, and workmen, as the storm winds pitched the submarine around on the sea's surface. Still, though, she was glad to be headed for deeper, smoother, safer waters. She was also painfully aware of the irony of her rescue craft.

It was not the sudden evacuation or the rough ride that caused her to shudder as she looked around the cramped, crowded compartment. She was inside the beast that she hated so much. Hated not only the ship but all it stood for. Hated the fact that this war machine she was secretly plotting to help destroy was protecting her from the raging sea.

She took another sip of the acrid coffee but did not even

taste it this time. What could she do to strike a blow? What would Alexi or her father tell her to do?

Then, right there in the hated warship's torpedo room, surrounded by the machinery and systems designed to launch such lethal ordnance, inches from several of the horrible, death-dealing weapons, she felt her face flush at the mere thought of Alexi Markov. Felt that familiar funny flutter in her belly and her heart skip a beat.

Dear, dear Alexi. Where was he now when she needed him so much?

16

President Grigory Iosifovich Salkov re-read the terse report yet again. A slight smile slowly formed at the sharp corners of his mouth. Ignot Smirnov, the Russian Minister of Defense, and General Boris Lapidus, Chief of the General Staff, sat across the broad desk and watched as their leader digested the news.

The Russian president grabbed the remote and clicked on the large-screen TV at the far side of the room, flipping the channel over to the Russian language Al Jazeera channel. The picture flickered for a second and then focused on a large ship heeled over. Most of the screen was obscured by the smoke pouring from the burning hulk, but it was easy to see that the ship was sinking and that it was obstructing a very narrow channel. The talking head TV news reporter was jabbering about the ship striking a mine in the Suez Canal, something about the Al Firdar Reach and the canal now being totally blocked.

Salkov muted the audio. He rose from his desk and paced across the broad room, then turned and paced back again, looking lost in thought, as if he were planning his next chess move.

Then he mumbled, "Our Syrian friends got to Hezbollah.

And they actually pulled it off." Still pacing back and forth, Salkov went on, his voice a little louder, "Now we have two of the American carrier battle groups blocked out of the Atlantic. Only one more to go." A chilling smile appeared on the Russian leader's face. "And the most delicious part of this is that the Americans do not yet even know that they are in the game, let alone already in checkmate.

"General Lapidus, move as many armored and motorized divisions as you can muster to the Belarus-Lithuanian border," President Salkov directed, a grandmaster arranging his pieces on the board, arrayed for the final victory. "I want them ready to move on a moment's notice, prepared with plans to take Vilnius and establish a corridor all the way to the Kalingrad Oblast."

Next he turned to Smirnov and smiled broadly. It was all the Minister of Defense could do to suppress a fearful shudder.

"My dear Ignot," the president said. "I have two tasks for you. First, contact your agents in the *Generalnovo Shtaba*, the GRU. Have them stir up 'dissident' activity in the Kalingrad Oblast and in Lithuania so that we can claim it is necessary to come to the rescue of ethnic Russian citizens and protect other sovereign Russian property and interests in the region. Make very sure that this unrest and the ensuing violence is headlined in all the media."

Minister Smirnov nodded. The plan so far was the one they had long discussed and they and their predecessors had previously implemented with mixed results in other former Soviet countries.

"That will not be too difficult. We have personnel and plans in place already. And the second thing?"

"I need for you to jam the cork in the bottle," Salkov answered. "I want you to load out our new special missions submarine *Moscow* with all the mobile mines it can carry. If there is time to do so, load stealth equipment like we have on

Igor Borsovitch. Who is that crazy Cossack that commands *Igor Borsovitch*?"

Smirnov scanned his notes. "That would be Captain First Rank Konstantin Kursalin, Mr. President. Both submarines are in port in Polyarny, conveniently berthed next to each other. And with what exactly should we task them?"

Both Smirnov and Lapidus held their breath awaiting the president's answer.

"Both submarines will take the most direct course and make best possible speed to the US East Coast," Salkov responded. He was gazing at a map of the United States on his large computer screen. "Captain First Rank Konstantin Kursalin will protect the *Moscow* while she sends her mobile mines into the waters near the submarine base at Groton, Connecticut, the naval base at Norfolk, Virginia, and the submarine base at Kings Bay in the American state of Georgia. And then they will head south and plant the last few mines in the approaches to the Caribbean side of the Panama Canal. As the American term goes, 'that should put a real kink in their planning.'"

Smirnov and Lapidus gasped. They had guessed—even speculated between themselves—that this was where Salkov might be going. However, to actually hear the words from their president was disquieting. General Lapidus was first to speak.

"Grigory Iosifovich, this will be considered by most of the world, and certainly the Americans, as an act of war. And, of course, the Americans will never stand for such provocation well within their own territorial waters."

President Grigory Iosifovich Salkov laughed until he broke into a deep cough. He slapped the table in front of him with an open hand, spat into his handkerchief, and then laughed and coughed some more. The admiral and the minister could only sit there quietly until he finished.

"Gentlemen, there is no chance the US will do any more

than what they usually do nowadays. First, they will make certain their general public never knows of our daring mining of their submarine bases. They will never admit to the voters or to the world that they lack the ability to prevent such action. When we retake the territories that are rightfully ours, they will rant and rave in front of the UN Security Council, posture in their press, and make threats we know for certain they will never consummate. America has become a toothless tiger led by a mewling kitten who is more affected by his beloved opinion polls than by any actions we may take. After Vietnam and then Iraq and Afghanistan, the Americans no longer have the stomach for war. While their far right will fume and fuss, they will do nothing of substance. On the contrary, President Whitten will secretly come groveling to us, ready to do anything we ask while he tries to make himself look strong and decisive to the voters and the media. He must do that before they learn of what *Moscow* has accomplished at their most secure harbors."

"Mr. President, I must..." Smirnov began, but Salkov raised his hand, shutting off his protest.

"Ignot, I should not have to remind you that I am not merely guessing how the American leader will react. I know precisely how this crisis will play out because I know President Whitten. I know him by deed and by word. I know what he has told me in private. He is flailing politically. His party whispers of replacing him with a stronger candidate next election, one who will keep his promises about reducing world tensions and negotiating to avoid war at all costs. He needs a showdown with Russia to make him appear tough but without risking any kind of actual military confrontation, so he will avoid any more risk of clashes like he did with the most recent events between our respective submarines. He is perfectly willing to blather and posture and condemn while secretly avoiding conflict until we have reclaimed our lost union and, with it, our rightful place as the world's foremost power. The rest of the world? They will be no worry to us once we have called Whitten's bluff. They will not even have the means to enforce their laughable sanctions against us."

When the president paused for breath, his defense minister dared to ask a question.

"But why is it necessary to mine their bases? We might accidentally sink a warship. Not even such a weak and misguided president as Whitten could ignore such provocation. And mining the canal could bring an international condemnation."

Grigory Iosif Salkov smiled so coldly that both men shivered.

"No, Whitten will do nothing. Not even if we blow to hell several of their ships. That I know. But there are those in the US military who are not so timid. We must make certain they are not able to send stealthy submarines or some other warships to retaliate on the high seas. Control of the seas is vital. With their warships bottled up, they have no way to come to the defense of their NATO allies. And we must stop them from swinging their Pacific fleet into the Atlantic. That is the reason for the mining, gentlemen. And we need to make sure that we do not lose *Moscow* or *Igor Borsovitch*. We will need them, you see, for the next phase."

"The next phase?" both men asked simultaneously.

But now the Russian president had changed the map on the monitor to concentrate on a different part of the world, a collection of countries surrounding a large blue area marked "Baltic Sea."

Ψ

The hurricane's winds screamed like an enraged banshee. Bill Beaman had to strain to hear the flickering television over the noise, even though it was playing at full volume. The announcer, ensconced in relative safety at the ZNS Bahama station in Nassau, was showing video of surf crashing over the beach at the posh resorts nearby. Hurricane Penny was building to truly historic strength, packing winds estimated at better than one-hundred-sixty miles per hour. Storm surge of at least forty feet was expected on the outer islands. Devastation would be widespread.

With the hotel windows covered by thick sheets of plywood, it was impossible for the SEAL or Elliot to see what was happening outside. For a moment, a loud crunching, tearing crash overpowered the roar of the wind, and Beaman dared to crack open the door to take a peek. He used all his strength and braced himself against the jamb to keep the door from being yanked from his hands. The sky was black as a moonless night although the TV clock read a little past noon. A large, heavy metal roof, torn from some building downwind, skittered across the street as if it were nothing more than a piece of trash. Even through the wall of rain and darkness, Beaman could see surf crashing over the pier and seawall. Waters from the harbor rushed between what was left of the palm trees adjacent to the hotel and into the swimming pool mere feet from where he stood. It looked like a tsunami.

"Elliot!" he yelled above the wind as he wrestled the door shut. "We'd better get on the upper deck now. Otherwise we may get our feet wet."

"Thinkin' you may be right, Mr. B," the cabbie answered. "I been packin' the essentials already." He tossed a backpack to Beaman and lifted a pair of large duffel bags. "Let's be movin' our asses," he said as he stepped toward the door.

Beaman threw the backpack over his shoulder and grabbed his crutches. When Elliot opened the door, Penny ripped it off its hinges and flung it away. Both men stepped onto the walkway that ran in front of the ground-level rooms. Fighting the wind's sheer power and using every bit of strength they could muster, they moved as quickly as they could toward the stairs at the far end of the brick building. The stairway gave some meager protection as Beaman awkwardly made his way, one step at a time, up toward the second floor. He had help from Elliot, who braced him from behind until he got stable on each stair.

Once on the second landing, they crashed into the first room they came to. Since the hotel was long since evacuated, they had their choice of rooms. They shouldered their way through the door and flipped on the lights, which blinked once, twice, and then died altogether.

"Surprised the power lasted this long," Elliot yelled. "I better get the bathtub filled with water while we still have pressure."

"Funny time to be taking a bath," Beaman said with a quizzical look.

"Cap'n, once you been through as many of these blows as me, you learn a trick or two," Elliot responded. "Drinkin' water, she gonna be in real short supply for a while after this storm passes by. That bathtub will hold enough for several days if we be careful."

He stepped into the bathroom and turned the tap on full. By the time the tub was filled to the top, the water from the faucet was little more than a trickle.

Meanwhile, the two men sat on the floor in the dark, listening as the wind built in fury, the noise rising to almost unbearable levels. They heard the occasional crash as some structure broke apart and was hurtled past, or a palm tree gave up the fight, lost its grip in the sand, and blew into the wall facing the wind.

Then, just as the sound and fury hit an impossible peak, it

stopped, leaving an eerie, unearthly quiet. They could even hear the water dripping into the tub.

Beaman got to his feet and opened the door. There was bright sunshine and a beautiful blue sky overhead, but the destruction around the Peace and Plenty shocked him. The whole west wing and Ramon's bar were completely gone. So was the low office building that had stood next door to the hotel amid a garden of bougainvillea and stand of tall king palms. The vegetation had been scoured away, leaving nothing but a cement slab and remnants of plumbing and wiring poking up where the offices had been. A sizeable fishing boat now sat partially in the hotel swimming pool, listing to port. Water lapped halfway up the first-floor walls.

"Jesus, I've been in storms in my day, but this one was the worst," he said as he stepped out onto the walkway to survey more the damage.

"I believe we will find that this was only the first half," Elliot told him. "We now be in the eye. I reckon she will hit us again in a few minutes and it gone be even worse. Cap'n, you best get back in here and hold on to your shorts."

The cabbie was right. Beaman looked to the southeast and saw nothing but churning clouds and a barrage of rainfall quickly crossing the harbor and headed their way. He had no sooner shut the door than the rear wall of the eye slammed hard into the island. The howling, screaming wind did appear even worse, especially after the scant few minutes of silent stillness.

Without warning, the whole building started to shudder around them, the walls moving back and forth several feet and the floor bucking beneath them. Elliot grabbed Beaman by the collar and pulled him into the bathroom. The roof above them tore away and was gone in a second.

Bill Beaman had the barest glimpse of a swirling tempest of

a sky. It felt as if someone was dumping barrels of water on top of them. The force of the wind was lifting them off their feet.

Then everything went midnight black.

Ψ

The Norfolk waterfront was a madhouse of frenetic activity. Every Navy ship with any chance of getting underway was making every effort to escape the piers for the relatively safer open Atlantic waters. Every sailor knew that it was far better for the ships to be facing the wind-churned deep water than languishing with storm moorings holding them to the pier.

Fuel lighters scurried from ship to ship, topping off tanks while tugs pushed other ships out into the Elizabeth River. A steady stream of haze-gray ships filled the already choppy outbound channel beyond the Hampton Bay Bridge-Tunnel and Willoughby Spit. Aircraft from Naval Air Station Oceana and NAS Norfolk made a steady stream of similar gray-colored aircraft heading west to airfields far from Hurricane Penny's reach.

Pier 22, the submarine pier at the far end of the vast Norfolk Naval Base waterfront, was already empty. But that was pretty much normal anymore. With the majority of the much-diminished submarine fleet now homeported in the Pacific, the Atlantic-based boats were kept very busy. They were all out, forward deployed in the far north, off the coast of East Africa, or in the Arabian Sea.

The nearly new carrier *Gerald R Ford* sat bound to the pier. Deep in a planned maintenance period, both her reactors were shut down and her engine rooms were cold iron. It was impossible for the massive ship to get underway before Hurricane Penny visited the Hampton Roads area. Extra inflatable Yokohama camels were shoved between the carrier and the pier while massive wire cables were stretched from the ship to mooring bollards on the pier. Even the big vessel's anchors were walked out and now lay under the bow to help hold her as steady as possible against the expected winds and flood tides.

While the *Ford* was being braced to face the hurricane alongside the pier, the *Harry Truman* steamed past Chesapeake Light and headed out into the Atlantic while a bevy of destroyers rushed about to form a screen around the carrier.

It appeared much of the US Navy's assets in Norfolk were scattering ahead of the arrival of a mean-spirited gal named Penny.

Ψ

Joe Glass could actually feel the roll of *Toledo* beneath his feet. Incredibly, even six hundred feet below the maelstrom on the surface, Hurricane Penny still packed sufficient energy to slosh around a seven-thousand-ton submarine enough for its crew to notice.

Glass was in the middle of a slow tour of the boat to see that both his crew and his guests were all right. People were stuffed into every possible nook and cranny of his boat. Even the engine room had been pressed into service as a temporary lounge for evacuees from the barges.

Glass caught up with Doug O'Malley as he passed through engine room middle level aft. Some enterprising NUWCians had set up camp outboard of the R-114 air conditioning plants. The engineer was busy trying to convince them to not completely block the passage so his watch-standers could get by them on the narrow steel deck.

"How long we going to be playing cruise ship?" O'Malley whispered.

"Until SUBLANT tells us otherwise," Glass answered, then

pointed upward. "At least until that mess topside blows past and we can get into port somewhere to unload them. I think we best figure on the better part of a week."

"This is going to be one fun voyage," O'Malley commented drily. "I'm just glad that Sam Wilson and his NRRO weenies aren't anywhere close. He would have a shit fit if he saw all the people we got stowed back here."

Glass chuckled. "You know it. Count your blessings. Weps seems to think we may have the time to test some of our new wonder devices while we are out here under the storm. Think enough of the stuff is installed to do anything?"

"Sure. Most of the work packages were closed out before we got underway. Give my guys a couple of days with a few of the NUWC engineers and I think we can sign off on the rest of it."

"Good. We do have captive experts close by who don't have much else to do. I'm going to grab the Weps, the XO, and Dr. Smithski to come up with a plan. Why don't you meet us in the wardroom in half an hour?"

Joe Glass turned, climbed the ladder to engine room upper level, and disappeared forward.

Ψ

Sam Smithski was the last person to enter the wardroom. He brought Sarah Wilder with him. The two took seats at the far end of the table, opposite from where Glass sat with Billy Ray Jones, his exec, on his right and Doug O'Malley to his left. Pat Durand sat next to the XO. The Chief of the Boat, Sam Wallich, and Master Chief Randy Zillich, the sonar chief, sat across from Smithski and Wilder.

Joe Glass could still feel the slight movement of the submarine. So could the other crewmembers. The engineers did not seem to notice.

"Dr. Smithski, I expect that we will be stuck out here for at least a week. Maybe longer. It depends on how much damage Penny does to the pier facilities along the coast, assuming she is hitting stateside. As you know, this storm intensified and took a course that apparently surprised all the folks who are supposed to be able to predict such things. Anyway, it could be a positive thing for us even if it is ruining a lot of folks' day at the beach. I'd sure like to get some of the testing done out here to save as much schedule slippage as we can. What do you think?"

Before he answered, the NUWC scientist riffled through his pile of notes and cleared his throat several times, needing adequate data before confirming any postulation. The submariners sipped coffee as he studied. Sarah Wilder sat quietly, her face expressionless, as if her thoughts were a thousand miles away.

She was a beautiful woman, Glass noticed. Beautiful and obviously book-smart. But something about her gave him a bit of a bad feeling, though he wasn't sure what it was. But there was something. As a commander of men confined in close quarters and under tense situations for long periods of time, Joe Glass—like most good submarine skippers—had developed uncanny abilities when it came to sensing all the aspects of a person's demeanor, character, and likely performance when things got tough. He would figure out this attractive egghead before this adventure was over, too.

Finally, Smithski removed his thick-lensed and unfashionably-framed eyeglasses and began idly cleaning them with one of the wardroom napkins.

"Well, Captain, I believe we do have the opportunity to do some testing. I suggest we see if the ELF radar will operate within specified parameters. That is the most crucial system not yet verified. The only problem is we don't have any way to tune it in order to calibrate any returns. We really need a target at a known range to do the final adjustments."

Pat Durand spoke up. "Doc, we don't need any target to tune our BPS-15 radar. We just tune it into a dummy load."

Smithski smiled at the Weapons Officer with just the slightest hint of condescension.

"Normal radars such as your BPS-15 operate in the gigahertz range. We have dummy loads able to very easily handle their relative low power at that frequency. At the same time, the wave guides provide adequate shielding from electromagnetic interference that is necessarily generated. On the other hand, with the ELF system we are dealing with much lower frequencies, below one kilohertz, and with much higher power levels. A dummy load that could handle those frequencies and power would necessarily be much larger than this submarine, I am afraid. And if it was not adequately shielded, the EMI would instantly fry all the electronic circuits onboard the ship."

Durand was mid-sip. He almost strangled on the coffee.

"Whoa! You mean I have panels down there in the torpedo room that could generate enough EMI to make charcoal out of all our electronic systems?"

Smithski nodded. "Yes. That is precisely what I mean."

Durand set his cup down on the table, his eyes wide.

"Doc, those are warshot weapons down there! Each one of the torpedoes has enough PBXN in the warhead to have us singing with the angels if something, like stray EMI, sets it off. The electronic circuits would be the least of our problems if something glitches."

Smithski smiled again, now comfortable in his element, explaining complicated subjects to those not in the know.

"Don't worry, Lieutenant. We built those systems with triple redundant shielding and automatic cutouts if there is any fault. You and your weapons are perfectly safe."

Joe Glass had been quiet, deep in thought.

"I think I may have an idea for a target that we might be able to use for calibration. Let's get us a refill on the coffee and maybe we can still make some chicken salad out of all this chicken shit."

Sarah Wilder had remained silent throughout the conversation, apparently listening. But now she had the merest hint of a smile on her lips. Those around the table might have assumed she was pleased with the efforts to stay on schedule with the project in which she was such a key cog.

Not at all. She now saw her chance to do what she had agreed to do, for the cause of peace, for Alexi.

Now she just had to find a way to be well clear and safe when it all came crashing down.

17

The long, broad pier at the Polyarny submarine base was a clamor of frenzied activity. Captain First Rank Konstantin Kursalin, commanding officer of the submarine *Igor Borsovitch*, was most appreciative that the entire facility was hidden beneath a huge roof. Otherwise, the American spy satellites would have long since warned their military that something unusual was afoot here, something major. That would have assured that the US submarines perpetually hovering just outside the mouth of Kola Bay in the dark, cold Barents Sea would be on high alert, waiting for him to emerge.

Kursalin was also thankful for the cover because it shielded him from the heavy sleet that was falling. Though it was still early October, winter had arrived in the Murmansk Oblast.

While his ship was getting its share of attention, the gigantic new submarine *Moscow* garnered most of the activity. Tractor-trailers lined up beneath the cover of the big shed to await their turn to disgorge cargoes of deadly cylindrical SMDM Mod 6 mobile mines.

The dark-green weapons looked sinister even sitting on their cradles. Guided by GPS, the mines would swim more than fifty kilometers into enemy harbors before sinking to the bottom at the precise location where they could do the most damage. There they would lurk, awaiting their prey. These killers could blow the bottom out of any ship unlucky enough to come close. But these mines were both smart and tenacious. They carefully selected their prey and even stalked it once the selected victim floated by. When triggered, the mine could rise and swim down the target's backwash, just like a wake-homing torpedo, before blasting the target with nearly five hundred kilos of high explosives. Properly placed, the mine would not only sink the ship but also assure its victim would block the ship channel for a very long time.

Kursalin turned to watch the latest batch of mines being hoisted aboard the *Moscow*. He could see that Captain First Rank Igor Nomor, the skipper of the newer vessel, stood at her brow, also watching the ongoing work. As young men, Nomor and Kursalin had been classmates at the N.G. Kuznetsov Naval Academy in Saint Petersburg. Later, they had competed for command at their alma mater's Advanced Specialists Officers Course for Submarine Command. Though not exactly friends, the two officers knew each other well. Nomor had used his family influence, in addition to his innate skills, to take the plum assignment as commander of the *Moscow*. Despite how the assignment came about, Kursalin was also well aware that Nomor was a good submarine commander and fully deserved the ship, unlike many others in his navy who received their assignments by bribe or birthright or both, not ability or promise.

At nearly nineteen thousand metric tons, the *Moscow* dwarfed Kursalin's *Igor Borsovitch*. The giant black submarine had only recently completed an extensive conversion from a Delta IV ballistic missile submarine into a special-purpose boat fully capable of carrying out a dazzling variety of potential missions. She could deploy whole companies of armed Spetnaz fighters in mini-submarines or launch swarms of deadly cruise missiles. Of course, she was also able to launch torpedoes and a host of other weapons at enemy vessels or spread sensors and other detection devices like seeds. Today she was being loaded as a submerged mine layer.

"Igor, my friend," Kursalin shouted, and waved for his counterpart to join him on the pier. When Nomor got there, Kursalin enveloped the smaller man in a powerful bear hug. "It has been a long time!"

Nomor could not move. He could do little more than nod and try to breathe.

"Yes," he managed. "Now...we are to sail together." Finally, Kursalin released his grip and Nomor stepped back. "Will you come aboard *Moscow* and enjoy a glass of vodka while we discuss this mission?"

The two officers climbed the brow together, crossed the submarine's broad main deck, and then dropped through a hatch, descending into the black beast's innards. They talked as they made their way below.

"We are finally almost done loading all those mines. Can you believe it has taken almost three days to take on all one-hundred-fifty-five of them?" Nomor said. "We have enough ordnance to plug up most of the ports on the American East Coast with sunken ships. We can only imagine what our president is hoping to accomplish." He glanced around quickly to make certain no one else could have heard his words. It would be bad if certain persons interpreted his remarks as in any way questioning the wisdom of President Salkov's orders. "We have been so busy loading the mines the engineers tell me they will not be able to complete the work on the *stels ustroystvo* device before we have to get underway. We will have to finish it on the transit."

Kursalin noticed that the boat still smelled of fresh paint and warm electronics. The aroma of hot hydraulic oil, rancid cooking odors, and sweaty sailors had not yet permeated every niche and recess of the ship. That would happen soon enough.

When they stepped into the commanding officer's stateroom, Nomor waved Kursalin to a seat while he retrieved a bottle of vintage vodka and two glasses. Kursalin took a big swallow then smacked his lips. Both men remained quiet for a moment, savoring the fiery liquid.

A television set built into the bulkhead flickered. The scene on the screen immediately caught Kursalin's interest.

A crowd milled about some kind of large, gray government building. The graphics said it was in Vilnius, Lithuania. A few people carried signs, pacing back and forth along the plaza in front of the building. The newscaster, reading from a script, said the small group was peacefully protesting some grievance or another perpetuated by the Lithuanian government against the country's ethnic Russian minority. The announcer went to great lengths to expound on the justness of their cause and the benign nature of their nonviolent demonstration.

Both officers were about to take their last drink of the vodka when the activity on the TV screen suddenly went askew as the camera jerked wildly. The unmistakable crack of gunshots could be heard. Some demonstrators ran while others fell to the ground. The camera lurched violently as it panned the crowd even as the operator was clearly running, backing up, trying to find safety from the sudden gunfire.

Several marchers were on the ground. The others had scattered in panic. The camera whipped back toward the building, focusing on a line of Lithuanian police who had their weapons at the ready as they watched the chaos before them. Their helmet shields prevented anyone from seeing their faces.

The inference was obvious. The police had fired into the

pacific, innocent crowd of protesters. Fired suddenly, viciously, for no apparent reason.

Kursalin watched wide-eyed as the scene played out until the camera finally fell on its side, motionless, leaving only a close-up view of weeds poking through cracks in the cement and, in the distance, four bodies lying stock-still, crimson blood already seeping from beneath them.

The submariner slammed his empty glass onto the tabletop and shook his head.

"Damn them all!" he growled through gritted teeth. "The Westerners with their high and mighty so-called democracy. Democracy so long as you follow in lock-step." His face was red as he glanced sideways at Igor Nomor. When he spoke again, his voice was little more than a raw whisper. "Soon, my friend, we— you, me, our brave crewmen—will have the opportunity to avenge this latest spilt blood."

Ψ

President Grigory Iosifovich Salkov watched the very same news coverage. As he took in the images, the president leaned back in his big, padded chair and smiled broadly.

The TV newsman talked breathlessly over a scene of pure pandemonium. Lithuanian police in full riot gear marched abreast, forming a long line, shoving aside what was left of the protesters and others who had somehow appeared. Smoke and tear gas drifted by in great clouds, obscuring most of the scene. Even so, several bodies could still be seen, lying there in the street, not moving at all. Clearly no one had come to their aid. The police seemed near panic themselves, looking up, pointing, gesturing wildly, but with guns still drawn, ready to fire again into the helpless crowd of protestors. The Russian newscaster was irate, screaming off-screen about the indignity, injustice, and death that the Lithuanian police had set loose on the peaceful ethnic Russians. Against innocent human beings who had done nothing more than march tranquilly in Vilnius to object to the way they were being treated by the former Soviet Republic's corrupt, Western-backed government.

Dimitry Sharapov, the Minister of Sports—but more often President Salkov's master of deceit and treachery—allowed a look of satisfaction to flash across his face.

"Grigory Iosifovich, our plan could not have gone better!" he crowed. "Our team of snipers did very good work. It was brilliant to have them fire into the crowd from above and behind the police lines. Silenced rounds, of course. The world will have no doubts it was the police who fired on the peaceful and lawful demonstrators. We are already hearing that some of the more friendly American cable networks are reporting it as a massacre by government police."

"Well done!" the president told Sharapov as he continued to watch the frenzied video.

"One more thing, my president," Sharapov said, proudly puffing up his chest and jutting out his jaw. "You will soon learn that among those so tragically murdered by the fraudulent regime are the very agitators that we sent to infiltrate and stir up these protests in the first place. Now, there will be no way to trace anything back to us."

Salkov nodded.

"Excellent work. Now, we will let this stew simmer for a few more days before we move the troops into positions to protect the other Russians in Lithuania who remain true to their ethnicity and loyal to the former union." The president turned to the other man who had been quietly sitting in the room, watching the afternoon's events. It was the Minister of Defense, Ignot Smirnov. "Will the tanks be ready to roll in five days? And those two submarines? Will they be underway tonight?"

President Salkov's tone made it very clear that these were not questions at all.

Smirnov merely nodded and said, "Da." Then he took a very large gulp from his glass of vodka.

Ψ

Admiral Tom Donnegan was so frustrated and angry that he smashed the top of his heavy oak desk with his big fist. A water carafe jumped and jittered toward the edge. It would have crashed to the worn carpet if Jon Ward had not deftly reached out and steadied it. Ward had caught many other objects sent flying by an angry Donnegan over the years.

"Jon, have I died and woken up in some damn alternate universe? Grigory Salkov has now put every damn thing in his navy that floats out in the Norwegian Sea and heading down toward our backyard in the North Atlantic! He's not sending a subtle message. He may as well be skywriting 'Screw you!' over the White House!"

Donnegan picked up and immediately slammed right back down a thick, heavy intelligence report. Ward watched the carafe, but it remained in place this time. "And the son of a bitch has better than fifty divisions sitting on high alert in Belarus. Add that to the hundred divisions he has stretched along the Ukrainian border from the Crimea all the way to Kharkov."

Donnegan had worked himself into an especially powerful rage as a worried Jon Ward tried to calm him down.

Donnegan finally slumped down in his chair, breathing hard, his face flushed purple. He made fists with both hands, willing himself to calm down, to breathe deeply for a few moments. Ward watched Donnegan carefully. It had occurred to him that his mentor and surrogate father might be on the verge of a heart attack or stroke. And now, with Ward's son, Jim, in critical condition over at Bethesda from his wounds suffered in Exuma, the commodore was not sure if he could handle another member of his "family" going down.

Donnegan suddenly looked up, his eyes wide, and leaned forward again, studying his notes. Ward thought it might be an aneurysm. But an odd smile appeared on the admiral's face.

"Jon, before you came in, I was on the phone with Brad Bradburn over at Fleet Forces. The *Truman* battle group is limping back into Norfolk. When Penny made that sudden jog north, they steamed right into the heart of the worst category-five hurricane in the last hundred years. From what Brad says, we are very lucky to have not lost several ships. Two of the *Arleigh Burkes* are under tow. The *Truman* is so badly beat-up that she will be out of commission and in the yards for a year or more. Right now we have no carrier in the Atlantic at all and won't for several weeks. The *Stennis* is making best speed to round the Cape while her battle group and the *Essex* head for the Panama Canal.

"Jon, I need you to load up *Toledo* and *George Mason* with whatever weapons and gadgets you have. Get them out there in the middle of Salkov's fleet, wherever it is by then, and do whatever is necessary to convince them to go home."

"That leaves plenty of leeway, Tom," Ward responded.

"I know."

Tom Donnegan studied both hands, looking at them as if this were the first time he had noticed them there, attached at the end of each arm. "One thing is for sure. We have to keep the shipping lanes to Europe open or Salkov will make sure NATO ceases to exist once and for all. And if we don't call Salkov's bluff, the whole balance of power on this planet will shift in a damned dangerous and unfixable direction. Now, if we can just do it without starting a fire we have no hopes of ever putting out..."

Large droplets of condensation rolled down the sides of the water carafe, adding even more dark stains to the old admiral's ancient, war-scarred desk.

Ψ

Doug O'Malley stood and stared at the great black machine. Only minutes before it had been humming quietly, transforming the roaring steam from the reactor into electrons to drive *Toledo* through the deep. The starboard DC drive generator, one of a pair coupled to *Toledo*'s main turbines and sitting on the frames that had previously supported her massive reduction gears, was supposed to power two of the four huge jet pumps housed out in the aft mud tank. The pumps, in turn, shot high-pressure water out the stern nozzle, jetting the submarine through the ocean. Theoretically this brand-new technology was supposed to be simpler, quieter, and more reliable. But right now, the reliability claim had fallen under serious doubt.

"I don't know what happened, Eng," EMC Stan Gromkowsky, *Toledo*'s leading electrician, confessed. "Damn gizmo just tripped off-line. Throttleman didn't see a thing."

He kicked the generator in frustration but only succeeded in stubbing his toe. It led to a colorful stream of epithets directed at the offending machine and the engineers who designed it.

O'Malley could not suppress a laugh. Chief Gromkowsky was legendary among the crew for his creative harangues, and this one was particularly inspired. Finally, the grizzled electrician ran out of words and breath at about the same time. He calmed down as he glanced over at O'Malley.

"What's so damn funny, Eng? You don't have to figure out how to fix this newfangled pile of crap. I don't figure those NUWCian eggheads will be much help either."

"Probably not." Doug O'Malley shook his head in agreement. "They specialize in sensors, not stuff that drives a ship. I'm going forward to brief the captain. Get your guys mustered and this thing 'danger-tagged.' I'll see if we can come up on 'chat' with the engineers at Surface Warfare Center, Philly. They're the guilty ones that designed these things. Maybe one of them can tell us how to fix 'em."

The Engineer stepped down onto the catwalk and headed forward, listening over his shoulder to a whole new set of colorful oaths concerning egghead engineers and their parental heritage.

O'Malley found Joe Glass in his closet of a stateroom. The Engineer eased down on his haunches in the narrow doorway as he tried to explain the problem they had encountered. The boat rocked gently, a very subtle reminder of the storm that was still lashing the surface of the ocean six hundred feet above their heads.

"So she tripped off-line. We are not really sure why. The diagnostics from that computerized troubleshooting gadget they gave us is puking out nothing but gibberish. All I know for sure is that we are on single main engine at the moment and limited to fifty percent power. We can probably do twenty knots running downhill with a stiff tailwind."

The Engineer's frustration was obvious. O'Malley took a great deal of pride and personal responsibility in keeping his engine room humming as it was designed to do. And he was damn good at it. Glass had a thought.

"You don't suppose the IETM would tell you much, do you?" The skipper was referring to the *Interactive Electronic Tech Manual*, a computerized detailed guide to the system.

"Skipper, you know how it goes. Like most of our new gear, the IETMs haven't caught up yet. Just one of the problems with having serial number one of a system. Some genius must have the idea this stuff can't break. I think our best plan would be to come up on 'chat' with Philly."

Glass nodded upward, toward the surface of the sea.

"Not for a couple of days. I don't want to sit up there in that soup blender unless we really have to. Let's wait until Penny blows over and things calm down a bit. I'm with you, though, Eng. This new stuff is great but I sure miss the old days when we had a real paper tech manual you could take to the head and read, and a big old 'crescent hammer' to fix what was broken. We could fix about anything, and for the knottiest problems we could just jury-rig something. I know you heard about *Nautilus* using radiator stop-leak to fix a pesky freshwater leak when they were on the way under the ice to the North Pole."

"Crescent hammer?" O'Malley asked with a sideways look.

"A-gang term. Adjustable wrench you use to beat on things with."

They were interrupted just then by the 1MC speaker.

"Loss of port DC drive generator. Loss of propulsion. Engineer lay aft. Captain, contact the conn."

O'Malley was shaking his head as he charged aft. He found Gromkowsky staring at the port DC drive generator, also shaking his head.

"Same damn thing as the other one," the electrician grunted. "Piece of crap tripped off and we can't figure out why. Damn computer is spewin' out the same babble as the starboard one. They are consistent even if they are both broke!"

"I see you at least figured out not to kick it this time," O'Malley offered, managing somehow to keep a straight face.

"I might yet. That does about as much good as anything else I know to try."

"Well, staring at the problem won't fix it. We at least have the installation wiring diagrams. Grab them and meet me in the wardroom. Maybe we can figure something out before resorting to the 'crescent hammer.'"

"Maybe." Gromkowsky was obviously familiar with the fictitious tool of last resort. "Guess that means no 'chat,' huh?"

"Hurricane Penny is still on top of us. No way we can go up in that mess. And especially not without an engine. Meanwhile the outboard is only going to push us at two knots, so we can't even run out from under the storm. It'll be a couple of days before we can safely give them a call."

A few minutes later, Chief Gromkowsky showed up in the wardroom carrying a large roll of old-fashioned blueprints. He plopped them down on the table.

"I'm sure glad the yard birds who worked on us were old school. They left these with us when they wrapped everything up for that sudden underway."

Joe Glass and Doug O'Malley each grabbed a sheet, studied the legend, and started tracing circuits. Billy Ray Jones, the Executive Officer, stepped in, followed by Dr. Sam Smithski. The NUWC scientist was grinning.

"I thought I would butt in and offer to help. Power electronic controls are a lot different from sensors, but wires are wires."

The group welcomed Smithski as they all sat down and tried to concentrate on whatever the paperwork might tell them. The going was mind-numbingly tedious as they worked through miles of complex circuits. Fueled by gallons of hot, black coffee and an occasional sticky bun from the nearby galley, they worked through the night and into the next morning. The gentle rolling was a constant reminder that a massive hurricane was still spinning away over their heads.

Joe Glass finally stood up and stretched aching muscles, rubbing his stinging eyes. He was about to call an end to the fruitless endeavor and let them all get some rack time, assuming nobody wanted to be the first to abandon the effort.

"Hmmm. Look at this." It was Jones, the XO. He blinked, shook his head, and took another quick look, tracing a series of lines with his index finger. Then he held up one of the drawings and pointed at a circuit card that appeared to be almost identical to the hundreds of others each man had considered so far. "This board controls the magnetic bearings on those generators." He looked around the room to see only blank expressions. "You know, the magnetics that hold the generators up. They use a magnetic field to replace the old journal bearings. They are supposed to be quieter, cooler, and work better." He pointed to one of the symbols representing a relay on the card. "Anyway, the note indicates that this relay trips the generators off-line if it senses a failure of the bearing. Correct me if I'm wrong, Doc, but those are exactly the indications we are getting."

Smithski nodded, still thinking. "Makes sense," he finally said.

Chief Gromkowsky was nodding. "Makes a hell of a lot of sense. At least more than anything else we've thought of. I can swap those modules out, retest, and have them back up online in an hour or so."

He grabbed the appropriate prints and headed aft to make it happen.

Glass looked over at Jones and grinned.

"Where'd you learn that, Bama?"

"I figured out a long time ago to pay attention to the folks who actually do the work. Took me all night to find the right drawing, but I remember some of the techs talking about how that system should have some kind of highly-visible status indicators since it could shut us down cold as a wedge."

"Shut us down what? Aw, never mind. Good catch. I hope it works."

"Me, too," Jones said. "Me, too."

18

_____

His first sense was that the whole world was still spinning wildly, just as it had the last time he thought he was awake. His perspective was complete blackness. He had no feeling of time or place, no sense of up or down. He could not move to brace himself for a landing. Then, when he finally came up to a new level of consciousness, when he could feel the muddy earth beneath him and something heavy and oppressive pinning him down, it was the smell that overwhelmed his senses.

Bill Beaman had smelled that same stench many times before. Manmade stuff, ripped apart, redistributed by some powerful force. Before, it had been war that had so brutally rearranged people's homes, buildings, cities, and lives. It was a sickening mix of raw sewage, strewn garbage, unleashed dust, sour mud, and death.

He fought the urge to retch and lost the battle.

He could not guess how long he had been buried beneath the rubble, the remnants of the Peace and Plenty Hotel. He knew that he had passed in and out of consciousness several times. More than once he was certain that he was dead. Or would be soon. Now, though, the odor and the gagging assured him that he was still living. For a little longer, anyway.

He was on his back and something very heavy lay across his body. Try as he might, he could not move it or slide out from beneath it, even though the ground beneath him was soggy. At first the weight had been intensely painful, pushing down on his chest, trapping his arms and legs. Now the throbbing only nagged at the edges, more annoying than agonizing, like an itch that he could not reach to scratch.

He lay motionless, listening. Still only silence. Deathly silence.

He thought of Elliot. The big SEAL had last seen the cabbie in the seconds of tumult when Hurricane Penny smashed the hotel down all around and then on top of them. He had no idea where Elliot was or even if he was still alive. Beaman could not remember if he had tried to shout out for him or not. He thought so, but was he dreaming then? Dream or reality, no one had answered him except blackness and silence.

Beaman had started to drift off again when he thought he heard something. Noises, something moving. Was he actually hearing it or was he dreaming again?

Then there it was again, a little louder this time. He tried to shout, to call out for help. So little breath was left in his lungs, though, that he was not sure if he actually made any sound.

He was just drifting off again when he thought he saw a flicker of light. The slightest glimmer, barely visible, even when he forced his eyelids to open, even as dirty water dripped onto his face and a fine dust filtered down from somewhere above him.

Then the light was blindingly white. A faint, warm breeze blew across his cheeks.

No doubt about it, Beaman thought. He had died. He was at heaven's door.

Then he heard noise. A loud voice, shouting.

"Over here! I found the other one. He's still alive!"

Someone pushed aside more debris, grabbed his shoulders, and started trying to pull him out. Beaman groaned, attempting to tell whoever it was that he was trapped, pinned, that he would be pulled in half before he would be freed. Then someone or something lifted and pulled the heavy beam off him. The man with the loud voice dragged him out of the rubble and into the clear.

Beaman sucked in the first deep breath of air that he had been able to manage since—well, he did not know how long. Minutes, hours, days? He had no sense of time.

Had his SEAL training helped him hold on to life? Beaman dismissed that idea. He was just damn lucky to have made it this far.

He blinked rapidly, trying to adjust his eyes to the brilliant tropical sunlight. Slowly a fuzzy, shadowy form came into focus, blotting out the sun. A hand holding a water bottle trickled a small cold stream onto Beaman's parched lips. He opened his mouth, allowing the liquid to wash over his tongue and down his throat. It was delicious, better than anything he had ever tasted. Though he coughed and almost strangled, he bobbed his head and grunted, begging wordlessly for more.

"Captain? Captain Beaman?" The voice was faintly familiar. "You okay? Can you tell me where you be hurt?"

Beaman swallowed hard, tried to tell whoever it was that he was fine, and struggled to get his elbows in place and push himself up. Gentle hands held him down. Someone threw a blanket over him. He felt the sharp pinch of an IV going into the vein in the crook of his arm. He lay back and allowed his rescuers to tend to him. That came from SEAL training. Fight the bastard enemy, not the good guy trying to help you get back into the battle.

Everything was almost into focus as he was lifted onto a stretcher. Nothing around him looked familiar. The hotel was gone. So were the tall palm trees that had once surrounded it. As far as Beaman could tell, there was nothing but devastation.

He looked over to the man walking alongside the stretcher. It was Raul, Elliot's twin brother.

"Elliot?" Beaman moaned. His head was beginning to spin as the drugs slowly took effect.

"We found him a couple of hours ago," Raul answered. "He is already on his way to the hospital. You two what don't have sense to come in out of the rain will be roommates for a while longer, it be lookin' like."

"How?" Beaman asked. "How did you...?"

"Searched for three days for you two. Just about decided that whirlwind took you both to the Triangle and made you food for the fish out there. Then we see Elliot's hack peekin' out from under a pile of what be left of the Peace and Plenty at first light this morning. Took us a while to clear a bunch more rubble and that be when we find you."

"Raul, thank...you," Beaman gasped. "I have to go look...got to find..."

The Bahamian patted the SEAL on his dirty, bloody hand.

"Lie back, my friend. We get you patched up, then you can go back to work chasing your bad dude."

But Bill Beaman did not hear any of it. The meds had taken him into a deep and blissfully dreamless sleep.

Ψ

Joe Glass stared intently into the eyepiece of his submarine's Type 18 periscope. The container ship was still there, hull down on the horizon. A little quick mental math and Glass estimated that the large merchant ship was about twenty thousand yards away from USS *Toledo*, steaming on a course that nearly paralleled his.

He glanced over at Sam Smithski. The NUWC scientist was hunched over his laptop with a pronounced scowl.

"Please tell me you are getting something, Doc," the sub skipper said.

Smithski looked up and shook his head in frustration. Sweat beaded on his forehead and his eyeglasses were fogged. The scientist pulled them off and wiped them on his lab coat.

"We are getting a return all right. Range is nineteen-thousand eight-hundred yards. But the bearing is all over the place, at least plus or minus thirty degrees, and the return is mushy as hell."

Glass couldn't resist. "Mushy? Is that one of those scientific terms?"

Smithski, apparently unaware of the attempt at humor, answered, "The return is not sharply defined in the time domain. With the slow rise above the noise floor, the algorithm could easily reject a smaller or more distant contact as merely background noise. We need a longer antenna if we hope to get better definition. And at these frequencies, I need an antenna that is at least a mile long."

Glass shook his head. "The bearing error is what worries me. We can see this surface ship, but plus or minus thirty degrees on a submerged contact? About the only thing I can use that for is to tell me the guy is approximately in the same ocean."

They had been testing the underwater radar for better than two days now. The system seemed to be working remarkably well, except for one little problem: they could not get a usable return.

"Doc, we already have the ELF floating wire antenna out," Glass added. "Between that and the hull arrays we bolted on back in the shipyard, we're dangling almost two thousand feet of wire out there. We don't have anything aboard that even comes close to a mile long."

The NUWCian grunted and slammed the laptop shut.

"Well then, we might as well quit and go home. This idea is a dead end right now."

Billy Ray Jones, *Toledo*'s executive officer, had been standing nearby, leaning against the BYG-1 fire control system and eavesdropping on the conversation. He cocked his head sideways and then, cranking up his thick Alabama accent, prepared to speak. Jones found the affected twang came in handy, putting the listener off guard before he said something unexpectedly profound.

"A while back I was readin' up on them ISAR radars. Y'all know, the system that the P-8s use. Seems to me that they have dern near the same problem you seem to be havin' here. Gettin' the picture in focus. Way they explained it in the paper I was looking at even made sense to an old country boy like me. What they do is they take a whole passel of radar snapshots and then they put them all together into one picture, just like they was all taken at once. Seems I remember that they call it a 'synthetic aperture' or some such. Anyway, would that be something that y'all might want to give a try?"

Sam Smithski sat there with an odd look on his face.

"Well, I appreciate the thought, but I doubt that..." he started, then hesitated, his jaw dropping.

He quickly opened the laptop cover and grabbed a notepad and pen and started scribbling madly. Every few seconds, he would look up from the scrawled notes and punch a few keys on the computer.

Joe Glass glanced over at Jones and suppressed a grin. Jones gave him a broad wink. Glass had seen his XO employ the country-boy dodge several times before but never quite as effectively as he had just done with the NUWC geek.

Nobody spoke as the scientist worked. Every once in a while, Smithski would mumble something about Nyquist numbers or half-lambdas. Then he would scribble some more. Glass looked at the rapidly filling notepad, but all the mathematical symbols were so much gibberish.

Finally, Smithski looked up and smiled crookedly. This time he rubbed his thick glasses clean on his paisley tie as he spoke.

"As nearly as I can tell theoretically, I think it will work. We will have to reprogram the algorithm, increase the sample frequency, add a time delay factor and displacement factors in the 'X,' 'Y,' and 'Z' planes into the time domain equations to shift the trans-positional vector and then run a simple multi-dimensional summation. It'll take a little work to bring everything into focus, but I don't see why it would not solve our... uh... 'mushy' bearing problem. I would guess we would need a couple of days writing and de-bugging code, then a couple more testing everything. The good news is we have everybody we need right here onboard, passing time in your torpedo room right now."

Smithski snapped shut his computer and bolted from the room, clearly anxious to get going on the XO's solution.

Glass punched Jones's shoulder.

"Country boy from South Alabama, huh?"

"Y'all best recollect it was a bunch of country boys from Alabama that put that great naval aviator Neil Armstrong on the moon." Jones winked again and headed out of the submarine's control room, looking back over his shoulder at his skipper. "'Roll Tide' and 'Go Navy.'"

Ψ

Jon Ward peered through the glass into the hospital's ICU. His son lay in there, connected to a bizarre array of tubes and wires and machinery. Jim Ward had been in a coma since he had arrived in DC on the MEDEVAC flight from the Bahamas. Except for the quick trip over to the Pentagon to meet with Admiral Donnegan, Ward had pretty much been standing right there in that same spot for the last four days, looking through the glass and praying that his boy would awaken and be his usual self.

Ward's wife, Ellen, had not left the hospital at all. She was either at his side or reconnoitering the hallways and nurses' station, talking to doctors, interrogating nurses, sneaking peeks at her son's charts. Like her husband, she was frustrated that she could do nothing to help her boy.

The lead doctor, a world-renowned neurosurgeon, stepped into the small alcove where the Wards waited. Both turned toward him, hopeful.

"Any change at all?" Jon asked.

"Nothing yet. As we have discussed, concussions like this are very challenging. We've done all the diagnostics and looked at all the pictures we can but we really won't know anything until he comes around on his own. We see no bleeding and no signs of elevated intracranial pressure. There is a possibility that everything will be fine, but you need to steel yourself. An explosion underwater can cause considerable trauma. There may be permanent brain damage. We simply don't know if there is any, what it might be, or what issues it might cause. Only time will tell."

"And prayer," Ward added. "If prayer helps, our boy will be fine."

"I'm with you on that one," the doctor said as he stepped out of the room.

Jon Ward turned to pull Ellen close to him. He could feel

her trembling, fighting to keep control. She was always a trooper, but Jim was her baby boy, regardless of how big and strong he was and what he now did in service to his country.

She leaned back and looked up at her husband, deftly wiping a tear from the corner of her eye.

"Okay, Commodore, you have something else on your mind. Spill it."

He smiled and kissed her forehead.

"That mind-reading thing of yours. You know it's not fair." He pulled her back to him. "I hate to do this to you, babe, but I've got to leave for a bit. Something has come up."

Ever the good Navy wife, Ellen Ward nodded stoically, patting him on the back, consoling him.

"I figured something was going on. It was that meeting with Papa Tom, wasn't it?"

"Yeah, something hot, or you know I wouldn't leave you, nor would the admiral have asked me to. He needs me to go out for a few days on a mission. He promised me that he would keep an eye on you two and get me back if... well, if anything happens."

He gently kissed the top of her head. Then he pulled away, told her he loved her, and quickly left the room before he could see the tears he knew would soon be streaming down her cheeks.

But he looked back anyway. She was standing there, eyes misty, a slight smile on her face as she waved to him, just as she had from piers so many times before when he left her.

He turned and walked away quickly, before he had the chance to change his mind. Or allowed her to see the tears that had welled up in his own eyes.

19

A full moon hung high in the night sky, illuminating everything below with a soft, silvery glow. A warm breeze brought scents of the Atlantic Ocean to the Newport News shipyard. The fitting-out pier was even busier than usual. No one took time to enjoy the nice evening, even after the recent bashing from Hurricane Penny.

A giant tractor-trailer backed cautiously down the pier, its alarm blaring a warning to any unwary bystander. A flagman stood in front of the tractor, waving two red-coned flashlights to guide the driver around myriad crates and CONEX boxes that littered the pier. Five more trucks stood by in a snaking line, waiting their turn to disgorge their cargo. A pier crane trundled down the tracks from the other direction, bell clanging, its long boom swinging around to prepare for when the first tractor-trailer was ready for unloading.

Jon Ward ignored all the noise and activity as he made his way past the pier-side hustle and bustle. He was deep in thought as he headed toward the brow that joined the new submarine *George Mason* to the pier. He had made one more call to Ellen before entering the main gate. No change with his boy.

Now he had to shove those worries aside to deal with the pressing business that brought him down to the waiting sub.

As he crossed the brow and saluted the sailor on topside watch, Ward spotted Brian Edwards a short distance away, standing on the deck of the submarine he commanded, keeping an eye on all the commotion that swirled around his boat. With sea trials abruptly halted—or "technically" interrupted—and the quick trip back to port, the young skipper had not expected his boat to be loaded and sent back out on assignment so quickly. Or for his men to be restricted to the boat while they were there. They could not even call home to tell wives or girl-friends that they were in port.

This was the first time that his crew would be loading weapons into the new *Virginia*-class submarine's payload modules. Doing it at night added another layer of difficulty to an already complex operation. Four giant, seven-foot-diameter holes stood open on the submarine's main deck behind the sail. Another two apertures waited in front of it to receive the trucks' large yellow containers.

As Ward stepped off the brow onto the deck, Edwards spied him, saluted smartly, and smiled.

"Commodore, it's great to see you again. Welcome aboard the *George Mason*."

Ward grinned as he returned the salute. Young Edwards had a gleam in his eye. Ward knew the feeling, like a kid on Christmas morning with a bright new toy. He had felt much the same way years before when he first took command of the old *Spadefish*. He was convinced that his initial command was the best boat in the fleet and he was the best skipper. And he meant to prove it to everyone else. He could not blame Brian Edwards for having the same thoughts about the *George Mason*.

"Thanks, Brian," Ward answered. "Happy to be aboard. Now, I would wager that you're just a little bit curious about what's going on with all this stuff we're loading onto your boat. Normally I would save the briefing for when we get to sea. Right now, though, make sure you get this stuff onboard and then get us ready to be out of here and mixed into the shipping traffic before first light. Then let's chat."

Edwards raised an eyebrow. This was the first confirmation he had that they were going to sea. He had even suspected that the loading process was some kind of test to see how they handled sudden, unexpected underways. The commodore's words were also the first news he had that he would have a guest aboard for whatever was in store for him and his ship.

"Commodore, we have work details assigned to get everything stowed as quickly as possible. As quickly as we can, that is, without even knowing what is on all those trucks lined up over there." He nodded toward the line of tractor-trailers. "As ordered, *George Mason* is ready for sea, the reactor is on line, and all shore connections are disconnected. Also as ordered, we have already completed loading stores for two weeks at sea. As you probably know, that is all we've been told. I just assumed we would not have been ordered to have the jalopy warmed up if we weren't going out for a spin."

Ward smiled. "Okay then, let's head below. First order of business is a cup of real submarine coffee for me. Then we can get together in your stateroom. I suggest you invite your XO, COB, and Nav to our little discussion, too. That way I won't have to repeat myself. By the way, I'm expecting a bunch of NUWC engineers to show up on the pier in a few minutes. Tell your guys to get them below decks as quickly as you can. I don't want them lollygagging around topside. Too much chance for stray questions or overheard conversation."

As Edwards relayed the order to a member of his crew and the two men dropped down the hatch, an unmarked van rolled to a stop on the pier. Six men climbed out, went around to the back of the vehicle to grab their bags, and carried them up and over the brow onto the submarine's deck. With only a few words of quick greeting, they were hustled over to a hatch and quickly disappeared into the bowels of the submarine.

Ψ

Eight hours later, Jon Ward stood on the top of the sail as the *George Mason* slipped easily down the James River, bound for the deep, vast waters of the open Atlantic. A thin sliver of gold faintly rimmed the Eastern horizon. There would be a new sunlit day in another hour or so with the sky clearing after the recent brush with Hurricane Penny. This was always the submariner's favorite time—getting underway, a mission before him, a well-trained crew working away inside the hull of the engineering miracle that was a nuclear-powered submarine.

Ward was unable to stifle a yawn even as he sipped yet another cup of strong coffee. He was taking advantage of the first moments of quiet since leaving the hospital. The night had been hectic with the short, hurried flight to Newport News and hustle down to the docks. Then he had to explain all the details of their mission to Brian Edwards and his team. And wrap up the harried work of getting the submarine loaded and headed down the river, all before the first light of dawn. It was imperative that they be away, hopefully hidden among all the shipping and fishing traffic around the busy port, before the next Russian spy satellite swept overhead. Best everyone else assume the new boat was still out doing sea trials and not questioning why she had made this unplanned pit stop.

The sub turned into the Elizabeth River, then into the Chesapeake Bay, before passing Fort Story to starboard. They would soon be swimming in the waters of the Atlantic. Jon Ward took another sip of the coffee and bowed his head for a short prayer.

Jim would be all right. Ellen, too. There would be good news upon his return from this mission. From this successful mission that would pull the world's two major military powers back once again from the brink of an unthinkable war. And most of the world would never even know how close they had come.

All those things were covered in the quick prayer Ward whispered into the warm, fragrant morning breeze just before he climbed down from the bridge and headed below. Time to get some sleep. Soon enough things would heat up, leaving very little time for rest.

And almost certainly no opportunity to say any more prayers.

Ψ

President Grayson Whitten stared across the great oak desk at his Secretary of State, Arthur Samson, and his Secretary of Defense, Paulene Wilson. The two cabinet members sat in hard-seated, armless, straight-backed chairs across from their boss. Bright sunlight glared through the thick, bullet-proof glass behind the president, giving him a halo but effectively blinding the other two. They tried to squint to see Whitten's expression, but they could not. The uncomfortable chairs and backlighting were an often-used tactic by the president to keep whomever he was meeting with off kilter. It worked very well.

Secretary Samson fidgeted nervously as he began reading aloud—as the president had asked him to do—from the heavy document he held.

"The people of the Russian Federation, in order to protect the safety and sovereignty of their naval forces while engaged in lawful and legal operations in the international waters of the world's oceans, in view of the repeated hostile acts of various nations toward those naval forces, call out the rights agreed to by all parties in Article 51 of the United Nations Charter, to wit, these forces have and shall exercise their inherent rights of self-defense. Under the provisions of Article 51 and generally recognized international law, the naval forces of the Russian Federation will henceforth regard all air and naval units operating within two hundred kilometers of said Russian forces and identified as military or operated in a manner that could be interpreted as military in nature as hostile forces. These units will be engaged and destroyed without further warning."

Secretary of Defense Wilson chimed in almost before Samson finished reading the menacing final sentence.

"Mr. President, we can't allow this to stand. We have to call an emergency session of the Security Council and protest in the most forceful manner. This is a threat to attack any of our naval vessels—or anybody else's, for that matter—without provocation or good reason. President Salkov could set off an accidental war with actions like this."

Secretary of State Samson, beads of sweat glistening on his bald pate, nodded vigorously.

"I am in complete agreement with Madam Secretary. We must put this before the United Nations and allow them to take corrective actions."

The president stood and paced in a circle around the desk. When he spoke, he seemed to be talking more to himself than the two cabinet members. "Of course, this whole thing comes just when we were getting some momentum in Congress on the highway and infrastructure bill. That's the key to swinging the midterm elections our way. Putting enough money and jobs into the districts where we are in danger of losing good, loyal representatives."

"You mean it's the key to paying off some of our best donors and the unions," Wilson said with a smirk, straightening her skirt and leaning back in her chair. "Realpolitik. Can't let the world and its sordid problems get in the way of financing our re-election."

Whitten stopped pacing and gave her a cold stare.

"Paulene, I don't need your cable-news-channel cutting-edge political analysis right now. I need for you to keep your bunch of wild-eyed admirals in check until Salkov shoots his wad and backs off. I can only fool the electorate so long by talking tough and glaring into the press pool camera. Somebody's going to eventually start carping that we should have stood up to the bastard. We do not need to see in the press that some Russian admiral is crowing about sinking one of our ships that allegedly attacked them and Grigory Salkov is on the evening news accusing us of trying to start a war."

He turned to his Secretary of State. "And Art, you are to see that nobody on our side says a word about what's going on or even hints any kind of response to this harangue from the Russians. Salkov can't box a shadow. And the American people will only hear about positive things, like what we are doing to rebuild the nation's crumbling infrastructure and create good-paying jobs."

The sun slipped behind a dark rain cloud. It was no longer blazing through the window, distracting the two cabinet members.

The meeting was over.

Ψ

Captain First Rank Konstantin Kursalin stepped back from the periscope and braced himself against a chart table.

"First Officer Garlerkin, do we have all the message traffic aboard?" he asked.

The Norwegian Sea was being its usual stormy, wind-tossed self, with massive seas rolling over the *Igor Borsovitch*. The planesmen struggled to keep the Russian submarine at the ordered depth as it pitched and heaved in the midst of the mountainous waves.

"Captain, we have received and receipted all the message traffic," Kaarle Garlerkin answered. He had wedged himself into a space just outside the radio room door favored for just such occasions. A particularly large wave shoved the submarine over hard. Tools and several coffee cups rolled across the now steeply inclined deck, crashing noisily into the pipe manifold on the other side of the space. The men ignored all the upheaval. "Not much new. Only that we are to escort our fat friend down to the American coast." The officer read another line from the message. "Here is one thing, however. There are orders to take a new route. We are to stay at least a thousand kilometers to the west of the mid-Atlantic ridge until further notice."

Kursalin cocked his head.

"I wonder what that is all about. It is curious that they are sending us so far west so soon. There must be something going on. We know the American ships are supposed to be in port. Supposed to be." Another wave tossed the boat. The captain braced himself against the roll. "Anyway, it is not our place to ask questions. Let us get deep and out of this mess before it beaches us somewhere." Lowering the periscope, he turned to the control room and ordered, "Make your depth one-hundred-fifty meters, steer course two-two-five. Make your speed forty-five kilometers per hour."

The submarine sank back into the quiet depths and headed southwest. Kursalin rubbed his eyes. He was desperately tired. The loading of the weapons, the work required for the rapid underway, and the tension of the rendezvous with the *Moscow* had taken more out of him than he would acknowledge. If he was going to be ready to do what was being asked of him and his crew, he needed to sleep, to be sharp.

Turning to his first officer, he said, "Mr. Garlerkin, contact the *Moscow* on the underwater telephone. Relay our orders to steer at least one thousand kilometers to the west of the mid-Atlantic ridge and to make best speed to arrive off of New London in the United States in seven days."

As he headed out of the control room, Kursalin turned once more to Garlerkin and added, "First Officer, take station off of *Moscow* and maintain at least a one-kilometer separation. Make sure the *stels ustroystvo* device, the stealth device, is working correctly. Remember, the *Moscow* will not be able to detect us, so you will need to follow their lead. Call me if you gain contact on any American warships. I will be sleeping in my stateroom, maybe dreaming of a holiday on the Black Sea."

The tall officer did not even bother to smile as he turned and disappeared down the warship's narrow passageway.

20

Kapitan Fedya Orlov eased back on the controls of his spanking new TU-160M *Blackjack* strategic bomber. He glanced out the cockpit window to see the other ten planes in his squadron. As he watched, a pair of Ilyushin IL-78 tankers dropped away and quickly fell behind them before heading back to base, their refueling tanks now empty. Fifteen thousand meters below, the rough, ragged Murmansk coastline stretched out before them. Soon it would mark the starting point of their mission this day: agitating members of NATO in general and the Americans in particular.

Orlov glanced across the cockpit at his co-pilot, *Starshiy Leytenant* Eduard Polzin. "This should be interesting, 'ey, Eduard. Kick the NATO hornets' nest, raise their collective blood pressure, and then we celebrate with a week of cold rum, warm sunshine, and hot senoritas in Caracas."

Polzin laughed softly as he continued to watch the navigation display on his main monitor.

"Why can we not teach the senoritas that we prefer a civilized drink, like vodka? Not cactus juice." He swiped his gloved finger across the touchscreen display. "Twenty seconds to the

turn. New course three-two-one. Signaling Eagle Flight now."
He paused for a second, watched the display intently for a
moment, and then continued, "Mark the turn. Execute...now."

Orlov applied pressure to the stiff stick nestled in his left
hand. The big bomber banked smoothly left and turned to the
new course, heading for a point just north of the Norwegian
coast. The rest of the aircraft in the flight obediently followed
suit.

As the big plane settled out on its new heading, Orlov
continued the conversation. "Maybe you need to engage in a
cultural exchange program, *Leytenat* Polzin. You teach the
senoritas the joys of vodka and they can teach the Russian
women how to do the truly nasty things they willingly do for
us." As he spoke, the pilot pulled back on the four throttle quadrants. "Increasing speed to Mach 1.5. Signal Eagle Flight to
comply."

As the TU-160M accelerated, its variable-geometry wings
swung back into a deep V shape. With a blue-white blaze, the
four Kuznetsov NK-43 afterburning turbofan engines pushed
the aircraft up to and then neatly through the sound barrier.

"Fourteen minutes to next turn," Polzin read from his nav
display. "New course two-two-five."

"Signal Eagle Flight to commence military flight procedures," Orlov ordered. He reached over to the communications
display and flicked off the IFF transponder, then shifted his
radars to combat mode.

Instantly, on air traffic control screens all across Northern
Europe, the tagged contact designating his formation of aircraft
disappeared.

Almost immediately, the *Blackjack*'s radar early-warning
receiver began chirping. Simultaneously, a tab on Polzin's touchscreen flashed yellow. The co-pilot swiped the tab and an information dialogue window popped up. A yellow arrow flashed

from his aircraft icon to a point on the Northern Norwegian coast.

"The Globus II station at Varno has picked us up," he read aloud. "And they have shifted to track mode."

"All as expected," Orlov grunted. "Allowing fifteen minutes to scramble, I expect the F-16s that belong to our friends from the Royal Norwegian Air Force will be joining us in about half an hour. I believe we have time for a cup of tea before the fun really starts." The pilot reached behind his seat to retrieve a heavy aluminum Thermos and poured himself a cup of steaming black tea. He looked toward his co-pilot and nodded to the thermos.

Polzin snorted and shook his head.

"Fedya, my tea-drinking friend, do you not know that stuff will rust your pipes and cause you to piss every half hour? Now, if you only had some vodka! I would willingly accept your kind offer." Suddenly he was distracted by a text that flashed up on his screen. Polzin glanced at it. "*Kapitan* Pilot, Aerospace Defense Operational Strategic Command reports that four fighters have scrambled from Andoya Air Station." His touch-screen display automatically shifted to a god's-eye tactical display. Four blips were rapidly closing from the southwest. "ETA...three minutes. And...I have them on radar now. Range three-five-zero kilometers. They have accelerated to Mach 1.5. Closing rate is Mach 3. Bearing one-nine-zero." The co-pilot's fingers danced expertly across the screen as a tab flashed red. "They are active on AN/APG-68 radars. Eighty-percent probability of detection."

Orlov keyed his throat mike. "Eagle Flight, take air combat positions. Stay on me." Behind him, like a flock of huge, white, supersonic geese, the other ten bombers spread out in a loose wedge, spaced so that every plane had room to maneuver without fear of hitting anyone else.

"The F-16s are swinging around to get on our tail," the co-pilot called out, a touch of concern in his voice. "Increasing speed to Mach 2. Thirty seconds to ETA."

Just then the radio speaker in the Russian aircraft squawked. The voice spoke in Russian but with a Scandinavian accent.

"Unidentified aircraft, flight of eleven, this is Norwegian Air Force. You have entered Norwegian Air Defense Identification Zone. Immediately identify yourself."

The Russian pilots ignored the warning, busying themselves with setting up their electronic defense systems.

"Unidentified aircraft, flight of eleven," the radio speaker bellowed again. "This is Norwegian Air Force. You are approaching Norwegian sovereign airspace. Turn right to course north or we will engage."

Orlov glanced over at Polzin and smiled. "Are our Viking friends in position?"

"Yes, *Kapitan*. They are ten miles astern, closing at Mach 0.4."

"Good." Orlov nodded. "Signal Eagle Flight to increase speed to maximum combat and engage electronic defenses. Come to course south. It is now time to demonstrate to them that should we desire to do so, we can obliterate their homeland with absolute impunity."

The bombers swung around on a course that had them pointed directly toward the Norwegian coast. When Orlov pulled fully down on the throttle quadrants, the *Blackjack* leaped ahead noticeably. Then, as the Russian bombers passed through Mach 3.2, the F-16s fell farther and farther behind.

A buzzer started to scream in the cockpit. Polzin shouted to be heard over the alarm.

"The F-16s have launched missiles. I hold eight air-to-air missiles inbound. Classified as AIM-120 missiles. I am now engaging electronic defenses."

The co-pilot swiped across his touchscreen to activate a dropdown menu. A transmitter housed in the big aircraft's tail section pulsed out a series of signals. Three miles astern, the flight of missiles fell over and corkscrewed downward into the ocean, fifteen thousand meters below, as if they had run into some kind of invisible barrier in the sky.

Seconds later, the Russian bombers crossed the Norwegian coastline, hammering the land below with a thunderous sonic boom. At Mach 3.2, the flight down the entire spine of Norway lasted barely twenty minutes. Directly over Oslo, Norway's capital, the formation swung around as if thumbing their noses at the Norwegians, and then headed southwest on a direct course toward London.

Four minutes after leaving Oslo, over the North Sea, the cabin radio that was tuned to the international air traffic frequency again sounded. This time the voice spoke in English.

"Unidentified aircraft, flight of eleven, you are about to enter British airspace. Identify yourself or you will be engaged."

Leytenant Polzin checked his screen.

"Contact on four aircraft inbound at Mach 1.3. Capture-E radar, best classification British Typhoons. Electronic defenses auto-engaged."

Orlov laughed heartily, as if someone had told a particularly funny joke.

"Now we shall see if the Motherland's engineers are any good. Commence jamming their radars. Employ electronic spoofing on the air search radars."

The Russian pilot lowered his face shield. A dark mask now hid his smirk. Polzin looked up from his screen and glanced toward the command pilot.

"*Kapitan*, you are aware that jamming is considered a hostile act. We could be starting a war here. They will fire on us and try to shoot us out of the sky."

"*Leytenant*, I will say this once only," Orlov retorted sharply. "Our orders are to test the British air defenses to the maximum. They are exactly the same as the Americans. They lack the spine to shoot. Besides, our technology is vastly superior. We are invincible here."

The co-pilot nodded, a sheepish look on his face as he returned to his screen. His fingers played a furious dance across the touchscreen. After several seconds, he glanced over at his captain, smiled, and reported, "Spoofing the air search radars. Lakenheath should now see several hundred aircraft going off in all directions. It will take them hours to figure out where we are in the midst of such a mess."

Then another insistent alarm began bleating and the on/off flashing of a light on the display intermittently lit up the co-pilot's face.

"The Typhoons have commenced counter jamming," Polzin yelled. "I am having difficulty tracking." Sweat rolled off the co-pilot's forehead and gathered around his nosepiece, fogging the face shield, as he tried desperately to keep contact with the approaching British fighter jets. "Their DRFM jammers are hopping frequencies faster than our radars."

"Try infrared tracking," Orlov ordered.

"Do you think I am straight out of *Voyenne-Voz dushnye* flight academy?" Polzin shouted. "Of course I am trying IR tacking. You fly the aircraft. I will handle the electronic defenses."

Orlov ignored the man's near-panic. He glanced out the cockpit window just in time to see four faint dots on the horizon grow to become onrushing aircraft at astonishing speed. With a combined closure rate of over 6,500 kilometers per hour, there was no time to even think of evading, only a split second to register the danger and pray they did not collide.

The British fighters were already starting their turn just as they passed a scant hundred meters below the Russian bombers. However, at the speed they were traveling, the two flights would be a hundred kilometers apart before the British could start their tail chase. With over a 1,500-knot speed disadvantage, they had no hope of catching up.

The four fighters emptied their air-to-air missile racks of their Mach 4 Meteor missiles in a last-ditch effort to protect their homeland. Sixteen active radar-guided missiles streaked toward the Russian bombers from astern. The missiles each locked on to a selected target and aimed unerringly at it. The advanced electronics they carried bored through the bombers' jammers like the signals were mere extraneous noise.

Yet another loud buzzer yelped in the cockpit.

"Missile warning alert!" Polzin shouted. "Our jammers are ineffective! Deploying electronic decoys."

He swiped a couple of tabs and a drop-down menu on the display. An antenna on each wingtip began to transmit a series of even more complex signals. The Meteors' onboard computer interpreted the signals as a radar return from a target that was diving while making a sharp turn to the left. The incoming missile dutifully performed a tight, high-G turn and dived to intercept the target, just as it was programmed to do. By the time the processor recognized a lost target, it was too far below and astern of the Russian aircraft to reacquire contact. Each of the other Meteors followed a similar flight path, trying to do what they were supposed to do, but it was too late. All of them plunged into the North Sea when their fuel was expended.

Leytenant Polzin flipped up his visor and wiped the sweat from his forehead with the back of his hand. "That was entirely too close," he murmured, mostly to himself.

Orlov heard him, though.

"Good Russian engineering," he said. "We were never in any danger. It looks as if we are feet dry over the United Kingdom and there is not a damn thing they can do about it. I do suggest that you compute the best vector to our refueling rendezvous over Greenland. At this rate of speed, we will be burning nothing but fumes in a few minutes." Orlov laughed again and winked at his co-pilot. "It would be embarrassing should some of us end up in the drink after we have just handed a couple of mighty NATO member nations their haughty asses."

The Russian pilot took a deep, satisfying swallow of black tea as he looked down on the wind-blown sea that stretched out ahead of the magnificent formation of mighty warplanes.

21

Sarah Wilder was well beyond frustrated. She had now spent more than a week on this disgusting, sea-going sewer pipe, with no reason to believe the claustrophobic nightmare was going to end anytime soon. She was amazed that the ordeal did not seem to be bothering her fellow engineers and scientists as much as it did her. Most of them saw it as a grand adventure, an opportunity to actually work in real time on the systems they usually designed, tested, and then handed over to the fleet for trials and use. Or, for her fellow female hostages, it was a chance to flirt openly with the sailors.

Hell, even her supposed mentor, that near-sighted geek Sam Smithski, was up to his skinny ass in the testing of his new radar system. He had long since lost sight of the fact that they were virtually prisoners aboard this submarine.

Wilder stretched and put her book on the mess table at which she sat. She had been only half paying attention to the lust and avarice and backstabbing going on in the bodice-ripper novel she was reading. The rest of her mind was mulling over how she might be able to get off of the *Toledo*.

She had much to tell Alexi. She needed to warn him that the

Americans had implemented the secret new stealth system on their submarine. She needed to inform him how she had taken the initiative to rig it so that the Russians would easily be able to defeat it—once she had activated the "bug"—and then locate the American vessel.

She had tried to sabotage the EMI filters on the underwater radar, but that had proven both too difficult and too dangerous to accomplish. She could not come up with a good method to trigger the sabotage after she was well clear of *Toledo*. It was one thing to help bring about world peace; it was an entirely different matter to become a martyr for it.

The bug idea was perfect. Smithski and the other fools would have no idea it was there until some Russian submarine triggered it. Then it would be far too late. They would have no opportunity to find it and reverse it. She would be a hero. She would have struck a mighty blow against the military/industrial complex that made the rich and powerful even richer and more powerful at the cost of innocent lives.

Finally, with this glorious victory, Alexi could step away, leaving behind all the intense pressure and dangerous work, swoop her up, and carry her back to his dacha in Russia. They could then make up for lost time, making passionate love until they were too exhausted to carry on and then bringing beautiful children into a far more peaceful world thanks to their defeat of the Western warmongers.

The engineer felt that familiar warm tingle in her belly when she thought of lying next to Alexi. She shivered slightly, swallowed hard, and then glanced at her wristwatch yet again. Nowhere to go, nothing to do. It would be four more hours before Liz Begally vacated the narrow bunk bed they had been forced to share. Sixteen females were marooned on this cramped tub, and they had been relegated to sharing bunks in a space no larger than Wilder's bathroom back home. The submariners called this compartment the "nine-man berthing room." Sixteen women and nine bunks. That required them to do something the sailors called "hot bunking." The bedding would still be warm and reek from the odor of that cow Begagly when it was finally Sarah's turn to attempt to sleep there. Or at least get a few hours of privacy, if anyone could consider what that thin blue curtain provided as any semblance of privacy.

Sarah Wilder was working on some options. One was a plot for an imagined illness. She had also thought about pushing Begagly down a ladder. Either might force Captain Glass to pull into port somewhere and let them off. She had even considered some kind of explosion, something that would not endanger anyone but would create enough smoke and collateral damage that they would have to head for a port somewhere.

As she pondered the possibilities, she spotted the submarine's executive officer, Billy Ray Jones, making his way across the mess decks toward her. She considered Jones to be about the only worthwhile scenery on this big steel tube. And his slow Southern drawl was downright sexy.

"Ma'am, I have some good news for you. We'll be doing a PERSTRAN tonight. I need y'all to get the ladies ready as quickly as you can."

"PERSTRAN?" The Navy and their damned acronyms! Why in hell did they not simply speak English?

"Personnel transfer. Looks like we will not be hosting y'all aboard *Toledo* much longer."

"Why, Commander Jones," Sarah answered, coquettishly mimicking his drawl, "if I didn't know better, I might imagine you were trying to get shuck of us."

Jones blushed. "Ma'am, not a'tall. It's just that we are not provisioned for so many riders and for so long a time. That hurricane has had us deep and rocking around down here longer than we thought."

The submarine officer blushed even redder when Wilder smiled and winked at him and his unintentional double entendre. He cleared his throat. "Anyhow, another couple of days and we'll be down to nothing but peanut butter and canned ham. We're about a hundred miles off Cocoa Beach. We'll surface and offload all the women and most of the NUWC men in a couple of hours. You should be back in Newport by tomorrow sometime."

"Most of the men?" Wilder asked. Why the hell would anyone voluntarily stay onboard this submerged dungeon for one second longer than they had to.

"Yes, ma'am," Jones answered. "Dr. Smithski and several of the radar engineers are staying aboard to help us operate and refine that system now that we have it operating in spec. A couple other engineers will help us put the other toys through their paces, the ones we haven't had a chance to learn about yet. For everyone else, it's time to go home."

Wilder did her best Scarlett O'Hara imitation, batting her eyes and touching his arm. He wore no wedding ring. He obviously worked out, though she could not imagine where on this glorified bathtub.

"Well, Commander, if you insist, but we were just starting to enjoy the hospitality." She winked again, enjoying how uncomfortable it made him. "Okay, so I had better tell the ladies to start packing. Although most of us have very little to pack since we left the barge in such a hurry. I haven't had underwear to put on in a week now." She rose from her seat and handed Jones her sultry novel. "Maybe your wife will enjoy this."

"Well, ma'am, I don't have…"

But she had already turned and was sauntering out of the mess decks, swaying her hips provocatively as she left.

The NUWC engineer giggled to herself as she rushed to the nine-man berthing. Good to know she could still get a rise from a man anytime she wanted to. Even one who was trained and determined to kill innocents in the name of global dominance. At the compartment she yelled at the women to get up and get packed. It was especially satisfying to drag Dr. Begagly from whatever disgusting dream she was immersed in.

Wilder grabbed her own small grip and retrieved her laptop from her locker. She rushed out to find a secluded spot to work, somewhere no one could get a glimpse of her computer screen and question why she would visit that particular system at this point. The only place she could find was a cramped corner in the torpedo room. Her fellow engineers were bustling around, preparing to leave, but they hardly noticed her. A few had tried to hit on her when she first joined the group back in Newport. She quickly earned the reputation for being unfriendly, stand-offish, and even downright hostile. Now they generally kept their distance unless required to interact.

Wilder quickly logged into the submarine's LAN and began to click through a maze of multi-level file folders with cryptic names. She only had a few minutes to finish her alterations to the stealth device program. Then, with one click, she would activate it. Her fingers flew across the keyboard as she glanced at the computer's clock. Time was the issue now. She simply had to complete the work. The future of the planet depended on her. Alexi depended on her. The world would continue to plunge toward fiery nuclear conflict unless she accomplished her mission here on this damnable warship. Her forthcoming personal happiness rested on getting this work completed without being discovered, too. Her dream life with Alexi once she had pulled him away from the other crusaders, bound for a far more peaceful future in each other's arms.

Sarah Wilder breathed a deep sigh of relief as she uploaded the hastily revised program and then checked the tiny box to activate it. She was done. She had just struck a mighty blow for a more sane future for planet Earth.

Just as she clicked the mouse, a shadow fell over her. Sam Smithski. She recognized his cheap cologne before she even looked up to see herself reflected in his thick, black-rimmed eyeglasses.

Wilder could not suppress a shudder as he asked her, "Sarah, what are you doing back here?"

She snapped the laptop shut.

"I was... just... that is..."

"Getting that 'I'm coming home' email ready to send to your boyfriend?" he asked, flashing a goofy grin.

Jesus. How long had that dork been standing there? Surely he had not had time to see what she was working on. At least not enough to get suspicious. Otherwise all was lost. She fought to control her trembling hands before her boss noticed.

But he had joked about her "boyfriend." Nobody at NUWC knew about Alexi. Of that she was certain. Smithski's joke was most likely intended as a cruel one. Sarah knew they talked about her and her frigid personality behind her back, that they even questioned her sexual orientation. God, if they only knew!

"Oh, no. Just tidying up my notes, trying to get a head start on catching up on work when we get back."

"You're a trooper, Wilder," Dr. Smithski told her, and he sounded sincere. "I wish we had a couple dozen more like you. But you better get going. They have already called for everyone to go topside. You don't want to miss your ride home and have to spend another week out here with us techies doing all this boring testing, do you?"

"No. No, I don't," she replied. And she had never given a more heartfelt answer to a question in her life.

Ψ

General William "Winking Willie" Willoughby sat at his desk and watched the scene playing out on the large-screen monitor that covered most of the office's far wall. A news reporter was railing about the injustice suffered by the poor Russian ethnic minority at the hands of the vengeful, bloodthirsty Lithuanian government. The talking head was speaking in Russian but an English translation scrolled across the bottom of the screen.

In the background, a large force of heavily armed police in gas masks appeared to be swinging hefty truncheons back and forth as they moved in a phalanx through a cloud of tear gas. They were forcing back a larger crowd of civilians who reluctantly gave way to the vicious onslaught. Several slower-moving participants were receiving individual attention, being beaten to the ground by the police. The TV news camera panned across women and children trying to run from the inexorable police onslaught. The video lingered on a child, lying motionless in the street, blood staining the asphalt beneath him. Two women carrying a limp man's body scurried past, both of them wailing. A burning car in the midst of the chaos added a heavy layer of black smoke to the gas clouds.

All the while, the news reporter droned on about innocent civilian casualties piling up in hospitals around Vilnius. He ended his diatribe with a plea for Russian President Salkov to send troops to protect the poor defenseless ethnic Russians being massacred by the Lithuanian fascists.

General Willoughby shook his head, snorted, then looked over at the computer monitor on his desk. He scanned for the fifth time the email displayed there. It had gotten no better since the last read. It was a classified situation report from the Army general who ran the United States European Command (EUCOM).

Or, that is, what was left of it. Over the years, US strength in

Europe had dwindled to only one armored division and a couple of F-15 squadrons. Now, thanks to President Whitten's "downsizing," that was reduced to a battalion, with all the tanks lined up in German storage warehouses. The Air Force had long since packed up and gone home.

The email the general was perusing discussed the Russian armored divisions that were already massing on the Belarus side of the Lithuanian border. It also confirmed that the Lithuanian government would soon issue a plea for NATO protection if and when those troops began firing or advanced across the border. The former Soviet republic had been a North Atlantic Treaty Organization member since 2004. An attack on any of NATO's twenty-eight members triggered a response from the others. Peaceful resolution, including working through the United Nations, would be the first goal. If that failed, nothing was off the table to ensure that the member nation received protection against the aggressor.

Willoughby held his head in his hands and looked down at a blank sheet of paper on his desk. This latest provocation by Russia and her president was already approaching the "nothing off the table" stage. Diplomats had been arguing for days at the UN, yet the troop buildup continued. Should the Russians begin shooting, there was only one possible response. And the world still did not know of the submarine hostilities out in the Atlantic, or that shots had already been fired in the wake of unprovoked Russian aggression in the deep waters of the Barents.

The general knew that he needed to fill that blank sheet of paper with his best advice for the President of the United States on how to deal with this crisis. His gut—backed up with plenty of data and past experience—told him that now was the time for strong, decisive action. That was the only effective way to deal with Salkov and his stooges. Call their bluff. Inaction, indecisiveness, and waffling would only encourage the Russian president. He and many other world leaders were already convinced that America lacked the will to step in and be bold. Once the images of dead US troops showed up on CNN, the Americans would be demanding "no boots on the ground" and a quick settlement. Any settlement, regardless of the political or diplomatic cost.

Indeed, Willoughby was well aware that the current resident at 1600 Pennsylvania Avenue would do all he could to avoid any kind of military action, despite what membership in NATO might require. President Grayson Whitten would dither and prevaricate, urge those in that part of the world to meet and talk and negotiate and then talk some more, tread water in the United Nations, all while people died, Russia gained territory, influence, and power, and the president searched for some kind of political alternative that would play well in the press and the polls and with his voter base. Whitten could not care less about the strategic outcome.

The Chairman looked up from the still blank page when his aide suddenly burst into his office.

"General, we just received this COSMIC NATO warning message from NATO Allied Air Command. A flight of eleven aircraft, verified as Russian TU-160 *Blackjack* bombers, just tore down the entire length of Norway, flew right over Oslo, then across the UK, and caused sonic booms directly over London." The Air Force Lieutenant Colonel read breathlessly from the message, and then he paused, frowning. "This can't be right. General, it reports tracking the Russian bombers at better than Mach 3.2. That's almost a thousand miles an hour faster than our intel rates them for. The flight danced away from all the NATO interceptors. And it looks like they played havoc with everything the Norwegians and the Brits could throw at them."

"Damn!" Willoughby exploded. "Salkov is thumbing his

nose at us again, big time. Plus he's letting us know in a rather spectacular way that he has capabilities we did not even suspect. Where are those damn bombers now?"

"We tracked them out over Greenland. They had tankers rendezvousing with them there," the aide answered. "At the kind of speed they can make, we expect them off the East Coast by afternoon."

Willoughby grabbed his phone, punched a button, and then yelled, "Get me NORTHCOM immediately. I need to speak with General Thomas now!"

Within seconds the Chairman was on the speaker with Air Force General Mike "Stick" Thomas, Commander of United States Northern Command. Willoughby dispensed with hellos.

"Stick, how quickly can you get those F-22s of yours airborne? We've got a flight of eleven Russian *Blackjack* bombers heading our way."

"You think we've been napping over here, Willie?" General Thomas shot back. "We assumed they would be coming this way and we already scrambled the squadron out of Langley just in case. We gave the order as soon as we got the warning from Lakenheath."

"I assume your guys will follow protocol if they approach our airspace?"

"Damn right! If we can do any good. You heard what they did over Norway and the UK?"

"Uh huh," Willoughby grunted as he hung up.

His right eye beat uncontrollably as, under his breath, the Chairman muttered, "Damn Russians! Always poking the hornets' nest. But this time...what the hell is Salkov really playing at? And that task force he has loose in the Atlantic... diversion or is he really ready to launch World War III?"

Willoughby pounded his desk. He did not have the luxury of the president, sitting there in the Oval Office demanding a diplomatic solution, calling up the Russian president and urging him to back off or we might get our feelings hurt. There had already been actual shooting skirmishes between Russian and American submarines practically beneath the cruise ship lanes off of Virginia Beach. An invasion of a NATO member nation seemed imminent. A Russian task force was steaming directly for the Atlantic Coast of the United States. A flight of unbelievably fast and powerful bombers were now on the way, too. How did he know that they did not plan on unleashing something much worse than a few thunderous sonic booms, something that would do far more than rattle the fine china in the White House dining room?

It was the general's job to know these things. Right now, he did not know shit.

Willoughby again punched a button on his phone and growled, "Get me Fleet Forces."

Ψ

Captain Kursalin carefully watched the submarine *Igor Borsovitch*'s sonar screen. The first real offensive strike of this particular mission was about to take place. Three thousand meters ahead of his vessel, Captain First Rank Igor Nomor had maneuvered his submarine, the *Moscow*, beyond Montauk Point, into Block Island Sound. Both submarines were well within US sovereign waters. A few meters above their sails, fishing craft and pleasure boaters were skittering back and forth across the calm surface of the sound, taking advantage of the first sunny days after the recent scare from the massive Hurricane Penny, which had thankfully made another unexpected but welcome turn to the northeast.

It was a fact that if the Americans found the two Russian submarines, they would attack without warning or mercy. And the waters between Long Island and the Connecticut and Rhode Island shore were far too shallow to effectively evade.

The sonar screen showed a spike of acoustic energy on the bearing to the *Moscow*. Superfluously, the sonar operator reported, "Captain, the *Moscow* has launched her first mine. We are tracking it running normally, headed for the Thames River."

The Thames was home to the US submarine base and training school at Groton, the Submarine Force Museum, where the world's first nuclear submarine, the *Nautilus*, was berthed as a museum ship, and Electric Boat Company, the facility where many submarines were built, modified, and repaired. The United States Coast Guard Academy was across the river on the New London side.

In a slow, methodical sequence, five more acoustic pulses followed from the blip that represented the *Moscow*. Then the new Russian sub made a slow turn to the east and headed back out toward deep water.

Kursalin finally allowed himself to breathe deeply as he brought the *Igor Borsovitch* around to take station astern of his charge.

From there, they set a course for Norfolk and their next delivery.

22

The dark-blue shape dropped away from its mooring beneath the broad, flat keel of the Russian "oceanographic" ship *Pushkino*. The unmanned underwater vehicle plunged sharply away, nosing down into the deep darkness. One hundred meters above the abyssal plain, the craft's on-board processor ordered it to level off and for the high-definition side-scan sonar module to break loose, drop away, and unreel behind. Its four propulsors pushed the UUV's nose up so that it leveled off and hovered precisely fifty meters above the flat, muddy ocean bottom. As the boat passed over its programmed datum, a small acoustic sounder fell free and sank to the sludge. A thin fiber-optic line connected the sounder to the *Pushkino*, rocking back and forth up on the unsettled surface of the ocean. The UUV and the sounder exchanged acoustic pulses, shaking hands from thirty-five hundred meters below the mothership.

With acoustic communications established, the UUV began a slow, precise spiral search, circling the sounder while incrementally moving outward, away from the datum. The side-scan sonar pinged at 147 kilohertz as it painted a picture of everything lying out to four hundred meters on either side of the module. Meanwhile, the gap-filler sonar that was attached to the UUV's belly searched the swath directly beneath the module, the area in which the side-scan was blind. The digital information was sent acoustically to the sounder, and then up the fiber-optic cable to the *Pushkino*'s control room.

That was where some half dozen technicians sat, staring at high-definition monitors each scanning a "snapshot" of the barren sea bottom far below. The side-scan sonar painted a detailed, high-resolution picture of the bottom with high-frequency acoustic energy. The advanced computer processors picked up every detail down to shreds of debris no larger than a crushed beer can. Search algorithms automatically drew red boxes around objects that might fit the pre-programmed criteria, freeing the operators to investigate only the high-priority contacts. The team settled back into a comfortable, if boring, routine. From experience, they knew that this particular search could take many hours, depending on just how accurate their initial information was. That was the data that had been used to program the search criteria.

A small-scale, bottom-contour chart of the North Atlantic Basin decorated the forward bulkhead of *Pushkino*'s control room. Thirteen lines zigzagged across the chart's representation of the basin, each connecting a point on the east coast of North America with various parts of Europe. Twelve of those thirteen lines had a broad red X painted across them somewhere along their paths across the abyssal plain. That meant *Pushkino* and her crew had already successfully located whatever the lines on the chart represented. There was only one line left to find.

This search was a little different from the previous dozen, though. There was a palpable sense of urgency now. It was not quite panic, but the air aboard the ship was far from the calm complacency of the past few days, and it permeated the control room.

A large twenty-four-hour analog clock hung on the forward bulkhead, strategically placed just above the chart. A red hand was set for seventeen hours in the future. The technicians regularly stole glances at the clock as the hands indicating the current time moved inexorably toward the looming red one. At a speed of five kilometers per hour, they would only be able to search about four square kilometers within each sixty minutes. From experience, they knew that the combination of their own navigation imprecision and inaccuracies in the charted locations for the cables meant that they would likely need to search hundreds of square kilometers before finding what they were looking for. And there was always the possibility that it was buried so deep beneath the bottom muck that even their sophisticated gear would never see it. Technology notwithstanding, such a hunt still had a huge element of luck.

Many in the upper reaches of the Russian Navy and branches of the government that oversaw the service did not believe in luck or tolerate it as an excuse should a mission fail.

With three hours still to go, an image suddenly appeared on one of the screens. It was a long, thin, straight line cutting diagonally across one of the snapshots. The UUV changed course on its own in order to pass directly over the object. The technicians were already smiling as a highly sensitive magnetometer measured the electric field surrounding the object.

Then, as the UUV maneuvered back and forth, one of the technicians threw up his hands in disgust. The object was nothing more than a length of iron pipe, something that had likely fallen off some transport ship sometime in the distant past.

The clock above the chart marched ominously on, hour after hour.

With less than sixty minutes before X-hour, another image flickered on the screen. The line was so faint that it was almost indiscernible, well below the algorithm's minimum sensitivity. Only the operator's well-trained and keen eye noticed a faint, familiar pattern.

Once again, the UUV maneuvered so it could cross the line on the perpendicular. This time the magnetometer chirped loudly. They had found their target.

Once confirmed, a manual command from the ship caused the UUV to drop down to five meters above the bottom and maneuver itself until it was hovering directly over the almost imperceptible cable. Lights on either side of the vehicle flashed on, illuminating the darkness of that one small spot in the ocean, almost certainly for the first time in all of history. Two cameras focused on what could be seen of a big, thick cable just below, almost covered by mud. Three pods fell away from their housings on the UUV and settled quietly alongside the dense bundle of wires. Tiny plumes of silt were barely visible on the screen in the control room.

Its job completed, the UUV climbed up and away, heading back to the *Pushkino*. The unmanned vessel was in the process of docking with the mothership when its acoustic beacon registered a small underwater explosion almost directly below them.

Within seconds, stations on both sides of the Atlantic Ocean were excitedly reporting and confirming a complete loss of communications via all of the trans-Atlantic cables. Ninety percent of the communications traffic between the two continents—including all of the truly secure communications between NATO and the United States—had suddenly and unexplainably ceased.

Communication-wise, it might just as well have been the middle of the nineteenth century once again.

Ψ

Sarah Wilder was so frustrated she was on the verge of a major meltdown. She had been stuck there for hours in a decrepit chain motel at a noisy interchange off I-95 in St. Marys, Georgia, north of Jacksonville. It had not taken her long to reach the point of desperation.

Most exasperating was the fact that Alexi was not answering his phone. Nor was he responding to her increasingly shrill and frantic voicemails and texts. No one even answered at the emergency contact number that he had given her that awful night in the Connecticut casino. The night he told her they could not see or contact each other for a while and then proceeded to walk right out of her life. The night she had struggled to convince herself that he had not abandoned her. That the plans for their own dacha on the Caspian Sea were not just a dream erased in the wisp of cold reality.

Her dad seemed happy to hear from her but had an odd tone in his voice.

"Sarah, when you get back home, we need to talk," he told her. "Your friend? I'm starting to wonder if he is totally aligned with how you and I feel about things. He may be pushing too hard."

She had no idea what he was talking about.

She knew what she had to do. She had to reach Alexi. If not him then the other Russians he had introduced her to. She had to let them know what she had done to the submarine's systems. Otherwise, they would never locate that American war machine in time. From what little she knew, she was aware that such a lack of knowledge could prove fatal to the Russians if it came to an underwater showdown.

Then all the work she—she and Alexi—had done, all the

risk and danger, all the pain would be for nothing. World peace would have suffered a daunting blow. And the outcome might even lead to the very nuclear confrontation Sarah, Alexi, and the others were fighting to avoid.

She also knew she could no longer continue on with the charade of being a loyal, patriotic NUWC engineer. She would not make the trip the next day back to New England. Things had gone too far already. Even if her efforts had been a waste, even if they were ultimately unable to take advantage of her work, someone would certainly find the trail of what she had done to the system code. It would be obvious who had done it and why. That made it even more critical that she reach Alexi. Or someone who could take her to him.

Sarah took another swig from the bottle of cheap wine and wiped her lips on her shirtsleeve. This foul-tasting stuff had been the only excuse for alcohol she had been able to find in the Walmart across the access road from the motel. That is unless she wanted to drink Budweiser or Colt 45.

She had also purchased some underwear, a bottle of bubble bath, and some kind of off-brand perfume. While she waited for Alexi to return her calls, she would soak away her troubles, washing off the horrid stench of that nasty submarine *Toledo* that seemed to follow her like a putrid cloud. As she unbuttoned her blouse, she also thought how pleasant it would be— despite her despicable surroundings—to lie there in the hot water, to imagine the soap bubbles were Alexi's hands on her body, caressing her, bringing her to...

There was a booming knock on the motel room door. Sarah Wilder jumped and stopped breathing.

"Miss Smerchanski, are you awake?" The voice was faintly familiar, low and gruff, with a trace of an Eastern European accent. "You called for a pickup for the airport."

Sarah was confused. She had not called anyone about a ride to the airport. And then it clicked. Smerchanski. That was her emergency call sign. Whoever was on the other side of the door was a friend. He was here to take her to Alexi. She shook her head, trying to remember the counter-sign.

"You must be Gregor," she finally said. "The company said you were on your way."

"No, Gregor is sick. I am Bill."

That was the proper confirmation. She breathed again. The bath would wait. Soon she might even be able to enjoy one with her love, not just his memory. She fumbled with the buttons on her blouse and then fiddled with the latch as she rushed to open the door.

A small, mousy man was patiently waiting on the other side.

"Come, Miss Smerchanski. We must hurry. You must not miss your flight." He grabbed her Walmart bag and the small valise she had not yet bothered to unpack and gently ushered her down the sidewalk to the waiting car.

Ψ

Kapitan Fedya Orlov eased back in the pilot's seat of his *Blackjack* aircraft. Every muscle now ached, the result of this long, tense journey. The formation flight down the east coast of the United States—always reluctantly remaining just outside the Air Defense Identification Zone—had been an anti-climax after the initial leg of the mission, the adrenaline rush of blasting over both Norway and England, unafraid of any repercussion. He had wanted to flash directly over Washington, DC, as well, to toss the American president right out of his comfortable bed in the White House with a thunderous, multi-aircraft sonic boom.

However, his orders had been explicit. Stay outside the ADIZ. Come as close to the line as possible without tempting some gun-happy Air Force pilot to respond. Make a statement. Show the Americans what his aircraft could do. And only then, after duly impressing them, proceed to the planned landing point.

After successfully blowing past the waiting F-22s at Mach 3, Orlov did just as he had been instructed. He could only imagine the Americans' jaws dropping as he and his flight left them in their contrails. That had been fun, but in the process of toying with the cocky Americans, they had missed another rendezvous with the IL-78 tankers over the Atlantic waters east of the Bahamas. And again, the speed required surprisingly large amounts of fuel. The dalliance had left his aircraft with a serious thirst. They would not have been able to even reach Cuba on the vapors, let alone fly all the way to Venezuela. Tankers were hurriedly dispatched from Russia's Cuban outpost to meet them.

The refueling aircraft had now dropped away, flashing them a safe-journey signal as they peeled away and headed back toward Cuba. Just then, *Starshiy Leytenant* Eduard Polzin informed his captain of incoming messages.

"We are receiving an encrypted text on the secure channel. On the center screen."

Orlov shook his head, looking puzzled. This was very unusual. Even for a mission as out of the ordinary as this one. The secure channel was designated as "war-reserve," a frequency and signal mode intended to be used only in case of actual conflict. So why was it encrypted? The Americans would know nothing about the channel, so they would have no way to intercept the signal, let alone decrypt it.

Then Orlov realized the reason. The only purpose for re-encrypting an already highly coded message was to make sure no one on the Russian side could intercept and read it either.

The captain spun the lock on the tiny safe outboard his seat and removed the off-line encryption key. He inserted the device into the comms slot. The center screen flashed and blurred before finally snapping into focus.

"*Kapitan* Orlov: You are to load tactical missiles onto all of your squadron immediately upon landing in Caracas. Refuel concurrently and stand by your aircraft. You will maintain a ready fifteen-minute status until further notice. Target packages will be hand-delivered upon completion of tactical load-out. Further orders will be delivered with target package. War deployment procedures apply."

The message carried a one-word signature: "Salkov."

A message on a war-reserve channel directly from the Russian president? Tactical missiles, war deployment procedures, along with a hand-delivered target package? What did it all portend?

A cold shiver went down Orlov's back as he glanced over to his first officer in the next seat. Polzin was staring back, wide-eyed.

"I seriously doubt that we are going to have the opportunity to drink rum or enjoy the affections of any senoritas on this trip," Orlov told him, then checked his bearing for Caracas once more before slumping down into his seat.

He had no interest in contemplating what the next few days would require him and his squadron to do. But no matter how hard he tried to think of other things—of his wife and two boys back in Russia, of his second home in the mountains where the air was so clean and fresh, of his elderly mother who kissed each night the photos of her own father, a World War II casualty at the hands of the invading Nazis—he could not shove away the thoughts that he and his crews may soon be called upon to ignite a wildfire that could quickly engulf the entire planet.

This was no longer mere saber-rattling for the Americans and NATO. This was growing ominously close to a game of chicken, and the potential results were too awful to contemplate.

"That's a damn act of war!" General William Willoughby thundered as he slammed the message down on the desk. "Ain't no way on God's green earth this is all one big happy coincidence."

Admiral Tom Donnegan stared at the piece of paper and shook his head in agreement.

"SOUSUS detected a series of minor explosions at precisely the same time that the fiber backbone went dark," he said. "Thirteen of them and the probability ellipses intersect each of the trans-Atlantic cables. This was clearly sabotage, but you and I both know that there is no way to prove it or finger the guilty bastard."

"Well, you can bet Salkov is sitting back, giggling so damn hard over all this he's choking on his borscht," Willoughby snapped. "Communications with Europe are down to a trickle. What's getting through is being funneled through the satellites. Stock markets are in a panic and the bankers are screaming. Meanwhile we are putting out crap about an underwater earthquake or some such bullshit." The general leaned back in his chair and ran both hands through his thinning gray hair. "And now the Lithuanians are formally asking for protection under the NATO treaty. You have any concept of the amount of data it takes to move a couple of armored divisions to Europe? No way we can do that and keep it secure. Salkov will know every soldier's service number, blood type, and girlfriend's bra size before they even get close."

Tom Donnegan's jaw dropped. He looked at his colleague in disbelief.

"Tell me you are not actually moving two armored divisions to Eastern Europe. There is no way you could ever get President Whitten's okay to do that."

Willoughby shook his head. "Naw, not yet. But it's either send the troops we promise in the NATO treaty or threaten to use nukes to stop Salkov from storming across Lithuania and claiming it for his very own garden patch. No one in his right mind would believe President Whitten if he got in front of a microphone and said anything at all about nuclear weapons."

"I'm just damn glad it's you instead of me that has to explain this to him." Donnegan paused, scratching his gray beard. "Willie, have you worked out the logistics on this thing? You got a Russian battle fleet sitting directly across your lines. Any troops would have to be air-lifted over airspace they control right now. If you were counting on the Navy to escort your transports by sea, sorry. We can't do shit right now after Penny slammed our last carrier. Willie, you got yourself one damn big problem."

"Winking Willie" Willoughby gazed out the window toward the Potomac, its distant waters glittering in the afternoon sun. "You can bet Whitten is sweating bullets. He has to know Salkov is testing him and that he is failing miserably. No matter that the Russian bastards have cut the trans-Atlantic cables, buzzed Norway and the UK, flirted with the East Coast in their new planes, and done all they could to sink a couple of our submarines, unprovoked. Any one of those deals calls for us to at least puff up and act like we are pissed off and not going to stand for it. But the president seems more determined to keep that one campaign promise to find common ground with Salkov and bring an era of sweetness and light to Planet Earth. He is being stubborn. Playing to the polls and press." Willoughby suddenly sat up and looked across the desk at Donnegan. "Wait a sec, Tom. You said 'just about everything' you got is in homeport. Something you ain't telling me?"

Donnegan shifted uncomfortably in his chair.

"I got two submarines out in the Atlantic now. The *George Mason* and the *Toledo* are both a few hundred miles off the coast. You should be aware, too, that they have a few toys onboard that may give them an unfair advantage if it comes to shooting at somebody who's threatening us."

Ψ

Sarah Wilder had worked her way into an even worse mood as she climbed down the narrow ladder off the little turbo-prop commuter plane and was almost overcome by the cloying heat and humidity. Her Russian minder had told her nothing, ignoring her questions, as they made the short run down I-95 from St. Marys, into Florida, and to Jacksonville International Airport. Then, with a nod, he handed her a boarding pass for this little puddle jumper, told her someone would meet her at her destination, and promptly disappeared. She stamped her foot and cursed out loud when she read on the boarding pass where she was headed—back to where she started this awful assignment a couple of months ago.

She was once again on Exuma Island in the Bahamas. Or at least what was left of the place after the storm. Did the Russians not understand her point, that she had to leave the country before whatever happened out there in the Atlantic happened? That she had to get to wherever Alexi was?

Wilder still had her Walmart sack and found her small carry-on bag waiting at the bottom of the plane's ladder. She had splashed on some of the off-brand perfume, and now the odor of the stuff was about to make her gag. God, please make sure whoever was meeting her had some clean clothes for her. And a place she could take a bath.

She grabbed the carry-on and trudged across the sweltering tarmac toward the tiny island terminal. When she stepped from the brilliant sunshine into the semi-darkness inside, she was almost blinded. If anything, it was even more stifling in the gate area.

She stopped walking when someone touched her shoulder, followed by a familiar voice whispering from just behind her ear, "Sarah, darling, it is so…"

She wheeled around and slapped Alexi Markov with all her might, catching him full across the cheek.

"Don't you 'dear' me, you bastard!" she hissed. But then she touched the ugly red welt where she had struck him and gently kissed his cheek. Leaped into his arms, forced him to stumble backward against a wall, and then tried her best to hump him right there in the airport terminal.

Alexi Markov held her tight to his body, not fighting her at all, allowing her to move against him. He returned her deep kisses, ignored the pain in his wounded shoulder, and finally, noticing others staring at them, breathlessly whispered, "Let's… let's go find somewhere we can be alone. I know just the spot."

He eased her down, took her hand, and ushered her out the door and into the waiting car. As they peeled out of the tiny parking lot, he firmly grabbed her upper thigh beneath her skirt. He steered with one hand as he moved the other upward, caressing her. Sarah Wilder leaned back in the seat and moaned, ignoring the storm damage that whizzed past her open window.

Hours later, as they lay in the bed they had by now almost destroyed, she waited to catch her breath before finally speaking.

"God, I've missed that... you... Alexi. Never again. You're not getting away from me ever again."

Markov laughed as he reached over and gently touched the side of her breast and tickled up and down her ribcage. Wilder giggled and pushed his hand away. "Hold on. We have some work to do. I have to tell you about what I did while I was imprisoned on that damned submarine. Then we can play some more."

Now back in spy mode, Wilder proceeded to tell her handler about the stealth device she had been working on and described the backdoor that she had snuck into its program. The more she explained, the more interested he became. Finally, she had presented him with the key he had hoped for since the first day he started turning her.

Now he actually had a way to get back in Moscow's good graces. He would snatch victory from the defeat that damn SEAL Beaman had saddled him with.

If this woman would quit reaching for his manhood yet again, he would need to figure out how to contact those who could certainly put this information to good use.

She was back on top of him but he managed to get his cell phone from the bedside table and check the signal. No bars. It had been that way since the storm. He had dared to use a mostly-hidden landline phone at one of the island's few remaining restaurants to report a cryptic version of what happened to the boat and UUV and to arrange to have Sarah brought here. He had hoped she would have information of some value, but he could not have gotten better news.

Alexi had also set up his own escape plan for the next day, hopefully before Beaman or the others could find him. A plan that did not include the woman now trying passionately to ride him to an early death.

"Sarah, my darling. Please. You can ride a good horse until he is worthless, you know."

"But it has been so long, Alexi. I'm making up for lost..."

"Look, lie back, rest, get a shower," he told her. "I must get your information to the right people at once so we can use it in the cause of peace. It is a critical time. And you, my dear, have provided the key." She groaned as she rolled off him. He leaned over and kissed her, long and deeply. "I will only be gone a few minutes. I will bring food for energy so we can pick up where we left off. I love you."

"I love you," she told him. "Hurry. But be careful. Be careful and come back to me, Alexi."

"I will," he promised. "I will."

Ψ

Bill Beaman was sitting up in his hospital bed, reading through a sheaf of paperwork he held in his lap. Most of the tubes and monitors were gone now. Only a single IV dripped saline solution and a preventative antibiotic cocktail into his arm. Even the monitor had been removed and turned off. He did not miss the constant beeping, always perfectly in time with his pulse.

There was a soft knock at the door and then Raul wheeled Elliot into the room. The big taxi driver had his left leg in a cast that poked straight out in front of him.

"Look at me and my broken leg. Now, I be like you, Cap'n Bill," Elliot said with a laugh.

"How about that?" the SEAL responded. "Yep, we can limp

into the bar together, maybe see if we can get some sympathy drinks."

After a round of sincere handshakes, Raul parked Elliot's wheelchair alongside the bed and grabbed a chair for himself.

"How you doin', mon," he asked.

"A hell of a lot better than I was when you pulled me out from under that rubble. This recuperating has given me some time for my bad leg to heal up some, too. Doc says he wants another few days of observation, mostly looking for infection. Then they're going to boot my lazy ass out of here. Something about needing the bed space for people who are really sick, but I suspect they're just tired of all my bitchin' and moanin'."

"Real good to hear," Raul answered. "Too damn many Anglo tourists not able to get off the island yet and they be hanging around while we rebuild this place. They be drinkin' all the rum. Ain't enough left for us workin' stiffs."

"Anglos. Got to love 'em," Beaman said with a grin. Then his face shifted to serious. "Any word on Markov? That bastard can't have just disappeared."

"Markov. Gorbenov. I get mixed up on the dude's name," Elliot answered. "But besides checking on your well-bein', that is why we're here. We been lookin' for him for sure, and it is not too hard, what with flights in and out so limited and our guys at the marina, watching the only places a boat could leave, even if he found one what had not been smashed to smithereens by that Penny." Elliot and Raul both broke into broad, proud grins. "Well, sure enough, he shows up at the airport this morning. But here be the thing. He ain't trying to leave. He is picking up some woman. Our man had no problem seeing him. The two of them, they made quite a spectacle of themselves. Too much public display of affection for the locals. That got the tongues wagging to be sure. According to the manifest on the incoming flight, his woman was named Wilder, an American."

Beaman almost choked.

"Sarah Wilder?"

"Yeah. You tellin' me you know her, Cap'n Bill? Guessin' you know all the fine-looking women."

"Not really," Beaman answered. "But she is one of the NUWC scientists that were out on the barge, one of the ones that got evacuated by our submarine just before the storm hit. If she is linked up with our Russian agent, it could be a bunch of bad news. Any idea where they are now?"

"Not for sure, but with the island as beat-up as it is, there are only a very few possibilities," Raul answered.

Beaman suddenly swung both legs over the edge of the bed and yanked the IV out of his forearm.

"Where you going?" Raul asked. "You're still in no shape to go chasing spies. Or fine-lookin' ladies, neither."

"Just try to stop me," Beaman retorted. "I got a lot of reasons for wanting to get my hands on that Russki son of a bitch. Now hand me my pants. And my sidearm out of that drawer over there."

24

Captain First Rank Konstantin Kursalin leaned back from his submarine's periscope and rubbed his eye. There were days when he was convinced that he was now far too old to continue this grind. Never any chance to really rest, never a time to sit back and nurse a vodka or three with friends and tell obviously embellished sea stories.

Fatigue was a factor and he knew it. Yet there were still many more days left for them on this highly taxing mission. He simply had to allow for some bunk time. What possibly lay ahead of them would require him to be alert and ready.

"Sounding?" he requested.

"Ten meters under the keel," the fathometer operator responded immediately.

So there was no room to maneuver here, Kursalin reflected. Even so, it was time to turn and head north again. Even the slightest change in depth would stick them firmly in the mud within spitting distance of the American coast. Such a catastrophe would be a long, slow, and deadly one if they were not able to get themselves out of the muck.

There was only one option. This would have to be a very

deliberate, easy turn, and they could only hope the current did not nudge them too deep. He willed his pounding headache to subside, but the pain disobeyed his direct order.

"Left five degrees rudder, come to course north," he commanded. The big submarine slowly swung around until its rounded nose pointed toward Polaris, the North Star. If only he could keep his bow headed for that star for a week. That would mean his stern would be toward the United States, and he would be tracking for home again, the mission in the past. But it was not to be. At least not just yet. There was still much more to do before he would once again see the bleak, rocky Murmansk coast through his periscope.

The last several hours had been very strange indeed. They were cruising just a few miles off the Chesapeake Bay entrance, the lights of Virginia Beach clearly visible on the Western horizon. They were kept busy, dodging the many merchant ships heading up and down the coast. One large sailboat had passed disturbingly close to their periscope. But not a single Navy ship —carrier, destroyer, submarine, or even a Navy tugboat—was anywhere to be seen. It was strange, indeed, to see no signs of the mighty US Navy. Even though he had been told in his final briefing that all assets were confined to port by storm damage, he still could hardly believe it. Nor could he necessarily trust it. He must remain vigilant, just in case.

The *Moscow* was out there, not far away, finishing up her work. The last of over one hundred mines were on their way up the channel. The weapons could be used to effectively block the harbor for a very long time if remotely ordered to do so. For whatever reason the American naval vessels were tied up, they would have to remain at their piers now. No captain would be foolhardy enough to run that daunting and deadly minefield.

First Officer Kaarle Garlerkin hurried across the control room, clutching the message board. "Captain, a dispatch of highest importance. Some spy for the *Sluzhba vneshney razvedki* (Foreign Intelligence Service) is reporting the Americans have at least two submarines deployed. Apparently not all their boats are tied up at their bases as you have been told. And one of them is carrying a new kind of stealth device. Captain, the message reads as if they have once again stolen our technology."

Kursalin grunted. It was the prevailing belief that the Americans stole nearly every bit of technology that Russia's engineers developed. Then they would crow that they had been the ones who originally developed and built these magnificent new machines.

"At least we now know how they were able to make that sudden attack from nowhere last..." Kursalin murmured, his voice trailing off.

"Sir?"

"Never mind. Is there more?"

"Our operative claims to have programmed what he is calling a 'backdoor' into the device," Garlerkin continued, reading from the text. "The system will broadcast a special pulse at 157 kilohertz once the stealth device is activated, giving us adequate warning that the American submarine is there, but her crew will have no idea that we have been alerted. Estimated detection range with our sonar is three thousand meters."

Kursalin shook his head. "Moscow and their spy have probably vastly overestimated our capabilities again." He scratched his chin as he did quick calculations in his head. "Set the sonar system up to closely monitor 157 kilohertz. Make the filters wide enough to detect two kilohertz either side of that frequency. And plan on initial detection ranges being closer to fifteen hundred meters." Now the submariner tried to rub away the sharp pain between his eyes. "And Kaarle, make the weapons system ready for an immediate launch when we detect the signal. We will not have very much time at all at that range. Even with the advantages given to us by our comrade, the chances of our ever seeing our wives and children are practically zero if we miss them with the first shots."

Ψ

Jon Ward squatted down and leaned back against the payload module to keep his balance. One of *George Mason*'s fire control technicians was busy programming the Large Diameter UUV housed inside the payload module. One of the NUWC engineers who had come aboard during the quick stop in Norfolk looked over his shoulder, carefully explaining each step as the FT worked the keyboard on his laptop.

Ward could not help but think how different this all was from the *Sturgeon*-class boat—the *Spadefish*—that he had commanded only a few years before. A few years in calendar time but decades in technological development. What was it the wonks liked to say? Technological knowledge doubles every five years?

The idea of UUVs that could be programmed to swim out of a submarine, complete a mission, and then swim back to the mother ship—all without a human operator in the loop— seemed more like something out of *Star Wars* than the submarine force. But there it was, right in front of him. Four UUVs were housed in the payload modules and two more rested up forward in the large-diameter missile tubes.

"Excuse me, Commodore." The COB, Master Chief Oshley, interrupted Ward's reverie. "Captain sends his respects, requests you come to the conn."

Ward rose, unlimbering slowly as he stood, easing the pain in his back. A thought flashed through his mind about how submarining was a young man's game. Likely always had been, even in the days of the diesel boats, but the stiffness in his knees and back confirmed that.

"On my way, COB," he grunted.

Brian Edwards was bent over one of the BQQ-10 display screens at the port side of the control room. He waved Ward over as he intently studied something on the monitor.

"Commodore, we're picking up hits on what looks like a surface action group. Contact is on the TB-29 towed array. We've resolved bearing ambiguity to the northeast."

Ward nodded as he watched the multi-colored images flicker on the screen.

"Classification?"

"We're still sorting it out. Right now, sonar classifies target Sierra Four-One as a *Kirov*-class heavy cruiser, bearing zero-two-two. Sierra Four-Three is another *Kirov*, bearing zero-one-six. Sierra Four-Two is classified a destroyer, probably a *Udaloy*, best bearing zero-two-three. Several other traces are way out there but still too weak to track."

Ward shook his head.

"Wow! That's a lot of firepower. Does intel have anything to say about it?"

Edwards nodded toward the large display over by the OOD.

"This correlates with the tactical intel picture. ENTR shows the two *Kirov*s, two *Udaloy*s, and six *Neustrashimyy*s at about the same location we are looking at. Range is about two hundred miles. I figure we will close them to engagement range while doing some TMA to nail down the range." The skipper paused a beat and then asked the obvious question. "But what do we do then? Scare them with our good looks? We don't have any torpedoes, you know."

Ward winked, but his grin was weak.

"That's when we use the new gizmos you're carrying, Brian. You know nowadays we don't always need to have something that goes boom to get the job done." Ward studied the glowing splashes on the monitor screen. "At least I hope not."

Ψ

Bill Beaman had not yet gotten accustomed to the walking cane the hospital had issued him. His leg had healed incredibly with the forced post-hurricane bed rest. The crutches and wheelchair were gone now, replaced by a cane to help bear some of his weight. But the thing seemed to always be on the other side of the room when he needed it. And he felt like an old man, limping along with that damn crooked stick.

Beaman and Elliot had been sitting together in the NURF BAL lobby, impatiently killing time. The cement block building had sustained little damage by Penny's ravaging winds, but the high-water marks well up on the walls showed that nothing here was immune to Mother Nature's destructive whims. Crews were already putting things back in order so all the high-tech work could get back on schedule. It would not be long before NURF BAL was once again in business. Beaman hoped the same held true for him and his bum leg.

The two wounded warriors were playing checkers, waiting for Raul to get back with some news. He was out, running down some leads, scouting for the pair of amorous spies. The afternoon had withered into evening with no word from the searching brother. Neither could understand the delay. Exuma was not a big place, and with Penny pretty much wiping it bare, there were not many places to hide. And since Raul knew most everyone on the island, he had plenty of reports on the man and woman and what they had been up to, some of which bordered on the pornographic.

Last they had heard, the two of them had abruptly left the little hotel where they had given other guests—mostly construction and disaster relief workers brought over from Freeport and Nassau—an earful with their recreational bouts. Beaman hoped the pair had not found a way off the island just when his little team was so close to catching them and finding out what they were up to. Besides trying to wear each other out, that is.

The SEAL had also spoken briefly with Ellen Ward. Still no change in young Jim Ward's condition. Even if there had been, his dad was off on some clandestine mission for Tom Donnegan and likely out of communications. Beaman tried not to think about the young SEAL, lying near death in the hospital. It only made him angrier and more determined to get to the Russian spy who had tried to kill the kid.

Finally, Raul burst through the lab's front door, looking excited.

"I've found them," he all but shouted. "They be holed up in one of those washed-up boats, high and dry on up Calvin Hill way."

Beaman jumped up and limped toward his cane. "Then what the hell we waiting for?" he bellowed. Raul pulled something from behind his back and tossed it across the room to Beaman.

"Here, Cap'n. This be more fittin' of a fightin' man than that wimpy little cane you got there. It's a hunk of pigeon-plum. Penny pulled up the tree. Found it layin' alongside the road. It be like your head, as hard as a rock."

Beaman examined the five-foot-long piece of wood. It was a good inch and a half in diameter. At one end it enlarged into a root burl that fit perfectly in his hand. The other end had been carefully whittled down to fit into a crutch end cap. The dark, purplish-red wood felt solid and smooth to the touch. It had the heft and balance of a very effective weapon as well as a fine walking stick.

"This will do very nicely," Beaman said with a grin. "Thank you! Now what say we go bust some heads?"

Elliot was still not physically ready for what they might soon find themselves in the middle of. He stayed behind, supervising the clean-up as Raul and Beaman climbed into a battered, much-used pickup that Raul had "acquired." He steered it toward Calvin Hill.

On an island the size of Exuma, no trip took very long. The drive to Calvin Hill, even allowing for dodging storm debris and wreckage, required ten minutes. Just past the north end of the tiny village, a large motor yacht sat incongruously on dry ground, alone atop a small, sparsely wooded hillock. It looked like some giant creature might have plucked his toy from the harbor, dropped it there, and then left it behind.

Raul shut off the headlights, eased the pickup to the edge of the road, and parked beside what had once been a small stucco dwelling but was now a cement slab and piles of wreckage strewn about the sandy yard. A child's bent, broken bicycle was tangled in a stubborn bush near where the front door might once have been. A huge West-Indian mahogany tree lay uprooted across the slab, hiding a great deal of the yard. It also blocked the view from the wrecked yacht to Raul's parking place.

"Cap'n, we walk from here," Raul told him as he climbed out. Reaching into the pickup's bed, he hauled out two sets of night vision goggles and a pair of M-4 carbine rifles. "It occurred to me we might be needin' these."

The pair set out in a broad circle around the hillock with the intent of approaching from the back side. The undergrowth extended all the way down to the white sand beach on that quarter.

With the night vision goggles, Beaman had a good look at the stranded boat. It seemed familiar. Then he realized it was the one the Russian spy, Markov, had been aboard the night they exchanged fire. The night Jim Ward had been so badly hurt by that murderous son of a bitch.

They were less than fifty yards from the boat, approaching in a slow, low crouch, when a shot suddenly rang out. Raul yelped and fell flat. Beaman dropped and scooted over to where his friend lay.

Just then another shot kicked up dirt and debris a few inches to his right.

He grabbed Raul's foot and dragged him behind a sea grape. Its straggly branches provided meager cover, but it was the best they had for the moment.

"Where you hit?" Beaman whispered as he tried to determine the extent of Raul's wounds.

"Got me in the leg," Raul grunted in pain. "Sorry, Cap'n, I stepped in front of that damn bullet. Now all t'ree of us be crippled."

Raul pulled his bloody hands away from a nasty-looking hole in his upper thigh. Blood spurted out with each heartbeat.

Beaman knew at once the wound could be fatal if the bleeding was not stopped. He clapped his hand down on the gouge, yanked off his shirt, and wrapped the makeshift pressure bandage tightly around the leg.

"My friend, we have to get you to the hospital quick," he whispered.

Another gunshot rang out and tore into the sand a few feet in front of the sea grape cover.

"No way, Cap'n," Raul told him, shaking his head. "You go get the bastard up there. I be all right here." He was already pulling his cell phone from his shorts pocket and punching numbers. "You not my only friend on the island, you know. And tonight, some of them be drivin' the ambulance."

Glancing down at Raul, Bill Beaman patted him on the

shoulder, then pulled his new walking stick close and crawled off into the darkness on his belly.

"Cover me if you are able," he whispered back to Raul.

"I be able. You just be careful, Cap'n. That Russian, he be one bad man."

Beaman continued to slither around to the left, the direction they had started, now hoping to flank the shooter while shielded by what little undergrowth the storm had left. Keeping low, he snaked ever closer to the high-and-dry boat. His leg had begun to ache and several of the sewn-up gashes from the hurricane debris were burning like hell. He did what he always did—called on his SEAL training, not allowing pain to distract or deter him. Bill Beaman had a mission to accomplish, and it would take more than a little discomfort to keep him from doing just that. And he could not help but think of Jim Ward, a kid he had known since the day Jon and Ellen brought him into this troubled world. Had watched grow up into a fine naval officer and tough, young SEAL, doing all the right things for his country for all the right reasons. And then had seen him severely wounded at the hand of the very son of a bitch that now had taken potshots at him and Raul.

Deliberately, Beaman crawled up almost to the base of the makeshift ladder that led up to the hulk's main deck. He was already mulling how he might get aboard without being seen. There had been no more shots. Maybe the Russian and his girlfriend had abandoned their hideout and headed off to look for a way to escape the island. Or maybe somebody was out there waiting for them now.

Then the big SEAL heard something off to his right. A rustle in the bushes, close by, just down the length of the wrecked boat.

He stiffened and started to roll over, his rifle already pointed to the spot where he hoped a pelican or a rat or a gust of sea breeze had made the noise. But he heard a low, familiar voice, one that carried an Eastern European accent, and realized the rustle in the bushes had been intentional, to let the SEAL know he was finished.

"Captain Beaman, you are a very difficult man to kill. But I think tonight I will do just that." Markov. Alexi Markov. And from somewhere in the moonless darkness, he had a deadly drop on the SEAL. "Rid yourself of all your weapons, starting with the M-4, and then stand up slowly. Very slowly. I am well aware of the tricks they teach you in order to extricate yourself from such a predicament as this."

Beaman released the rifle and shoved it away with his foot. Next, with thumb and forefinger, he carefully slid the Berretta 9mm from its shoulder holster and tossed it toward the Russian spy's disembodied voice.

"The other pistol in your back waistband, please. And the knife under your left arm also."

Beaman obliged. Then, using the walking stick for leverage, he slowly pulled himself erect, deliberately turning to face the Russian spymaster, bracing the stick in his armpit to shift weight off his bad leg and find balance in the deep sand. If the bastard was going to take time to revel in what he was about to do, as bad guys so often do in the movies, Beaman would certainly allow him to do so. Meanwhile he would try to figure a way out of this predicament. And do it quickly.

Markov raised the snout of his AR-15, his finger already on the trigger. The reveling had clearly come to an end.

A shot rang out, but it came from somewhere back down the hillock. The bullet instantly splintered wood from the boat's hull, right beside where the Russian stood. He flinched, turning his head and instinctively pointing his rifle toward the sound of the shot. That split second was all Bill Beaman needed. He grabbed the new walking stick, jerked it from beneath him, and whipped it around, all in one smooth motion.

The cudgel caught Markov at the kneecaps. With a grunt, the Russian collapsed forward onto his face, his legs taken from beneath him. Beaman snapped the war club around again in a big circle, using the hull of the boat against his shoulder for leverage, and smashed the hardened root burl at the top of the stick into the side of Alexi Markov's head. The awful blow connected just behind his ear.

Beaman knew from the loud crunch of the man's skull cracking open that the spy was finished. He lay still.

Suddenly an ungodly scream erupted somewhere above where Beaman stood. A dark figure, a woman, leaped from the main deck, sprawling in the sand but bouncing back up immediately, screeching all the while. She lashed out with all her fury at the SEAL, scratching and clawing with one hand and brandishing some kind of wicked-bladed knife in the other. She was going for his eyes with her fingernails and his throat with the knife.

He spun away, falling almost beneath the boat, feeling the nasty gash she left in his right bicep. He was stuck, trapped, nowhere to crawl away. Beaman tried to kick the woman's legs to knock her off balance, but she speared at his thighs, still screaming like a possessed banshee.

Finally, when a boot connected with her ankle, she fell back a few steps. He rolled over and, with all the strength he could muster, again kicked her away. She was briefly off-balance and staggering backward, but managed another slash with the blade, this time catching Beaman in the meat of his right calf.

But he ignored the pain and used the stick to leverage himself to his feet. Stood even if his right leg was suddenly reluctant to hold him up. And the pain was so intense in his arm and the sense of touch now so dim in that hand that he could not even be certain he still held the only weapon he had left.

Bill Beaman sucked in a deep breath, let loose his own ear-piercing, primal scream, and once again swung his war club with all the force he could muster.

He hoped it was the crazed woman he had struck. Hoped it was not the ground or the hull of the boat that he had clubbed.

But the dizziness overcame him before he could find out, and the SEAL collapsed into the sand beneath the hulk. As the swirling blackness claimed his consciousness, he thought he heard the distant wail of a siren.

Or was it the primeval howl of the crazed woman, moving in for the final kill?

25

President Grayson Whitten held his usual seat at the head of a long mahogany table. He calmly sipped hot tea from a fine cup, a gift from the current government of China, the value of which would pay a year's wages of a typical factory worker in that nation. To his right sat Secretary of Defense Paulene Wilson, studying notes on the computer tablet propped up before her. To the president's left, Secretary of State Arthur Samson fidgeted nervously with his cell phone, the inevitable beads of sweat already prominent on his broad forehead. There was no one else in the room. That was a rare occurrence. The president usually preferred plenty of backup.

"I will remind you both again to let me do the talking," Whitten said. "Grigory will fuss and bluster as usual but we must not engage in his favorite sport. That merely plays into his hands. That is also why we don't have a roomful of aides and a bunch of intimidating military sitting here with us. He must realize that he *can* deal with us and that he *will* deal with us, not a bunch of faceless minions or medal-bedecked military. He must know that I run this show."

As if on cue, the wall-size video monitor at the far end of the room flickered awake and came into focus. A gentle series of tones announced that the circuit was active and two-way. Russian President Grigory Iosifovich Salkov was there, staring into a similar setup from behind his desk in the Kremlin. No one else was visible in the video frame from Moscow.

It was not lost on any of them that this communication marked the first time that the two world leaders had used the so-called "red phone." The actual red phone had long since been replaced by a much more sophisticated dedicated video link.

"Good morning, Mr. President," Salkov said with a twisted grin. He had chosen to employ his almost perfect command of English for this call. He often pretended little fluency in the language when it best suited his purposes. "You will have to excuse the picture quality and annoying video delay. It seems that we have necessarily had to use as a backup the Eutelsat satellite, which is overcome by unusually heavy traffic this morning. I understand that the fiber links across the Atlantic are inoperative for some reason. Greedy capitalists foregoing maintenance in exchange for profits, I suppose."

President Whitten's face reddened. His jaw muscles tensed as he gritted his teeth.

"Good afternoon to you as well, Mr. President," Whitten finally responded, but chose to take a sip of his tea before moving the conversation away from the very sore subject Salkov had chosen to broach right off the top. Secretary of Defense Wilson took advantage of her president's pause to ignore his previous admonition and make her own point.

"A situation for which we have you to thank, sir. Our SOUSUS arrays pinpointed the failure locations and correlated them without question to operations by one of your so-called deep-ocean research vessels."

As President Whitten choked on his tea, Grigory Salkov

smiled benignly and literally waved off the comment with a flip of his hand.

"That, of course, Madam Secretary, is a charge that you have yet to prove. Nor will you ever be able to do so. At any rate, such allegations are meaningless. No one believes the lies of the mighty USA anymore. Since what you insist on calling the Cold War and the disaster of Vietnam and all the nation-building and regime-change and oil-nation colonization you have conducted, international opinion has come to distrust anything you Americans say and the motives of anything you do." The Russian president sat up straight in his chair, clearly pleased with himself and the stinging lecture he had just been given the opportunity to deliver. But before Whitten or the others could respond, he lifted his right hand, pointed to the camera, and changed tones, his voice diving deep and threatening. "But I did not initiate this call to exchange pleasantries about some hunk of deep-ocean fiber or to remind you of the failures of your once-mighty country over the past sixty years. No, the reason for this call is to politely urge you to stay out of European affairs for once. Take care of your own problems on that side of the world. Bluntly, I am telling you not to interfere in our reasonable and legal efforts to protect ethnic Russian citizens in countries which were once lawfully a part of the Soviet Union—those innocents who are being abused and tortured and killed by their fascist puppet governments, and all due to thuggery supported by NATO. NATO, a treaty I do not need to remind you is one to which your country is a signatory. I suppose that makes you one of the thugs."

President Whitten sat motionless, his tea cup still halfway back to the table, the sip unswallowed. Secretary Samson was open-mouthed. Never, in his long diplomatic career, had he heard one head of state so blatantly blister another. It was unbelievably lacking in the gentlemanly discourse that typically ruled such conversations.

Secretary Wilson glanced at the two men at the table, frowning, waiting for one of them to supply a rejoinder. Neither seemed willing to do so. She slammed her fist hard on the table.

"Mr. President, how dare you try to dictate to the United States about what should or should not be our foreign policy." Her high-pitched, squeaky voice—so often imitated hilariously by the comedians on *Saturday Night Live*—failed to add gravity to her riposte. She cleared her throat and tried again. "If necessary, we will employ the full might of our military to protect our interests and allies, whether it be in Europe or anywhere else on the globe."

Salkov grinned, then chuckled, as if the presidential cabinet member had just shared an amusing anecdote. When he spoke, he used a condescending tone, one he might employ in speaking to someone lacking the intelligence to fully understand what he was saying.

"Madam Secretary, let me assure you that what you so amusingly term 'the full force of your military' will do you little good." The Russian paused for a second and gazed steel-eyed at the three American leaders. The chill could be felt from almost five thousand miles away, and a bit of digital hiss on the Russian's words made them sound icily brittle. He locked his fingers together behind his head and leaned back, taking his ease, clearly enjoying the moment. "You are not the world power you once were. Certainly not the one you have convinced yourselves and a few hapless allies that you are. You are powerless to carry out your puny threats. If you have paid any attention to your intelligence reports, you will know that a Russian battle force of historic strength is patrolling the Atlantic sea lanes at your very front door. Be assured that any attempt on your behalf to send troops to Europe in support of NATO will result in your planes being shot down or your ships sunk."

Grayson Whitten swallowed. Finally able to speak, he interrupted the tirade.

"President Salkov, please, let us not resort to threats. We are all civilized here. Let's determine a date and location of your choice and meet in person to discuss our differences."

"Mr. President, with all due respect, *shut up!*" Salkov said, exploding at the end. The circuit was eerily quiet for a moment. Then the Russian president leaned forward, closer to the camera. The three American leaders could hear his chair squeak. He again poked his finger in the direction of the camera. "There is nothing to meet about or discuss or work out. We are well beyond that point. Instead, you will do exactly as I say. Your navy will remain in port, where that hurricane so helpfully forced them. You will soon be aware that we have already heavily mined many of the harbors that are home to those vessels. Any attempt to deploy any warships will result in a needless loss of life and ships. I am also certain that you noticed the squadron of advanced TU-160M *Beliy Lebed* bombers—I believe that you call them *Blackjack* bombers—that we have recently deployed to bases in Venezuela. I think they caused quite a bit of a stir on their outbound route. We were not very stealthy about that for a reason. Be assured that they are fully armed and ready to strike anywhere in the US at a moment's notice. The little demonstration on their journey south should have convinced you that you and your allies are defenseless to stop them. While you and your Congress have haggled over your military budget, the people of Russia have been preparing to defend ourselves and those who, through no fault of their own, have been held under inhumane fascist dictatorships in the former Soviet republics."

Secretary of Defense Wilson finally spoke up, her voice sputtering.

"But Mr. President, each of those threats constitutes an undisputed act of war! Should you so blatantly attack United States territory or military resources, we would have no choice but to consider the possibility of employing a nuclear response, if necessary."

Salkov laughed and slapped the top of his desk.

"Secretary Wilson, I salute you for being the one person in the Whitten White House with a set of balls. But even you speak of 'considering,' 'possibilities,' and 'if necessary.' Even if I were afraid of such idle threats, that very hesitation on your part would convince me you not only have no choice but you would never use serious force. And let us be completely honest. You, Madam Secretary, are not the one to order such a response. The man sitting next to you would, and we all know that is not going to happen. Therefore, your bluff is meaningless. And quite comical."

President Salkov dropped his right hand and the menacing finger. The video screen immediately went black. Face flushed with anger, Paulene Wilson looked sideways at her president, the presumed leader of the free world.

He sat there, mouth agape, ashen-faced, in a near stupor. His hands were trembling so badly that he dropped the tea cup he'd held for the entire duration of the dressing-down he had just received from the Russian president. It shattered. None of the three noticed.

After a few seconds, President Whitten shook his head and regained some color. He turned to Secretary of State Arthur Samson.

"Okay, Art, here is what we will do." But his voice was soft, his words mumbled. "You will hold a press conference. If I host it, it will send the signal that this is bigger than it actually is.

Invite our usual group from the favorable press. Tell them that we have commenced discussions with President Salkov's government to find common ground for a mutual decision to resolve any differences we may have." Whitten, always the politician, hesitated as he searched for the right words to put whatever might be said in the best possible light with the people, the polls, and the pundits. "Assure them that we are confident these discussions will lead to a peaceful resolution to the current European situation while ensuring the safety and freedom of all citizens in Europe and the rights of each nation to protect their citizens from harm and harassment. Get Scotty to help you with the words. He's great at this sort of shit."

Paulene Wilson stared hard at Whitten.

"But what about the mines? The threat to sink ships and shoot down aircraft? To send bombers to attack the US? We should have the Joint Chiefs on the phone right this damn minute!"

"Paulene, calm down. We will consult with the military when the time is appropriate. Grigory is, as I have previously noted, full of bluster and..."

"So you are going to do nothing but call a press conference? And you are going to ask Secretary Samson to lie to the American people and meanwhile let Lithuania—and who knows what next—fall to the Russians?"

President Whitten shook his head wearily and then lapsed into his oft-used professorial tone, as if lecturing a particularly slow student.

"Look, Paulene, spare us the drama, okay? Once Salkov sees that we are not rattled into doing something dangerously rash, we can get him to a table somewhere, in public, maybe at the United Nations with the world watching. Besides, what would you have me do instead, suddenly start a shooting war with Russia? And all over a tiny European country where a majority would probably vote to rejoin Mother Russia if given the chance? We have more important domestic issues to resolve. Gun nuts shooting innocent children in our schools. The infrastructure crumbling. Factories spewing dirty emissions into the air, global warming, polar bears—too many to list. We would do best to let this crisis pass, ignore Salkov's saber-rattling. We cannot step into his trap. We promised the American people—and by 'we' I include you, Paulene, in your nominating speech for me at the convention—to avoid confrontation and work toward peace and better understanding among nations. Not this 'shoot first and count bodies later' philosophy that has gotten us to this point around the world. The polls back us up. Besides, this isn't the first time we have misled the American people for the greater good."

The president had quickly recovered from Salkov's face-slap and was already back in usual form.

The Secretary of Defense could only shake her head and wonder how she could have been so wrong in choosing to ride this particular horse all the way to the White House. And try to figure out what she would tell the Joint Chiefs as soon as she could get out of that room and over to the Pentagon.

Ψ

Joe Glass dropped down the ladder into engine room lower level. He headed aft, stepping past the feed pumps, over the sill into the next space. Doug O'Malley, the Engineer aboard *Toledo*, stood there wiping grease from his hands, a sour look on his face. EMC Stan Gromkowsky was crammed up behind the drain pump, spinning it by hand while watching the meter jump on a sound analyzer. The crotchety chief was shaking his head in disgust and murmuring profanities.

"What's the problem, Eng?" Glass asked, dreading the

answer. With what they were likely facing, his boat needed to be operating flawlessly. The crew, too.

O'Malley nodded toward the drain pump set up on the port side of the narrow space.

"We got us a problem with the lower motor bearing on the drain pump. It's making a real racket. If we keep running it, I'm afraid it will just fail on us. E Div is breaking out their gear and M Div is setting up the rigging to lift the motor so we can take a better look. Best case, I'm afraid the pump will be OOC for a day or so."

Glass nodded. "Okay, we'll cross-connect the trim pump to the drain system for a bit while we..."

"Captain, please call the conn." The 2MC engine room announcing system abruptly interrupted their discussion.

Glass reached around O'Malley and grabbed a JA handset hanging there.

"Captain on the line."

"Captain, Officer of the Deck." Glass recognized Pat Durand's voice. "Sir, we are picking up some kind of transients on the towed array. Master Chief Zillich thinks they might be launch transients but they aren't like anything he has ever seen."

If Zillich had never seen the signature of whatever was out there, then it had likely not existed before now.

"Call away Battle Stations Torpedo," Joe Glass answered. "Get a leg on those transients. We may have found what we have been looking for." He replaced the handset and continued into engine room lower level forward, then stopped, thought for a few seconds, and called back over his shoulder.

"Eng, get everything ready to fix that pump, but don't break the coupling yet. I don't want that thing dangling up in the air if we have to maneuver."

By the time Glass reached the control room, the battle

stations tracking team had assembled and were busy doing target motion analysis on the curious new contact.

Pat Durand was in the process of turning over to Jerry Perez as the Battle Stations OOD. Durand quickly briefed Glass as well as Billy Ray Jones, who had come running into the room, fresh from the rack, still pulling on his poopy suit.

"The transients have been to the northwest, best bearing is three-one-two," Durand reported. "We counted eight of them and they seem to have stopped for now. Also we just picked up a forty-seven-hertz line on that bearing. That doesn't equate to anything in our data base but we are tracking it. Best estimate of range right now is fifty thousand yards."

"Good job," Glass said with a nod. "This gets curiouser and curiouser. Let's narrow down the range a bit and close this guy. We have to be careful and not charge in, though. We don't want any surprises like the last time."

Billy Ray Jones looked over Glass's shoulder as the skipper studied the VMS navigation chart on the horizontal flat-panel. He was trying to get a geographic perspective of their tactical situation.

"XO, look at this," Glass muttered as he pointed toward where they thought the contact lay—the mouth of the St. Marys River, the entrance to the Kings Bay Submarine Base from the Atlantic Ocean. "Somebody has decided to hang out around the Trident base. I doubt they are there to go water-skiing. I have to wonder what those transients are. Let's slip in real quiet like and see if we can find out. Get Dr. Smithski's eggheads to make sure the stealth system is working at the max to make us invisible. I'd prefer whoever or whatever this is doesn't see us and figure out that we are intent on crashing their picnic."

26

Master Chief Randy Zillich's face was twisted as if in pain as he pored over the sonar display screens before him. The USS *Toledo*'s BQQ-10 transient analysis algorithm was up on one screen and the narrow band was on the other. Zillich was trying very hard to tease any stray bits of information from the flickering pixels of light. A pair of headphones was firmly clamped over his ears, just in case the computers missed some bit of audible energy out there.

The grizzled old Master Chief muttered to himself under his breath as he tried to conjure up some of his typical magic. Nothing was working. The contact had been there and then it simply disappeared.

"Captain, I lost him," he finally reported, sounding like a surgeon whose patient had just expired on his operating table. "No more launch transients. I lost the forty-seven-hertz line, too. Last bearing three-one-zero."

Joe Glass leaned over the VMS flat-panel display and played with the keyboard. For the ten thousandth time, he mumbled something about the "damn electronic gadgets" and how he missed the old paper geo plot. When he swung the bearing cursor around to three-one-zero and the range out to fifty thousand yards it lined up very closely with the mouth of the St. Marys River, the entrance to Kings Bay Submarine Base.

Billy Ray Jones looked over Glass's shoulder and scratched his head. "Skipper, what you reckon's going on? Launch transients on a bearing to Kings Bay. That can't be a good thing."

"Agreed," Glass shot back. "Based on what Admiral Donnegan told us and what little intel we're getting, I'm guessing that our Russian friends are over that way, and if they are, they cannot be up to anything good. Get Dr. Smithski up here. It's time to use his radar toy. I figure we need to mosey over that way and find out what's going on. That patch of water belongs to the citizens of the United States of America, and it looks like we got trespassers on our property."

"How's about we let the boss know what's going on?" Jones suggested.

"Good idea, XO," Glass replied. "You draft up a message to Donnegan. Tell him what we have and that we plan on searching the area around the St. Marys mouth. Ask him to get us the water over there. We certainly don't want to bump into any of our friends by accident. When you're ready to send, we'll make a quick trip to PD. Meanwhile, I'm going to use our underwater radar to see what we can see while we close the area."

Glass massaged the taut muscles in the back of his neck. They were about to stick their nose into a very dark hole. No telling what kind of monster was waiting in there to bite it off.

Ψ

Admiral Tom Donnegan sat back and sourly contemplated the future. The next few days would be critical if events played out the way he calculated they likely would. President Salkov would have a very limited time window to make whatever play the megalomaniac was planning. His fleet, no matter how powerful, could not control the Atlantic sea and air lanes for very long, so he was obviously planning to do something grandiose soon. Then he would present the West with a *fait accompli*, some move he would use to dare the West to try to reverse. By then, he would have established some new beachhead that would be impossible to take back. Not in the climate in which the world found itself these days. And that would just make the guy even more recklessly bold for his next move.

But what exactly would Grigory Salkov's master stroke be?

Donnegan grabbed the latest intel estimate and scanned the summary. It did not take the admiral's intellect and vast experience to figure out that the Russian armored divisions sitting on the Lithuanian border were not there to take in the tourist sights. Nor did Salkov need any other kind of diversion to just go ahead and shove across the border in the name of protecting the Russian nationals in the former Soviet republic. No, that likely would not be his main thrust. Nor was it a diversion to draw attention away from what the Russian president really wanted to accomplish. If his big play was to march into Lithuania, he would simply do it and ignore all the hollow threats and newspaper editorials around the world. Without the promise of US armed intervention, nobody else would step up to put a stop to such a thing. The invasion would be a cakewalk.

Just then the secure telephone's shrill jangling interrupted Donnegan's thoughts. He grabbed the offending headset and growled, "Donnegan. Go!"

"Not very hospitable, Tom," General William "Winking Willie" Willoughby said with a laugh. "We need to talk secure."

Donnegan reached over and punched a button on his STE phone. It bleeped and chirped for a few seconds, and then the LED switched from red to green and the sound cleared to a flat silence.

"I hold you secure," Donnegan reported. "What you got, Willie?"

"Hold you the same," the Chairman of the Joint Chiefs of Staff responded. "I just left a small meeting with SECDEF. By small, I mean her and me. No staff. It was not pretty."

Donnegan rubbed his chin. This was interesting. Meetings with the Secretary of Defense had always entailed a full entourage on everyone's part. Even so-called one-on-one meetings always involved aides in the room just so there were other ears to remember what was said. And, of course, to blame for any possible leaks that occurred. Meetings with no staff did not happen.

"Okay, you got my interest," Donnegan told him.

"She had just come from a meeting with his Imperial Highness, our mighty leader," Winking Willie said with a derisive snort. "Although she didn't phrase it quite that way, you understand. Apparently, they had a VTC on the red phone. According to Paulene, Salkov really blistered Whitten's ass. Told him in no uncertain terms to butt out of Europe or pay the consequences. Of course, Whitten is going to paint this as 'constructive dialogue leading to further substantive discussions.' The interesting part from our viewpoint is that Salkov told the president that all our Navy ports are smart-mined and that he will use his battle groups to attack any transport heading to Europe. Those, by the way, would each be an act of war, but Salkov doesn't seem to care. Or at the very least he is calling our bluff. Our beloved 'negotiator-in-chief' immediately folded like a cheap Murphy bed."

Tom Donnegan's mind was swirling. "Go on. Something tells me there's more."

"Well, to top it all off, POTUS ordered SECDEF and his Secretary of State to take no action at all. And they were not to talk with anybody about anything that happened or anything that was said in the call. Not their folks. Not even the Joint Chiefs. Especially not the Joint Chiefs. God knows we might try to do something to save our precious country from that idiot Salkov. No, the president is more worried it would screw up his poll numbers and deep-six his plans for re-election. The SOB is more worried about getting his skinny little butt re-elected than he is in defending the country."

Willoughby paused in his tirade to catch his breath. Donnegan could imagine how his eye would be blinking to beat the band.

"Well, at least Secretary Wilson had the guts to tell you what's going down before the bullets start flying. You got any ideas?"

"I might. Tom, you still have those two boats out there?"

A discreet knock at Donnegan's door interrupted their discussion. His aide stepped through the door and handed Donnegan a single sheet of paper.

"Hold a sec, Willie."

"Admiral, just received this from *Toledo*," the aide said. "You need to see it right away."

Donnegan quickly scanned the few lines of text and slammed his fist onto his desk. The aide scurried back out the door.

"Son of a cockeyed bitch!" Donnegan bellowed. "Willie, it's already started. Message from *Toledo*. Joe Glass says that he detected a bunch of launch transients—ten or more—at the entrance to Kings Bay Sub Base."

"Well, looks like Salkov wasn't bluffing about the mines," Willoughby grunted. "I'm closing all the East Coast ports until we can sweep them. Any idea how long that kind of operation will take if we throw everything we have at it?"

"Best guess would be a month, if we have the resources in place to do it," Donnegan answered. "The few sweeps we have left are way over in the Gulf. But you need to talk to Brad Brad-burn down at Fleet Forces. Those all belong to him. Meanwhile, I'm telling *Toledo* and *George Mason* to shoot to kill."

Willoughby agreed. "See what you can do with your boats. I'll get Brad working on the mines and see if he can get any P-8s in the air to help you out. And I'll see if Stick Thomas has any birds he can use to screw with that battle fleet."

"Okay, Willie." Donnegan paused. "But advise everybody to be careful. This is no drill. Our best hope is we stop all this crap with minimal damage on both sides. Pray that Salkov has nothing he can crow about and the world never knows what he —or we—lose out there."

"And if we don't get what we are hoping for..."

"Your worst nightmare times a million. A nuclear shooting war. The kind nobody wins."

27

The MQ-4C Triton Broad Area Maritime Surveillance (BAMS) Unmanned Aerial Vehicle (UAV) orbited at 65,000 feet, high over the North Atlantic. Delta Echo Three's broad wingspan easily kept the aircraft aloft, even at such an extreme thin-air altitude. The aircraft was every drone fanatic's wildest dream.

At the moment, it was gazing down at the Russian battle group steaming in formation more than twelve miles below. Its Multi-Function Active Sensor (MFAS) radar painted each ship in remarkable detail while the bird's MTS-B multi-spectral targeting system fed high-resolution imagery and other data back to an actual human being, "Spanks" Smith onboard P-8 Tail Number 441.

Smith sat in the tactical radar operator's seat inside the P-8 *Poseidon* aircraft that was lazily circling at twenty thousand feet two hundred miles to the southwest. He was receiving a constant feed from not only Delta Echo Three but also from her sister UAV, Delta Echo Five, hovering four hundred miles farther north. The two unmanned surveillance planes dutifully matched every course change the Russian ships made. If Boris stepped out on the bridge wing of the *Pyotr Veliky* battlecruiser and flipped a finger up at the eye in the sky, Spanks Smith knew about it before Boris could drop his hand.

As Smith watched the scene play out far below his two bird's-eye vantage points, the AN/ZLQ-1 ESM feed from Delta Echo Three suddenly spiked and raspy alarms began buzzing loudly. Smith had barely glanced at the ESM screen before seeing that a Tomb Stone fire control radar aboard the *Pyotr Veliky* had locked on. Then the electro-optical screen bloomed brilliantly in the infrared mode.

"Oh, shit!" Smith mumbled as he punched the intercom button. "Skipper, birds launched from the *Pyotr Veliky*! Looks like a pair of SAMs. Initiating evasive maneuvers for the UAVs."

Even as he started the pre-planned maneuvers for Delta Echo Three, Spanks Smith knew that there was very little chance that his multi-million-dollar toy would survive the hell-fire that was racing toward it. He watched in fascination as the electro-optical camera on the UAV followed the two incoming missiles from launch all the way to their target. The same target on which the camera rode, relaying back images of its own imminent demise.

At better than Mach 3 closing speed, the Russian missiles' flight took a little over two minutes. Then the screen went blank. That was followed seconds later by the display showing the camera view from Delta Echo Five also going dark.

Spanks Smith's mouth remained open in amazement. He felt as if he had just lost two of his best friends.

Just then, the AN/ALQ-213 EW system blared a series of ominous alarms. Smith's head snapped back as he read the monitor screen.

"Jesus! Tomb Stone's locked on us! SAMs are away!" he yelled. "Skipper, get us the hell out of here!"

Even as he gave the warning, Smith began simultaneously punching buttons. Clouds of metal chaff billowed aft of the gray bird as brilliant flares lit up the sky. Powerful radar jammers slewed around, aimed at the rapidly approaching missiles. All this was designed to try to confuse or blind the incoming SAMs.

As he felt the plane accelerate and make a hard turn, Smith stared helplessly at two specks of light on the electro-optical screen. The image showed a pair of SA-N-9 Kinzhal surface-to-air missiles expanding rapidly to fill the full screen. Smith touched two fingers to his lips and then to the photo of his girl-friend wedged into the corner of the screen.

"I love you," he whispered.

The missiles raced right past the chaff and flares, stubbornly ignoring them. Once directly below the P-8, they detonated with simultaneous blasts.

The shock waves ripped the port wing off the big bird. Angry, hissing shrapnel riddled the cockpit and crew compartment, shredding the aircraft and the men inside.

Every member of the P-8's crew was dead long before the wreckage of their aircraft splashed into the cold, gray waters of the Atlantic Ocean.

Ψ

"Loud transient!" the sonar operator aboard the USS *George Mason* called out. "Best bearing zero-two-one."

The submarine's skipper, Brian Edwards, and his passenger for this trip, Jon Ward, ran squarely into each other as they both raced toward the sonar operator. Sure enough, the display showed a short, very bright spot to the northeast. The screen maintained that the sudden transient had lasted less than a second.

"It sounded like an explosion. Or a crash. Or...something," the operator reported, realizing just how vague his analysis appeared. "Hey, I have never heard anything like that."

"See what the computer's best guess is," Edwards ordered.

The sonarman brushed his finger across the touchscreen, toggling an electronic switch. The small pop-up display flickered, "UNKNOWN TRANSIENT."

"The transient analyzer doesn't have anything in the database that matches, either."

Edwards glanced over at Ward. The former submarine captain had heard just about every noise there was in his years at sea. But now, he could only shake his head, a puzzled frown on his face.

"That's in the general direction of the Russian warships," Edwards noted. "I hate to think it, but could something be going on over that way? Or is it just a coincidence?"

"Only way to find out is to get closer and see," Ward answered. "Let's ask the boss what he knows. Suggest you launch a comms buoy so we don't lose any time gossiping."

Edwards nodded and turned to the officer of the deck.

"Mr. Jennings, load a comms buoy in the forward signal ejector then slow to five knots when it's ready to launch. Come to course zero-two-one and depth one-five-zero."

Aston Jennings repeated the order and put his team into action. The pilot brought the *George Mason* around to the ordered course and depth while the torpedomen loaded a comms buoy in the signal ejector. Jennings then ordered the big boat slowed to five knots.

"Launch the comms buoy," Jennings ordered. The co-pilot touched a button on his flat-panel display.

Thirty feet forward, the signal ejector outer door opened. High-pressure water flushed the three-inch-diameter, forty-inch-long buoy out into the ocean water. As it slowly floated to the surface, a hair-thin strand of fiber spun out behind it. A similar reel in the signal ejector spooled out as the *George Mason* moved forward. The cumulative effect was that the fiber did not move through the ocean, but stayed stationery as the buoy floated up and the submarine moved forward. When the buoy pressure sensor determined a depth of ten feet, the upper section parted and a balloon inflated so that an antenna bobbed to the surface, held there by the floating balloon. A thin whip sprang up to reach five feet above the wave tops.

George Mason moved slowly away from the spot where the buoy floated. Each reel had enough fiber for the sub to travel about three miles before it all paid out, meaning they had about forty minutes for communications before they ran out of fiber.

"Captain, Radio. We are in sync on the broadcast. Admiral Donnegan is on 'chat' for Commodore Ward."

Ward moved over to a computer console and typed in his password. The screen flickered for a second before a pop-up appeared. Words flashed up in the window.

"Tom, what is your situation?"

Ward, never a fast typist, pecked away as best he could.

"Admiral: Closing Russian fleet. Best estimate range is 150 miles to northeast. We hold them on TB-29. Also heard a loud transient on that bearing 15 minutes ago. Unable to correlate transient to any known activity."

The screen flickered a second later. Ward could imagine the expression on his old mentor's face as he took in the information on his display.

"Understand. Things heating up here. Expect Russians to be hostile. We had BAMS bird dogging them but lost all contact few minutes ago. Your transient could explain why."

Ward grunted as he typed. "Orders?"

"Do what you can to stop Russians. Employ all assets in your toy box. We need to chase them away. Do it as covertly as possible."

"Aye, sir. Any more intel appreciated," Ward typed. "Commencing operations with toys."

His eyes were drawn away to the latest plot downloaded on the ENTR screen. The Russian battle fleet had steamed a few miles to the north from their last reported position, but not much else had changed. Ward turned to Edwards.

"Captain, it's time to launch the packages in the forward payload tubes. Set the Russians' present location as the target area."

Brian Edwards nodded, then scratched his head as he admitted, "Commodore, we have never used these UUVs before. Is there anything special we need to do?"

Ward gave him a weak grin.

"Brian, as hard as it is for a good nuke to understand, these things are called unmanned underwater vehicles for a reason. Once we launch them, they don't need us anymore. At least not until they're ready to swim back into the tubes and catch a ride home. The mission is pre-programmed into their onboard processors, and if they get confused they will call home for help."

"So all we have to do is hit 'Launch?'"

"That's pretty much it. They tell me the things are practically sailor-proof."

"I'll be damned," Edwards mumbled. In a louder voice, he ordered, "Mr. Jennings, launch the UUVs in payload tubes one and two."

Lieutenant Commander Aston Jennings punched a few buttons on the weapons control console. Up forward of the submarine's sail, a series of valves repositioned to flood and equalize the two big payload modules.

"Captain, Sonar. Sounds of modules equalizing."

The two big tubes were only a scant few feet aft of the sub's hyper-sensitive Large Aperture Bow Array. The noise of the tube flooding all but blanked it out from detecting anything else.

Jennings looked up from his screen and announced, "Tubes flooded and equalized. Opening outer doors. Launching UUVs."

Up forward, two giant eighty-seven-inch-diameter heavy steel doors swung up and out of the way, revealing devices that resembled either very small submarines or very large, fat torpedoes. They were stored vertically, each device nearly filling its tube. The bright yellow UUVs easily floated up and out of the payload tubes, then swung over to a horizontal position and swam away from the mother ship.

"Captain, UUVs appear to be operating normally. Hold both opening our position," the sonar operator reported.

"Commodore, they are on their way," Edwards relayed to Ward. "Now, do you have any idea what they are supposed to do?"

Ward's mouth formed a sideways grin as he scratched the new stubble on his jaw.

"I don't know for certain, but I expect they are going to give that Russian admiral the first of several massive headaches compliments of the United States Navy."

28

Joe Glass paced back and forth across the busy control room. He had lost track of how many times he had made the circuit. He could feel the tension building in his gut, the tight, uncomfortable feeling that he was forgetting something. Something important. Something that required attending to right damn now. But for the life of him he could not conjure up what it might be.

Toledo's skipper had just finished another "chat" session with Admiral Donnegan back at the Pentagon. After hearing about President Salkov's latest threats and correlating that with the mysterious launch transients they had been hearing, both men were certain that the Russians really were mining key US harbors that contained naval facilities. The Russian president's threats were not idle bluster. It was also obvious that they were using a submarine to do it.

No matter what the politically driven Commander-in-Chief —the one who received his mail at 1600 Pennsylvania Avenue— had said, Admiral Tom Donnegan was perfectly clear about what had to be done. Whoever was laying the mines had to be stopped. It was not just a provocation. It was downright dangerous. An act of war. Right now, unless some cruise ship out of Port Canaveral happened to have some armed depth charges on its lido deck, Joe Glass and his submarine were the only ones in a position to do anything about it.

Glass reached for his coffee from the cup holder behind the periscope stand. A random thought flitted through his mind: how did a submarine metal cup holder get named a "zarf?" He promised himself that he would have to look up the answer someday. Someday when he was not on the verge of trying to torpedo a Russian submarine that was placing deadly explosives near US naval bases.

He took a big swig of the black coffee. Ugh! Cold.

"Eng is on the JA, Skipper," Jerry Perez, the navigator, called from his position back by the nav stand. "He says he has everything ready to rig out the drain pump motor. Requests permission to proceed."

Glass nodded distractedly, staring into his cold coffee.

"Rig out the motor," he ordered. "Tell the Eng to get that thing on the deck and lashed down as quick as he can. We sure as hell don't want a half ton of metal swinging in the overhead if we have to maneuver."

As Perez relayed the message into the phone, Glass turned to the computer console where Dr. Stan Smithski and Billy Ray Jones were huddled together, whispering and gesturing. Another odd thought crossed Glass's mind. The two of them looked like a couple of school girls excitedly discussing their dates for the big dance. He caught snippets of conversation about "incoherent scatter" and "the pulse-pair correlation algorithm." The NUWC scientist and the Southern "good ole boy" XO had clearly bonded over the new underwater radar system. They had been busy plotting out ways to optimize the untested system's potential performance. Glass was about to tell them they might soon get their chance, but for real, not in a test.

First, though, the skipper stepped into Sonar to speak with Master Chief Randy Zillich. It was time to make sure that *Toledo*'s sonar system was operating at its best and that the big submarine was as quiet as a hole in the ocean. They were now busy trying to track a weak 43-hertz tonal. They had first picked up hints of the tonal on the same general bearing as the launch transients. Then, when the transients stopped, whatever made the noise seemed to have deliberately moved away from the mouth of the St. Marys River and headed south.

Initially, they had speculated that the submarine—and they were reasonably sure it was a sub—was heading down to mine the St. Johns River, blocking the Mayport Naval Station there. But they had not heard anything that sounded like a launch transient as the target continued right on past there and kept going south. Glass figured the Russians did not want to waste any mines just to bottle up a few littoral combat ships. They probably assumed the little LCS vessels were useless in the real world and would not pose any actual threat to the battle fleet if they got out of the barn.

But that did not solve the mystery of where the sub was actually going. Half-jokingly, Zillich suggested they might be headed to Cuba for some liberty. But that really did not make any sense. Not unless Salkov really wanted to rub the US Navy's nose in the steaming piles he had just left up and down the East Coast. Propaganda pictures all over social media of Russian submariners in Havana, smoking victory cigars, kissing Cuban girls, celebrating triumphantly after demonstrating just how remarkably the balance of military might on the planet had shifted.

But why be so covert in laying the mines and then announce to the whole world what he had just done? Even someone as craven as President Whitten would have to react with force to that kind of public provocation.

Glass quickly decided such speculation was outside the bounds of what he and his crew could control. They needed to maneuver *Toledo* into a position to stop this mysterious minelayer. But where?

Glass looked at the charts on the VMS display, zooming out so that he could see the whole of South Florida and the Caribbean Basin. Then it hit him.

Damn! The Canal! Salkov was going to mine the Panama Canal. That would prevent the Pacific fleet from charging through to the rescue.

"Officer of the Deck, come to Flank, course south," he ordered. "Nav, give me the best course to get to the Windward Passage."

From what precious little intel that Glass could piece together, the interloper was most probably the Russians' newest submarine, the *Moscow*. It was the only boat large enough to carry enough mines to effectively shut down all the ports on the East Coast where naval ships were tied up. That also fit perfectly with the 43-hertz tonal. That particular signature did not show up in the library of known Russian submarines. This would be something new.

Joe Glass almost took another sip of the cold coffee but stopped himself. The last time he had gone toe-to-toe with one of Salkov's undersea toys, the son of a bitch had employed some sort of cloaking device, technology very similar to what now hid *Toledo*. Clearly the *Moscow* did not have such protection. They could hear her just fine, if weakly.

But the Russians never sent a boat out alone. Even when their boomers were hiding beneath the Arctic ice, they always had an SSN lurking around to help protect them. They would certainly have an escort on such a dangerous mission as the one that they were trying to pull off now.

Was his cloaked friend actually out there right now,

protecting the *Moscow?* If so, how would he handle this? How could they engage the minelayer knowing an invisible, deadly vessel was prowling the area, ready to shoot back?

Then the thought hit him. How could he be so dense? Even if *Toledo* was invisible to the Russian sonar and the Russian submarine was invisible to *Toledo*'s sonar, Glass had two big advantages over the bad guys.

First, the sons of bitches had no idea *Toledo* was even out there. All US Navy vessels were, so far as the Russians knew, tied up at the dock. Nor did they know that *Toledo* had a cloaking device. The last time, the Russians only got a shot off because the new technology had failed.

Even more importantly, the Russians had no inkling of the underwater radar system *Toledo* carried. If they could make the radar work, that gave *Toledo* a tremendous advantage in finding the "undetectable" Russian submarine. She might be invisible to sonar but she would be right there, bright and beautiful on the new radar.

Okay, so they had a couple of advantages to help them find the Russian. But then what? The Mark 48ADCAP torpedoes that *Toledo* carried used the most advanced sonar in the world to detect and home in on their target. But that sonar, as good as it was, would be useless against the protector sub if the torpedoes could not "see" her. Also, once they fired the first torpedo, both Russian vessels would not only know *Toledo* was crashing their party but also know exactly where she was. Even though the submarine would remain unseen, the fish and their launch point would be perfectly visible the instant they emerged from the tubes.

Glass turned back to where Smithski and Jones were still chattering away. The only possible answer was the underwater radar. The mostly unproven radar. They would have to rely on it to show them where to aim so the first shots would be true, lessening the chance of retaliation.

But how could they possibly lash up some way to put it to use? And even if they figured that out, would it actually work the way some engineer at the Naval Undersea Warfare Center designed it to?

Glass had no way to be sure, but at the moment, he had no other choice. He could only hope that Smithski and his XO would be able to figure out something. And that no one who worked on the system had a bad day and left some bit of computer code disconnected or pointed to the wrong line somewhere in the program.

Once the shooting started, there would be no time to de-bug software.

Ψ

UUV GM-1 had proceeded as programmed since leaving the submarine *George Mason*'s payload tubes. Now it slowed and came shallow, precisely as instructed. When it sensed the lower sea pressure, the control processor—the brain—sent an antenna up to take a deep sniff of the electronic spectrum. After a few minutes of gathering all the electronic bits and bytes, the brain sorted out the Russian radar signals and data streams from the classic rock broadcast stations, the amateur radio operators, the cell phones, and all the other radio-frequency energy across the spectrum, and calculated a bearing to the convoy of Russian warships. Then it uploaded all its data to an orbiting satellite high in the sky overhead. After a millisecond's calculation, the brain ordered a new course for GM-1 that sent the UUV just west of the Russian battle group.

Deep in the bowels of Fort Meade, Maryland, under tons of concrete and dirt, GM-1's bits and bytes were captured and fed into the world's largest and fastest super-computer. Even with the National Security Administration's massive computational power and database, reducing the terabytes of digitized information to usable intelligence took an hour of precious processor time.

Meanwhile, fifty miles away from where GM-1 was already changing course, GM-2 performed a very similar set of precise maneuvers. It then dutifully pointed its bow toward a spot east of the Russian battle group.

Two hours later, the UUV GM-1 again slowed and came shallow. And again it deployed its antenna, gathering all the electronic signals that were out in the environment. But this time, GM-1's controller, sitting in a bunker just a few feet from the shoreline in Dam Neck, Virginia, sent a series of orders to the unmanned underwater vehicle's brain. The UUV acknowledged the new instructions and injected a short series of codes into the Russian data stream.

An hour later and sixty miles farther east, GM-2 slowed and came shallow. The canary-yellow unmanned submarine performed a very similar series of operations of its own. Then, on command, it, too, injected more data into the Russian data stream.

The two unmanned undersea warriors repeated their tasks diligently as they moved to take their stations to the northwest and east of the battle group. Each time they came shallow to sniff the electronic spectrum, they injected a little more of their own special ingredients into the Russian data stream.

The lines of code the Russians were swallowing were slowly building up.

Ψ

Ellen Ward had hardly left the spot she had claimed for

herself in the hospital's ICU waiting room. That assured she would be able to see her son during the short visiting times she had been allotted and could be easily found if there was any update on Jim Ward's condition.

She could see no change at all when she stood by his bedside. He looked so strong, so indestructible, but his closed eyes and all the tubes and sensors and probes indicated that he remained a very sick young man. The nurses could only tell her his vital signs remained stable, which the readouts on the various monitors confirmed. The doctor had been busy and could only repeat what he had already told them.

They would have to wait to see if her boy would ever wake up again. And what kind of shape he would be in if he survived.

A particularly loud group of family members was carrying on an argument with a judge holding court on the waiting room's TV. They were so into the show that Ellen almost did not hear the nurse calling her name.

"Mrs. Ward!"

"Yes?"

"The doctor wants to speak with you. Consultation room three. Right down the hall. He'll be there in a few minutes."

Ellen held her breath as she gathered her purse and shawl and tried to read the young nurse's expression. It revealed nothing. She wished yet again that Jon were there with her. But this was nothing new. She had been on her own through many difficult times over the years while he was away, doing what he did.

She was aware she was about to get very good news or very bad news. Either way, she would have to bear it alone, and for who knew how long. She did not know where on the planet her husband actually was. Whether he was above or below the ocean's surface. No idea when he would be someplace where she could share with him what she was about to learn.

Even so, Jon was with her in spirit. He always was. She knew that and drew strength from it.

The nurse held the door open for her as she stepped out into the broad hallway. She felt a cold breeze from somewhere as she made her way toward the consultation room and the rest of her life.

29

Kapitan Fedya Orlov kicked the foot of the rusty metal bed hard, jarring awake the sleeping *Starshiy Leytenant* Eduard Polzin.

"Time to wake up from your sweet dreams," the pilot roared. "We have our orders."

Co-pilot Polzin groaned, rolled over, and rubbed the sleep from his eyes before finally sitting up. He looked around groggily, as if he still was not sure where he was. The two men shared a small, corroded metal trailer parked mere feet away from the revetment that protected their parked TU-160M bomber.

"Orders? What orders?" he mumbled as he slowly stood, stretched, and stepped into his flight suit. "Please tell me we are headed home. Even if so far we have not seen any naked senoritas, a drop of rum, or even a good cigar. Some vacation for the Rodina's finest warriors."

Orlov finished throwing his meager kit into his flight bag and opened the door. It was still dark outside. Dark and stickily humid. The grumbling air conditioning unit in the trailer's lone window had kept the air just tolerable during the short night's sleep.

"Grab your stuff, warrior," Orlov shot back over his shoulder. "Wheels up in fifteen minutes."

Two minutes later, Eduard Polzin emerged from the trailer into a world gone mad. Lights blazed, cutting through the pre-dawn darkness. A thick layer of misty fog hid the night sky. Red lights flashed on fuel trucks scurrying down the taxiways. Other transporters were busily topping off the fuel tanks of the bombers lined up in neat order along the concrete apron. Still more vehicles—weapons carriers—loaded missiles into the waiting warbirds.

The co-pilot jogged across the tarmac, then pulled up abruptly to avoid getting flattened by a lorry loaded with a flight crew that came zooming toward him out of the swirling fog. He finally climbed up into the sleek, deadly, supersonic bomber and struggled into his harness. Orlov was already sitting in the pilot's seat, working down the pre-flight checklist.

"Any idea what is going on?" Polzin asked. He had never seen such frenzied activity around his aircraft.

Orlov shook his head. "I do not know. Our orders are not so specific. All I know is that we are loading tactical missiles on all the squadron. We are to complete the tactical load-out and be airborne before 0500 local time. We rendezvous with the tankers east of here to top off our fuel tanks and then take an orbit out over the Atlantic. That is all I know. Now, quit asking questions I cannot answer and help me with this pre-flight."

Fifteen minutes later, eleven Russian TU-160M bombers lifted off from Venezuelan soil, roaring into the air one at a time with an ear-splitting rumble. Then, in perfect formation, they turned as if joined together and headed northeast into the hazy sky. Once above the fog banks, just a hint of orange and pink glinted off their right wings as yet another day announced its imminent arrival in the Peoples Republic of Venezuela.

Ψ

Six hours earlier, as that same sun was just starting to raise its arrival banner over the Republic of Lithuania, a thousand Russian T-14 Armata tanks spewed blue smoke into the crisp pre-dawn air. Their massive A-85-3A diesel engines coughed to life, crushing the morning quiet. Another couple of thousand Uran-9 robotic battle tanks roared as their engines kicked over. The smaller, unmanned war machines intermixed with the huge main battle tanks.

At the same time, ominous sonic booms and flaming contrails streaked high across the pink-gray sky, rivaling the appearance of the sun, marking the paths of hundreds of Mig-35 Fulcrums and Su-35 Flankers heading northward from Russian territory.

Below the fast movers, closer to the green farmland, Mi-28 Havoc attack helicopters rose and buzzed away like a very large swarm of angry, steel-spitting hornets. A long line of troop-laden Mi-24 Halo transport helicopters, stretching for miles to the south and east, followed the Havoc choppers over the invisible line that marked the Lithuanian border with Belorussia. They all headed north, toward the capital city of Vilnius.

The invasion continued as the Armata tanks and their unmanned companions wheeled out and slewed away in the same direction, their steel tracks churning the newly seeded winter wheat fields into an ugly sea of mud. Just behind the battle tanks, battalions of BMP-3 infantry fighting vehicles and BTR-4 armored personnel carriers followed.

Over thirty thousand Russian troops crossed the border without a shot being fired in defense. The sleepy residents of Vilnius rose to find the streets filled with troops dressed in drab green combat gear. The Russian press and a small crowd of ethnic Russian civilians were already gathered in the giant courtyard at Vilnius University to cheer deliriously the "liberating heroes." Those images of a grateful populace were for the homeland media consumption but would soon also be seen on CNN, Fox News, the BBC, and every other media outlet in the world.

Meanwhile, a few blocks away, the members of the Lithuanian government—many still in their night clothes—made a panicked evacuation, carrying what documents they could hastily gather, grabbing whatever official vehicle they could commandeer. They hastened across the Neris River toward the city of Klaipeda on the Baltic Coast on roads already clogged with terrified citizens.

The tiny Lithuanian Air Force was caught totally by surprise. Their one combat aircraft, a Czech-made attack jet, managed to struggle aloft only to crash in flames seconds later. A Russian Mig-35 performed an insolent victory roll low over the runway at Šiauliai Air Base before rocketing straight up. The last gesture was a final "screw you" before the fighter jet disappeared into the rising sun, headed back to its home base for a celebration and to receive medals of valor.

A few platoons of the Lithuanian Iron Wolf Mechanized Brigade managed to get their ancient Mark 113 armored personnel carriers armed and out into the field. Their light armor and Mk-2 50-caliber machine guns were not even a speed bump for the Armata tanks and Uran-9 robots. It was not long before burning hulks dotted the landscape.

By noon local time—about the time the Russian bombers were clearing Cuban airspace—the invading Russian troops had consolidated their positions and swung around to head west toward Kaliningrad. Before the sun set in the west that afternoon, a fifty-kilometer-wide corridor existed from the Belarussian border to the Kaliningrad Oblast. The Russian troops settled in to enjoy their leisurely parade through

Lithuania. Tomorrow they would mop up whatever meager resistance the Lithuanian army and their NATO allies might muster.

Tonight they would revel in the successful liberation of Southern Lithuania and its oppressed Russian ethnic minority.

* * *

President Grayson Whitten had grown tired of being in the White House Situation Room. Lately he seemed to be spending all his time in this cave deep below his Oval Office, out of sight of the press and the electorate. True, he was supposed to be here at times of crisis, doing his part to solve the world's problems. However, he was still convinced that all the hoopla over the Russian president, his idle threats, and even his haughty words were only a test, trying to see how far he could push the US president before Whitten did something dumb and reactive.

President Whitten was determined to show Salkov that he could not be bullied, that he would remain rational and not try to counter the Russian's intimidation with foolish, threatening harangues of his own. No, Whitten was going to demonstrate true resolve, take the high road, stay the course, allow the world community to align and show Salkov what he would face in the form of censure and sanctions if he continued his ways. Besides, the voters had chosen Grayson Whitten specifically because he promised to no longer involve America's troops in every skirmish in every far corner of the planet. No, he had guaranteed to put people back to work, get the economy back on track, and he had a long list of government programs that would do just that if he could only get them past that stubborn bunch that now controlled both houses of Congress.

But now, here he was, wasting time and energy on another

damn emergency that demanded his attention instead of taking his case for the new programs to the people.

"Okay, okay," Whitten said impatiently, waving his hand at the video screen. "Let's get on with this."

A grim-faced Secretary of State Arthur Samson sat next to President Whitten, looking at the same video screen at the far end of the Situation Room. Staring back at them was Darijus Kestutis, President of Lithuania, and, next to him in the same frame, Maxine Williams, the new US Ambassador to the country.

Kestutis was a short, paunchy, balding man. He began speaking, pounding the table in front of him for emphasis, stating his case in rather good Oxford English. The man was obviously in shock, his disheveled appearance adding urgency to his pleas.

"Mr. President, we need the military assistance of NATO immediately. And we all know by NATO I mean the United States of America. Under the terms of the NATO Treaty, we are officially calling upon the United States and all other members to join you in coming to our defense. As I am sure you know, Russian military forces invaded our country this morning with overwhelming force. At this time, they occupy almost a quarter of our nation, including Vilnius. The government has evacuated to Klaipeda."

Whitten kept silent, studying his manicure. Secretary Samson finally decided the president was not paying attention so he directed a question to Ambassador Williams.

"Madam Ambassador, what is the situation from your perspective?"

Maxine Williams was a middle-aged matron who usually wore too much makeup. This morning she appeared to wear none. And she was clearly on the verge of panic.

Williams had presented her credentials as ambassador only

a few short weeks ago. She was a long-time party hack and, prior to this appointment, had served as chairman of the party, using her rather extensive and considerable influence to help get Grayson Whitten elected. This ambassadorship was meant as a reward for her loyalty, a plum assignment where most duties were purely ceremonial or boringly routine and there was little danger of her messing things up.

"Art, I didn't sign on for this job to find myself in the middle of a shooting war," she screeched. "Get me out of here right now. Send the Marines. Send the Navy. I don't give a damn what you send, just get me out of this mess."

"Maxine, please don't get all excited," Samson told her. "I'm sure it's not that bad. We can work this out. Just some misunderstanding with President Salkov."

"Misunderstanding, my ass!" Williams thundered. "I had to evacuate the embassy. There were Russian tanks with their guns aimed at me. All my furs and clothes are still in the official residence. Some damn Cossack's bitch is probably strutting around with them even as we speak."

"President Whitten," Kestutis interrupted. "While I appreciate and sympathize with Ambassador Williams's concerns, I really think we need to discuss military intervention for the defense of our sovereign territory. When can you have troops and fighter planes here?"

"President Kestutis," Whitten answered, speaking slowly, forming his words carefully as he spoke. "The US military simply cannot be used in this manner. We will need to first attempt to resolve this situation through peaceful channels. We have an organization specifically tasked with bringing the world community together to solve territorial disputes..."

"Territorial disputes?" Kestutis sputtered. "This is an invasion! Lithuanian citizens have been murdered! Our government is on the run and..."

"Darijus, please," Whitten said, holding up a hand to the video screen. "Stop this now. We gain nothing by becoming irrational and rushing to a violent retaliation. We have already requested an emergency session of the United Nations in order to gain a consensus, and, with the collective strength of the world's nations, we will then seek remediation. I assure you this unpleasant episode is merely a temporary..."

The Lithuanian president went from pale to red-faced, livid with anger.

"You are abandoning us! You are turning your back on your treaty obligations!" he stormed. "President Salkov is right. You are spineless. My people will fight on to defend our country. Fight on to the last man and woman. And you, sir...you and your NATO can go straight to hell!"

The video screen went blank just as Ambassador Williams seemed ready to once again plead for rescue.

Secretary Samson was the first to speak.

"Well, in my experience, that was about the worst video conference with a friendly foreign leader that I have ever witnessed."

President Whitten shrugged. "So, what exactly would you have me do that I am not already doing?"

"I might suggest that you issue a tough statement for the press. The news channels are already speculating why you haven't said anything yet."

"Give me some credit, Art. Mike's already requested TV air time for this evening, prime-time coverage. He's circulating a draft statement to all our media advisors and polling analysts now. Tammy's waiting right now in the Oval Office to work on my expressions and gestures to be sure they are appropriate. With the right words and a good performance on my part, we should get some positive spin from the usual friendly networks and columnists. Nothing I can do about the others. We'll watch the polls, but with the right messaging, we should be able to come out of this with a net gain."

"Well, thank God for that," Secretary Samson said, not even attempting to hide the sarcasm. "At least the American people will get the right spin. The Lithuanians are left with their collective asses in their hands."

Whitten looked sideways at him.

"So what would you suggest I do, Art? Start a nuclear war over some little patch of farmland in Eastern Europe? That's the only option that Salkov left me, and we all know that is what he's trying to push us into. I won't go down in history as the president who started a nuclear war."

"Well, Mr. President, I do suggest you get the military involved, just in case we do have to call Salkov's bluff. If it is a bluff. And I am in serious doubt about that right now. I believe the bastard truly intends to annex Lithuania and God knows what else if we don't respond. And if things go haywire, we can blame any downside on the bungling military."

"All right! All right! I get the message. Call General Willoughby and Secretary Wilson and get them over here. Maybe for once they can come up with a useful alternative course of action that doesn't involve blowing up hell's half acre and getting us bogged down in some backwater republic for a decade or three."

30

The *George Mason* sat motionless and silent, one hundred and fifty feet beneath the surface of a particularly empty patch of the Atlantic. In a careful, slow sequence, each of the four payload tubes behind the boat's sail swung open, allowing a yellow UUV to float up and out of its tube into the open ocean before swinging over into a horizontal position. The four newly launched UUVs swam clear of the *George Mason* and immediately headed northeast, each unmanned vessel off on its individual mission. Jon Ward watched the sonar display as they faded out in the distance, then turned to Brian Edwards.

"Skipper, it's time for us to get into position. We need to be just over the horizon from the nearest Russian ship, say fifteen thousand yards. But first, I need you to get in closer and do it very, very quietly. Come around to course north and close the group at best quiet speed."

Edwards ordered the changes in course, speed, and depth as the two men stepped over to the large horizontal flat-panel VMS display. Edwards moved the cursor to a drop-down window and selected a god's-eye view. The screen shifted so that from their perspective it appeared that they were riding a satellite orbiting high over the Atlantic Ocean. The blip representing the *George Mason* was about twenty-five miles south and west of where the Russian battle group had spread out. Those warships were still stubbornly straddling the primary shipping and aircraft routes between Europe and North America.

The four UUVs *George Mason* had just launched showed up on the display as little green dots steadily moving away from the submarine, toward the Russian war group. The other two UUVs —the ones they had launched the previous day—were to the north and east of the Russians, now circling slowly as they awaited their next commands.

Ward pointed to a spot to the west of the battle group.

"This is where we need to be for the next phase of the attack. We certainly don't want to be hanging around anywhere near the UUVs."

"Why not, Commodore?" Edwards queried.

"It's probably going to get real hot in their vicinity," Ward replied with a chuckle. "I expect there will soon be lots of ordnance flying around. We sure don't want to suffer collateral damage from any of those fireworks. And Captain, please load the signal ejectors with those special buoys we brought aboard. We need to see if we can add a little more confusion to the mix."

Ψ

Captain First Rank Kursalin expertly danced the brass dividers across the navigation chart, measuring the distance that the *Igor Borsovitch* and their giant playmate, the *Moscow*, needed to travel beneath the surface of the Caribbean Sea in order to reach their next destination.

The much younger First Officer Kaarle Garlerkin, clearly amused at his captain's outdated ways, could not resist commenting, though such input sometimes led to a fierce rebuke.

"The computer would give you the answer much faster," he said quietly, so that only Kursalin could hear. "And the result would be far more precise."

Kursalin snorted and waved him off.

"I know that, First Officer. But I do not need a precise, instantaneous answer. I need time to think, to figure out our next move. The old ways offer me such an opportunity. The digital solution does not." The captain pointed to a spot on the chart a few kilometers off Colon, Panama, the Caribbean entrance to the Panama Canal. "If we are going to fulfill President Salkov's orders, we need to be here by dawn tomorrow morning. To get there in time, we will need to make fifty kilometers per hour. Easy for us, but the *Moscow* will need to go to Flank. It is a thousand kilometers straight across the Caribbean Basin."

"But will the Americans not hear us?" Garlerkin responded, worry evident in his voice. "We will be running across their back porch, and they have to know what we are up to by now. If not, our direction of travel and speed will certainly alert them."

Kursalin shook his head.

"Maybe. But we have no real choice in the matter. Our orders are to be near the canal entrance by dawn tomorrow. We must do everything we can to be there. Signal *Moscow* to come to Flank and steer best course through the Windward Passage. Then double-check the stealth device. We want to be sure they can see only one of us so we can better do our job and protect *Moscow*."

Ψ

"Winking Willy" Willoughby grabbed the STE phone and

punched hard at the buttons. He was so angry that the device skittered across the desk from the force. As he pulled it back and held on as he dialed, his eye was blinking at near Mach speed.

The phone was answered on the second ring.

"Office of the Secretary of Defense."

"This is General Willoughby. Patch me to Secretary Wilson right now!"

"I'm sorry, General," the receptionist politely answered. "She is in a meeting and asked that she not be disturbed. May I...?"

"I don't give a damn!" the Chairman of the Joint Chiefs of Staff shot back. "Get her on the phone right damn now."

The line went dead. General Willoughby idly pounded the desk with the heel of his hand, watching the flickering images on his television set. He had just about concluded that the receptionist had hung up on him when Secretary of Defense Paulene Wilson came on the line, sounding miffed.

"General, this had better be something earth-shattering. I am in the midst of an important meeting with the Chairman of the Senate Armed Services Committee, and with the budget hearings coming up..."

"Madam Secretary, is World War III important enough for you?" General Willoughby smacked the desk even harder. "Turn on Channel 7 News. They are reporting a ship sinking after a mysterious explosion. It is a container ship named the *Maersk Evening Dawn*. You can skip a rock from Virginia Beach to the hulk, it's that close. The TV station even has their chopper up, shooting video of it sinking and the Coast Guard pulling crewmembers out of the water. If your senator and the rest of the American people find out that a Russian mine is to blame, that gutless wonder in the White House will have hell to pay trying to explain why we are meeting with the Russians, not shooting at them."

Willoughby could hear a brief commotion as Secretary Wilson turned on a television and watched for a few seconds.

"Oh, my God," she groaned. "It's true. And it's started."

"Yeah, it's started," Willoughby shot back. "And right now there isn't much we can do about it. Thimble Shoals Channel will be blocked for weeks while they try to clear that ship out of the way. That's after they clear the mines, and that, by the way, will take a month or more."

"Oh, my God," Wilson repeated, then paused as she attempted to gather her wits. "Okay, General, what do we do now?"

He almost responded with something snide, such as, "So, you want us to do something *now*?" But he did not. Somebody had to do something. And it had to be the right thing or this whole mess would explode. Literally.

"First, I suggest that the Department of Homeland Security close down all the ports on the East Coast to all shipping," Willoughby answered. "Right now, we have no idea which ports are mined and which ones are not. I've got fifteen MH-53E mine-sweeping helicopters available and maybe twenty MH-60S mine hunters. They are ramping up to sweep Norfolk first and then head up the coast."

"The president is going to ask what he should say, how he should respond," Wilson predicted. "What do I tell him?"

"You could start with the truth," Willoughby responded, the sarcasm heavy in his voice. "But he won't do that. Tell him to say it could be an accident of some kind but that we cannot rule out a terrorist attack. We have to confirm that possibility, of course. We are taking it seriously. Blame the terrorists. They'll probably claim credit for it anyway. Everyone will believe that. Meanwhile, we have to be sure nobody else gets their asses blown out of the water. Or that the general public finds out that we are about this close to a shooting war with Russia."

Ψ

"Captain, we're starting to get hits again on that 43-hertz tonal," Master Chief Randy Zillich reported. "Looks like you guessed right."

The *Toledo* had just completed a mad dash down to the strait separating Cuba from Haiti and had slowed to start a barrier search across the narrow strip of deep water between the two island nations. The route had long been a passageway for submarines. In World War II, boats headed for the Pacific through the Panama Canal ran submerged there as well as near the canal, mostly to avoid friendly-fire incidents that claimed several vessels when ASW aircraft mistook them for German U-boats.

"Good thing," Joe Glass responded. "Otherwise, we'd be too far from anywhere to do much good. If we had not taken the chance, though, we could not have caught up either. Is he going anywhere in particular?"

"If we had the base frequency right at 43.1 hertz, I'm showing a big upshift in Doppler," the sonar expert reported. "He's making close to thirty knots in the line of sight. He's hauling ass."

"Any sign of his friend?" Glass asked, hoping that the escort would not be his stealth-equipped adversary.

"No, nothing else showing up out there except a couple of distant merchs, Sierra two-seven and three-one."

"Roger," Glass answered, and turned to Billy Ray Jones. "XO, man battle stations, torpedo, silently. Make tubes one and two ready in all respects. And get Dr. Smithski busy with the under-water radar. I'd say we are really going to need to start collecting return on investment on that bad boy now."

Ψ

The red phone in the White House Situation Room came on line for the second time in a week. The large flat-panel screen revealed President Grigory Iosifovich Salkov sitting behind his familiar massive, ornate desk in the Kremlin.

"My dear friend, President Whitten," the Russian leader began, opening the conversation without as much as a "good morning." "I am calling to inform you that a squadron of our TU-160M Beliy Lebed bombers are, as I speak, taking station off your coast. They are armed with tactical cruise missiles. In the pursuit of world peace, I urge that you make no move that could in any way be construed as hostile toward any of our assets in or above international waters or in response to our recent liberation of the Lithuanian people. Talk all you desire before the United Nations, issue whatever statements you wish to your press, but any military action toward Russia or its citizens will be considered blatant aggression and will result in immediate and deadly response."

The screen went black, the audio circuit dead.

President Whitten had not even uttered a word.

31

UUV GM-6 had the shortest distance to swim and arrived in its operation area first. The yellow unmanned submarine maneuvered slowly on an arc around the Russian warships that steamed to the robot vessel's northeast. As it moved, the UUV ejected small buoys from its large cargo bay at predetermined locations. Each tube floated to the surface and then waited patiently just below the wave tops. Once all the buoys had been deployed, UUV GM-6 came shallow and deployed its electronic sensors mast to take a look at the electromagnetic environment. Detecting the Russian radars to the north, GM-6 slowly turned and headed in that direction.

Further to the east, GM-5 and GM-4 performed the same series of operations, planting their cargo of buoys, sensing the Russians' radio-frequency noise, and then swimming directly toward them.

Only GM-3 had a different mission. That particular UUV made its way north with its sensor mast exposed, keeping the enemy warships just on the horizon as it warily circled the fleet.

Off to the north and east, GM-1 and GM-2 maintained their watch, keeping a steady eye on the fleet, sending their data back home, and intermittently injecting more of their own bits and bytes into the voluminous Russian data stream.

All the time, with no idea of the presence of the unmanned American drone vessels, the Russians diligently watched the sea and sky in all directions, awaiting any US or NATO ship or plane that might try to pass, but not really expecting to see or hear anything at all. Satellites had shown nothing. Intelligence reports said all US Navy vessels remained tied up in ports, many penned in behind perfectly placed clusters of mines. Even the Atlantic Ocean seemed unusually placid since the waves from the recent hurricane had subsided.

From the lowest snipe deep below decks to the fleet commander high on the bridge of his flagship, the Russians were confident their unprecedented show of force, their bold move to liberate their fellow citizens in Europe, and their president's strong stance in the face of so-called "world opinion" had worked even better than they could have ever hoped.

They had cowed the American president and his "superior" military. NATO was nothing more than a social club now. History had been made.

The balance of power on Planet Earth had not so subtly shifted to Moscow.

Ψ

Tom Donnegan watched the movements of the UUVs play out on the wall-sized screen in the situation room at the Dam Neck control center. In his own from-on-high view, he tracked the *George Mason*'s litter of unmanned vessels as they circled the unsuspecting Russian battle fleet. Meanwhile, their submerged mother ship stood off, just over the horizon, close enough to observe but deep and far enough away to minimize the chance of being detected.

The tactical display in front of the admiral flashed a red icon resembling a Monopoly house. The blip moved swiftly from the south, approaching the Russian battle group. Donnegan aimed his mouse pointer at the NTDS symbol and clicked on it. Immediately a pop-up window said that the symbol on the screen was a flight of eleven hostile aircraft—the Russian TU-160 M bombers—that were heading north at a speed just under Mach 1, on the way to rendezvous with their fellow countrymen.

Grim-faced, Donnegan tapped the desk with his fingers, pursing his lips as he mumbled, "All the players are on the field. It is time. Let the games begin." Then, in a louder voice, he ordered, "Start the false target sequence. Stand by for first data injection. Tell *George Mason* to go ahead and shut down the Russian comms."

Operators were hunched over keyboards and peering into computer screens all around the room. Tension was palpable. At Donnegan's command, they began furiously punching buttons and zipping through drop-down menus, clicking and dragging an amazing barrage of confusion and chaos onto the unsuspecting Russians.

Halfway between where the *George Mason* sat at periscope depth and where the Russian battle group steamed happily along, the first of the buoys planted by the submarine began performing the next step in its mission. In response to signals from the *George Mason* transmitted over the attached fiber optic line, the buoy began sending out a series of precise commands. Those instructions immediately blocked the Russian communications paths to their orbiting satellites.

The battle group was now on its own in the middle of the Atlantic with no electronic tether to anyplace else on Earth. However, no one in the fleet had any idea what had just happened.

At that same instant, ten thousand meters to the south of the

Russian anti-submarine warfare (ASW) cruiser *Varyag*, a periscope suddenly popped up on the ship's sophisticated detection equipment. Within a second, the cruiser's periscope detection radar began sounding the alarm. The sonar operator did not hesitate. As he had been trained to do, he immediately slewed his 3-kilohertz active MGK-335EMZ sonar to the bearing of the periscope and began beating away with high levels of acoustic energy. At 1,500 meters per second, the pulse reached out through the water and bounced back in a little over thirteen seconds, confirming the presence of an unknown submarine exactly where the detected periscope said it was.

They were being stalked by a submarine! What happened next was virtually automatic.

One minute after the initial radar detection, two RPK-2 *Vyuga* anti-submarine missiles blasted out of launchers on either side of the cruiser's deckhouse. Three seconds later, two more missiles shot out. All four left behind an arrow-straight, arcing trail of flame and smoke aimed directly at the detected submarine.

At the same time, the pilot of a KA-27 Helix ASW helicopter was already pulling back on the collective to lift off the vessel's flight deck. He could see the missiles as all four struck the surface of the ocean, roiling the water with a series of massive underwater explosions. The helicopter hurried that way to attempt to visually confirm the kill and take care of anything that might pop to the surface in the wake of the sudden, vicious attack.

No submarine—and especially one hovering at periscope depth—could have survived such an ambush. A school of blue-fish, in the wrong place at the wrong time, paid the ultimate sacrifice.

But then, mere seconds later, another submarine periscope was detected poking up above the sea surface. This one was about 8,000 meters to the east-southeast of the destroyer *Admiral Levchenko*. Again, the well-trained sailors aboard the warship quickly had RPK-2 *Vyuga* missiles arcing toward the target. And they, too, launched a Helix helicopter into the air within seconds, just as the projectiles struck the spot in the water where the offending periscope was likely still protruding.

But before anyone could cheer the first two successful attacks, yet another submarine periscope caused multiple alarms to sound on various vessels in the fleet. This one was to the east of the *Sovremenny*-class destroyer *Nestaychivy*.

But wait. There was another one to the north of the fleet. Another to the southwest. To the northeast. Still another one popped up halfway between two warships that were only five hundred meters apart!

As they were programmed to do, RPK-2 rockets were launched from multiple ships at every single detected 'scope. RBU-6000 rocket salvos arced off at the close-aboard submarine contacts with a dozen splashes surrounding the target seconds before the ocean boiled up from the concussion. And Helix helicopter pilots lifted their aircraft off and began vectoring toward the better than half dozen lurking enemy submarines, even as they were getting astounding reports of still more.

Radio traffic was frantic. How could this be? How could there possibly be so many submarines out there? But for the chopper crews, the immediate concern was how could they dodge all the missiles that suddenly zoomed past, going in all directions?

The sky was full of deadly rockets and dodging helicopters!

Ψ

Tom Donnegan watched the situation unfold on the wall-size display screens. Except for the slightest glimmer in his eye, he did not show any emotion.

"Okay, before the damn Russians figure out we're screwing with their ASW systems, let's go to the next stage." Donnegan turned to a pair of sailors sitting in front of a console to his left. "Launch the killer bees." Then, turning to his right, he ordered, "Tell Jon Ward that it's time to throw some of their shit into the game."

To the north of the Russian fleet, UUV GM-1 released its cargo on command. A dozen small drone aircraft climbed up into the air, spread out, and headed toward the Russians. Each of them trailed a thin wire with a series of tiny transducers. To the west of the fleet, GM-3 simultaneously launched a dozen similar drones.

Jon Ward was bent over the flat-panel tactical display in the *George Mason*'s control room. He grunted when he received the text message from Donnegan, then turned to Brian Edwards and ordered, "Start jamming GPS. Wait ten seconds then inject the new coordinates into GLONASS."

The second buoy that *George Mason* had cautiously planted near the Russians began selectively jamming the four civilian GPS frequencies. Immediately, the Russian navigation systems lost their position source. However, as they were programmed to do in such an unlikely event, they automatically shifted to the less accurate Russian GPS system, the one with the unfortunate acronym of GLONASS.

Seconds later, every instrument on every ship indicated that the fleet was steaming along in the middle of the Kalahari Desert in Southern Africa.

Ψ

Before they had an instant to respond to the deluge of

confusion, the Fregat 3-D air search radars on the *Pyotr Velikiy* and *Varyag* began sounding their own frantic alarms. Operators aboard the ships could not believe what their screens were reporting.

Dozens of cruise missiles were attacking from the north! Even more from the west!

The missiles were down low, barely skimming the wave tops, clearly trying to sneak in for an attack. But from where? Why had they not been detected before getting so close?

What the...?

Blaring alarms proclaimed that a squadron of bombers was rushing in at high altitude—15,000 meters—obviously intent on attacking from the south. They were only one hundred kilometers out and closing fast! How could the Americans have...?

The battle group had only seconds to respond to the two-level attack. Launch tubes on the *Pyotr Velikity, Varyag,* and *Marshal Ustinov* belched out smoke and flame as salvos of *Shtil* long-range SAMs soared skyward to look for and destroy the aircraft and enemy rockets. The destroyers added to the unbelievable fireworks display with salvo after salvo of shorter-range *Tor* missiles, all aimed to intercept and destroy the on-rushing cruise missiles.

The *Pyotr Velikity*'s S-300FM missiles were hitting Mach 6 by the time they passed through a thousand meters. The *Marshal Ustinov*'s S-300F missiles lagged behind at a more leisurely Mach 4.

The voices on the radio channels approached panic. All that ordnance had to do the job! Otherwise, according to the various detection systems, the Americans had more than enough firepower in the air—even with the submarines destroyed—to do serious damage.

A war was fully underway in the middle of the Atlantic Ocean.

Ψ

High in the sky, *Starshiy Leytenant* Eduard Polzin's bomber squadron was closing in on their friends in the Russian battle group at Mach 1. The pilot watched in amazement as his radar screen suddenly lit up with clamorous warnings. Missiles were being launched from directly ahead and 15,000 meters below. Coming from his fellow Russian warriors!

He had only seconds to ponder what might be going on. His sensors did not register any other contacts in the air around them. Only Polzin and his squadron of TU-160 M bombers were flying in that part of the world.

He quickly glanced at the IFF. The green lights showed that it was operating normally, supposedly assuring the ships in the battle group that his bombers were friendly. There could be no mistake. Besides, they were expected. So why would his own countrymen be shooting at them?

But there was no doubt about it. The missile tracks were zooming straight toward them!

"Fedya, I do not know why, but..." Polzin yelled as he began punching out countermeasures. "But why...?"

Both pilots knew instinctively that their efforts were futile. The Russian missiles were far too smart and far too fast. And they had far too great a head start.

Thirty seconds after they launched, and before the pilots could do little more than begin a sharp evasive turn, the first missile detonated a mere two meters from the big white bird's cockpit. The continuous-rod warhead expanded at lightning speed, tearing the aircraft in half. The two aviators were already dead when the plane's fuel detonated.

Ten seconds later, the last of the squadron of bombers was destroyed. Nothing remained but a few smoldering pieces of wreckage fluttering down toward the ocean far below.

Ψ

The battle group's A-213 *Vympel-A* close-in weapon systems were now fully engaged with radar tracks of a dozen low-altitude cruise missiles. Those weapons had amazingly leaked past the *Tor* barrage as if it were nothing. AK-630M Gatling guns on many of the ships whirled around on command, spewing death at 3,000 rounds a minute in every direction. The Helix helicopters—the ones sent out to confirm the submarine kills—had no chance against the six-barreled thirty-millimeter cannons. But that was not all. With bullets screaming all around, they also sprayed the bridge and topside of any sister ship that happened to be within range.

Hell had been unleashed.

Ψ

Commodore Jon Ward watched and listened to all the confusion and chaos happening above him. The operation had worked even better than they could have hoped. But now it was time for phase three of Admiral Donnegan's plan.

"Brian, raise the electronic attack mast," he directed the *George Mason*'s CO. "It's time to really screw with these guys. Train the beam on the *Pyotr Velikity*. We'll mess with him first. Use the alpha signal."

Up in the *George Mason*'s sail, the after-most port side UMM raised a trash can-shaped mast until it was well clear of the wave tops. The mast electronically steered itself until its beam was pointed directly at the huge Russian battle cruiser. The signal emanating from the submarine was received by the *Pyotr Velikity*. The automated systems onboard the Russian vessel obeyed the digital instructions and promptly ordered all the computer systems onboard to shut down and execute a self-destruct routine.

The huge battle cruiser, the pride of the Russian navy, went completely dark, gliding to a stop within a few meters. No amount of effort by her sailors would get the ship moving again no matter how feverishly they tried. Their big warship was dead in the water.

"Okay, now use the bravo signal on the cruisers," Ward commanded.

Suddenly, and in response to no order from their captains, both the *Varyag* and the *Marshal Ustinov* jumped to a flank bell, their powerful turbines whining desperately from the intense effort required to push the big ships through the water at top speed. That was merely the beginning.

No sooner had they leapt forward than their rudders swung over hard, causing the cruisers to heel over and steer around in impossibly tight little circles. No effort by the crews had any effect. It seemed as if their mighty warship had a mind of its own. And had lost that mind.

The turbines sped right on through their normal and design speed limits. Not only could crewmembers not stay on their feet from the centrifugal force but then the huge turbines also started to fly apart, sending the hardened-steel blades flying like shrapnel around the engine rooms. It took almost five minutes to reduce both warships to little more than powerless hulks, lifeless, drifting with the current and wind.

"Only thing left is the destroyers," Brian Edwards noted. "I can't wait to see what you have in your bag of tricks for them."

Ward grinned. "I almost feel sorry for them. We are going to use the X-ray worm on those bastards."

Seconds later the remaining Russian computers on the various ships in the battle group began spitting out gibberish printed in Mandarin Chinese characters on the ships' display screens. Without their computers or communications with the rest of the world, the destroyers were useless as warships. They had no idea what damage might have been inflicted on all the ships, helicopters, and aircraft as a result of the crazy things that had happened in the last half hour. They were hardly able to even steam around in a vain effort to assist their bullet-riddled and powerless larger brethren.

Ψ

Back in Dam Neck, Admiral Tom Donnegan pushed back from his tiny desk in the command center and struck a flame on his ancient lighter. He lit whatever tobacco concoction he had in the bowl of his pipe and puffed contentedly for a full minute.

A broad smile broke on his grizzled face.

"Boys, that was not a bad afternoon's work. We just left the largest Russian fleet in modern times heavily damaged, mostly powerless, and in complete disarray. We also eliminated an entire squadron of the most powerful and sophisticated aircraft the Russians have in service." He puffed even harder at the pipe. The thick smoke virtually hid his face but not his deep, hearty laugh. "And you know what else? We damn well did it without firing a single shot."

32

Joe Glass was getting more and more annoyed with all the Buck Rogers experimental systems that seemed more to infest his boat than help them survive what had become a treacherous situation.

First the cloaking device—designed to hide them from any enemy sonar—had crapped out at the worst possible time. Then the highly-touted electric propulsion system had left them crippled. Now the underwater radar was giving them fits again. And the latest failure had come just when they needed such capability the most.

That damn Russian attack sub was still out there somewhere, and probably close, but he was invisible to the *Toledo*. The Russian navy's cloaking technology seemed to be working just fine. Thankfully, so was *Toledo*'s.

Until Dr. Stan Smithski and his coterie of eggheads could wave their magic wand to get the underwater radar system working again, there was absolutely nothing Joe Glass could do. He could only hope the Russian captain might develop the same problems with new systems that he was facing. Otherwise, he would remain invisible on sonar, no matter how close he got.

A sudden report interrupted Glass's wishful thinking.

"Conn, Sonar. Possible target zig, Sierra two-seven, upshift in received frequency on the 43-hertz tonal." Master Chief Randy Zillich's voice was flat and unperturbed on the 7MC. He easily could have been reporting a pod of whales in the distance instead of a move by one dangerous adversary, matched by the likely feint by another enemy vessel that just happened to be imperceptible. "Definite zig toward. Increasing bearing rate. Right 0.3."

Glass glanced at his watch, noted the exact time, and nodded. This big guy was nothing if not predictable. He cleared baffles and came to periscope depth every twelve hours, pretty much on the dot.

"Conn, aye," Pat Durand, the current OOD, answered. "Slowing to seven knots."

Glass allowed himself the slightest of smiles as he watched his well-drilled team take this maneuver in stride. If he could just get the damn radar to work, he could find this guy's playmate, the vessel that really worried him. The son of a bitch was not staying in stealth mode for nothing. And Glass knew the first time they might find out the second Russian submarine's exact position would be when he launched torpedoes at *Toledo*.

Glass stepped quickly back to the nav table. Dr. Smithski and Billy Ray Jones were still huddled over a pair of laptops, flipping through schematic drawings. EMC Stan Gromkowsky had joined them. Glass could hear him mumbling profanities under his breath, the gist of which seemed to revolve around damn civilians messing with the load-sharing on his boat. Even so, Gromkowsky was pitching in, tracing out the intricate drawings for the power supply to the radar system.

Glass turned to the OOD.

"While our Russian friend is up top calling home, let's do

the same and see what home base has for us. Launch a comms buoy from the signal ejector."

Pat Durand set his team to work. A few minutes later, the comms buoy floated up, its antenna bobbing on the surface, receiving and then sending *Toledo*'s mail down through a hair-thin fiber to the boat's radio room.

The traffic had barely begun to arrive when the MJ growler beside Glass barked. When the skipper picked it up, the radioman of the watch said, "Captain, come to Radio. We have a 'Personal for, eyes only' for you."

Joe Glass got to the radio room in time to read the traffic as it scrolled across the screen.

"Holy shit," he muttered as he read Admiral Donnegan's missive to him. "All hell has broken loose in the Atlantic. We've got the Russian fleet all screwed up, shooting themselves in the foot." Glancing up, he noticed that Billy Ray Jones had followed him into Radio. "XO, looks like the shooting has started. We're tasked to immediately and without warning take out any submarines that display hostile intent. That big mother we've been trailing sure fits the category. Trying to mine the Panama Canal sure as hell qualifies as 'hostile intent.' It's time we went to war."

Jones had been reading the screen's contents over Glass's shoulder.

"I'd say it's sure gonna get interesting around these parts, too," he drawled. "What's the game plan, Skipper?"

"Well, Admiral Donnegan has pretty much given us the green light to respond to anything we deem 'hostile,'" Glass replied. "Only thing is, I sure don't want to shoot the big guy before I know where his little friend is. I don't like a two-on-one brawl even when it's a fair fight. I like it even less when the other guys have a clear advantage, like one of them being a ghost. We need to move the element of surprise over to our side. Get the

Eng up here to relieve the Weps as OOD. Tell the Weps to load a MOSS in tube one and those new Mod 9 ADCAPs in the other tubes. While that's happening, we damn well need to get that underwater radar gizmo working."

"Got it, Skipper. We'll make the weapons moves happen. Meantime, suggest you come out to control and listen to Chief Gromkowsky. Amidst all his usual bitchin' and cussin' it looks like he is on to something."

"It's those damn power spikes," the electrician chief explained to Glass. "When you light that bitch off, the instantaneous power draw is more than the turbine can handle. That wouldn't be a really big deal when we are only doing a single ping, or even a couple. The turbine can handle that because it's really quick-like. But when you guys go to continuous search, the turbine is swamped." Gromkowsky crossed his arms over his chest and smiled proudly. "Hence your damn problem."

Glass rubbed his chin in thought for a second. "Just a sec, Chief. We don't see that spike on the meters. You sure about this?"

"You bet I'm sure, Skipper. I thought the same thing until I put a chart recorder on the bus." He unfolded a roll of shiny chart paper covered with a red grid and dark, jagged traces. "See those huge spikes? See how quick they are? Way too fast for the meters to even flicker. Too quick for the breakers to sense them and trip, too. But after a few cycles, the load and heat plays hell with your voltage control. Design flaw is all I can say. What we need to do is drop the peak power by, say, thirty percent. That should keep the spikes down to where they can be tolerated by the system. It won't heat up enough to screw with the voltage controls. That should work."

Glass nodded but had one more thought. He turned to Stan Smithski, who was listening to the electrician's diagnosis with great interest.

"What would a thirty-percent reduction in power do to performance, Doc?"

Smithski punched a few numbers into his machine and studied the results.

"If we use the FM-modulated signal, we get maybe a ten-percent reduction in max range. That is certainly within acceptable limits since we're invisible ourselves and operating pretty close to these guys anyway. In fact, it may actually be beneficial in getting a better bearing definition."

"Okay, do whatever you have to do to get it back on line. We need it real bad if the shooting is about to start!"

Ψ

Konstantin Kursalin watched as his sonar team tracked the *Moscow*'s maneuver back to the surface for another check-in. Despite all the dizzyingly advanced technology in use at the moment, it was not lost on the veteran submariner that he and his American adversary were relying on old-fashioned deduction and calculation, similar to that used by their counterparts a hundred years earlier in far simpler underwater vessels.

If the two Russian submarines were being trailed by that American sub—the one with the stealth device—now was the time to draw a bead on him. The American, still assuming he could remain invisible with his cloaking device engaged, would probably move in close so that he did not lose contact with the *Moscow* while it was maneuvering.

Kursalin would simply move *Igor Borsovitch* in close as well. But not too close. Just near enough so he could reliably trip the trigger in the American submarine's stealth-system program. The one that the spy had so helpfully planted. Then the American boat would be perfectly visible on sonar, an actual sitting duck.

To launch the bug in the device, he calculated that despite what the scientists back at Polyarny had suggested, he needed to be within about 1,500 meters. That would be much too close for comfort. There would be a real chance for a collision if the American did something crazy or if the computer-code routine the spy inserted did not work. Though his superiors assured him it would not be possible, Kursalin also had to consider the Americans may have found the fractured code and fixed it.

No, it would still be prudent to keep depth separation between them. But at what depth would the American be?

Kursalin tapped the rim of his tea cup as he pondered the problem, then he had a sudden thought. He was asking the wrong question. The problem he needed to solve was actually at what depth would the American submarine *not* be? That answer was easy. He would not be shallow. That was where *Moscow* was operating.

"First Officer, bring the ship up to thirty meters," the captain ordered. "Close to two thousand meters astern the *Moscow* and about thirty degrees off her port quarter. Energize the spy pinger and begin the search for the American vessel."

First Officer Garlerkin opened his mouth to question the order but remained silent when Kursalin raised his hand and scowled at him. The captain did not entertain questions about his orders. Not even from his second-in-command. It was always best to obediently carry out the commands and then make a suggestion later, when they were alone.

Kursalin sat back and prepared himself for a long search. They would be looking for a very small needle in a very big haystack. However, the *Moscow* made a very enticing bleating lamb with which to bait the wolf. A very brief smile flitted across his face as Kursalin enjoyed the mixed metaphors, both a reflection of his childhood spent on a collective farm.

Minutes later, as the *Igor Borsovitch* was still maneuvering into position, the sonar operator reported contact on the 157-kilohertz pinger, the device the spy planted aboard the American submarine. The contact not only confirmed that the vessel had dared to come within range but also that it was employing its stealth technology.

The bearing put the American on the other side of the *Moscow*, somewhere off her starboard quarter. So the wolf was indeed tracking the lamb. Now it was time to spring the trap.

"First Officer, make tubes one and two ready. I want to shoot immediately after we turn off his stealth device. Stand by to send the signal."

Garlerkin looked at the tactical display and gulped. No time to be diplomatic here.

"Captain, are we not too close to the *Moscow*? She will be inside the acquisition cone. We will be shooting right across her stern! We might hit her by accident."

"We'll discuss your insubordination later, First Officer," Kursalin muttered, not even trying to hide his anger. "Now, do as I have ordered. Send the signal and launch torpedoes the instant the American submarine is detected by our sonar."

Garlerkin swallowed hard, nodded, and went off to do his captain's bidding. Someday, though. Someday the arrogant commander would get his comeuppance and Garlerkin would earn the respect so long due him.

Ψ

Joe Glass looked over Stan Smithski's shoulder as he fine-tuned the underwater radar controls. The NUWC scientist finally looked up and smiled. His forehead was sweaty and his thick-lensed glasses once again fogged.

"Okay. All set to give it a try. You ready, Captain?"

"No time like the present. Let's give it a go."

Glass held his breath as Smithski clicked on the system's transmit control. Then both men watched as the screen showed the radar signal propagating out from the *Toledo* in a series of concentric circles. Everything seemed to be working exactly as predicted, but they would not know for sure until the beam found something it could bounce the signal off.

Then one blip appeared in the display, right where the large Russian submarine—the sonar contact designated Sierra two-seven—was located, finishing up her regular trip to periscope depth to copy radio traffic.

Then another blip suddenly appeared a couple of thousand yards behind Sierra two-seven.

"Got you, you bastard," Joe Glass said in a rough whisper. Then, in a louder voice, he continued, "Time to initiate the plan. MOSS?"

"Captain, MOSS is in tube one. Ready to shoot." Pat Durand gazed over the weapons launch console. "MOSS is programmed to run astern of Sierra two-seven, then up her port side. Weapons in tubes two and three ready in all respects."

"Very well. Launch the MOSS," Glass commanded.

The small ten-inch-diameter submarine simulator swam out of tube one and crossed over ahead of the *Toledo* as it commenced its mission. A hydrophone spooled out behind the MOSS to precisely three hundred and sixty feet, the distance equal to the real submarine's length. It immediately began transmitting a recording of *Toledo*'s distinctive sound signature. Anyone listening on conventional sonar would swear that the MOSS was really the *Toledo*.

Joe Glass was on the verge of ordering the torpedoes to be launched when he was interrupted by multiple reports, all coming in rapid succession.

First, Stan Smithski yelled out, "Damn! Son of a bitch tripped off!"

Right on top of that came the cry of, "Torpedo in the water! Two torpedoes!" It was Master Chief Zillich. His normally calm voice was heavy, laced with a mix of fear, excitement, and strain. Then the sonarman added, "Best bearings two-seven-one and two-seven-two."

The Russians had beaten them to the punch. Explosive death was already headed their way.

Glass glanced at Smithski's underwater-radar screen. Sure enough, the second blip—the one the new radar had just spotted—was sitting at bearing two-seven-zero, the bearing at which Zillich had heard the sound of torpedoes in the water.

"Shoot tubes two and three on radar contact bearing two-seven-zero, range two thousand. Set straight run, acoustics off."

"Set," Pat Durand replied as he input the orders. "Acoustics off? Acoustics off!"

Then, a second later, he said, "Shoot!"

Two loud impulses momentarily drowned out conversation in the control room as tubes two and three hurled their deadly loads out into the Caribbean Sea.

"Both weapons running normally in high speed," Durand reported, looking up at Glass questioningly. How was a straight-running, "acoustics-off" torpedo supposed to find a target? Even one as big as the newly-located Russian submarine. It was shooting in the dark. He knew enough not to question the skipper when the chips were down and there was no time for debate.

But was this the right tactic? How would it work?

Glass, of course, did not have time to explain. Too many things were happening too fast.

Now, with weapons away, the skipper turned to ask about Smithski's problem. The scientist was pale, his mouth open in consternation.

"Radar?" Glass asked. Or maybe the scientist had just realized he was being shot at by a potent enemy.

Smithski shook his head and swallowed hard.

"No, the cloaking device. It's off. It was command-disabled. I can't get around it to re-initiate. We are totally visible!"

"Inbound torpedoes, bearing two-seven-two and two-nine-five," Master Chief Zillich's voice boomed over the 7MC. "Looks like one weapon is chasing the MOSS. The other"—Zillich paused an awful instant to confirm what he was hearing—"is heading for us."

Joe Glass looked at the run time on his own two weapons. He did a lightning-fast calculation.

"Weapons, run one weapon up to one hundred feet, the other to six hundred. When they get to nineteen hundred yards, command detonate both."

He did not wait for confirmation. He turned and yelled at Jerry Perez, the battle stations officer of the deck.

"Ahead Flank. Course north, depth sixty feet. Put that big mother between us and that fish hiding on the other side of her!"

Men grabbed hold of anything solid as *Toledo* leapt ahead and angled sharply up. Cavitation from the sail—air bubbles rushing down the submarine's hull as she picked up speed—sounded for all the world like they were being pelted with barrages of buckshot.

"Incoming weapon, bearing two-six-nine. Range gating."

Twenty-five knots, thirty knots. The sub was going all out. Still, the Russian torpedo was coming fast and true.

"Launch evasion devices. Reload and launch again," Glass ordered in a desperate attempt to confuse the onrushing weapon with a wall of noise.

"Skipper, we're about to get real close to the Russian!" Perez yelled. "Inside a couple of hundred yards."

"I don't care if you take paint samples!" Glass answered. "Drive right alongside her and wave as we go by."

"Loud explosion, bearing two-six-three. I think the MOSS just ate one," Zillich reported.

"Command detonating both weapons," Durand hollered.

"Incoming weapon going into final attack sequence," Zillich announced in an amazingly calm voice.

Glass's quick prayer was interrupted by a pair of explosions. Both seemed well aft of them.

Then, only a second later, there was a massive blast. The impact knocked the skipper off his feet and sent him sprawling across the deck. He hit his head hard on something immovable.

The lights inside the *Toledo* blinked off and then back on. It was surprisingly quiet inside the submarine's control room. No yells. No screams.

Joe Glass shook his head as he struggled upright. He wiped blood from a cut on his temple. Otherwise, he seemed okay.

He looked quickly around the control room, fully expecting to see catastrophic destruction and hear frantic reports of damage and of his boat breaking up.

There was nothing.

"Conn, the Russian weapon hit the big guy. Think it took out his screw," Chief Zillich reported from Sonar. "He's DIW. I'm hearing sounds of flooding. Sounds like he's blowing to the surface."

The *Moscow* was dead in the water, blowing tanks to get to the surface. The torpedo from the *Igor Borsovitch* had missed *Toledo* and instead struck the Russians' brand-new submarine.

Glass shook his head to clear the cobwebs. Someone handed him a piece of gauze to apply to his bleeding wound. He needed to slow the boat down and figure out for certain what was going on before there were more torpedoes in the water aimed at his vessel. The stealth boat was still out there somewhere. And *Toledo* was no longer invisible to that vessel's sonar.

"Ahead one-third. Come around to course zero-nine-zero. Report all contacts."

"Conn, Sonar. Only contact is Sierra two-seven, bearing two-two-one. Contact is DIW."

"Conn, Radar," Smithski responded, employing his best imitation of submarine jargon as he reported what he was seeing on his underwater radar display. It would have been funny had it not been so serious. "Hold two contacts, one at two-two-zero, range five hundred yards. Equates to Sierra two-seven. Other contact bearing one-nine-five, range nineteen hundred yards. Equates to the stealth sub, designated Romeo one. I don't think he's moving, either."

Glass nodded and reached for the red ring in the overhead.

"Raising number two scope."

The chief of the watch called out, "Speed five," as Glass shifted the ring and waited for the periscope to slide up out of its well beneath him. He put his eye to the eyepiece as soon as it emerged and spun around as the scope came up. He was greeted with a beautiful, sunny afternoon, aquamarine skies and deep blue ocean. He had it all to himself.

That is, except for the two submarines he could now see bobbing on the surface. The nearer one was a truly huge vessel, larger even than a *Trident*. It was, as Zillich had reported, sitting dead in the water and significantly down by the stern. The boat was clearly in trouble.

The more distant submarine was a sleek black Russian fast-attack. A *Severodvinsk*-class was Glass's best guess. It was off in the distance, about a mile away, also sitting perfectly still, clearly without power.

"XO, get on marine band and tell both our Russian friends to stay on the surface and remain dead in the water. Any attempt to dive or run will be deemed hostile and we will finish what they started."

As Billy Ray Jones was speaking into the marine band transceiver, Glass was already busy formulating his message to inform Admiral Tom Donnegan that he and the crew of the USS *Toledo* had survived a hostile attack.

And, in the process, they had captured two Russian submarines.

EPILOGUE

President Grigory Iosifovich Salkov read the message once again. Then he tossed it away as if it might be infected with something toxic.

"Who is this American Admiral Thomas Donnegan who has the gonads to contact you, the Minister of Defense of a—no, *the* —major military power and do so directly, not through back channels? Who has given him such authority? And why are we wasting time even considering his demands?"

Ignot Smirnov could only shrug.

"He is head of the American Naval Intelligence. Believe me, the GRU is quite familiar with Admiral Donnegan. I expect you will be as well, Mr. President, once you read the report on the incident surrounding our fleet in the Atlantic. We believe he was the instigator. But what is our response to him?"

Chief of the General Staff, General Boris Lapidus, stepped in.

"Donnegan 'suggests' that since our fleet is destroyed we should abandon the foothold we have established in Lithuania and return all our troops and equipment to behind the previous border. He says—and we have confirmed—that the Americans are already sending many aircraft across the Atlantic. Sir, after what they caused us to do to our own ships, after we witnessed the new technologies we had no idea existed, what might they next unleash on our troops? This Donnegan is hinting the debacle in the Atlantic was only a precursor."

Lapidus was a battle-hardened old warrior, yet it was clear from both his tone and expression that he was nearly in a panic. The one thing that most frightens even the bravest soldier is the unknown.

President Salkov laughed, but it was devoid of humor.

"You two worry far too much. We will ignore this low-level functionary and his veiled threats. We will dig in and stay precisely where we are. That is probably exactly what this... what is his name?... Donnegan actually expects. We will have the media continue pushing the story that our valiant troops are liberating and protecting the heavily oppressed ethnic Russians in a corrupt capitalist country. Seed the stories with reports of atrocities and first-hand accounts of starvation and torture. News outlets worldwide will thank you for such lurid and view-ership-enticing information. Then, what we did not capture by conquest, we will achieve in the peace talks. This admiral may have *gonadys* but he will not be sitting across the table from us. His president and those in his control will be, and they might as well wear skirts."

Salkov finished a tumbler of vodka with one big swallow and slammed it down hard on his desk. Then he licked his lips as he turned to Dimitri Salkov.

"Speaking of skirts, I believe I need to conduct yet another interview with that delightful gymnast, the one who wants so badly to be a part of our Olympic team."

Ψ

The blazing-hot tropical sun beat down without mercy on the men standing on the decks of the two hardworking tugs. Dwarfed by the mammoth submarine, the smaller vessels smoked and strained mightily as they labored to push the powerless warship up against the long, empty pier. A second smaller submarine floated idly in the outer harbor as the *Moscow* was shoved into her berth and gingerly moored.

A pair of littoral combat ships stood guard at the entrance to Ensenada Bay, the seaward side of the long-abandoned Roosevelt Roads Naval Station on the remote east end of the island of Puerto Rico. Fishermen, pleasure boaters, and sight-seers were not welcome just now.

The badly faded sign at the end of the pier read, "Welcome to Roosevelt Roads Naval Station, Pier 3."

A squad of heavily armed US Marines arrayed themselves along the length of the pier, warily watching the Russian sub as the line handlers tied it up. The rest of the Marine company manned sand-bagged gun emplacements at the rusty access gates to the pier, monitoring the steady stream of shipyard workers and trucks full of repair equipment. Just visible farther in the distance, atop a hill where the old officers' club once stood, a pair of LAV-25 armored vehicles protected the scene in the harbor and at the pier from any prying eyes. All troops were especially observant of the movements of the Russian sailors aboard the two submersible vessels.

Two other submarines, the *Toledo* and the *George Mason*, were already moored at the old Pier 2, a little deeper inside the harbor. Admiral Tom Donnegan, fresh from a very fast flight down from Norfolk, bounded across the brow to the *George Mason* the moment the portable crane lowered it onto the sub's deck. He ignored the waiting salute and instead grabbed Captain Jon Ward in a tremendous bear hug. Then the old spy proceeded to dance the commodore around the deck, much to the wide-eyed amusement of the sailors who were tending the lines.

Finally, apparently remembering decorum—or what passed for the expected decorum of the submarine admiral—Donnegan released Ward and began congratulating everyone else in sight. Then as he headed down the ladder and toward the new submarine's wardroom, he continued to slap every back and shake every hand he encountered.

Finally, in the wardroom, alone with Jon Ward, Brian Edwards, and Joe Glass, who had come over from *Toledo*, he tried to explain why he was so effusive with his greeting. None of the officers, including Ward, who had known Donnegan since boyhood, had ever seen the admiral so pleased or so proud.

"All you guys have done is make naval history. You totally defeated a major battle force without your assets scoring a single hit or directly causing a single casualty. You have ushered in an entirely new era of naval operations. Very, very well done." Still sweating and breathing hard from the dance on the deck in the raging sun, Donnegan paused for a moment to absorb some of the air conditioning from an overhead vent and take a sip of an offered cup of coffee. He frowned and stared hard into the black liquid. "Thanks for the joe, but if it wasn't so damn weak I'd think it was horse piss and mud! Fighting men like you deserve better coffee than this."

The admiral eased down into a chair, pulled a handkerchief from his pocket, and wiped at the sweat on his forehead.

"Admiral, I'll do a memo," Jon Ward offered. "I'm sure we can redesign that coffee pot for a few million dollars and it will only take five years."

Donnegan winked and grinned.

"Now, much as I appreciate you boys, and as much as the citizens of the United States of America would, too, you understand that very few people will ever know what you did out there. At least not in your lifetimes. Way too sensitive. But I'll tell you that because of the way you and your crews performed, you stopped the Reds right in their tracks. Oh, there will be talks and all sorts of bullshit carryings-on at the U damn N and lots of hemming and hawing. And in the end, the Russians will probably keep that corridor they cut through somebody else's backyard, at least for now. They'll save face and we'll save face, but I don't think we will see Salkov and those bastards mining harbors or launching torpedoes at our boats again anytime soon. Long as we can keep them guessing about what we have and what we can do with it, the more of a deterrent it is and the less likely it is that they will do something like this again. It's a far bigger victory than most will ever know. And you boys did it."

Each man at the table nodded.

"Thanks, Admiral," Jon Ward said. "But we were…"

"Commodore Ward, what the hell are you still doing here?" Donnegan shot back.

"Well, I was…"

"Jon, get your ass off this boat and in the air right this minute! I have a car and driver at the pier gate and a C-37 waiting for you at the airfield. That wife and son of yours need you a damn sight more than me and this mangy bunch of sub sailors do!"

Ward knew not to object. As he beat a hasty retreat, Donnegan gave him a forceful thumbs-up. Next the admiral turned to Glass and Edwards, the two submarine skippers.

"Looks like you boys are going to be stuck here for a few weeks. It'll take that long to sweep the Russian mines, so you can't go back to Norfolk until then. Meantime, you can take full advantage of being trapped here in this tropical paradise. We might tap some of your crew to help the Russians fix their boats, too." He winked. "Maybe you can look around a little as you do."

Joe Glass gazed over his coffee cup at the normally gruff, taciturn admiral.

"Boss, what gives over there?" Glass nodded in the general direction of the pier where the Russian submarines were being tied up. "Can we actually keep the Russkies here against their will?"

Donnegan grunted with contempt.

"Well, Joe, your little *tête-à-tête* with them left both ships in no shape to sail home. The big mother—which, for your information, is their newest special purpose boat, the *Moscow*—lost her screw and has major engine room flooding thanks to that torpedo hit from the other boat, the *Igor Borsovitch*. They're damn lucky they aren't all at the bottom of the Caribbean for eternity. I'm not even sure yet what all is wrong on the *Igor Borsovitch*. Best we can tell on what little they have told us, she suffered some pretty hard knocks from those two close-aboard explosions. Looks like the Russian UNDEX designs are in need of some revisions."

Donnegan took a big swig of the coffee. He was so enjoying the nature of his report to the submariners that he forgot this time to complain about its taste and texture.

"The skipper on the *Moscow* demanded that we tow them all the way home to Polyarny. He is mad as hell that we have the audacity to actually block his communications. He says his government will tell family members that the boat is lost with all hands now that they have failed to report in on schedule, and that Geneva Conventions require that we let them know they are okay. Well, I doubt the Russians will tell anybody about anything that has happened in the last couple of days. And anyone from their battle fleet or off either one of these boats will be shot if they ever so much as breathe a word of it. We'll let them go in good time, after we've fully made our point, taken a good look at their equipment, and when they are able to slink home under their own power. Meanwhile their navy is demanding to know the status of their boats and we can only stall them so long."

"How about the other guy?" Glass asked. "You know he tried to sink us twice."

"Yeah, he's some crazy Cossack named Kursalin. Konstantin Kursalin. He is actually playing a little nicer. He is very quietly asking for political asylum. I think the guy is afraid Salkov is going to blame him for shooting the *Moscow*. And he's probably right. I'd guess his XO will take that boat home while Captain Kursalin will share many interesting facts and figures with us before the taxpayers set him up in a nice beach house on Lake Michigan or somewhere where it gets cold enough for him. Or if we distrust the accuracy of the information he offers, we can always send him back to his president to explain what he's been doing back in the good old USA."

Donnegan finally seemed to notice again the quality of his coffee. He scowled as he glared at the residue in the bottom of the cup.

"You boys sure this ain't something you scraped off the crapper ball valve in the head? Yech!" He spit the foul mixture back into his cup and slammed it down. Rising, he grabbed his hat. "All right. You guys should have some fun with these Russians. I got to get back to DC and face the shit storm there. It's not just Salkov who is raising hell. I'll eventually have to explain this whole deal to the president and his SECDEF. I expect I'll have to employ my well-known charm and legendary diplomacy to keep my ass from getting put in front of a firing squad."

Joe Glass stood and shook Donnegan's hand.

"Admiral, thank you for believing in us and what we could do."

"No, Joe, thank you. You and your crews and the folks who designed and built these ships and all those gizmos that helped us kick those bastards in the teeth. Now I got to get back to the Pentagon and my office so I can finally get myself a damn decent cup of coffee!"

Ψ

The President of the United States finally looked up from the sheaf of papers he was studying. His Secretary of Defense, Paulene Wilson, and Chairman of the Joint Chiefs of Staff, "Winking Willie" Willoughby, sat in straight-backed chairs across the table, squirming slightly like two schoolkids called before the principal. Secretary of State Arthur Samson slouched patiently in a wing chair off to the side, safely out of the line of fire.

General Willoughby could wait no longer. He coughed politely and started to brief.

"With the Russian war fleet no longer a factor and the air corridors to Europe now open, we have the forward elements of three divisions airborne and heading that way. They will land in Ramstein, Germany, in three hours. There they will be married up with their heavy equipment and be in place on the Lithuanian border by end of day tomorrow. The remainder of the divisions are geared up and ready to follow. Secretary Wilson concurs that this show of force will be so effective that we will not have to fire a shot. That should put a pause in President Salkov's power grab until we can sanction and negotiate them into a retreat."

Grayson Whitten's normally glowing pink complexion flushed a deep crimson red. He slammed the papers down, sending them skittering across the table and into Secretary Wilson's lap.

"I suppose you two think you are heroes!" he yelled, but his angry, high-pitched voice was more a squeak than a roar, far from the well-practiced, stirring intonation he used in public. "You go off half-cocked, and without my authority, and come about this close to starting World War III. You totally screwed up my foreign policy initiatives, which were on the verge of finally achieving the basis for a lasting peace for the whole planet. So, you tell me, after all this, how are the Russians ever going to be willing to trust us now? Why would they want to peacefully negotiate if we are reacting to every perceived threat with bared sabers and loaded and cocked weapons?"

"But what about Lithuania and our NATO commitments?" Paulene Wilson started to protest. "Salkov blatantly invaded a member nation's..."

Whitten interrupted her, vigorously waving his hand for her to shut up.

"I don't give a damn about Lithuania or any rusty old remnant of the Cold War like the NATO treaty. You will turn those troops around this instant before President Salkov and the press get wind of it. There will not be a single American boot on European soil. Not while Grayson Whitten is Commander-in-Chief. And I expect both your resignations on my desk before you leave the White House today. The Press Office will assist in drafting them and composing the releases and talking points for the media."

President Whitten next turned to his Secretary of State, employing a much more controlled voice.

"Art, get hold of Salkov's people on the back-channel. Tell them we need to meet and discuss all that has taken place recently. Assure them that we are not going to ask that he give up any of the territory he has taken so far. We will only request respectfully that he leaves enough land that we can arrive at a negotiated peace. As you well know, Art, we need to remain well clear of these foreign bog-holes and concentrate on domestic politics, as we promised in the last election. Otherwise, we are going to get our asses handed to us in the midterms."

Samson nodded vigorously in agreement.

"I'll get right on it. A few days of useful discussions with the Russians over some wine and cheese in a swank beach resort somewhere ought to do the trick. Then we can set up a fancy signing where you swoop in, claim your part in achieving world peace by remaining strong but flexible, give Grigory an opportunity to do likewise, and then watch your poll numbers soar."

"Perfect, Art. Perfect. Make it happen."

Ψ

She dreamed Alexi was calling her name from somewhere far away in a swirling murkiness. But no matter how hard she struggled, she was not able to reach him. It was as if she were tied down.

Then she was reliving the last moments she could remember. Alexi was struggling with someone in the darkness beneath the beached boat. Again she tried to get to him, to whoever was fighting with him. But she still was not able to do more than try to get free, screaming all the while to attempt to frighten away the murderous bastard.

Then, suddenly, Sarah Wilder's eyes blinked open. The bare white walls and harsh lights that shone so bright it hurt. The wires and tubes that ran to her body. The restraints that held her to what appeared to be a hospital bed.

Slowly she tried to sit up. No use. Waves of nausea and dizziness and palpable frustration washed over her. Then grief. She remembered. Alexi was dead. She had seen him lying there next to her, his blood being wicked up by the sand. The other man was standing over her, about to swing his awful club again as she blacked out.

A disembodied voice spoke to her from somewhere in the middle of the bright room.

"Well, you are finally awake... let's see... inmate number N4763. Maybe you'll quit all that screaming and crying now."

She could not tell who was talking. At first, she thought she might still be dreaming.

"I would tell you to enjoy your stay with us, but I doubt you will. Even so, this place is a far sight better than where you'll go when you get all better."

Wilder opened her eyes as much as she could stand. A woman was seated in a chair at the far side of the room. But she was in some kind of uniform, not scrubs. Could she be a nurse?

"Where... where am I?" she mumbled through thick, dry, unresponsive lips.

"You are the guest of a maximum-security women's penal facility operated by the Federal Bureau of Prisons. The exact location doesn't matter. After all, I don't imagine you'll ever have an opportunity to see the local sights. Apparently you did something really, really bad, darling, because you will not see the outside of anywhere for a very long time."

"I want to see a lawyer!" Wilder screeched, still struggling weakly, trying to break free.

"I'm sure they'll get you one someday, maybe. But again, the word I'm getting is they got you dead to rights. Don't get too used to my face, either. As soon as you're off the vitals monitors, you're on the way to solitary. We'll still be watching you twenty-four seven, but you won't see anyone again. No, you won't be able to go anywhere out of that room. We're going to make real sure whoever it was you worked for won't enforce their own death penalty. About the only way you'll ever be out of this particular slice of hell and serve your time in a more pleasant environment is to share with the FBI all the names and numbers and email addresses you may remember. Your former friends know that, of course, and they'll want to try to keep you from giving in to that temptation. If we do our jobs, though, you'll get to live to fully enjoy your four walls, Miss N4763. Enjoy them for a really long time."

Ψ

Bill Beaman maneuvered his wheelchair down the hospital corridor and into the doorway of the intensive care unit. The small room was so overcrowded that he could barely see the bed where Ellen Ward sat, smiling as she held her son's hand in her lap. Young Jim Ward was pale and drawn, but his eyes were open and he was grinning weakly.

"How you doing, kid?" the big SEAL asked him as he grabbed the young man's other hand. Jim Ward barely nodded before settling instead for a broad wink.

"Shot at... missed... shit at..." was all he could manage.

"Hey, there are ladies in the room, Toad!" Beaman growled.

Ellen laughed. "I'm married to a submariner, gave birth to a SEAL, teach college-level students, and have had riffraff like you, Bill, hanging around for most of thirty years. I'm immune to any amount of grossness by now."

"I know, but getting himself blown up is no excuse for bad manners in front of his momma!" Beaman took Ellen's hand. "How's he really doing?"

"He's having trouble talking yet. Doctors say that will come soon. They say he's going to be all right, but it's going to take a while before he's chasing women and saving mankind."

Beaman nodded. "He's a real fighter, Ellen. But you know

that. He'll get through this. A SEAL doesn't know how to quit. Neither does a Ward."

"I know. I know. I do want to thank you for what you did, Bill, getting him out of the water and air-lifted out in the middle of the hurricane. All with a broken leg and bad guys shooting at you."

"Aw, you know we never leave a team member behind. Not even your precious tadpole! I only wish we could have…"

Just then, Jon Ward rushed in and joined the group in the cramped ICU room. He headed for Ellen, hugged her close for a long moment, then leaned over to embrace his son as best he could. Only then did he grab Beaman's hand and pump it vigorously.

"BB, I'm glad to see you made it back, more or less in one piece. Between that tree in Costa Rica, the hurricane, and that little fight on Exuma, I'm surprised you are still 'a-jyle,' 'mo-byle,' and hostile!"

"Jon, I have to admit that I ain't feeling any of those things right now." Beaman grimaced. "I may as well tell you first. I've decided that I'm going to hang it up. Sit back and soak up some sun for a bit. Elliot, Raul, and I have been discussing buying the land and rebuilding the Peace and Plenty on Exuma. We figured we'd run the bar and hotel, sit in the sun, drink a few beers, relax, and get fat."

Ward laughed, but there was obvious doubt in his voice when he spoke.

"Bill, I can't believe what I'm hearing. You were born to be a SEAL. I just don't see you playing the beach bum for very long. You're not exactly Jimmy Buffett, you know."

Beaman leaned back in his wheelchair and checked every face in the room. He knew them all. Only then did he go on.

"Well, to tell you the truth, Jon, I'm hedging my bets just a little. Tom Donnegan promised me that he might have a little something or other that he might want me and my partners to do every once in a while. I think the brothers and I will make a pretty good team. Those two guys...well."

The hospital room was quiet for a moment. Then, from the bed where he had so recently been close to death, Jim Ward struggled to make his lips form the words of the unofficial SEAL motto.

"Only... easy... day... was... yesterday."

FINAL BEARING

From the authors of the novel Hunter Killer, now a major motion picture starring Gerard Butler and Gary Oldman

Commander Jonathan Ward and his crew on the old attack sub Spadefish are on one last mission. A US Navy SEAL team is inserted into South America. Their orders are to destroy the secret laboratories of the world's most notorious drug cartel, and the Spadefish has been sent to provide assistance.

But Juan de Santiago, the violent billionaire drug lord, has an entire private army and a futuristic new mini-submarine of his own. He will do anything to protect his empire.

And he knows the Americans are coming...

★★★★★ "Suspenseful, thrilling, and non-stop action!"
★★★★★ "I could almost feel the heat in the sub's nuclear reactor!"
★★★★★ "Reminds me of the late Tom Clancy—fast paced and suspenseful. Great read."

Get your copy today at Wallace-Keith.com

JOIN THE READER LIST

Never miss a new release! Sign up to receive exclusive updates from authors Wallace and Keith.

Wallace-Keith.com/Newsletter

YOU MIGHT ALSO ENJOY...

The Hunter Killer Series

Final Bearing

Dangerous Grounds

Cuban Deep

Fast Attack

Arabian Storm

Hunter Killer

By George Wallace

Operation Golden Dawn

By Don Keith

In the Course of Duty

Final Patrol

War Beneath the Waves

Undersea Warrior

The Ship that Wouldn't Die

Never miss a new release! Sign up to receive exclusive updates from authors Wallace and Keith.

Wallace-Keith.com/Newsletter

ACKNOWLEDGMENTS

As with any project, a number of people contributed mightily to bringing *Fast Attack* to you. The people at Severn River Publishing have been fantastic in their support. Andrew Watts has put together a wonderful team and a stellar business plan for a twenty-first-century publishing house. Their publishing director, Amber Hudock, is a joy to work with. So is our editor, Cara Quinlan. And thanks to our literary agent, John Talbot, for introducing us to these forward-thinking folks who have a knack for doing well the very thing that book publishers should do: get stories in front of readers who want to consume them.

The astute reader may wonder why we started this book with a quote from Admiral John Richardson, our thirty-first Chief of Naval Operations. Admiral Richardson—maybe inadvertently—gave us the inspiration to tell this story. In his prepared remarks at a Naval Submarine League conference a few years ago, Admiral Richardson said that we need a good adventure novel that really tells the story of modern submarines and their capabilities. Probably being the only novelist in the crowd, George took that as direction. And now we have *Fast Attack*.

We are often asked if there is any classified information in our stories and we anticipate hearing that question a lot with this book. First off, our stories are FICTION. We make them up. For any real capabilities that we include, they would have never shown up in a story unless we had found an open-source discussion of that technology. Even then we ratchet back on the actual capabilities and their details. The VIRGINIA-class payload modules are an example. Then some "capabilities" are the product of our overheated imaginations. The "cloaking device" and the "jet pump propulsion" are examples in *Fast Attack*. The plots and the tactics are simply more examples of our white-hot imaginations.

Could all this actually happen? It already may have. We don't know. But yes, it could. The authors firmly believe that a well-trained, well-equipped military makes it far less likely. And that even if it does happen, those brave men and women will do all they can with the technology at their disposal to assure it is contained to the point that most of us will never know or suspect how close we came to Armageddon.

We thank all of those men and women, too, for their dedication and service.

George Wallace and Don Keith

ABOUT THE AUTHORS

Commander George Wallace

Commander George Wallace retired to the civilian business world in 1995, after twenty-two years of service on nuclear submarines. He served on two of Admiral Rickover's famous "Forty One for Freedom", the USS John Adams SSBN 620 and the USS Woodrow Wilson SSBN 624, during which time he made nine one-hundred-day deterrent patrols through the height of the Cold War.

Commander Wallace served as Executive Officer on the Sturgeon class nuclear attack submarine USS Spadefish, SSN 668. Spadefish and all her sisters were decommissioned during the downsizings that occurred in the 1990's. The passing of that great ship served as the inspiration for "Final Bearing."

Commander Wallace commanded the Los Angeles class nuclear attack submarine USS Houston, SSN 713 from February 1990 to August 1992. During this tour of duty that he worked extensively with the SEAL community developing SEAL/submarine tactics. Under Commander Wallace, the Houston was awarded the CIA Meritorious Unit Citation.

Commander Wallace lives with his wife, Penny, in Alexandria, Virginia.

Don Keith

Don Keith is a native Alabamian and attended the University of Alabama in Tuscaloosa where he received his degree in broadcast and film with a double major in literature. He has won numerous awards from the Associated Press and United Press International for news writing and reporting. He is also the only person to be named *Billboard Magazine* "Radio Personality of the Year" in two formats, country and contemporary. Keith was a broadcast personality for over twenty years and also owned his own consultancy, co-owned a Mobile, Alabama, radio station, and hosted and produced several nationally syndicated radio shows.

His first novel, "The Forever Season." was published in fall 1995 to commercial and critical success. It won the Alabama Library Association's "Fiction of the Year" award in 1997. His second novel, "Wizard of the Wind," was based on Keith's years in radio. Keith next released a series of young adult/men's adventure novels co-written with Kent Wright set in stock car racing, titled "The Rolling Thunder Stock Car Racing Series." Keith has most recently published several non-fiction historical works about World War II submarine history and co-authored "The Ice Diaries" with Captain William Anderson, the second skipper of USS *Nautilus*, the world's first nuclear submarine. Captain Anderson took the submarine on her historic trip across the top of the world and through the North Pole in August 1958.

Mr. Keith lives with his wife, Charlene, in Indian Springs Village, Alabama.

You can find Wallace and Keith at
Wallace-Keith.com

Ψ

CPSIA information can be obtained
at www.ICGtesting.com
Printed in the USA
BVHW031048151119
563959BV00002B/227/P